KATRINA

The Canleigh Series – book 3

CAROLE WILLIAMS

Amazon Paperback Edition

Copyright 2019 Carole Williams

All rights reserved

No part of this book may be reproduced in any form without the prior permission in writing of the author, except for brief quotations used for promotion or in reviews.

This is a work of fiction. Names, characters, places and incidents are used fictitiously and any resemblance to any persons, businesses, locales or events is entirely coincidental.

PROLOGUE

FEBRUARY 1998

Lady Delia Canleigh, the Countess of Glentagon, often thought about her wedding, which had been held two months ago in Blairness Castle, her magnificent home in the heart of the Scottish Highlands.

Brian, her wonderful new husband, had been amazing, his eyes locked with hers, full of love and tenderness as he said his vows in the solemn ceremony in the grand hall of the castle and later, toasted her with champagne and declared his undying love for her in front of all their guests.

It had all been so perfect and the wedding breakfast in the beautifully decorated hall was a huge success. The caterers had surpassed themselves, the wine and champagne had flowed freely, the ceilidh had been stimulating and exhausting and then, tired, happy and full of love, they had driven back to Brian's cottage on the estate to consummate their marriage. It had been the best day ... the very, very best day, of Delia's life and she would never, never forget it.

Then, just hours into their marriage, their lives had taken a dramatic turn. It had been hard, getting their heads around the fact that they were so quickly elevated to the positions of Earl and Countess only twenty-four hours after they had exchanged their vows.

They had been enjoying themselves in the cosy bubble they had created in the cottage with Meg, Brian's much-loved elderly chocolate Labrador, when a knock at the front door had changed their lives forever.

Delia had been in the kitchen, making a pot of tea, enveloped in Brian's dressing gown, having not long pulled herself out of the circle of his arms in his delightful feather bed. Her mouth had dropped open when she opened the door to find Lucy, her daughter, standing on the threshold, wringing her hands and with tears in her eyes.

"Whatever's the matter, darling?" Delia uttered worriedly, not having expected to see anyone from the castle during the two days she and Brian were 'honeymooning' at his cottage.

"I'm so sorry," Lucy said miserably, "I really didn't want to disturb you but it's Brian's family. The estate manager at Glentagon has just been in touch. He tried your phone here but couldn't get through."

"Brian pulled it out of the socket last night and turned off our mobiles so we wouldn't be disturbed," Delia said, turning to look at him as he emerged from the bedroom, having pulled on a pair of jeans and a sweater.

"What's the matter, Lucy ... what's happened," he said, guessing that whatever she had to impart was going to be bad news. Bob Willis, whom Brian had known since he was a small boy, would never contact them unless something was seriously amiss at Glentagon and he was unable to get hold of the Earl, Brian's brother.

"I'm so very sorry, Brian. I ... I don't know how to tell you this but it seems your brother, with his wife ... and the children ... they were on a sightseeing tour of the Grand Canyon. The light plane they were in ... it crashed. I'm afraid ... I'm afraid, everyone on board was killed."

Delia would never forget the horror of that day. Brian, white-faced and grief-stricken hadn't allowed his feelings to prevent him from doing what had to be done. They had packed immediately for the long drive up to Glentagon. Delia had offered to take the wheel but Brian had insisted he was okay and it would be quicker as he knew the roads, which as they grew nearer to his ancestral home, became no more than single tracks meandering through the hills and mountains, covered in snow and ice. They had taken Delia's

Range Rover rather than Brian's Volvo but even so, the vehicle struggled through some of the testing terrain and they were both relieved when they finally reached their destination.

Delia's first sight of Glentagon, which was a twelfth century castle, much older than Blairness, made her sigh with pleasure. Brian had shown her photographs but they didn't do the place justice. The castle wasn't particularly large but it was certainly impressive and she fell in love with it immediately. Old, gnarled oak trees stood like sentinels flanking the long, straight drive, with fields covered in several feet of snow beyond them. The drive had been cleared by estate staff so a single vehicle could get through to the castle itself, which Delia looked upon with awe as they drew up outside. The centuries old, square building was made of solid grey stone, with towers in each corner. On the roof, in between the two towers at the front, a flag with the Glentagon crest was flying at half-mast.

They slid reluctantly out of the warmth of the car into the icy air, Brian taking Delia's arm and leading her up the steps beneath the portcullis, into the castle courtyard and straight across to a door in the far left-hand corner, which led into an ante-room. There was a door on the right and another on the left and a set of winding stone stairs in the middle. He opened the door on the right and gestured for Delia to go in.

"This is the sapphire drawing room, which has splendid views over the gardens. We don't tend to use this room much in the winter as it's beautiful but not exactly cosy. Let's go through there." He pointed to another door at the far end of the room.

Delia had looked around her with interest as they moved through the sapphire drawing room. It was lovely. Two Waterford crystal chandeliers hung from the ceiling, the walls were adorned with a sumptuous shiny blue silk and the four sofas in front of the two marble fireplaces were covered with velvet of the same colour. Various portraits hung on the three inner walls of people whom Delia guessed, from their features, were Brian's distant relatives.

The outer walls possessed three sets of French windows overlooking a huge rectangular lawn, covered in snow, with two statues of lions sitting with their backs to the castle on either side, only feet from the building.

Brian gave a wry smile as he saw Delia glance their way. "My father had them put there. Goodness knows why but I suppose they must be pretty off-putting to anyone approaching the castle from the rear. In a certain light, they can almost look alive. Ah, this is better," he said, instantly feeling the heat from the flourishing fire when he opened the door they had been heading for and entered a much smaller room.

"This is the scarlet drawing room, where we tend to congregate far more as it's always much warmer and gets such lovely light, facing south and west."

Delia was immediately taken with the room. It had a relaxing feel, obviously helped by the roaring fire and also because the colours were so much more cheerful and warming to the soul. Brian took her coat and guided her over to the red and cream chintz sofa only feet from the fire.

"Get yourself warm. I'll just pop through to the kitchens and tell Brenda, the cook/housekeeper, that we're here and in need of something hot inside us. I'm sorry no other staff are here to greet us, although I had expected Donald, he's the butler and Brenda's husband, to make an appearance but perhaps he never heard us arrive. Anyway, I sent instructions earlier that everyone else was to only do what was necessary today and then get home. It's going to be an awful night, with more snow forecast and there's nothing for any of them to do here this evening. Brenda and Donald have a flat on the top floor so at least they don't have to venture out."

Although Delia had soon come to think of Glentagon as home, the first few days had been a strain on both of them, Brian, in particular, since he had lost all his family in one hit. The bodies had been flown back to Scotland a few days after the tragedy and were buried in the graveyard beside the village church, all five of them; Brian's brother, his wife and their three young boys, all lined up, side by side. With the weather being so bad, many mourners had been unable to make the journey into the wilds of Scotland so it was mainly locals who attended and came back to the castle for refreshment afterwards.

Delia had felt the usual discomfort in the presence of people she didn't know well, fully aware they all had knowledge of her past and were probably wondering why on earth the new Earl had decided to marry her. However, Brian had introduced her to them all, smiling fondly at her and making it perfectly plain he was deeply in love, she was going nowhere and if they didn't like it, it was their problem and not his.

So, their married life began. Not as they had expected, at Blairness as plain Mr. and Mrs. Hathaway but at Glentagon as the Earl and Countess, and although Brian was deeply saddened by the loss of his family, they were happy … ecstatically happy … and were convinced nothing and no-one could ever burst their bubble. How wrong they were!

* * *

Thirteen-year-old Katrina Gregory was fascinated by her Aunt Delia, even more so since she had watched her marry in that splendid ceremony in Blairness Castle. Katrina envied her madly. Aunt Delia was beautiful, had a stunning husband who was an Earl, who was rich and owned a castle and vast estates but she had money, status and property of her own and not just any old property but a beautiful Scottish castle.

Katrina knew all about Aunt Delia's torrid past, resulting in spending many years incarcerated in Holloway prison, where she had been sent long before Katrina was even born, but it only made her seem more fascinating, especially now she had put all that behind her and was living a somewhat charmed life.

Katrina wanted that for herself, not the torrid past of course, but everything else Delia had ... the property, the status, the cash but she didn't particularly want a man to get it for her. She was ambitious and wanted to do it for herself and not share her success with anyone. She was utterly selfish in that respect, had no wish for a husband and children. She just wanted to indulge herself and she knew it wasn't going to be easy and she would have to use every trick in the book to get what she wanted ... and at this moment in time the only way she could see to do it was to become a rich and famous actress. She had harboured ambitions along those lines for a while, star-struck from watching Catherine Zeta Jones in Darling Buds of May and other famous actresses. That was the life she sought, where she would be centre of attention, everyone would know her and envy her and she would be rich enough to buy anything in the world she wanted ... but she had to start somewhere ... and that was at school, in the plays the drama teacher put on two or maybe three times every year. She joined the drama class.

It had been difficult at first. The drama teacher, Miss Ferguson, didn't seem keen to give her parts, even small ones, and Katrina became frustrated and annoyed. Then suddenly, and without warning, things had changed.

At the end of school one day, while she was waiting to be picked up by her mother, she had noticed Miss Ferguson heading in the opposite direction to where she usually caught the bus home after school. Intending to catch her up and beg for a chance to play the lead in the next school play, she had followed her and was intrigued to see her hurry down the next street and jump into a maroon Jaguar. The car remained stationary and Katrina moved closer, her curiosity getting the better of her, especially as she recognised it as belonging to the husband of Mrs. Delaney, Thistledown's much loved and revered English teacher. So, what was Mr. Delaney doing down here, away from the school? He certainly couldn't be waiting for his wife as he would have parked outside the school, not down the next street ... and why was Miss Ferguson jumping into the car so readily, almost as if she didn't want to be seen?

Katrina moved as close as she dared and couldn't believe her eyes. They were kissing ... Miss Ferguson and Mr. Delaney. Really going for it, oblivious to anyone who was near enough to see. He was stroking her face and Katrina watched wide-eyed as his hand moved down to Miss Ferguson's bust and then further down her body. Katrina didn't hesitate. She walked right up to the car and stood blatantly outside, staring down at Mr. Delaney's hand as it travelled down to the hem of Miss Ferguson's skirt and disappeared inside. Miss Ferguson was wriggling provocatively and Katrina grinned as she watched her teacher squirm in her lover's arms.

Devilment made Katrina knock on the window and laugh out loud as the pair broke apart and Miss Ferguson stared disbelievingly at Katrina with an expression of shock and dismay. She sprang out of the car and grabbed Katrina's arm.

"Katrina! It's not what you think," she gasped, her face flushed with passion and shame. "I ... we ...,"

Katrina laughed again. "Oh, come on, Miss Ferguson. It's exactly what I think ... and now I know what you get up to after school, I think you will have no reason whatsoever in not offering me all the juicy roles in every school play from now on. After all, we don't want the Head or Mrs. Delaney knowing what is going on, do we?"

A chastened Miss Ferguson gasped and leaned back on the car, horrified at what the thirteen-year-old Katrina Gregory had said. Christ! She was being blackmailed ... by a child! There was no way out. She was desperately in love with Nigel Delaney and was hoping upon hope he would leave his wife and move in with her but she didn't want the situation getting out of hand and Verity Delaney finding out what was going on just yet. It was too soon. She and Nigel had only been seeing each other for six months and although she had known how she felt about him right from the start, he had never declared his love for her. If this ghastly child spilled the beans now, he would probably take fright and the affair which had taken over her whole life, would be over … and she would get the sack. It was school policy that if there were any hint of extra-marital affairs or any scandal concerning any of the staff, they would be dismissed immediately to avoid gossip and speculation amongst the very often spoilt, over-confident and snooty girls whose parents paid whacking fees for them to be educated at Thistledown.

"So, we have a deal, Miss Ferguson. I keep my mouth shut and you give me every good part that comes up in the future … until I leave Thistledown in five years' time and go off to Radley. That will all look very good on my application form, don't you think?"

Katrina had walked away, a huge, self-satisfied grin on her face, knowing her threat would work. Miss Ferguson had too much to lose, especially her job if Mrs. Robins, the Headmistress, found out what she had been up to and who with. Katrina also knew that the school staff were highly paid and the likelihood of her drama teacher finding another post with such a good salary was pretty unlikely if she were given the boot. No, she had the woman just where she wanted her and her acting career would start to take off and she would be in a great position when it came to attending Radley, the best drama school in the country. Fame and fortune were going to be hers and one day she would be as wealthy as her aunt, Lady Delia.

CHAPTER 1

OCTOBER 2003

Eighteen-year-old Katrina Gregory stormed out of the prestigious Radley Acting School building in the heart of London and slammed the heavy oak door behind her. It was raining hard and she had forgotten to bring a brolly. Within seconds she was soaked but she didn't care. She was angry. So bloody angry. How dare those ignorant, stupid people say she couldn't act her way out of a paper bag, how dare they not give her a part, even a small one, let alone the lead, in the Christmas play?

She was furious with the tutor, the thin, weedy looking Anne Meriott with the steely grey permed hair, the wrinkled face and a determination to give her favourites her full attention … and for some reason, Katrina hadn't made the grade. Anne had made it perfectly plain she had no time for Katrina, right from the first day of term but Katrina had every intention of finding a way to push the old girl into giving her what she wanted, just like she had at Thistledown but it was the taunting of the other students that really got to her. They were always laughing at her behind her back. She had heard them; imitating her walk, the tossing back of her auburn hair, her 'posh' voice … and just now she had finally snapped and let them have it.

The cast list for the Christmas play had been placed on the noticeboard during break and she and her fellow students had dashed to read it. Not to see her name on it, let alone at the very top, was the most crushing disappointment Katrina had ever suffered and then that awful Cissy Nelson had opened her mouth to gloat and the humiliation was hard to bear.

"Oh dear, *Miss* Gregory," Cissy had purred. "No place for your talents on the stage this Christmas then. Never mind. You can come out and join us for the applause at the end … although you will have to remain at the back ... no room for you at the front with all of us."

The rest of the class had stood and sniggered. Not one of them had made any attempt to befriend her since the term had commenced. Not one kind word from anyone. No support at all. She looked around at them, all laughing at her and then she saw the Meriott woman advancing on them with a haughty smile playing around her lips.

"I'm sorry, Katrina. I know you wanted to be included but it's just not possible this time. You can help out backstage ..."

Katrina cut her off, her fury difficult to control. She so badly wanted to slap the woman and then pummel Crissy to the ground and give her a good pasting but maintaining her dignity, she pulled herself up to her full height and gave them all a contemptuous stare.

"You're welcome to your pathetic play," she said with as much scorn as she could muster. "I'm far too good for you anyway."

She glared at Anne Meriott. "So, you can forget your poxy classes. They're a load of old rubbish and you wouldn't recognise talent when you saw it. You'll see my name up in lights long before this course is complete. You'll see."

"I presume from that remark that you won't be continuing with your education here then," remarked Anne, pleased as punch that the silly girl with such a high opinion of herself was about to walk out of Radley. She had known Katrina would be a problem from the first moment she had set eyes on her and she had been right. She always had to have her own way, always had to push herself to the forefront, was always upsetting the other students and putting them down, assuming that because she was the daughter of a Lady and the granddaughter of a Duke, that she was far superior to all and sundry. It would be a relief not to have her in the class any longer.

"You presume right," Katrina spat back, turning sharply on her heel and marching back down the corridor to the cloakroom to collect her coat and bag, ignoring the sniggering behind her back.

"Bye Katrina. See you soon on the silver screen. We'll buy the best seats in the cinema," called Cissy.

The stifled laughter became a roar and Katrina flew into the cloakroom, gritting her teeth and trembling with anger and frustration. She grabbed her things and headed out of the building, uncaring of what she was throwing away but it was just too bad. She had burnt her boats with all the over-confident, pushy people in that place. She was going to make it on her own. She didn't need them in her life and she was going to ignore what they said. She *was* gifted. She *did* have talent! Bugger them all. She would show them! She *was* going to become famous and wealthy. Definitely. There was absolutely no question about it.

Bristling with rage, she dashed along the street to the nearest taxi rank. She needed to get back to the flat to think and decide what to do next. She couldn't tell her parents that she had walked out of Radley. Not yet anyway. They would be furious after spending so much money on fees and paying the exorbitant rent on a lovely flat in Kensington for her to live in. Thank goodness they couldn't keep an eye on her as they had sold the nearby club they had owned for years, severing all their connections with London. That meant she could hide what she had done from them for a while and in the meantime, she was going to sign up with as many agencies as she could and get a decent part in something so she could show them she knew what she was doing. Obviously, as inexperienced as she was, apart from school plays, she wouldn't get any leading roles just yet ... but in time. With patience, fame and fortune would come.

It was still and silent in the flat. She stepped into the hall, which was nearly as big as the largest of the two bedrooms and made her way through to the bathroom where she ripped off her sodden clothes and stepped into the shower. The powerful gush of water rid her body of the tension and anger and by the time she had towelled herself dry and pulled on the pyjamas she had abandoned earlier that morning, she felt somewhat chastened and silly. What had she done? What had she thrown away? Just because she didn't like being ribbed by her fellow students and hadn't obtained a part in the stupid Christmas play.

She wandered into the lounge and pulled out a gold lighter and a packet of Benson and Hedges from her red leather Gucci bag. She lit up a cigarette and inhaled deeply, wishing it was something a little stronger but this would have to do for now. Meandering over to the window she stared outside. It was eleven thirty in the morning and the traffic in the street below was heavy but as the windows were triple glazed it was impossible to hear the noise from inside the flat.

She still couldn't believe what she had just done, walking out of the one place she had wanted to attend for so long. Ever since she could remember she had wanted to be an actress. Catherine Zeta Jones had really set her off. She had so wanted to be like her; beautiful, charismatic, wealthy, desired by men all over the world, bagging a wealthy, famous husband. Then she had watched an old movie starring Maureen O'Hara. That really did it. The flame-haired actress darting about in fabulous gowns or dressed up as a man, was a sight to behold and captured the young Katrina's imagination. Her own hair had always been dark until she reached her teens and then it had started going a boring shade of brown. Disliking it intensely she had dyed it auburn, allowing it to grow longer than it had ever been before and using tongs to wave it, just like Maureen O'Hara's. She had stupidly thought her beauty and her hair would impress all her contemporaries and tutors at Radley and help her get most, if not all, of the lead roles in any plays that were put on but crushingly it hadn't worked.

And now she had scuppered it. She had let her temper get the better of her … again. Mother had always told her she would get into serious trouble one day if she didn't watch what she was saying ... and she hated to admit it but her mother was right. There was no way she could go back to Radley. It would all be too humiliating, having to eat humble pie. No. She was going to have to make it on her own now.

She fished around in the sideboard, knowing there was a Yellow Pages buried in there somewhere. She found it, beneath a pile of videos and CDs. She thumbed through, looking for acting agencies. There were a few, probably some which were on the dicey side, which she would steer well clear off. She would go right to the top first, to the best. They would see what talent she possessed. They would find her starring roles, of course they would. She was a natural. She didn't need to spend years wasting time at acting school. Katrina smiled as she picked up her mobile. This was it. She was going to be just like Catherine Zeta Jones and Maureen O'Hara. Oh, she was so excited!

* * *

Delia was out riding. It was cold today and she was glad she was wearing thermals beneath her cashmere sweater and thick jodhpurs. Her face was flushed and sore with the bite of the stinging wind but her spirits were high. She pulled up Charlie, the beautiful gelding Brian had bought her five years ago, just after they had moved to Glentagon as the Earl and Countess. Charlie was spirited but not as difficult to handle as Demon, her crazy, mad and sometimes bad, previous horse, whom everyone had been scared off and other animals hadn't cared to be too near. Charlie had a much gentler side to him and no-one, nor any of the horses he associated with, were frightened of him.

The dogs caught up and sat down beside horse and rider. The two black Labradors, Rosie and Petal, Delia and Brian had inherited from his brother's family, remained by Delia's side constantly. They had taken to her as soon as they discovered her presence at Glentagon, loved her unconditionally and were in their element romping around the estate by the side of Charlie and their mistress.

Delia looked around her with pleasure as she smiled at the dogs and patted Charlie's chestnut neck. He snorted, pawed the ground and then raised his head and joined her and the dogs in surveying Glentagon castle and estate from their vantage point high up on the hills above.

Delia loved Scotland. She loved Blairness, her very own castle further south in the Highlands but Glentagon she loved even more … probably as much as Canleigh. She didn't know why. Perhaps it had something to do with being Brian's wife, being made to feel secure, loved and deliriously happy. Her wonderful husband had proved to be everything she could possibly wish for, right from the moment they had married at Blairness Castle.

Delia had slipped neatly into her new role as the Countess of Glentagon. There was still Blairness to consider but with the able assistance of Crystal, who was promoted to general manager, with a good many staff accountable to her, and a new estate manager, Gerald Ponsonby, it ticked along nicely and made a healthy profit. Delia tried to get down to Blairness for a few days every month to keep abreast of things. Occasionally Brian accompanied her, sometimes he didn't, as since Bob Willis had retired not long after they took over Glentagon, Brian had decided to dispense with hiring another estate manager and do the work himself.

The years had passed by in a blissful haze. She and Brian had relaxed into their new positions with ease, although their social life was kept to a minimum. Delia had no wish to hobnob with the neighbours and Brian was inclined to agree. He had the odd drink in nearby hostelries with people he had known for years but never invited anyone back for dinner and as a result, invitations, which had been plentiful in their first few months of residence, soon dried up. Delia wasn't sorry. She didn't want to be paraded around as the notorious Lady Delia Canleigh and have to suffer the indignity of being sized up at the dinner table.

As a result, Delia often spent her days alone until dinner, just with Charlie and the dogs for company, while Brian saw to estate matters. She didn't mind one bit. She loved sharing a good hearty Scottish breakfast with him every morning and once he headed off into his office she would stride down to the stables for Charlie with the dogs at her heels, all of them ready and willing to explore the local area, whatever the weather. She would come home to the fabulous old castle, exhilarated and looking forward to dinner with Brian, when he would update her on Glentagon matters and she would tell him where she had been and what she had seen. In the warmer, lighter months, they would stroll down to the lake after dinner or just sit on the lawns outside the sapphire drawing room, and watch the sun go down, the dogs never far from their sides. In the winter they would settle in the scarlet drawing room with huge log fires and watch television or read until it was time to go up to their luxurious bedroom above the sapphire drawing room where they would make love and cuddle up together, safe in the knowledge that their love for each other was fast and true and would never die.

Yes, thought, Delia as she, the dogs and Charlie surveyed the countryside before them now, she was deliriously happy and hoped to God it would never end. Brian had been her absolute saviour. He was her best friend, her lover, her soulmate. She adored the very ground he walked on and could never thank him enough for what he had done for her since the very first day she had set eyes on him at Blairness when he was her estate manager. She couldn't imagine life without him now and didn't know what she would do if anything happened to him. It simply didn't bear thinking about. So she wouldn't.

She looked at her watch and thought about heading back to the castle. It became chilly quickly in the afternoons now it was nearing the end of October, with the clocks due to go back at the weekend. It wouldn't be long before it was Christmas either and she was really excited about this particular one as Lucy had invited them to Dingle Dell, the fabulous bungalow she had built on the Canleigh estate. They had been down to stay twice in the last two years, when the authorities were assured by Ruth and Philip that they would be safely abroad on holiday. However, even though Delia's five-year licence had now expired, going anywhere near Tangles and the two people she had nearly murdered twenty-two years ago was still a no no, which didn't concern her unduly. She had no interest in them any longer but agreed, for Brian and Lucy's sake, that she still wouldn't go to Canleigh unless Ruth and Philip were away … and Lucy had advised her that they were off to Spain for Christmas and New Year so the coast would be clear.

So, as much as she adored Christmas with Brian at Glentagon, it was going to be extra special this year, being down at Dingle Dell, with Lucy engaged to David Jenkins, her general manager at Canleigh, which they had so successfully turned into a spa hotel. He seemed utterly devoted to her and a million miles away from doing anything remotely dreadful like her first husband, the ghastly Jeremy. He was a bit straight laced and stuffy for Delia but Lucy loved him and he obviously loved her and that was what mattered. Delia had been extremely worried about Lucy's mental health for a long time following Jeremy's death. She had descended into a deep depression and had been reliant on pills to help her for many months. A burgeoning relationship with David had started to change all that and since the engagement, she had been able to exist without relying on her medication, for which Delia was exceedingly grateful.

Delia looked down across the landscape at the castle and shivered. Sitting still was making her feel really cold. It was time to go home. She felt a thrill of excitement. Brian would be home soon too. It was one of the best parts of the day, meeting up with him after a few hours apart.

"Come on kids," she called to the dogs, who had grown bored and were sniffing in the trees on the hunt for something to eat or to chase. "It's time to go."

As she turned Charlie in the direction of the castle, she caught a movement in her eye. Brian was driving their new Range Rover towards the castle, along the winding back road. If she galloped all the way back down, she could catch up with him, perhaps even overtake him as he never drove very fast on the estate, always careful in case there were any deer or sheep about to cross his path.

Excitement began to mount in her tummy as she and Charlie, in perfect rhythm, cantered down the hill until they could straighten up on the flat and increase the pace to a gallop. She always felt like this when about to see Brian. It had never changed, feeling warm and glowing every time she grew near to him. She urged Charlie on. There was no second to waste. She wanted to be with her husband.

* * *

Brian smiled. He had seen Delia canter down the hill and knew what she was going to do, try and overtake him. He drove slower, wanting to see her fly past him. He loved watching her ride. She was breath-taking in the saddle, always in perfect harmony with the horse, as if she was born to it and it always gave him such pleasure to see her looking so ecstatically happy when she was doing something she most loved in the world.

He still loved her, as much as he had when they had first come together at Blairness. He would do anything for her, absolutely anything, if it meant she was happy and could never be hurt again.

He knew all about her past, trying to kill Ruth and Philip and even though she had never told him exactly what happened when her brothers, Richard and Rocky had died, he had guessed that she had deliberately set out to kill them too. But he had seen ghastly things while in the SAS and had to do things which made him squirm, however much he was hardened and trained. He had killed, albeit in the line of duty and who was he to judge and condemn her? She had paid for and suffered enough for her crimes and he had never seen anything but love and great compassion in her eyes and he would do anything to keep it that way and protect and shield her from any hurt or rejection in her life. Perhaps she would tell him all about it one day but if she didn't, it didn't matter. It was all in the past and they had a wonderful present and a great future to look forward to. As his wife, Delia was all he had hoped and expected her to be and that was what mattered.

She flew past him with a grin of triumph, Charlie eating up the ground furiously while the dogs did all they could to keep up. He grinned. They were going to be shattered and snore their heads off when they lay in front of the fire in the scarlet drawing room this evening.

"Hello, darling," called Delia, as he stopped the car and she turned Charlie and trotted back to him. "Have you had a good day?"

"Not bad. I've been visiting some of the tenant farmers to make sure they're all happy with their lot for the winter and there aren't any problems. You look as if you've been enjoying yourself."

He put out a hand to rub Charlie's nose. Charlie snorted and stamped his feet. He was hungry and eager to get back to the stables now he had enjoyed a good gallop.

"Yes, we have," replied Delia. "Been miles today … managed to get to the beach but it was too cold to stay long. Much better inland." That was another thing she loved about Glentagon, being so close to beautiful sandy, unused beaches. They often drove out in the summer and went swimming, the dogs by their sides or she took Charlie for a long ride. It was a pity it hadn't been so welcoming today.

"Well, we are heading for winter … it's only a few weeks to Christmas."

Delia grinned. "I know. I can't wait. It will be so good to see Lucy and Selena at Dingle Dell. I do love that name," she laughed.

Brian smiled. "Yes, it will be lovely to see them again … and didn't Lucy say something about Katrina visiting too? It will be nice to see her. I suppose she's grown up into quite a young lady and it will be interesting to hear all about her experiences at Radley … our future star of the silver screen."

Delia grinned. "I wonder if she's over her fascination with me by now. I do hope so. She was positively nauseating at our wedding. I don't think she took her eyes off me whenever we were in the same room. Oh, I'm so looking forward to going down, Brian … and maybe, if the weather is kind, we can get out a bit again … maybe go up to Malham Cove?"

Brian smiled. "That would be good. Now, come along, Your Ladyship. I think it's time we all went home."

CHAPTER 2

Katrina wasn't having much success with the acting agencies she contacted. They didn't seem particularly impressed by her looks or that she had been allocated the lead role in every school play for the last few years. They were also horrified she had chucked in her course at Radley.

"That was a rather silly decision," remarked one woman who peered at her over the top of her designer glasses. "Very unwise of you, my dear. You would have learned such a lot."

"Yes, I know," Katrina admitted, "but …"

"There you are then," the woman had interjected. "And we really can't help you at the moment. You have limited experience and you are very young. We simply don't have anything suitable for you apart from the odd extra and I don't think that's what you are really looking for, is it? I have an idea you think you are going to be the next Meryl Streep or Cate Blanchett."

"Well …," Katrina had squirmed. "Not just yet, of course, but in time."

"Oh, my dear. Have you any idea how many girls we see just like you? You all go to the cinema and think it is so easy to become like your favourite stars. Let me tell you, it isn't. They have all studied hard and worked their socks off to become who they are …,"

"I'm determined to work hard too," replied Katrina sullenly, realising she was getting absolutely nowhere. The woman had obviously taken an immediate dislike to her and the whole interview was a complete waste of time.

Miss Jenks drummed her long fingers with scarlet nails on her desk and stared hard at Katrina.

"That's all very well but it's just not good enough I'm afraid. I'm so sorry Miss Gregory but I simply can't offer you anything at this moment in time. Perhaps if you come back in a few years, having attended some kind of course somewhere … it would certainly be in your best interests to return to Radley ... we have many able students from there who have gone on to have very successful careers."

"So that's it then. You're not going to take my experience in school plays into account."

"No. I'm afraid it's just not good enough for us. We need to know you have studied acting seriously and have a degree to prove it."

Katrina stood up abruptly. "Right. Well, thank you for your time," she muttered, turning on her heel and leaving the woman's office, ignoring the smiling receptionist and heading out into the London street with a mixture of relief and anger. So much for that agency. There were others. She would try them all.

She did. In the next few days she rang all the decent ones, some turned her down immediately, not even offering her an interview, others saw her but the result was always the same. They wouldn't consider her with her limited experience.

She was becoming desperate and knew it wouldn't be long before her parents found out that she was no longer at Radley. In fact, she was surprised they didn't know already, expecting the school to have contacted them about the monthly fees for her tuition. She was also becoming concerned about money. She received a monthly allowance from her parents but now she didn't have all her meals at Radley, which were included with her course, she had to cater for herself, and as she disliked cooking and ate out in nice restaurants every day, her cash was disappearing at an alarming rate, especially with the constant trips around London to visit the agencies. She kept telling herself that it was all going to change in the next few weeks, as soon as someone took her on and she began to get a decent salary. Then she could happily contact her parents and show them how successful she was going to be and how she could run her own life without their help.

Then she received the phone call she had been dreading. She had just returned to the flat after yet another day of visiting agencies and getting nowhere, apart from being offered a role in a porn film. The ghastly man in that particular establishment had leered at her, his eyes lingering over her bust and her legs and she didn't hang around any longer. She was determined not to consider that kind of role for herself, however desperate she was.

She showered immediately she got home, wanting to wash away the grime of the city and the prospect of using her naked body to earn a living. Not intending to go out again in the evening, not that she had any social life in London, she pulled on her pyjamas and sank despondently onto the sofa in the lounge, flicking the television from channel to channel with the remote. She would have liked to have gone out to enjoy the sparkling London nightlife but had no-one to go with. She didn't know anyone apart from the students she had met at Radley and she certainly didn't want to socialise with them. It was now three weeks since she had marched out of the acting school so hastily, eagerly expecting a life far more exciting than the one she had. Desperation and depression engulfed her and she could feel the tears welling up when her mobile rang. It was her mother. Oh God! She was for it now. Katrina picked up her mobile and answered it, wincing as she heard her mother's clipped tones.

"Katrina! Will you please tell me what is going on? I had a letter from Radley today, cancelling the direct debit for your tuition and when I rang them, they informed me that you left a few weeks ago. What on earth are you playing at? What are you doing with yourself? I do hope you're not in any trouble."

Katrina gulped. "Well, I'm sorry, Mother, but I just couldn't stand it. They were all so bloody pompous and scathing of my abilities. They just couldn't see I had talent and am going somewhere ... I just felt I was wasting my time."

"For goodness sake, Katrina! They are one of the best drama schools in the country and you've wanted to go there for years. I just don't believe you, I really don't ... so what are you doing with yourself all day?"

"I'm very busy, Mother. I'm popping into all the acting agencies and it seems there will be parts for me ... in time."

"You mean they won't look at you with no experience and as your A levels won't count, no qualifications."

"Um ... something like that ... but it's only a matter of time ... I promise you. I'll get something soon. I know I will."

"And in the meantime, I suppose you expect us to pay the exorbitant rent on that flat and keep sending you a monthly allowance."

"Please, if you will ... just until I get on my feet ... and once I'm rich and famous ..."

"Oh, for goodness sake, Katrina. Wake up! Your father and I will pay one further month's rent and allowance. Then, if you haven't achieved some kind of paid employment by then, you will have to return home and work at The Beeches. I'm going to insist on it. London is a dangerous place for a young girl to be on her own and I simply won't allow it or support it. Do you understand?"

"You were quite happy to keep me while I was at Radley and I was still effectively on my own here," argued Katrina.

"Yes. But you had the support of Radley, the tutors, the pastoral care ... and fellow students. Now you have nothing and no-one. You really are a silly girl."

"Thank you for that, Mother. I'll prove you wrong," Katrina bridled. "I'm going to get work as an actress and I'll do it in the next few days. I have some really important interviews lined up and I'm sure once they see what I can do, they will take me on without hesitation."

"Oh, Katrina. I despair of you, I really do. You always were headstrong but just be careful that trait doesn't get you into hot water."

"It won't. Really. Please don't worry. I'll ring you as soon as I have a role in something. Promise."

"You have one month and that is all. If nothing suitable has cropped up by then, I'm coming down to fetch you home. Is that clear?"

"Yes, Mother. Now goodbye. I must have an early night as one of these important interviews is first thing in the morning," Katrina sighed, desperate to get her mother off the phone and get some peace.

"Ok. I'll ring you in a couple of days. See how things are going … and make sure you eat properly!"

"Yes, Mother," Katrina sighed again, switching off her phone, a wave of deep depression engulfing her. There were no important interviews lined up. She had been to every decent acting agency in London with no success. Some had taken her details but she knew there was very little chance of them contacting her. There was too much competition out there and what that first woman had said, Mrs. Jenks, was right. Without serious study of acting and proof that she had done so, there were few, if any, agencies that would consider her. There were the seedier agencies, of course, those that dealt with pornographic films but she really didn't want to go down that route and if her family ever found out, they would probably disown her. So, what the hell was she going to do? She had exactly one month to find something as she had no intention of returning to The Beeches with her tail between her legs. It would be thoroughly humiliating after she had boasted for so long that she was going to become a famous actress. No. She wouldn't do it. She couldn't and she wouldn't.

She wandered into the spacious bedroom and sat down at the dressing table and studied her features. She was lovely … beautiful … striking .... irresistible … at least she liked to think she was. She hadn't been on many dates but the boys she had been out with had obviously thought so, always wanting to get into her knickers at the earliest opportunity. She had only succumbed once … when she had drunk too much at a party one night and ended up in a bedroom with a rather luscious young man called Mark. She couldn't remember much about the actual experience, apart from a lot of fumbling, but spent two weeks afterwards terrified she might be pregnant and was so grateful when her period came, she promised herself she would never, never have sex with another man again without some form of protection and promptly paid a visit to the local family planning clinic and got herself on the pill. She had also considered the possibility of having contracted HIV but Mark had appeared to be a decent young man, who had probably not had many sexual partners so the possibility of that was pretty remote so she pushed that thought from her mind and kept a fairly safe distance from other boys who had seducing her in mind unless she decided she wanted to jump into bed with them, which seemed to happen more frequently as time went on.

Katrina studied her profile. She stood up and looked at herself in the full-length mirror on the wardrobe door. She was gorgeous, with her perfect figure, long flowing wavy auburn hair, which she pushed back so she could study her face in more detail. Horrors. A spot was appearing on her chin, which would have to be dealt with pretty promptly but apart from that her skin was clear. She had always been lucky with that, recalling some of the dreadful problems that some of her school friends had endured with acne, whiteheads and blackheads galore. Perhaps it was something to do with her diet. She had never eaten badly, ignoring all the fast food her friends devoured readily. She had kept to fresh fruit, yoghurts and as much of a vegetarian diet as she possibly could, not wanting to devour red meat, not because she cared about the animals who suffered but for health reasons and it had seemed to pay off as far as her skin was concerned.

She looked at her nose. She liked it. It was small and neat, unlike some of the hooters some people had to live with. Her lips were full and even without lipstick were a nice shade of pink. Her eyes were beautiful. Violet. Much prettier than boring old blue. Her brows were well defined and her lashes long, her cheekbones were high and her neck was long and elegant, almost swanlike.

She could see no reason at all why she couldn't find success as her eyes trailed down her body in the mirror. She was reasonably tall at 5'8", her figure was perfect, her bust measurement the same as her hips and her waist, the required ten inches smaller. She had worked hard to keep it that way, not just through diet but also exercise. It had been handy when at The Beeches as she could join any of the classes held either in the pool or the gym but since she had been in London, she had let her routine slide and she could certainly feel the difference. It was true, she was walking more since being in London, dashing from one agency to another, in order to save a little on bus or tube fares but it was not enough. She needed a gym to keep her vital statistics in trim but the fees were exorbitant and she just couldn't consider joining one until she found some kind of work.

Throwing herself on the bed and staring at the ceiling, she thought hard and long about her predicament. She could try another line of work, just to pay the bills and keep her in London until an acting job came up. After all, that's what other would-be actors did. She wouldn't be alone but what could she do? She wasn't qualified for anything and only had a couple of A levels under her belt. Who was going to take her on and give her a decent job which would pay the rent and the bills? A lowly waitress or bar job wouldn't do it. Secretarial work might. She could type but that was about it so wouldn't exactly slot easily into one of the top jobs to anyone important. So, what the hell else was there? It always came back to porn. That would make her a decent living … and no-one up in Yorkshire need ever know. None of her family watched sleazy films so there was little chance they would discover what she was up to. She didn't want to do it but she might have to if she wanted to keep this flat and remain in London waiting for her chance to shine.

Her thoughts kept returning to the man who had offered her the film this afternoon. What would it entail? How many men would she have to sleep with? What would she have to do? Oh

God! The thought was nauseating but would have to be given serious consideration if nothing else turned up. She took a deep breath. She would give herself another fortnight to find a part in a play, a film, a television series ... anything, anything at all which would keep her on the path she had chosen. After that she would have no choice but to head for somewhere such as the 'Harlequin' agency and beg someone for a job. God forbid but if the pay was generous, she might be able to save enough in a few months to get herself to Hollywood. Surely she could make a name for herself there?

* * *

Lady Victoria was deeply worried about her daughter. Katrina had been a bit of a headache ever since she was old enough to talk and as she grew older, she was becoming worse and now she was alone in London with nothing concrete to keep her occupied, she was really like a loose cannon and goodness knows who she might pick up with and where it might end.

Vicky had lived in London for years ... at the club she had run in Kensington, firstly with her first husband, the cheating, violent Barrie and following his dramatic death, with Alex, who eventually became her adored second husband. She and Alex had made a fabulous success of the club, enabling them to have enough funds to buy further establishments in Edinburgh and Cardiff and then, of course, The Beeches, the jewel in their crown ... the fabulous old abandoned stately home which they turned into a flourishing spa hotel. However, with businesses all over the country, it had meant their marriage suffered as Alex had to be away a considerable amount of time but two years ago, Vicky had put her foot down and insisted they sell all the clubs and just concentrate on The Beeches and enjoy a much more stable family life.

It had worked and although she had been relatively happy beforehand, having Alex with her every day and every night was the icing on the cake. They had had their ups and downs, of course, the worst episode being Jeremy, their adopted son from the age of six, who had married darling Lucy, had turned out to be something of a rotter and died in that awful crash with those awful men. Vicky had been so ashamed of the way in which he had treated Lucy and hated to admit that along with the grief of his death, she had felt a tiny bit of relief that he had gone and they could draw a line under the ghastly scenario.

Thankfully, Lucy had made a good life for herself afterwards and Vicky was extremely proud of her for what she had achieved at Canleigh. The Hall, as a spa hotel, was becoming famous and Lucy had done a great job with it, with the aid of David Jenkins who had proved to be a brilliant general manager, a little advice from her and Alex of course … and, apparently, the odd comment from Delia.

Vicky's thoughts turned to her sister. The whole family, had been sick with worry that once released from prison a few years ago, she would carry on as she had before and probably finish what she had started with Ruth and Philip. But, surprisingly, she hadn't. She had settled down at Blairness, concentrated on creating a good business, somehow charmed her estate manager, who had turned out to be a member of the Scottish aristocracy, married him and was now the Countess of Glentagon and lived in a castle further up in the Highlands.

It had all been a tremendous shock to them all and Vicky often wondered what kind of man would have taken on Lady Delia Canleigh as a wife with her reputation. He must be an absolute saint.

Vicky's reflections on the doings of Delia and Brian were interrupted by the telephone on the table beside her. She realised with a start that she should be downstairs in her office, not reclining on the sofa upstairs and drinking coffee.

"It's Suzanne for you," said Gillian, the head receptionist.

"Oh, lovely," replied Vicky managing a smile. "Put her through please, Gillian."

A chat with her adopted daughter, the elder sister to Jeremy, was always a pleasure. Vicky had adored Suzanne who came to live with her and Alex when she was eight, two years older than her little brother, Jeremy. Suzanne had been a lovely child, and traumatised by her experiences in foster homes and care homes while trying to look after her little brother, had been utterly relieved to find a permanent home with Vicky and Alex and had given them no cause for concern the whole time she was growing up. She had even been a huge help when Katrina was born, happily sharing motherly duties with Vicky. At a very young age she was skilled in changing nappies and bottle feeding.

Vicky had been pleased for Suzanne when she was offered a job on a cruise ship once she was qualified to be a hairdresser, even though it meant she wouldn't see her for months on end but her marriage to Todd, an Australian colleague, as nice as he was, was a bit of a blow. They held the wedding ceremony at The Beeches, no expense spared, but it was tinged with huge sadness that once the happy couple disappeared off on their honeymoon, that would be the last Vicky and Alex would see of them, apart from the odd holiday if they could manage to get away.

When Suzanne had a baby just a year later, Vicky had managed six weeks in Australia, which had been pure delight. Little Daniel was gorgeous, happy when he was awake and slept solidly for hours at a time. He had grown into a boy who was just as delightful and Vicky was looking forward to welcoming the whole family back to The Beeches for a four week stay in the very near future. No doubt Suzanne was ringing about that. She was as excited as Vicky was and neither of them could wait to see each other again.

"Mum?" came Suzanne's voice, now with an Aussie accent mixed with a hint of cockney and Yorkshire from her earlier life in London and then at The Beeches with Vicky and Alex.

"Suzanne, darling ... how are you ... how is Daniel ... and Todd? I can't wait to see you all again," said Vicky, with excitement.

"Oh, Mum," wailed Suzanne.

Vicky's heart plummeted. Something was wrong and they weren't coming. She felt the disappointment keenly. She had been so looking forward to having them all at The Beeches for a whole month.

"You're not coming," she said despondently.

"Yes," Suzanne sobbed. "Yes, I'm coming ... and Daniel ... but ... but not Todd ... oh, Mum. We've split up!"

"No," Vicky gasped. "But why? You've always been so happy ... whatever's gone wrong?"

"He's been having an affair ... with Julie of all people!"

"But ... she's your best friend ... you worked together on the ships. You've known her for years ... and she was one of your bridesmaids," recalled Vicky, remembering the pretty young woman who had looked so lovely in pink as she followed Suzanne down the aisle on her wedding day. "How could she do that to you? How could Todd do that to you? I had expected far more of both of them. Oh, Suzanne. I am so very sorry."

The pain in Suzanne's voice was acute. "Thanks," she said, so quietly Vicky could hardly hear her. "Anyway, I can't stay here ... in Australia ... any longer. Can I ... can we, Daniel and I, ... please can we come and live at the Beeches ... just until I find a job and a flat ... somewhere in Harrogate or Leeds?"

"Oh, darling, of course. You will both be very welcome and we have masses of room here so there is no need for you to find somewhere else to live. You can stay here. Alex and I would love that ... and as for a job ... I have an idea about that too. I've been wanting to add a salon to our facilities here ... how ... how would you like to run it for me?"

Suzanne was crying and laughing at the same time. "Oh, Mum. I don't know what to say ... you've always been so generous ... and I think it's a wonderful idea. You don't know what a relief it is and I don't know how I can ever thank you."

"Just keep our guests happy, darling. That will be thanks enough. Now. How soon can you get here ... do you need me to send you the money for the journey?"

"No, thank you. I have enough. I've booked a flight from Adelaide for the end of the month as I have to give the salon where I've been working some notice ... and then there's all the packing, etc., etc. I'll check what time we will be landing at Heathrow and let you know."

"Great. I'll get down to London ... it gives me an excuse to pop in and see what Katrina is up to ... the silly girl has walked out of Radley and God knows what she is up to down there all by herself. It really is a bit of a worry. I can stay with her until it's time to get over to Heathrow and meet you."

"Thanks Mum. I really do appreciate it. I can't wait to see you again."

"I know, darling. I feel the same. Keep your chin up, at all costs remain dignified and get yourself back here where you belong."

Vicky replaced the receiver and then picked it up again and rang Katrina. Meeting Suzanne and Daniel was a damned good excuse to visit her youngest daughter and see exactly what she was up to.

CHAPTER 3

"Alex and I have been discussing what we should do about helping Suzanne ... now she is divorcing Todd and has to bring Daniel up on her own ... with every possibility that Todd won't be the responsible parent we had all hoped he would be," stated Vicky.

Ruth looked up from the canvas she was working on. Both women were in her studio on the top floor of Tangles, Ruth working quietly on the painting of Canleigh lake she was exhibiting at the next Harrogate show while Vicky sat beside her, drinking coffee.

"As you know," Vicky continued, "we're going to let her live in the cottage in the grounds at The Beeches rent free, which will be part of her remuneration package for helping us launch the hair salon but we've also decided we're going to re-write our wills and leave everything equally between Suzanne and Katrina."

"Um," Ruth murmured. "I don't think Katrina will be too happy about that."

Vicky sighed and pulled her hand through her hair. It needed cutting and she would be glad when Suzanne did eventually arrive. She was a damned good hairdresser and no matter how much Vicky spent, she could never find another who could do her hair the way Suzanne did.

"Well, that's just too bad. I wasn't too worried about Suzanne while she was settled in Australia with Todd but now she has to depend entirely on herself and care for Daniel, she needs all the help she can get. She's adamant the marriage is over and that Todd is just a waste of space. Who would have thought it? He seemed such a nice young man with a good head on his shoulders and they were so much in love. I feel so very sorry for her and want to do all I can to make life easier for her."

"And when are you going to tell Katrina that she is going to have to share her inheritance?" asked Ruth, putting down her palette and picking up her mug of coffee. "You know she isn't going to like it ... not one tiny bit."

"I'm going to pay her a visit on the way down to collect Suzanne and Daniel from Heathrow. I need to find out what she is doing. I'm so damned cross with her for jacking in Radley and now she's roaming around London looking for work, she could end up in all sorts of trouble. You know how headstrong she is and if she decides she is going to do something, she will. I am so frightened for her, Ruth. She is so attractive ... and so young and there are so many predators out there, especially in the line of work she wants."

"But what can you do? You can hardly drag her back to Yorkshire."

"I'm giving her a month to try and find work and then we're not paying the rent on that flat any longer and if she can't do so, she will have no option but to come home. She can have a job at The Beeches ... learn the ropes ... after all, she and Suzanne are going to end up with it one day and she needs to get this silly nonsense out of her head that she is going to be a famous film actress and buckle down to some real work. To be honest, I never did rate her performances very highly and could never understand how she always ended up with the best parts in all the school plays when some of the other kids were obviously much better."

Ruth smiled. "Well, your daughter can be very persuasive when she wants. That poor drama teacher probably stood no chance."

Vicky grinned. "Yes, I know what you mean. When madam wants something, madam is going to get it." She sighed. "Oh, Ruth. I do envy you this room. It's so relaxing up here, listening to the birds through your open window, with gentle neighs from the horses up at the stables or trotting past the house. Tangles really is a lovely place to live."

"I know," replied Ruth. "We're so happy here ... especially Philip. Although he never complained, he found it a struggle having to live at Canleigh while Stephen was growing up."

Both women fell silent for a few minutes, thinking about young Stephen's childhood and then that terrible time when he, the young Duke of Canleigh, with a brilliant future to look forward to in the British army, died at the hands of drunken thugs on a platform at a London tube station. It had been a senseless and brutal attack, leaving Stephen dead and his friends badly injured. Ruth had been inconsolable for months after his death, suffering from a depression which had been difficult to shake. She still felt incredibly sad at the loss of her son but time had helped ease the raw pain a little and she could talk about him now without dissolving into tears.

"Coming to Tangles certainly helped. I think if we'd stayed at Canleigh much longer, I would have been a terrible wreck. This place has been such a comfort. It's wonderful just being here with Philip in this lovely old house, full of his grandparents' bits and pieces. It's so homely and cosy ... and having the responsibility for Canleigh taken from my shoulders was a huge relief. I can really concentrate on my art now and it's such good therapy. I forget all about the world while I am up here, painting away. Lucy offered to let me keep my old studio at Canleigh before she turned the place into a hotel but as much as I loved my den, I didn't want to keep going back. This is much better."

Vicky finished her coffee and placed her mug on the table beside her. "Lucy has done so very well with Canleigh. It's been a remarkable achievement."

"I know," smiled Ruth. "It was so hard for her after ... after that awful time with Jeremy, Felix and Matthew. She did the right thing, concentrating on turning Canleigh into a hotel and then building her own home. I love Dingle Dell. It's so right for her and Selena."

"Dingle Dell. It's a lovely name. I wonder how she came up with that one."

"Some story she was reading to Selena, I think. Yes, I like it too. It sounds a bit ... magical ... and it is ... out in the middle of a damned great field, surrounded by woods. I was there the other week and you could hear the badgers shuffling around at night … it was like something from Wind in the Willows."

Vicky grinned. "It would be a bit isolated for me. I like people around me."

"Well, she has plenty of security. A state-of-the-art alarm system was installed when it was built, tons of security lights outside and a panic button which goes straight through to the police … I do wish she would get a dog though … it would be nice for Selena too. I know she has Coco, her lovely little cat, but she could have more fun with a dog … going for walks and playing in the garden. Philip could easily find a suitable one from all the rescues he has down at the kennels."

Vicky pulled a face, not being keen on anything canine. All that mud, dog hair, poo and wee were not for her and although she had been asked time and time again to allow dogs to stay at The Beeches, that was one rule she was not about to break.

Ruth grinned. Charles' daughter was very beautiful and elegant and although she was a member of the aristocracy, she appreciated the countryside for its beauty rather than being part of the hunting, shooting, fishing brigade who owned umpteen dogs and horses. Vicky enjoyed an amble around the lake but that was enough outdoor exercise for her. She much preferred to swim in the pool at The Beeches when she often joined in with the aquarobics classes. Having enjoyed ballet lessons as a child, she had also recently taken it up again and had private lessons twice every week.

"Right," she said, standing up and stretching. "Let's go down and have some lunch. Philip will be in a minute and he's always famished. I can finish this off later. There's plenty of time before the exhibition."

"Why don't you come with me … to London," suggested Vicky. "Then we can stay a couple of days, do a bit of shopping, take in a ballet ... or an opera ... I haven't been to the Royal Opera House for at least a couple of years."

"Um. I don't know," replied Ruth, thinking hard. It would be good to get away for a few days and Philip wouldn't mind. He was always urging her to get out and about.

"Go on. I can see you want to. Let's go stay at the Ritz or the Savoy for a few days. Really treat ourselves."

Ruth smiled at her step-daughter. "Go on then. I'd love to have a bit of time in London and Philip wouldn't want to go. He would hate it ... all those people ... all that hustle and bustle. I can't say I'm overly keen and wouldn't want to stay longer than a few days. It's exciting to begin with, all that buzz but then it begins to grind one down. I have no idea how you could have lived there for so long ... and run a busy club."

"I was young then ... and loved it but I know what you mean. I don't think I could do it now but just a few days, with you for company, that would be nice."

"Right. That's settled then. Let's go down and tell Philip. I must admit it will be lovely to see Suzanne and Daniel ... and Katrina of course."

"Oh yes, Katrina," Vicky rolled her eyes. "She who wishes to be the next star of the silver screen."

* * *

Katrina could have cried. She was becoming utterly desperate now, not getting anywhere at all with landing some kind of role in any kind of performance. She had tried all the agencies and no-one wanted her. No-one was prepared to give her a try or a helping hand. London was a washout. Perhaps she should just chuck it all in and get herself to Hollywood. Surely there was someone there she could bowl over with her talent ... and she might just bump into Catherine Zeta Jones ... God, how fabulous that would be.

However, there was a massive problem with that idea. She had no money. She couldn't go to Hollywood ... she couldn't go anywhere. She looked in her purse despondently. There was a lonely looking ten-pound note, two fifty pence pieces and four 2p pieces. It was all she had in the world until her parents paid her allowance into her bank account, and that day couldn't come soon enough. On checking it earlier she had been horrified to see there was only £8.32 left from last month's allowance.

Things were beginning to look desperate, especially in the fridge. She only had a lump of cheese, a couple of yoghurts and three eggs. That would get her through the day ... she could have a cheese omelette but what about tomorrow?

She was just mulling over her massive financial problem as her mobile rang. She looked at the number, not having a clue as to who it was but she answered it anyway. She wanted another human being to talk to and anyone would do if it would take her mind off her problems for a little while.

"Miss Gregory?" came a sunny female voice.

"Yes," replied Katrina.

"It's Maria, from the Starlight agency in Greenwich. You contacted us a week or two ago and sent us your c.v and photos. We wondered if you would like to pop out and have a chat ... tomorrow would be good. About 10.30? We might just have something for you ... a couple of new films coming up and you might just fit the bill." She omitted to say her bosses were after females with ample busts, long slim legs and a good head of hair, all attributes which Katrina possessed.

Katrina's heart leapt. This woman was giving her a lifeline. Thank God there was enough cash in her purse to get to Greenwich. "Yes," she said with a rising sense of excitement. "Oh, yes. Thank you so much. I'll definitely be there."

"Good. I look forward to seeing you," the woman said. She sounded nice ... kind and warm ... with a smile in her voice.

Katrina caught the bus to Greenwich. She would have liked to have gone by river ... on one of the tour boats but couldn't afford it today but her spirits were so high, it didn't matter too much. When she was rich and famous, she could buy her own boat ... a speedboat maybe, to zip up and down the Thames. She would buy a brand-new car too ... a Porsche would be good ... a silver one. As she sat on the bus, full to the brim with people from all walks of life; some smelling sweetly, some not so fragrant, some fat, some thin, some noisy and some quiet, some laden with shopping, others with annoying children, she let her mind wander to how different things were going to be in the future when she would never have to set foot on a public bus again. She was going to have beautiful clothes, a wonderful apartment with fabulous views in London, there would be an Italian villa, another in California. She would travel the world in style, perhaps even have her own private plane. She would be feted and dined, have men drooling at her feet. Everyone in the world would know who she was and what films she had starred in. All the women would envy her and all the men would want her in their beds.

As a smelly, fat woman slumped onto the seat beside her, Katrina edged nearer the window, trying to prevent their coats touching. Oh yes, life was going to be very different from now on. As soon as she walked into the Starlight agency, she was setting herself on the road to dazzling success. She didn't stop to think why Maria was offering her roles when they hadn't met and had made no mention of her lack of experience and her young age. Katrina was too wrapped up in visualising the bright and sparkling future that was ahead of her.

CHAPTER 4

Katrina had to go down two flights of steps to find the door to the Starlight agency. It hadn't been easy to locate, sandwiched between a dry-cleaners and a newsagent and she wasted quite a few minutes asking various people where it might be and to her surprise no-one seemed to have heard of it. Then a sorrowful looking young woman in cheap ill-fitting clothes with two bawling children in a pushchair, pointed it out to her.

Cigarette butts littered the road outside and there was a lingering aroma from a fish and chip shop two doors down. Not exactly the kind of start to her career that she had visualised, Katrina thought, with a vague sense of unease as she looked at the grubby sign on the doorway stating it was her destination. Still, she was here now and she had no choice. Things were growing desperate and work, any kind of work, would be gratefully received she thought, with a gulp of despair but please God, don't let this be anything untoward. She really didn't want to go down that route if she could possibly help it.

With growing trepidation, she pushed open the door at the bottom of the stairs. Suddenly the world above seemed a much safer place and she wanted to run back up, scurry off to the bus stop and head back to the flat but her steps lead her on, down a dimly lit passageway and then through another door and then she was in what appeared to be the reception. Two other girls sat on seats thumbing through magazines while a smiling woman was talking to someone on the telephone. Katrina recognised her voice. It was Maria … the woman who had rung her yesterday. Feeling a little reassured, she smiled back and sat down next to the other two girls who didn't even bother to look up from scrutinising their mobile phones. One was chewing gum and the other looked as if she had been drinking, finding it difficult to stay upright in her seat. Katrina wrinkled her nose with distaste.

Maria put down the phone and turned to Katrina.

"Hi. You must be Katrina. I hope you didn't have much trouble finding us."

Katrina smiled back nervously. "No, not at all," she lied.

Maria stood up. She was wearing tight jeans and a white shirt; a ton of make-up and her wrists were adorned with a number of silver bracelets. Her long dark hair was dead straight and flowed around her shoulders. She certainly didn't look like a typical receptionist but at least she was friendly. "Right, Katrina ... come with me and I'll introduce you to Bill and Roger and they can tell you more about what you will be doing."

Katrina followed her through a door on the right of the room, down another passage and then Maria knocked on a door and marched right in. Katrina followed but even with Maria by her side, she felt a growing sense of unease. This certainly didn't look like any of the agencies she had visited in the last few weeks. It was too quiet and tatty. All the rest, apart from that place she had been yesterday, which was not dissimilar from this, had been buzzing with excited people and sparkly signs and photographs of famous actors and actresses everywhere.

"This is Bill and this is Roger," Maria stated with a quick smile at Katrina. "They will look after you," she said and left the room, shutting the door firmly behind her.

Katrina gulped and stared anxiously at the two men. The young black one had risen to his feet with a flash of brilliant white teeth while the other, a white thirty something with greasy hair and a huge whitehead on his chin, remained in his chair at his desk and looked her up and down, spending more than a few moments eyeing her bust and legs.

The black one moved around his desk and came towards her. Katrina wanted to run but stood her ground, her heart pounding hard.

"Hi, I'm Roger," the man said, holding out his hand for her to shake. It was sweaty and revolting and feeling a need to throw up, she pulled hers away, resisting the desire to run it down her skirt to wipe away his perspiration.

"Hi," she said tremulously, attempting a smile.

"And I'm Bill," announced the other man, still not rising from his seat.

"Hi," repeated Katrina, wishing Roger would return to his. He was standing far too close to her and she didn't like it. She took a step nearer to the door.

Noticing her movement, Bill waved a hand at a chair opposite the desk. "Sit down, Katrina ... let's have a chat. Roger, come back here. I think you're making the poor girl feel a little anxious," he grinned.

Roger gave a grunt but did as he was told, still staring hard at Katrina.

"We make a lot of films here, Katrina," said Bill, "and you can make a lot of money if you stick with us ... and I presume that's what you want ... cash and a step on the ladder to success in the film industry?"

Katrina nodded and clasped her hands together primly in her lap. Her knees were knocking and she hoped neither of the men would notice.

"Good. Then we should all get along famously. We're starting on a new film this morning actually and you can certainly have a part in that."

"What ... what is it?"

"Well ... let's say, it's on the romantic side."

Roger sniggered.

"Yes. Romantic," continued Bill with a glare at Roger. "You are in love with this guy, who you will meet in a moment or two, and all you have to do is make love to him ... it's all very easy ... Leo will look after you ... and you will enjoy the experience with him ... all the girls do."

"You mean ... you mean ... you want me to have sex with this man ... in front of the camera?" breathed Katrina, her worst fears realised.

"Well yes, darling ... we all have to start somewhere and just a couple of hours of your time will bring you a wad of cash and a starring role ... come on sweetheart. You are perfect for this. You are extremely beautiful and are going to make a real impression ... and you can't tell me that most of the stars of stage and screen haven't taken their clothes off at some time in their lives in order to promote their careers."

Katrina gulped. He might be right but she really didn't want to do this. She wanted to make a bolt for it but Roger had stood up again and walked towards the door where he stood with his arms folded, a big grin on his face. Katrina felt the terror sweep over her. She had never felt so scared in her life. She was totally at the mercy of these two and even if she did scream, it was doubtful if she would be heard and even if she was, she couldn't imagine any of the three women in reception would lift a finger to help her.

Bill was fiddling in the top drawer of his desk. He produced a packet of pills, removed one and poured a glass of water. He stood up and handed them to her.

"Take this, sweetheart. It will relax you and help you on your way to huge success."

"What about ... what about my lines ... surely I have to learn some?" Her voice rose shrilly in panic as she tried to play for time.

"Don't you worry your head about that. We don't need you to learn anything. Just go with the flow with Leo and everything will be fine ... now, take the damned thing!" he commanded with a flash of annoyance in his beady eyes.

"What is it?" squeaked Katrina.

"Nothing that will hurt you. Just a relaxant ... help you enjoy what you are about to do. Really. All the girls take them ... swear by them as a matter of fact ... now, stop messing about."

Roger moved behind her. "If you don't take the blasted thing, girl, I'll shove it down your bloody throat."

Katrina stared at Bill with horror. He grinned back at her. He had a tooth missing and the pimple on his chin seemed to grow bigger by the second. She felt so sick. What the hell had she done? Why the hell had she come to Greenwich? Why the hell had she walked down those blasted steps? She was done for. She couldn't get out. They weren't going to let her go. She was going to have to go through with whatever ghastly scenario they had devised. She looked at the pill. If it helped her through whatever was in store, she had to take it. Please God she saw the light of day afterwards. She took it from Bill's hand, threw it into her mouth and downed the water. Within a few seconds her mouth was awash with moisture and she felt a lovely sense of wellbeing, floaty and warm. The pimple on Bill's chin seemed to be receding and he looked almost desirable. She turned to look at Roger. Why hadn't she noticed he was rather a stunner. She put out a hand and ran it down his face. He smiled and pulled her towards him.

"Right. It's about time we got your clothes off, darling," he purred. "Let's really see what you have to offer."

* * *

Maria put Katrina in a taxi afterwards, paid the fare and told the driver to take her home.

"Don't lose your money," she warned. "You've earned it."

"I won't," replied Katrina blearily. The effects of the pill were wearing off and she was absolutely exhausted, her breasts and vagina were as sore as hell and all she wanted was a long, hot bath and then get into bed and sleep until she could sleep no more. She could only remember bits of what had happened to her in the Starlight agency but on checking her bag and seeing a wad load of cash, she felt a little better. At least she could afford to eat now and as she couldn't remember much of what had happened, perhaps it had been worth it, after all.

The taxi dropped her outside her block of flats and she slumped into the lift gratefully, desperate to get back into the security of her flat. She caught sight of herself in the glass panels. She looked an absolute fright. Her hair was a mess, her eye-makeup had run and her clothes were awry as someone else must have dressed her. She hoped she wouldn't bump into any of the other residents of the prestigious block of flats. She was hardly presenting as an up and coming young actress. She looked more like a tramp who had been out on the tiles all night ... and it was four o'clock in the afternoon.

She put her key in the lock and entered her flat with a sigh of relief and then nearly collapsed with shock. Her mother was standing in the kitchen doorway staring at her with dismay, Granny Ruth behind her with her mouth open. No-one spoke for a second and then Vicky walked towards her, a look of sheer horror on her face.

"Katrina! Where the hell have you been and what the hell have you been doing?" Vicky demanded, throwing her hands up in despair.

Katrina groaned, dumped her bag on the floor and headed towards the bedroom. "Oh God, not now! I need a bath."

"Yes, I think you do, young lady ... and as soon as you finish, you can get back out here and give us an explanation as to what you have been up to ... and more to the point, who with."

"Whatever," mumbled Katrina, banging the bathroom door and locking it behind her. She threw off her clothes, catching sight of her body in the mirror as she bent down to turn on the bath taps. Her skin was covered in red marks, there was a love bite on her neck and her nipples were red raw. What the hell had they done to her ... and who? She could vaguely remember a large naked white male with slicked back dark hair, a cheeky grin, a fabulous six pack and a well-tanned body advancing towards her as she entered a room with an enormous bed ... and there was another man sat on a chair holding a big camera but she couldn't remember anything else. Would it come back to her? Did she want it to? Probably the less she knew about it the better.

She sank into the foaming water, wincing as all the sore parts of her body were covered. They hurt like mad but gradually the warmth of the water began to ease the pain. Her brain seemed to be clearing too and she began to consider her position ... and all that money in her bag. There must be at least three or four thousand pounds in there. Not bad for a few hours work ... well, at least if you could call it work ... as she had no idea what she had actually done. She wouldn't make that kind of money waiting tables or doing secretarial work in such a short time. Perhaps there was something to this after all. If she could survive it once, she could survive it again. As Maria had put her in the taxi, she had said Bill and Roger were pleased and would be in touch. So, if they did contact her and she could cope with a few more sessions like today, she would soon have enough money to get to Hollywood and keep herself until she could really set the world alight with a proper film career.

As she began to gingerly apply body wash to her skin, she grinned. Perhaps, just perhaps, she had just struck gold.

CHAPTER 5

Katrina crept out of the bathroom, hoping to get to her bedroom and nod off before her mother cottoned on. She could hear her talking to Granny Ruth. Their voices were low but it was quite possible to make out what they were saying.

"I've been worried sick about her ever since I heard from Radley that she had walked out. I just don't know what to do, Ruth. I can't exactly drag her back home but I fear for her here, especially after the way she appeared just now … at this time of the day. I dread to think what she has been up to."

"Well, she is still young and you know what we were like … parties and more parties, etc. The Oxford scene could be pretty wild at times," grinned Ruth, remembering their university years with a sigh.

Vicky smiled half-heartedly back. "Yes. I know but we were in a crowd of people we knew and who would look after us. Katrina has no-one in London now she's not at Radley any longer. She's floating around in a cesspool and goodness knows if she can keep her head above water … and …," Vicky didn't finish her sentence as the bathroom door clicked shut loudly as Katrina moved towards her bedroom.

"Katrina … come in here please. I want to talk to you," Vicky called. "Now."

Katrina could have kicked herself for not having been more careful closing the bathroom door. She had no choice now. She had to face her mother and she really didn't feel like it. Her body was so tired and desperately needed rest. She walked reluctantly into the lounge, pulling her bathrobe around her tightly, her expression sullen and obstinate.

"Sit down," her mother commanded, "before you fall down … and I want you to explain exactly what you have been up to, coming home in that state. Have you been taking drugs?"

"No," said Katrina, slumping into the chair next to Granny Ruth, who was looking a little more sympathetic than her mother.

"Well, if you haven't, you've certainly had too much alcohol and you know how dangerous that is. Not having full use of all your faculties in London, especially on your own, is sheer stupidity."

"I wasn't on my own. I had friends to look after me ... we went to a party ... didn't you ever party when you were young?" Katrina managed to get out before her mother launched into her usual tirade about the evils of drink and how not to succumb, no doubt her fear of too much alcohol brought on by what her first husband, the philandering Barrie, had done, running off with Aunt Delia and then crashing his car into a tree on Canleigh drive and killing himself, long before Katrina was born. Having heard this particular lecture so many times before, she switched off and looked around for her bag. Where had she dumped it?

"What are you doing? Sit down. I want to talk to you," snapped Vicky.

"I want my bag. I need a cigarette if I have to listen to you going on and on," Katrina muttered, spying it on the floor in the hall where she had dumped it. Bending down to pick it up, her head began to swim and she needed to sit down again ... fast. Returning to the lounge, she slumped back down into her chair, trying to open the bag but for some reason the clasp wouldn't work. She pulled it, she twisted it and then with a quick jerk it flew open, fifty-pound notes flying all over the cream carpet to rest at the feet of her mother and Granny Ruth.

For a second no-one spoke. They all stared at the cash with disbelief and then Vicky turned her head to look at her daughter.

"What on earth? There must be thousands of pounds there ... exactly what have you been doing to get your hands on so much money? It certainly can't be anything legal."

Katrina groaned and grabbed her cigarettes and lighter from the bag. She daren't bend down to pick up the money or she would throw up.

"Well? I'm waiting."

"It's ... oh, for goodness sake, if you want to know, I did a bit of filming ... for a cash payment. Nothing to get on your high horse about."

"Filming ... what film? What company? Where did you go?"

"Greenwich ... it's a sloppy romance," Katrina lied, remembering Bill's description earlier.

"That I don't believe ... I'm sorry, Katrina but I'm not happy. I want you to come home with us tomorrow."

"No. I'm not going anywhere ... especially back to Yorkshire. I want to stay here ... I need to stay here ... I'm earning some decent money now ... and you said I could stay here if I got a job. Well, I have one."

"A somewhat dubious one by the look of it. What you had to do exactly for this kind of money doesn't bear thinking about," said Vicky, on her hands and knees picking up the cash and then counting it. "There's four thousand pounds here, Katrina. Four thousand pounds! You told me yesterday you still haven't got a job so to earn this amount in such a short space of time can only mean you were doing something completely untoward and I'm still not convinced you haven't taken something."

"Oh, for God's sake, Mother. Do stop keep going on. I have a headache," groaned Katrina, puffing hard on her cigarette.

Vicky threw the money on the coffee table, marched to the window and opened it to let in some fresh air. She closed it again quickly, the noise of the traffic and the fumes from the car exhausts worse than the cigarette smoke. She stood staring at her daughter, fear and anger enveloping her. She knew it was all her fault. She had indulged this girl from birth. Katrina had been spoilt and petted and look at the result. She was now a young woman with a somewhat wild streak about her. Vicky's thoughts flew to her elder sister, Lady Delia. Katrina was so similar in many respects. She was very beautiful, knew she was very beautiful and played on it which resulted in her getting virtually everything she wanted and if she didn't, woe betide anyone who stood in her way. The girl also possessed an unhealthy interest in the doings of Lady Delia, her wayward aunt, which had always unsettled Vicky. The last thing she wanted was for Katrina to emanate Delia.

"What are you doing here, anyway?" asked Katrina. "There was absolutely no need to come and spy on me."

"We came down for a couple of days to take in a ballet and do a little shopping and then we're picking up Suzanne and Daniel from Heathrow tomorrow," said Ruth, seeing Vicky was struggling to overcome her anger.

Katrina raised her head and looked at Ruth. "Suzanne and Daniel? What are they doing back here? And why hasn't Todd come?"

"They've split up ... Todd has gone back to the cruise ships and their marriage is over. Suzanne is bringing Daniel home and they're going to live at The Beeches," explained Vicky, managing to keep a lid on her emotions. "In fact, that is something else I wanted to talk to you about and you're not going to like it."

"Oh, God. Another lecture on how I'm supposed to be nice to them, I suppose."

Vicky ignored her and continued. If they were going to have a row, it might as well be now while they were cross with each other. "Your father and I have decided that in the light of Suzanne's new circumstances, she's going to need a lot more security if she's going to bring up Daniel alone. We're offering her the chance of opening a salon in The Beeches and also learn the hotel business."

"Bully for Suzanne," Katrina said sulkily, not giving a toss about her adopted older sister and what happened to her.

"That's not all," remarked Vicky, throwing a despairing glance at Ruth, who grimaced back, guessing there was about to be an almighty row. "We've decided to draw up a new will. We're going to split everything ... including the Beeches between you."

Katrina leapt to her feet, her bathrobe falling open to reveal the nasty marks on her neck and cleavage. "What! You can't. It's mine. Everything is mine ... it's always been that way. She's only adopted ... I'm your real child ... you can't do this to me!"

Ruth and Vicky were gazing open mouthed at the sight of the wounds on Katrina's skin. She realised and pulled her bathrobe around her quickly, stubbing out her cigarette in the ashtray on the coffee table and lighting another immediately. She took a deep drag and glared at her mother.

"I'll never forgive you for this and I'll fight it tooth and nail when the time comes. As far as I'm concerned Suzanne's not going to get what is rightfully mine."

"Might I remind you that your father and I can leave our possessions to anyone we wish to. In fact, madam, we don't have to leave you anything at all," said Vicky coldly, deeply ashamed of how Katrina was behaving and those marks on her skin ... who had treated her so badly? Her fear for her daughter was growing by the second. She had to get her away from London and back to the safety of the Beeches as soon as possible before she disappeared into the abyss of the seedier parts of London life never to emerge.

Ruth was listening to the conversation with growing despair. Katrina was belligerent, angry and obviously exhausted. Vicky was stressed and anxious. Nothing was going to be achieved with both of them in this state.

"I think Katrina needs to get some rest," she said quietly, looking at Vicky with concern. "Why don't you and I return to the Ritz and have something to eat before the ballet this evening? We can come back here early in the morning and discuss this properly when everyone has calmed down ... before we go to the airport for Suzanne and Daniel."

"That's a bloody good idea, Granny Ruth … but I'm really fine. I can manage now," said Katrina, waving a hand at the cash on the coffee table."

Vicky wanted to shake her. "That won't last five minutes in London, especially with the rent on this place, you silly girl … and then you're going to have to earn some more pretty quickly."

"And so I will. Really Mother, don't worry your head about me. After all, you're going to have your hands full with your precious Suzanne and her kid and while you're drooling over them, I'm going to save as much as I can and once I've enough, I'm going to Hollywood."

"Oh, Christ," Vicky blasphemed, running a hand through her hair. "You're being so stupid, Katrina … the only thing you will be good for are pornographic films … when are you going to realise you have no damned talent? You have been deluding yourself for years. You were terrible in those school plays … how the hell you got those parts I have no idea. Miss Ferguson must have been blind and deaf!"

Katrina stared hard at her mother. "Oh, believe me, she wasn't. She would never have given me all those lead roles if I hadn't found out she was having an affair with Mrs. Delaney's husband." She gave a hollow laugh. "Oh yes, Mother dear, I blackmailed the silly bitch. I told her I would tell on her if she didn't give me the parts I wanted. It worked a treat. She didn't want to lose her cushy job … and she probably wouldn't have been able to get another …. so I got what I wanted … easy peasy."

Vicky looked at Ruth with growing horror. It was like listening to Delia, the nastiness, the manipulation …. It was all there. Just as it had been years ago with her sister. Where the hell was Katrina going? Please God, not down the same path.

"I can't listen to this," she uttered, grabbing her bag from the side of the sofa. "I need to get back to the Ritz. Go to bed, Katrina. I will do as Ruth suggested and come back tomorrow morning and then we'll talk properly."

"I shan't be here. I'm going out."

Vicky glared at her daughter and headed for the door, Ruth following.

"Get some sleep, Katrina," she said sorrowfully. "And make sure you're here in the morning. You owe your mother that much."

The front door closed behind them and Katrina threw herself on the sofa. She wanted to cry, with rage and disappointment. Her own mother didn't believe she had any talent. That was hard to swallow but even worse was the knowledge that her parents were planning on giving half her inheritance to bloody Suzanne and her brat. However, there was nothing she could do about that now and as her mother and father were in good health, she had plenty of time to work on them but they would have to see sense. They would have to change their minds. There was no way on earth she was going to give up so much to Suzanne, who was not of their aristocratic blood and had come from goodness knows where. Why should she?

Katrina bridled with indignation, quite forgetting how Suzanne, a good few years older than her, had helped look after her as a child, had played with her, had helped her with schoolwork, had been like a second mother to her. She was too annoyed. Blast Todd. Why hadn't he been a decent husband and kept his wife happy and thousands of miles away? As if there weren't enough problems to sort out and now there was her inheritance too. Bugger. Anyhow, there was time to work on that. For now, she had to concentrate on securing her career and just had to obtain more money to kickstart it. London was a washout as far as that was concerned. She had to get to Hollywood. The Americans wouldn't be so stuffy. They would see her potential. There was no way she was being dragged back to The Beeches, and have to watch her mother fawning over Suzanne and her kid.

She scrabbled in her bag for the card Maria had pushed at her earlier. She found it and stared hard at the phone number. She didn't want to do it but there was no other way at the present and it would be quick. In a short time, she could have enough to get her to Hollywood. Just a few more sessions with Leo ... she could remember his name now ... could remember his hands on her body, probing, prying, kissing, sucking. Perhaps it hadn't been so bad after all. She might have a few bruises, which could easily be covered up with make-up, but she also had a wad of cash and it was the quickest way to get what she wanted.

She found her mobile and keyed in the number. "Hi Maria," she said. "It's Katrina. Please could you tell Bill and Roger that if they want me, I'm available for more work from tomorrow."

CHAPTER 6

Suzanne looked at Daniel, sleeping beside her on the huge plane that was taking them nearer and nearer to the U.K. Her heart turned over with love for him. She felt so guilty that he probably wouldn't see his father again for many years but then, she reasoned, why should she? Their marriage had proved to be a complete disaster but it hadn't been her who had messed it up. Todd had simply never matured and was unable to settle properly when they had given up their life at sea to live in Adelaide. At some point in one's life one had to grow up and that was the trouble. She had and he hadn't.

Would she ever see him again? Her errant husband. It was doubtful. He would be revelling in having a good time with his new shipmates and then there would be the girls, loads of them, crew and passengers. All looking to have a good time and many not caring about the consequences … and her husband, good looking, charismatic Todd, would be in the thick of it.

Her emotions were a mixture of extreme sadness and intense anger. The life she had envisaged in Australia was disappearing fast with every second. She had been so happy when they had married, found a little place to live, obtained jobs and the icing on the cake had been becoming pregnant with Daniel and then, gradually, all that hope, all that expectation, had melted away to be replaced with worry over her husband's inability to hold down a job for very long and whether he intended to stay with her.

If it hadn't been for Felicity, her boss at the hair salon, she doubted if her marriage and her residence in Australia would have lasted as long as it had. Felicity had been a tower of strength and wonderful support right from the moment when Suzanne set foot in the poshest salon in Adelaide for her interview. She had dressed Felicity's long, blonde hair in the latest fashionable style and blown her away. Felicity hadn't hesitated. She didn't want to lose such a find to her competitors and appointed Suzanne as her senior stylist immediately, offering her an exceedingly generous salary, which with Todd's inability to hold down a job for very long, had managed to keep their heads above water financially.

Suzanne had walked out of the salon for the last time a week ago with deep sadness. She and Felicity had become good friends in the few years they had worked together and it was a terrible wrench to have to leave it all behind. Felicity had tried to persuade her to stay but as much as Suzanne loved Australia, she craved to go home to the U.K. She longed for the countryside, damp days and freezing winters. She had had enough of heat, sometimes relentless and dizzying in the summer months. It was all very well having a beach not far away but she was always so busy at work, and looking after Daniel and the house, that it was rare she had any time for herself and Todd had been no help or support whatsoever.

He had changed so much once they were married. He had been such fun on the cruise ships and they were inseparable but once confined to Adelaide, he was restless, couldn't hold down a job for long and went on and on about how he missed the ships and couldn't they go back? Having Daniel hadn't helped as they certainly couldn't take a child with them. After a tense few years when Todd had walked out of job after job after only a few weeks or months, they had yet another blazing row when two weeks into his latest as a debt collector, he came home and announced he had had enough, had obtained a job on the excursions desk on a ship with the Princess line and was departing for a cruise of the Caribbean the very next day.

"I'm going and that's that," he said belligerently, "and you can't stop me. There's no need to panic, anyway. We'll still have the joint account and you will be able to access my salary."

"That's if you don't spend it on women and booze first," Suzanne had screamed, so angry with his casual attitude to their marriage and their son, that she bordered on hitting him.

Todd had ignored her. He had flung clothes into a suitcase and left their rented bungalow with a stubborn expression on his face and little else. No hug, no kiss, no apologies. Nothing. He just went. The gorgeous young man she had fallen in love with just walked out of her life. She knew he wouldn't come back. She knew she was on her own and left with total responsibility for Daniel. How she hated and despised her husband, leaving her with no support as he didn't even have a family she could turn to. His mother had died when he was in his teens and then his father had turned to drink in a big way and ended up in his grave far earlier than he should have done. Todd had no siblings and wider family so there was no-one Suzanne could lean on. She was on her own, totally and utterly … apart from friends, especially Felicity. But she needed more than that now. She wanted the security and warmth of people around her who really cared and there were only two who truly did. Darling Vicky and Alex, the two most wonderful people in the world as far as Suzanne was concerned. They had rescued her and Jeremy, her younger brother, from a life of misery, having been shuffled from one children's home to another, from one foster carer to another. It had been a fraught and stressful time until they were adopted by Vicky and Alex and taken to live with them in London and then later on, to The Beeches.

Suzanne had fallen in love with her new parents immediately and couldn't do enough to show her appreciation for the time, money and attention they lavished on her and Jeremy. Then little Katrina arrived. Suzanne had never been jealous of the new baby. She adored her and being allowed to help care for her was a real treat and she had rushed home from school every day to spend as much time with her as she could before bedtime.

Jeremy hadn't been so enamoured of course but then he was a boy. Jeremy. What a rotten little bugger he had turned out to be, to poor Lucy. Suzanne felt so ashamed of what he had done and it even went through her mind that she might be a bit to blame. If she had remained in or near to Harrogate and been around for her brother, he might not have been so easily swayed by Felix and Matthew and things might have been very different. Still there was no point thinking along those lines now. What was done was done and nothing could be changed. Jeremy was in his grave, at least his ashes were, buried in the grounds of The Beeches and that was that.

The Beeches. Suzanne couldn't wait to get there, to be surrounded by people she trusted and loved and who felt the same about her. She was exhausted from all the recent upheaval, with boxing up personal possessions for shipment to the U.K, giving the rented bungalow a good clean before handing in the keys, and saying a final, emotional farewell to Felicity who had bought Suzanne's car and then driven her and Daniel to the airport.

So, there was no turning back now. She and Daniel had finished with Australia. They had a new life to look forward to with Vicky and Alex, Lucy and Selena, Granny Ruth and Grandpa Philip ... and Katrina of course. It would be really good to see her little sister again.

She glanced back down at Daniel who was still asleep. It would be a few hours before they landed. She shut her eyes and followed her son's example.

* * *

"Your attention please," came the Captain's voice over the loudspeaker. "We will be landing at Heathrow in just under twenty minutes. I do hope you have enjoyed your flight with us today and I would ask that seatbelts are now fastened as a matter of priority and any loose items put away safely. Thank you and thank you for flying with us."

Suzanne did her belt up immediately with a nervous rush of fear. She hated flying but she hated taking off and landing even more, always terrified something was going to go wrong and the plane would crash on the runway and burst into flames and they would be unable to get out. She much preferred to travel by sea. At least she would stand a bit more of a chance if the ship went down as she was a strong swimmer and might just survive until help arrived.

She pondered on whether to wake Daniel but as he had kept his seat belt done up and they had another twenty minutes or so before landing, it seemed unnecessary. He was oblivious to what was going on and there was no need to disturb him for a little longer.

The cabin crew bustled up and down the aisles, making sure overhead lockers were shut properly, checking seat belts were fastened, smiling and efficient, hurrying to get to their own seats and do up their own belts. They all looked tired and would no doubt be as glad to land as the passengers. It had been a long flight.

Suzanne looked out of the window. They were approaching London. She could recognise certain landmarks; the Thames, looking cold and grey, busy with boats, meandering through the capital; the Tower, Buckingham Palace, Westminster. Sights she hadn't seen for years. She remembered her childhood when she lived with Vicky and Alex in their flat above the club in Kensington. She and Jeremy had been taken all around London at one time or another to see anything and everything of interest and it would be good to do the same with Daniel. They could catch the train down from Yorkshire every now and again and have a few days here. He was an inquisitive little boy. He would love it and it would be something to look forward to.

Daniel stirred and Suzanne woke him up properly. He had enjoyed taking off and would probably do the same with landing and would be disappointed if he missed it and anyway, she wanted the comfort of holding his hand.

"We're nearly here, Danny," she said, a bubble of excitement welling up inside her. "We're going to land in a minute. See, look, that's London down there. We'll be with Granny Ruth and Granny Vicky very soon now."

The flight landed without incident and after what seemed an age, they were through passport control, had collected their baggage and were being hugged tightly by Vicky and Ruth.

"Oh, Suzanne, you don't know how good it is to see you," exclaimed Vicky, "And you, young man," cuddling Daniel. "I haven't seen you for months. Gosh, you've grown."

"Hello, Daniel, I'm your Granny Ruth," Ruth smiled warmly at the child. She hadn't met him, never having been to Australia, so it was a real pleasure to finally see the little boy Vicky was always enthusing about.

"Oh, Great Granny, if you please," grinned Vicky. "I'm his Granny."

"Oh, don't," grinned Ruth. "That makes me feel really old."

"So, you're my Granny and you're my Granny," said Daniel with a puzzled expression on his little face, "but I already have a Granny … in Australia … although she's dead."

"Yes, darling, I'll explain it all to you later," said Suzanne, suddenly feeling exhausted now they had reached their destination.

Vicky looked at her sympathetically. She had been to Australia every year since Suzanne settled there and knew how she felt. "Come on. We have a room booked for you at the Ritz, next to ours. You can have a good rest and something decent to eat and we'll journey back to Yorkshire tomorrow. I need to see Katrina again before we go anyway."

"Katrina … oh, how is she getting on at Radley? Is she enjoying it?"

Vicky grabbed one of Suzanne's suitcases, while Ruth picked up the other. "That, Suzanne, is something I shall tell you about later, when you've had a good rest."

* * *

Katrina had woken that morning feeling stiff and sore but after a half hour yoga session, a banana smoothie and a long, hot shower, she felt more herself. Maria had rung to say she should present herself at the studio by midday, which gave her far more time to get ready than the day before as she had enough cash to afford a taxi all the way there rather than having to sit with the hoi polloi on the bus with very little money in her pocket.

She played with the four thousand pounds. If her parents weren't going to pay the exorbitant rent on this flat, even this amount wouldn't last long and she needed to save for Hollywood. Perhaps she should look for something cheaper, share with others. She shuddered at the thought. She wasn't good at sharing anything, let alone somewhere to live. But needs must. Getting herself to Hollywood, buying the type of clothes she would need to get noticed, renting somewhere decent, etc., etc., would need funding well. She didn't want to run out of money over there, although she knew damned well that if she really called for help, her parents would bail her out however much they said they wouldn't. But she didn't want to rely on them any longer. She wanted to show them she was capable of making a life and career without running to them all the time. So, she would have to compromise somehow. She would have a look in the letting agents on the way to work.

On the way to work, what a joke. Her stomach lurched. What would she be expected to do today? Would it be with Leo again? She pushed it all to the back of her mind. The money was good, more than good. It would get her to where she wanted to be and then she could forget all about this seedy episode of her life. After all, as the delightful Bill had pointed out, how many others had started this way? She certainly wasn't the first and was damned sure she wouldn't be the last.

It wasn't Leo today. It was two big black guys who leered at her horribly when she sashayed into the room with the enormous bed, devoid of clothes and the tablet Roger had given her a few minutes earlier taking hold. Their leers turned to smiles as she lay on the bed with them, grinning wickedly at Kevin, the cameraman, as the powerful effects of the drug made her want to do things to the two men and allow them to do things to her that she would never have dreamt of if she were in her right mind. The session went on for much longer than the day before and by the time they had finished with her, she was in a worse physical shape than the first time. Again, Maria called her a cab and handed her a wad of notes. It was more! Five thousand pounds! Christ! This was getting better and better. How much would it be next time?

"I'm available tomorrow," she muttered to Maria as she staggered to the taxi. Maria smiled. "Good. I'll let them know ... I'm sure they'll want you ... you seem to be their favourite at the moment so make the most of it. Favourites don't last long unless they are really adaptable."

"Oh, I can be adaptable ... very adaptable," murmured Katrina, settling back onto the leather seat of the cab. It would take a while to get back to Kensington and she could have a good sleep on the way. She hugged her bag to her chest and dropped off as soon as the car pulled away.

* * *

"She's not answering," said Vicky, not knowing whether to be annoyed or worried. "I don't know what to do, Ruth. Should I go to the flat now or just leave it? We're going home early in the morning and I won't have another chance for a while."

"Leave it. You know how obstinate she can be. She's doing her teenage thing, wanting to be an adult and not really getting there. Leave her to stew for a little longer. Keep ringing her from home and then come down again next week ... I'll come with you again if you want me to."

"Um. You're probably right," agreed Vicky, "We're all tired and need to get home. I just can't stop worrying about her though."

"No, of course you can't. We never stop worrying about our children," replied Ruth sorrowfully, wishing her Stephen was still alive so she could be concerned about him but he was cold in his grave now and would never need her again.

Vicky sat down beside Ruth on the sofa in the lounge of the suite they had booked at the Ritz, which had cost a small fortune but was worth every penny. She placed her hand over Ruth's and smiled warmly.

"Sorry ... I do go on a bit."

Ruth smiled back. "No, you don't. It's perfectly natural and if Katrina was mine, I would probably do the same ... in fact, I might have nearly killed her by now."

"Have you noticed how much like Delia she is becoming?"

"God! I hope not," exclaimed Ruth, sitting up abruptly.

"It's that look in her eyes. Daggers drawn ... and you know how she has idolised my blasted sister for years. She has newspaper cuttings of the trials in her room at home and photographs of her ... lots of photographs ... I so wish she hadn't gone to Delia's flaming wedding. She had always been curious about her but after that little trip she became ... quite frankly ... obsessed. She talked about nothing else but Delia for days afterwards ... how beautiful she was, how she was so lucky having Blairness, marrying Brian ... and when we discovered they had become the Earl and Countess of Glentagon ... well, she went overboard. I became sick to death of hearing about them and had to tell her not to utter another word ... and she didn't ... thank goodness ... and I sincerely hope she never sets eyes on Delia again."

"Gosh, yes. I agree. Heavens, if those two got together, it would be hell on earth. That man must have nerves of steel, marrying Delia with her reputation. I don't envy him if he should ever cross her."

"According to Lucy, he idolises the ground Delia walks on so, for his sake, I hope it lasts. If she should go on the rampage again

…," Ruth shuddered. She would always be terrified of Delia and what she might do.

They were interrupted from further discussion by Vicky's mobile notifying her of an incoming text. She took the phone from her black leather bag at her feet and grimaced.

"It's Katrina. She says she's too tired for visitors, she's gone to bed, to go home and she will ring me at the weekend."

"There, you see. She has been in touch. She loves you really and knows how much you worry about her. Now, put your mind at rest and concentrate on Suzanne and Daniel for a while … and perhaps, just perhaps, Katrina will start to grow up and sort her life out."

"God, I hope you're right, Ruth," replied Vicky glumly. "But I'm still very concerned. I just hope she's not on a downward spiral to disaster. It just doesn't bear thinking about but I'll leave her alone for now … I want to see Suzanne and Daniel settled at home. I'll come back down very soon and see what's what but if Katrina hasn't sorted herself out by then, I really am going to drag her back to Yorkshire, whether she likes it or not," she said determinedly, totally forgetting that now Katrina was eighteen and an adult, she could do whatever she pleased without any restrictions from her parents.

CHAPTER 7

Katrina first came across Summer in Starlight's reception area when arriving for work the following morning. The young, blonde-haired girl with a fringe that hung loosely over her startling blue eyes was sitting opposite Maria who was behind the desk, typing furiously. The girl looked as nervous as Katrina had on her first day and unusually for her, she felt a wave of sympathy, knowing just how the new recruit was feeling.

Maria introduced them.

"This is Katrina," she said to Summer with a vague hint of a smile. "She hasn't been with us for long but is already a rising star. You will be working with her today and she will show you the ropes, won't you, Katrina?"

Katrina nodded. "Yes. Sure. It's nothing to worry about. Really. You won't remember much about it anyway. I never do … and it's worth it, for the money."

"I didn't want to come here," whispered Summer when Maria answered a telephone call and couldn't listen to what the girls were saying.

"Oh?" said Katrina, sitting down beside her, deciding to rest her body while she could. Roger had warned her that today's session would be a little more hectic, which meant she would leave here today with a shattered body … but with a bag full of cash again. She had to remember that. It was what was keeping her going … what would get her to Hollywood and to where she wanted to be.

"No. I've tried so many agencies but no-one wanted me. No-one seems to think I can act … but I know I can. I just need someone to see it … to give me a chance."

Katrina grimaced. "I know that feeling. I've done the rounds too and they all said the same to me … but I'm saving hard to get to Hollywood now … and this job is helping enormously. The money is so good. A few more months and I'll have enough …

that's if I can get somewhere cheaper to live. I can't afford the place I'm in now."

"I'm looking for digs too. My parents have disowned me. I've been sofa surfing for weeks but my friends are becoming fed up with it. That's why I need this job … so I can pay rent somewhere."

Katrina stared at her, wondering what Summer had done to make her parents disown her but now was not the time to ask. She seemed decent enough, wearing cheap but clean clothes, didn't appear to be on drugs or an alcoholic. Her bare arms were devoid of needle marks and her hands were motionless in her lap, even though she looked as scared as hell. Katrina thought quickly. If they were both working here and could get a flat together somewhere in the vicinity, that would save on travel costs and help her get the cash she needed much faster. She drew in her breath. Nothing ventured, nothing gained.

"If you get on okay today … and want to come back … how about we find a place together … somewhere near here?"

Summer raised her head, pushing her fringe away from her eyes and the strands that were brushing her cheeks, behind her ears. She was a stunner, Katrina thought, now she could see her properly. Her skin was soft and clear of spots, she had high cheekbones, beautifully formed eyebrows, long lashes and perfect white teeth as she smiled at Katrina with relief.

"Oh, that would be marvellous. I didn't want to live on my own."

"Right," said Katrina, taking charge. "We'll get on to it in the morning … that's if you survive today … we'll see how you feel later … anyway, there's no point in doing anything about flat hunting then as we'll be too exhausted. Believe me, all you want to do when you leave here is find a bed and sleep for hours." She gave a hollow laugh.

"Oh God," gasped Summer. "Is it that bad?"

Katrina sighed. "Just close your mind to what you're doing … Bill will give you a pill that will help … and if we are working together today, just follow my lead. The men ... they aren't so bad ... especially Leo ... he's a dream ... and as gentle as he can be under the circumstances."

Maria finished her phone call at the same time as the buzzer on her desk shattered the peace of the foyer. She nodded to Katrina. "They want you now."

Katrina stood up and smiled at Summer. "It's a bit scary when you first see Roger and Bill but just go with the flow and I'll see you soon."

Maria had been right. The girls were working together today. They were expected to cavort with Leo and Saracen, a big black guy with rippling muscles and dreadlocks. As the bed was huge, two king-sized fixed together, there was ample room for the four of them to show off their antics to the best advantage. Summer, once the pill Roger gave her had taken hold, was on fire and fondled Katrina willingly as the two naked men on the bed watched before joining in. Katrina had declined the enhancer. The pills gave her blinding headaches afterwards and now she had grown used to the idea of what she was doing, she was actually having fun and wanted to experience it with a clear head.

As she lay on the bed, Leo thrusting into her, and Summer, astride Rastus beside them with a look of sheer lust on her face, she wondered how much Roger and Bill were making out of all this. It must be a hell of a lot of money because if they were paying her what they did, they were probably paying the others the same, which amounted to an exorbitant amount every day. She hadn't really thought about it before ... where the films were ending up and who, exactly, were looking at them. Presumably, and hopefully, it was just dirty old men in the privacy of their own homes. It would be so humiliating if anyone she knew actually saw what she was up to, especially her family. Anyhow, she couldn't dwell on what might happen. She was making money, had a new flatmate once they found somewhere decent, and she was going to Hollywood. She smiled warmly at Leo and pulled his head down to hers, licking his mouth playfully as Kevin brought the camera in for a closer shot. Summer groaned in ecstasy beside her as her body shook and trembled with a massive orgasm. Katrina grinned. Summer wasn't faking it.

* * *

As they weren't expected at the studio until later the next day, Katrina and Summer met up in Greenwich just after nine a.m. to tour the letting agents.

Summer was obviously tired from the exertions of the previous day but, like Katrina, was ecstatic about how much she had earned and was keen to do it again. It hadn't been so very bad with Katrina by her side and whatever was in the pill Roger had given her, it had certainly taken away all her inhibitions.

"This one looks good … and that one too," said Katrina, pointing into the window at the row of pictures and details of flats and houses to let. She threw her abundance of auburn hair to one side to clear her vision, Summer almost pushing her nose into the window beside her as she stared hard at the particulars too.

"That one is cheaper … and has a bit of a garden … being on the ground floor. That would be nice, to be able to sit out in the summer."

"Um. True … but then we would have to keep it tidy and I don't know about you, but I'm not remotely interested in gardening … and after all, the park isn't far away if you want to sit outside … and it has that spectacular view over London."

"Yes. You're right, I suppose. Should we ask to view the other one then? It looks pretty decent and we would have a bedroom each."

"Yep. Let's do it and now. It would be great if we could get it all sorted before we have to be at the studio."

The letting agent was obliging. The flat had been empty for a week and he had an hour spare to show them around.

It was really handy for the studio, right in the next street above a florist. The heady smell of roses, sweet peas, carnations and dahlias accompanied them up the stairs to the side of the shop, which was nice, Katrina mused. Far better than fish and chips or some other kind of take-away and it would be quiet too as the shop would be shut at tea-time.

The flat wasn't exactly big but provided ample space for two single girls. Both bedrooms were the same size, one overlooking the street and the other, the rear of another row of houses. There was a tiny shower room which was adequate for their needs but the tatty grey shower curtain with mould along the edges, definitely needed replacing surmised Katrina with a shudder, thinking sorrowfully of the luxurious, spacious, beautifully clean flat she was about to leave. Never mind. She didn't intend to stay here long. She would grab every chance she could in the next few months to get as much work as Bill and Roger would give her. Then she would head for the stars … and be a star. Residing in this kind of accommodation would then be a vague and distant memory.

The lounge was a decent sized square room with two sofas in a dismal shade of brown, which had seen better days. There was no carpet on the wooden floor, just a lime green rug in front of the gas fire. The kitchen had everything a kitchen should and looked remarkably clean, which was something to be grateful for, thought Katrina, looking at Summer to see her reaction.

Summer was positively glowing and grinned at Katrina. "This is great. I love it."

"Ok. We'll take it," said Katrina, smiling at the letting agent, a middle-aged man in a brown suit, white shirt and sickly yellow tie. "When can we move in?"

He flicked through a few papers in the folder he was carrying. "We will have to take a few details, obtain some references, do credit checks, etc., but all being well, you could be in within a week."

"Oh," remarked Katrina. "We might have a slight problem there. I … we don't have any references."

"Ok. That's not a problem. Do you have anyone who could be a guarantor for you … a family member perhaps?"

Katrina grinned. "Oh yes. My mother. Lady Victoria Canleigh … Mrs. Gregory as she is now … or my father, Alex Gregory. They own The Beeches hotel just outside of Harrogate and are simply loaded. I'm sure they won't mind."

"Right. Come down to the office now and fill in the application form and then perhaps I can ring your parents and we can get the ball rolling."

* * *

Gary Chambers telephoned Vicky and then faxed the details of the flat through to her as she had requested. She read them thoroughly. It looked a decent place in a decent area with an affordable rent, quite suitable for two girls sharing. She did wonder who this other girl was with whom Katrina was going to live but would find out when she popped down to London next week. She was still desperately worried about her daughter but if Katrina was going to dig her heels in and not come home, there wasn't much she could do about it. As Ruth had pointed out, Katrina was eighteen years old now and could make her own decisions. Sighing deeply and hoping desperately she was doing the right thing and Katrina wouldn't get herself too deep into whatever she was doing, she picked up the phone and rang the letting agents.

"Yes, that's all fine, Mr. Chambers. I've signed the form and am faxing it back to you," she confirmed.

CHAPTER 8

Three weeks later, Suzanne and Daniel had settled well into life at The Beeches. Vicky and Alex had offered them a small cottage in the grounds to reside in. It had been used occasionally for the convenience of staff if they had to work late and couldn't get home or let to guests if they required somewhere more private than the hotel. It was perfect for Suzanne and Daniel as there was a small enclosed garden and a lovely view of the countryside to the rear of The Beeches.

Suzanne had no furniture as she had sold everything bulky before she left Australia, which was just as well as the cottage was already furnished, with exquisite taste. She was a bit concerned that Daniel might ruin something but Vicky was unconcerned and waved Suzanne's worries aside.

"This place is perfect for you and if something gets spoilt, it's just too bad. I'm so pleased to have you both here. I'm sorry about the circumstances but to have you near to us again is a real pleasure and I can't wait to have you working with us as well … and anyway, you need somewhere you can be alone. Working over the shop might be convenient but it does have its drawbacks," she said with years of experience behind her from living over the club in Kensington and then at The Beeches. "Believe me, you'll be glad to have a little place of your own to escape to after you have pampered our clients every day."

Vicky had whisked Suzanne into the area she had put aside for the salon as soon as they had arrived home from London and they had talked about little else since. Within a week the decorators had finished, the fixtures and fittings were in situ and all the paraphernalia for a top-class hair salon had been delivered. Suzanne held interviews for two top stylists to join her and just days later, it was all up and running.

Vicky purposefully kept Suzanne busy, hoping to distract her from the heartbreak of her ruined marriage. They also had Daniel to consider and had spent a day touring three different schools in the local area but decided it was best for him to attend the Parlham school for boys to the north of Harrogate, which had a splendid reputation. Following a long chat with the headmaster, a walk to see all the facilities and bumping into an enthusiastic games tutor, Daniel had seemed keen to go, especially as he was already showing a real interest in sport.

Once Daniel commenced at Parlham, he soon made friends, often bringing them home to play or to do homework together. Suzanne was pleased to see he wasn't missing his father very much, if at all, and seemed quite happy with his lot, not missing the sunshine of Australia and fascinated with the beauty of an English autumn, especially when they paid a visit to Lucy at Dingle Dell and she gave them a tour of the grounds of Canleigh and walked around the lake. Daniel loved it and commented that it was just the sort of place he would like when he grew up, which made them all smile.

Suzanne didn't hear from Todd. He made no effort to write to her or ring her, although she had sent him a text to say they had arrived safely in England. Somehow, she didn't think they would hear from him again and decided that she would have to visit a solicitor and set the wheels in motion for a divorce. It would be better for all of them as they would all know where they stood and Daniel could banish any hopes that his parents may get back together.

She was so lucky having had Vicky and Alex to turn to. Considering she wasn't a blood daughter, as was Katrina, they had really pulled out all the stops for her, giving her somewhere really nice to live … and a job. The support was tremendous and she was immensely grateful, determined to work as hard as she possibly could to make the salon a huge success to repay them.

It was easy. Suzanne was a brilliant hairdresser and once someone had been lucky enough to have her do their hair, they wanted her again and again, especially when they discovered she had looked after many famous people when at sea. She quickly gained a good reputation and not only did she have the hotel clients to look after, but many ladies living in the local area decided they would visit the salon and partake of refreshment in the hotel afterwards, lingering over lunch or afternoon tea, which made Vicky and Alex even happier. Visits to the beauty salon and memberships of the spa also increased as more notice was taken of the facilities in the hotel. The hotel had been doing well prior to the opening of the hair salon but within a few weeks of Suzanne's arrival, the footfall had definitely increased, along with a noticeable jump in revenue.

"I think I shall have to steal Suzanne away from you," teased Lucy a few weeks later when she had popped in with Selena after picking her up from school. "Canleigh Hall could do with a hair salon too. I think I shall have to look into it."

"I'm glad Suzanne's settled so well," replied Vicky, as she tickled Selena under the chin. Selena chortled merrily. She idolised her Great Aunty Vicky, especially as she always gave her such delicious things to eat and the cherry cake in front of her was one of them. She picked happily at the cherries and popped them into her mouth, leaving the sponge until last.

"I was so concerned about her but she seems to be really enjoying her work ... and Daniel is happy at school, so it all seems to be working out well ... so, it's just Katrina I have to worry about."

"Oh, and how is she doing?" asked Lucy, drinking her tea and picking up the teapot to pour another. It was Yorkshire tea, her favourite, and she could never stop at one cup.

Vicky didn't want any more and shook her head when Lucy waved the teapot in her direction.

"Honestly ... I really don't know. I was going to go down and see but what with settling Suzanne and Daniel in and all the normal day to day activities, I just haven't had the time. She's moved into a new flat with a girl called Summer and they are both working ...

but at what, I have no idea, and quite frankly, I'm not sure if I want to know anyway so while she isn't sending out an SOS, I think I will leave it for a while before I go down ... but then it's going to be Christmas soon and we're always so busy here. She's promised she will come home for a few days then .... and as this Summer hasn't any family, Katrina asked if she could come too. Naturally, I said yes."

"Well, there you are then. I shouldn't worry too much. As long as she has a decent roof over her head and is working, that's something."

"Yes, but at what, Lucy? I so wish she hadn't packed in Radley. At least I knew she was safe there and had decent people to support her, even though her studies would probably never come to anything."

"Oh, why not?"

Vicky looked at Lucy and bit her lip. She still hadn't recovered from the shock of hearing Katrina had blackmailed her drama teacher at Thistledown into giving her all those parts in school plays. It was too horrific to think her own daughter could do such a thing ... and she still hadn't told Alex. He would go ballistic.

Lucy was looking at her with a puzzled expression. "Aunt Vicky?"

Vicky gave Lucy a despairing look. "I never did think Katrina's career choice was the correct one ... you never did see her in the school plays, did you, Lucy?"

Lucy shook her head. The performances had always seemed to be when she was otherwise engaged.

"Well, quite frankly ... she was awful ... there were other students in lesser parts who were far, far better and I could never understand how she always obtained the lead in whatever play was put on."

"But the write-ups in the local rag ... they were always positive."

"Yes ... for the whole play ... not for Katrina's individual performance."

"So why was she chosen ... why didn't other students get the parts?"

Vicky hesitated. She knew Lucy would never breathe a word to anyone but even so, to actually tell someone what Katrina had done was humiliating and it was also admitting she was a useless parent if her daughter could get away with such dreadful behaviour.

"Aunt Vicky ... for goodness sake ... tell me, please ... you're beginning to worry me now."

"Promise you won't tell Alex. I will tell him ... in time ... but I have to pick the right moment as he's going to be so very angry."

"Okay ... but you really are worrying me."

"She was blackmailing her drama teacher," Vicky said quickly. "The stupid woman was having an affair with the husband of another teacher. Katrina found out and blackmailed her."

Lucy gasped. "Oh, my God! No! That's dreadful. How ... when did you find out?"

"Katrina told Ruth and I when we were down in London a few weeks ago. Oh Lucy, I never could understand how she got those parts but it makes sense now, although she was still deluding herself, insisting on going to Radley but as Katrina always seems to get what she wants, she naturally went. Someone there must have told her a home truth or two and knocked her down a peg, which was probably why she stormed out. She couldn't take it ... yet she still goes on about Hollywood, how she is going to get there, by hook or by crook ... and become rich and famous. She wanted us to fund her but we've refused. If she couldn't manage to knuckle down at Radley after all that cost us, bearing in mind she was still in this country, we flatly refuse to pay for her to go to America. If she can't make it here, I doubt very much she will there with all that extra competition ... and if she does manage to get to the States, I'm going to worry myself sick. At least I can get down to London easily or she could get back here but California is a different kettle of fish."

"Oh dear, Aunty Vicky. I'm so sorry. I really don't know what to say or what I can do to help."

Vicky smiled ruefully at her niece. "There's nothing, darling. We just have to pray Katrina will be sensible and eventually get onto the right path and be happy with her lot."

* * *

Katrina wasn't too happy at all. Roger and Bill were expecting her to work every day now, even at weekends and she was becoming utterly exhausted and even though the money she was stashing away was considerable, she could easily do with a weekend or even a day off. She didn't always work with Summer either, which was a mystery as Summer seemed to be spending a considerable number of evenings being picked up by a man with a black BMW and was very mysterious about where she was going. With no sign of Summer working during the day, Katrina was becoming miffed. She had been on the scene first and had helped Summer settle in. If she was doing something more lucrative, Katrina didn't see why she couldn't be part of it too. Surely it couldn't be any worse than what she had to do in the studio with Bill and Roger looking on, leering and sniggering in the background.

She finally caught Summer off guard as she sneaked back into the flat early one morning, looking like death, not even possessing the energy to make it to her bedroom. She collapsed on to the sofa, kicked her shoes off and was just about to close her eyes when Katrina emerged from her bedroom and sat down heavily beside her.

"Now. Will you tell me what the hell is going on and where you have been?"

Drained from the exertions of the night, Summer couldn't raise the energy to argue. "Oh, if you must know, thanks to Bill and Roger I'm the plaything for rich blokes of all colours and creeds in fancy hotels around London."

"Oh, really," Katrina pouted. "But why ... why are they pimping you out? Why didn't they keep you in the studio with me ... and why didn't they ask me?"

"Because you're great at what you do, I suppose. You look so damned good on camera, so sexy, so desirable ... and they are making a mint out of any film you are performing in ... whereas I ... I much prefer the privacy of someone's bedroom ... in fact, to be honest I quite enjoy it ... and you could just see what these men shower me with ... look at this bracelet I was given tonight ... must be worth a bomb."

Katrina stared at the gold band encrusted with several diamonds. Summer was right. It looked damned expensive.

"I had a ruby necklace last week, with matching earrings," Summer grinned. "And there's plenty of champagne and lots of lovely food if I want it ... beautiful baths and showers and jacuzzi's. It's not too bad a life at all."

"Hell!" exclaimed Katrina. "I'm talking to Bill and Roger today. I want a bit of this. I'm damned fed up with the studio ... it's so damned seedy .... and if you're getting all these extras and I can do the same, we can sell all the jewellery and with what we've saved we can soon get to Hollywood."

"Oh, Hollywood. That's all you ever talk about. You'll never get there. It will be a complete waste of time ... you and hundreds of other hopefuls trying to make it and not succeeding. I certainly can't be bothered with it now. I'm going to continue what I'm doing until I find some man who will be willing to set me up in a fancy apartment and shower me with gifts and cash if I keep him happy. Now I've seen what can happen and how possible it is, I don't intend to mess about trying anything else. If you've any sense, you should do the same. If you do go to Hollywood, you'll probably only end up doing exactly what you're doing now."

"Well at least the sun will always shine," groaned Katrina looking outside at the pouring rain and thinking about spending yet another day in that dreadful studio bonking for hours. God, life was so bloody depressing. She was going to have to talk to Bill and Roger about spending less time filming and see if she could get a bit of what Summer had ... she certainly wasn't going to miss out if she could help it and if they said no, it just wouldn't be fair!

CHAPTER 9

Katrina had marched straight into the office as soon as she knew Bill was alone. Roger hadn't deigned to make an appearance but as he was becoming heavily reliant on cocaine, it wasn't surprising. Bill didn't take drugs of any description, although he shot a copious amount of whisky into his coffee in the mornings and in his tea in the afternoons. What he drank in the evenings, Katrina had no idea as she was never around at that time and didn't want to know anyway.

He sat on the opposite side of his desk to her, leaned back in his chair and eyed her up and down. She was already devoid of her day clothes, ready for the next session which was due to take place and wore just an emerald green velvet dressing gown she kept at the studio to give her a little dignity when she wasn't writhing about on beds with various males and females. Bill was well aware she was naked under the dressing gown and licked his lips. He wanted, more than anything, to throw her over the desk and give her a good seeing to but so far, he had kept his hands to himself as she was too valuable an asset and he didn't want her marching out. She was a bloody good porn star, was in high demand and becoming more popular by the minute with their clients who bought the material they were churning out at a rapid rate. They had used what was probably hundreds of girls since they had been in operation but most ended up useless junkies or looked bloody miserable or tacky while they were supposedly in the throes of passion. Katrina was different. She actually had class, was bloody beautiful with a fabulous body, great boobs and an awesome head of auburn hair which fell way down her back and he was more than pleased she no longer wanted pills to help her through the sessions. She actually looked as if she enjoyed it and made the whole damned business so easy. He grimaced as he remembered how they had females screaming their heads off in the past, getting hysterical, crying and refusing to take the pills. He had had to smack one or two around but they had looked so bloody frightened, it hadn't been worth it.

"So, what's the matter, darlin?" he drawled, lighting up a cigarette but not offering her one. "I presume you want more money?"

"No, actually ... although anything extra would always be welcome," she said slowly, not sure how he was going to take what she was about to say. Bill had a nasty temper. She had seen him punch and threaten a couple of girls with a real pasting a few weeks ago and she didn't want to go there.

He looked up in surprise. "So, what is it you do want? Leo can't come in today ... damned dentist or something ... so you're paired up with Tyrone and Connor and that new girl, Veronica ... you should all look good together ... and do me a favour, give it your all ... I've some rather important Russian clients waiting to see this little showing ... we're getting in pretty tight with them and it's a damned lucrative market ... so there might be a bit extra for you too if you do well."

Katrina tried to prevent a shudder. She didn't like Tyrone much. He was really rough and she always came away from a session with him feeling she had done ten rounds with a champion boxer. Perhaps she could get Veronica to pair up with him and she could have Connor. He was young, the same age as her, and like Leo, possessed a good sense of humour and made sessions a bit more fun.

She gulped. It was now or never. "I wouldn't mind a bit of what Summer is doing."

"Oh, really?" Bill dragged hard on his cigarette. He exhaled slowly and eyed her up and down. "I prefer you fresh for the studio, darlin. You're a damned good little actress with your clothes off and damned popular with our clients. If you go out all night serving our other patrons, you'll be no good to us during the day.

"But ...,"

"But nothing! Just remember who is boss here and also, we have a rather nice little portfolio of your work now … and I'm pretty sure you wouldn't want darling Mummy and Daddy seeing exactly what you get up to, now would you? So, until I decide to dispense with you … in whatever manner I choose … you will do as I say and I want you in the studio. Do you hear?"

His voice was quietly aggressive and Katrina, for the first time since the day she had walked into this office, felt a real sense of fear. 'Until I dispense with you … in whatever manner I choose' he had said. What did he mean? Surely he didn't intend to kill her. She began to wonder what had happened to the girls who had worked here in the past. None of them were ever mentioned but there had probably been quite a few, the willing and not so willing. What had happened to them?

She pulled her dressing gown around her tightly as he stood up and walked towards her. "Now, come here," he grinned, throwing all caution to the winds. He had her now, threatening to show her parents what she was really like. He had seen the look of fear in her eyes. She would do anything to prevent that happening. Why the hell hadn't he thought of it earlier? She was all his now, for the taking, and he could do anything with her he wanted. He licked his lips.

"Let's have a bit of fun before you start work," he grinned, showing big, yellow teeth. "Warm you up a bit. I've been wanting to get to grips with you for a while now."

Panic gripped her. He was going to really hurt her. The look in his eye was terrifying as he advanced towards her, his hands outstretched ready to grab her, sling her over the desk and brutally rape her. He was going to do it if she didn't move, or do something to defend herself. For a second, she stood where she was, her legs turning to jelly.

"Get here," he ordered, his eyes glittering, his big lips moist as he licked them again. "I'm bloody well going to have you now. I've been lusting after you for months, and now you're going to give me as much pleasure as you do those other halfwits I employ. Get that bloody dressing gown off," he growled as he approached her and yanked at the belt but even though she was hanging on for grim death, it came undone and her robe slipped open. She stood, mesmerised, while Bill stared at every inch of her body. He put out a hand and ran it over her breasts, pulling hard at her nipples. She shuddered, the fear tight in her belly. She still couldn't speak, still couldn't move. He pulled the dressing gown off her shoulders and it slid to the floor. He grabbed her hand and pulled her towards the leather sofa in the corner of the room while he tugged at his trouser belt with his other hand.

Above the sofa was a shelf, overflowing with empty beer cans, ashtrays and three bottles of whisky. Bill was having difficulty with the zip on his trousers. In his frustration he bent his head to see what was wrong. Katrina saw her chance. She grabbed a full bottle of whisky and brought it down hard on his head. It shattered into pieces, whisky spilling all over him and the cheap brown carpet. With a deep groan, Bill slid to the floor and didn't move. Katrina, terrified she might have killed him, bent down to see if he was still breathing. With relief she discovered he was but she had no time to lose. She had burnt her boats now and had to get out or he really would kill her when he came round. She rapidly pulled her dressing gown back on, hurtled out of the room, down the corridor to the changing room and dressed quicker than she had ever done in her life before. Stepping fearfully into reception, she was relieved to see Maria had her back to her and was talking on the telephone. She sidled past and made her way quietly to the stairs to the street above. Then she ran.

* * *

As Katrina dashed out of the door and charged down the road as if all hell was after her, Roger emerged from the newsagents further along and looked at her with astonishment as she hurtled past him. He debated on whether he should follow her and find out what had happened to send her flying out of the studio in such a panic or go and find Bill and see if he knew what was going on. He decided on the latter. Katrina had disappeared rapidly and he wasn't feeling up to a chase and then dealing with a hysterical woman.

He walked into reception, ignoring Maria who was on the phone, and headed straight into the office. Bill was on the floor beside the sofa, groaning and swearing under his breath.

"That flaming Katrina … she did this," he spat, holding his head as he crawled unsteadily up onto the sofa.

"Christ! What the hell for?" asked Roger, staring at the broken whisky bottle on the floor and the blood on Bill's head which was now all over his hands as he tried to cover up the wound. "What the hell did you do to her?"

"Nothing! Bloody nothing!" Bill yelled, clutching his head. "Get me to the bloody hospital … I probably need stitches … and when we get back, I'm going after that little bitch."

"I presume you were going to rape her," remarked Roger. "You stupid bugger. She's too valuable for that. If we lose her, we lose a hell of a lot of money. You know that. None of those other girls are a patch on her. You stupid, stupid git."

"Shut up, will you? I know … but I couldn't bloody help myself. She stood there … her tits pushing out of that dressing gown …,"

"Oh, for Christ's sake! All those girls we have in here … all for the taking … and it won't matter a jot what you do with them … but no, you have to have a go at her. I can't believe you, man. We need her. We really need her. We'll never find another like her."

"Shit! My bloody head hurts like hell. Stop messing about. Ring an ambulance or something."

"Only if you promise to make it up to her. Apologise. Grovel. Send her flowers, chocolates ... jewellery. Just make sure she comes back."

"Okay, okay," groaned Bill as the pain engulfed him. "Anything, anything ... just get me some help ... bloody little bitch!"

* * *

Roger had rung her to apologise immediately Bill had left the studio in a taxi, heading towards the nearest Accident and Emergency department.

"He really is very sorry," said Roger, "and promises it will never happen again. Look, we realise we have been working you rather hard lately ... because you're so damned sexy and photogenic. Have a couple of days off, have a good rest and then come back to us. Please. I'm having a few things delivered to you and you'll also get more cash per session. How does that sound?"

Katrina had acquiesced. She didn't want to lose her job. She badly needed the money to get to Hollywood. Just a while longer and she could go. So, if Roger was promising Bill wouldn't try and touch her again, she could go back. She agreed and was highly amused when an hour later she received an enormous bouquet, a gold watch and a pair of diamond earrings.

However, even if she had wanted to, she couldn't have gone to work the next day as she woke up feeling like death. She had suffered a bout of flu five years earlier and knew instantly what it was. She had a temperature, ached all over, had a sore throat and a hacking cough.

Summer heard her and popped her head in when she arrived home from goodness knows where at 9.00 a.m., shattered and ready for her bed. She had kindly found a packet of painkillers, prepared a hot water bottle and a flask of tea and left Katrina to it. She dozed on and off for the remainder of the day and didn't fully wake up until there was movement in Summer's room indicating she was getting ready to go out in the evening. Dragging herself out of bed and into the lounge, Katrina peered blearily at her flatmate who was on the sofa applying a liberal layer of foundation to her face.

"I've got a blasted spot … look … right on my chin." Summer exclaimed. "God knows why, I eat well and spend a fortune on the right makeup and always cleanse. Do you think anyone will notice?" she said, holding the mirror one way and another to see her skin in the best light.

"No. I shouldn't worry about it. Somehow, I don't think any of your punters will care two hoots … they will be far more concerned with other parts of your body," sighed Katrina, settling into the chair opposite and watching Summer apply black eyeshadow with a silver highlighter, black eyeliner above and below her eyes and then three layers of mascara. Her lips were covered with bright red lipstick and a clear gloss. Summer tossed her hair back and examined her face thoroughly in the mirror. Katrina had to admit, she did look good.

Summer stood up. "What do you think of the outfit? I went shopping this afternoon while you were asleep. I hope tonight's punters are generous as I nearly had to take out a mortgage to buy this little lot."

"You look great," encouraged Katrina, wishing she felt and looked as robust as Summer in her peacock blue shimmery dress which was so short it barely covered her backside and left little to the imagination. The previous day Summer had treated herself to a spray tan and her bare legs, arms and shoulders were a gorgeous colour. She slipped on a pair of silver sling backs with six-inch heels and picked up her silver bag.

"So, where is it tonight … and who with?" asked Katrina.

"I think it's a private residence … not a hotel. Germans I believe … I've not done these before … but Bill seems to want to impress them as they're loaded and he wants to do a lot more business with them."

"That's a bit dodgy, going to their place. I'm surprised you agreed to it. You're not going on your own, are you?"

Summer gave a flicker of a smile. "Don't have much choice, do I? If I said no, Bill would probably go berserk ... but I'll be okay. Have been so far. Oh ... there's the car," she remarked, hearing a horn outside and peeking out of the window at the street below. "I'll see you in the morning. Try and have a good night's sleep and if you're lucky, I might cook you a nice breakfast."

"Um. Pigs might fly. Be careful," Katrina warned as Summer flew out of the door as the car horn sounded again.

Katrina went back to bed. She didn't even have the energy to lay on the sofa and watch television. She buried her head in the pillows and willed herself back to sleep. She had to knock whatever she had on the head as fast as possible. Being ill wasn't going to get her to Hollywood.

* * *

Summer didn't make it back to the flat. The car, with its monosyllabic driver, took her to a part of London she had no knowledge of, in the heart of Bloomsbury, to a block of Georgian flats. He dropped her at the entrance and told her to make her way up to flat twenty-three on the fifth floor.

She did as she was told, giving a wide smile to the concierge in the entrance hall who looked the other way and pretended he hadn't seen her. Stuck up bugger, she thought as she pressed the button to summon the lift for the fifth floor. Once inside she looked in the mirror on the wall. Outwardly, she appeared calm and in control. Inwardly, she was shaking like a leaf. However much she put on a brave face for Katrina, she found these private sessions a bit nerve wracking, especially when she was working alone, as she would be tonight. So far, she had only met men who treated her with a degree of respect but then they had mostly been English or American. She liked the Americans. They were the most generous. She'd had one or two French blokes too and they had been quite sweet and almost romantic but she had never had a German and they didn't come with the best reputation. The other girls Summer had met who had been with a few, flatly refused to do it again. "Bloody rough ... almost brutal," one girl told her "and they never speak English. Just gesture and shout and if you don't do what they want quick enough, they give you a slap ... bloody Nazis."

Summer's stomach churned as she remembered the girl's words. God, she hoped she wasn't in for a bad time ... but it was too late now. She was here and she had to get on with it. She looked at her gold Cartier watch she had bought last week from the proceeds of an evening with two Americans. It was nine thirty. At this time tomorrow morning she would be back in her own bed in the flat with Katrina, all of this a bad dream. She thought about the pills she had in her bag. Bill had given her a good supply but she didn't like to take them. They might make her feel extra randy and uninhibited but losing control of her faculties was bloody stupid, especially being in a place she didn't know and all alone with no back-up. No. She would only drink water tonight and make sure her head was clear in case she had to do a runner.

The lift reached the fifth floor. Summer stepped out and looked at the numbers on the brass plaques on the two doors in front of her. Number 22 was on the left and number 23, on the right. They must be enormous flats, she surmised, as there were only two on the whole floor and the building was vast.

She rang the bell on number 23. It was opened immediately by an extremely tall man with swarthy skin, long face and black rimmed glasses. He was slightly overweight with a protruding belly. His smile was more of a smirk as he stared at her appreciatively.

"You'll do," he said with a German accent. "Get in here and remove your clothes."

Relieved that at least she could understand him, Summer moved into the flat but turned cold when he shut the door firmly behind her and she saw three more men in the lounge. Surely she wasn't expected to service them all? Surely there was going to be other females here.

One of the men stood up and moved towards her. "Excellent," he said slowly, staring at her legs. "Bill certainly knows how to pick you girls. He sings your praises, Summer, and tells us that you will be able to keep us all of us amused until the morning. I do hope he is right."

Summer could have willingly killed Bill at that moment. The bastard had known there were more than two men here. She had managed two plenty of times but not four. She didn't think she could do it. Not all night.

She gave a nervous grin. Perhaps she did need those damned pills after all. She couldn't do what was expected of her otherwise. None of them were remotely attractive, which didn't help. One was grinning, showing off yellow teeth, and had really bad skin which seemed to cover most of his body as he sat with his shirt wide open. Another was grossly overweight, and his hair was thick with grease. She wondered when he had last washed it. Then there was the one who was standing beside her now, running a finger up and down her bare arm, smelling disgusting, a mixture of sweat and alcohol. He was perspiring badly, whether it was because the flat was overly warm or because of excitement at what was to come she had no idea but whatever it was, he was repulsive.

"I … I have to go to the bathroom first," she said, feeling nauseous and afraid. "I need a wee."

"It's through there," the first one gestured, pointing to a door on the opposite side of the hall, "and don't come back with your clothes on."

They watched her, sniggering and laughing as she moved quickly across the room and into the bathroom, shutting the door behind her and locking it quickly. She looked around. There was a window but she was five floors up. She couldn't jump. She couldn't get out. God, she was really scared now. There was no way they would let her make a run for it. She had to go through with it. With tears of fear welling up in her eyes, she fumbled in her bag and found the tiny box of pink pills. Perhaps she should take the lot.

She suddenly felt terribly tired and a wave of huge depression flooded over her. Was all this worth it? She hated herself for what she had become, although she always put a brave face on it. A whore ... a common flaming whore. That was what she was and she had a nasty feeling she would never be anything else.

She took the pills. Not just one, which would have given her the energy and carefree attitude to get through what she had to do, but two and then another and then another. She suddenly had no desire to live her life as she did and could see no way out. She hadn't met anyone who wanted to lavish money and possessions on her for her favours and keep her in the style to which she wanted to become accustomed and she might earn good money now but she always seemed to spend it. She wasn't good at saving like Katrina, who had a nice stash under the bed and counted it regularly, making sure she was on track to get to Hollywood but she didn't seem to be able to do that. Every penny she was given seemed to disappear so fast. Admittedly she bought a lot of very nice, expensive clothes but then she had to look the part when turning up at classy hotels but even so, it just seemed to slide out of her hands with increasing speed and it was frustrating she didn't seem to be able to plan for a more stable, decent lifestyle. So, what was the bloody point of it all? No-one would miss her if she ended it all now. Her parents didn't care a fig. She had no brothers or sisters and no real friends either. She didn't really class Katrina as a friend. She was just convenient for someone to share a flat with and help pay the bills. No, no-one would care. She took another pill. Her head was beginning to spin ... or was it the bathroom ... she took another ... it was the last. She had taken ten. Would that do the trick?

Someone was banging loudly on the door. "Get out here! Now! We haven't paid a fortune for you to hang about in the bathroom," the man shouted aggressively. "Snell ... Snell ... or I'll break the door down."

Summer couldn't move, even if she had wanted to. Her whole body felt as heavy as lead. Her fingers were twitching and wouldn't keep still. Her mouth was dry, she couldn't feel her tongue, her eyes felt as if they were popping out of her head. There was a terrible throbbing in her temples. Her heart was pounding. She felt sick. As the door caved in, the wood splintering loudly, she closed her eyes and passed out.

* * *

Katrina woke up abruptly. Someone was hammering on the flat door. She moaned. Who the hell was it at ten o'clock in the morning? She hadn't ordered anything and as far as she knew, Summer hadn't either so it couldn't be a delivery. She crept out of bed, her head throbbing but surprisingly she did feel slightly better than she had the day before. Her legs didn't feel so wobbly as she pulled on her fluffy white dressing gown and made her way to the flat door.

"All right, all right," she yelled as whoever it was bashed the door again. "I'm coming."

Her face dropped when she opened the door and came face to face with two police officers, a man and a woman. The man looked stern, the woman slightly more sympathetic.

"Hello. I'm P.C Bright and this is P.C Burgess," said the male officer, nodding at the woman in uniform beside him. He turned back to Katrina. "I believe a Miss Summer Carruthers lives here."

"Yes," replied Katrina, "but I don't think she's in actually. She was working last night and I haven't heard her come home."

"Can we come in?" asked the woman politely.

Katrina shrugged. "If you must ... why ... what do you want with Summer?" Her mind was in turmoil. What had the silly girl gone and done now?

"I take it you are her flatmate ... Miss ...?" enquired P.C Burgess as she sat down beside Katrina on the sofa.

"Yes. Katrina ... Katrina Gregory."

"And has ... Summer ... any family ... as far as you are aware, Katrina?"

"As far as I know her parents chucked her out and she hasn't any brothers or sisters. She's all alone ... apart from me, that is."

"In that case," said P.C Burgess, ignoring P.C Bright who had moved to the window and was examining what was going on in the street outside, "We will try and trace her parents but I need to tell you that Summer ... I'm sorry to have to tell you that a dog walker found her body down by the Thames early this morning. It looks as if she had taken something ... the toxicology report will tell us ... but she was beaten badly too so we are treating the case as murder until we know any different. Do you have any idea of where she was last night or what she was doing? You said she was working."

"Oh God!" whispered Katrina, finding it difficult to close her mouth. "Stupid girl. Going on her own. I knew it wasn't a good idea."

"Go where?" uttered P.C Bright, turning back to her abruptly. "Go where, Miss Gregory?"

"I ... I don't know ... I don't know where she went. A car ... it picked her up and took her ... she said it was a private residence this time ... she usually went to hotels ... but this was different ... she said they ... the punters ... they were German."

"So ... she was on the game," he said, his suspicions confirmed.

Katrina nodded, the shock making her whole body shake. P.C Burgess noticed and hurried to the kitchen to make tea, spooning in a lot of sugar. She took it back to Katrina and handed it to her. "Drink that. You'll feel a lot better."

PC Bright was sat on the arm of the sofa. He had whisked his notebook out of his pocket and stared hard at Katrina after she had taken a few sips of the tea.

"What more can you tell us, Miss Gregory? Have you any idea at all where Summer was going … where she was getting her clients from … who was controlling her … and maybe you?"

Katrina gulped. If she told them about Bill and Roger, she was going to be for it and if they were arrested and charged, she was going to lose her job. She couldn't say anything. She had to keep her trap shut. "I … I …,"

"Don't tell us any lies," P.C Bright warned. "You know damned well we're going to find everything out eventually so you might as well come clean now. It will save you a lot of trouble in the long run."

Katrina glared at him. "I'm really sorry but I know absolutely no more than what I've already told you. Summer didn't tell me exactly where she was going or the names of the people she was going to be with. So, I'm afraid I can't help you any further."

CHAPTER 10

She had to get out of London. If she didn't, there was every chance she was going to end up like Summer. No matter how ill she felt, she had to leave as fast as possible. It wouldn't take long for the police to find out exactly who had been pimping Summer and when they started to investigate Bill and Roger in more depth, they would discover the drug racket and quite possibly other crimes as well and they would more than likely be sent to prison. However, until that time, which could be months away, she was at risk because they would automatically think she had spilled the beans. They would never believe she had kept her mouth shut and would come gunning for her. Her life wouldn't be worth living … if they gave her the luxury of staying alive.

She looked around the flat. She hadn't any affection for it but it had provided shelter while she was stockpiling cash. She had just under £5,000 stashed away now and although she would have liked to have a lot more, it was enough to get her to Hollywood and fund her for a short while until she could find proper work. She should go now but knew she wasn't well enough to deal with getting ready, enduring a long flight and trying to get sorted at the other end. She needed to get better first, go somewhere she could rest in peace, regain her strength and plan her next move. She needed her mother.

She swallowed another couple of paracetamols, tried to ignore the fact that she was quite ill and should be in bed, and hurriedly packed her favourite items of clothing. The rest would have to remain here and the landlord could sort it. She found a writing pad and a pen and dashed off a letter to the letting agents, informing them of Summer's demise, that the police would provide details of Summer's parents so her effects could be forwarded, and that she was ill and vacating the flat, leaving instructions for them to do what they wanted with any of her personal possessions left behind. Luckily the rent was up to date and as far as she knew all the bills paid. Anything outstanding could be sent on to The Beeches and she could settle it from there.

She took a quick look in Summer's room, glancing around at all of her things; her make-up spilling all over the dressing table amongst bottles of expensive perfumes, a dress she had worn recently, slung over the back of the chair; her shoes, abandoned on the carpet by the bed. The bed itself, unmade, still with the imprint of her head on the pillow.

A deep sadness for Summer engulfed Katrina, even though they hadn't shared a deep friendship. Whatever had happened to her last night, she hadn't deserved it. Surprised that she wanted to cry for her deceased flatmate and sobbing was something Katrina rarely did, she pulled herself together, suddenly remembering all the jewellery Summer boasted of, all those presents men had given her. Without further ado, Katrina started going through Summer's drawers in the dressing table. Knickers, thongs, and bras spilled out and beneath them all was a big blue velvet box. Katrina opened it carefully and was thrilled to see the ruby necklace and earrings, a sapphire ring and a diamond bracelet and beneath, a wad of fifty-pound notes. Katrina counted them carefully. One thousand pounds, which could be added to her stash. She hurried back to her room and shoved the box into the bottom of her suitcase along with the big brown envelope containing her own cash.

Pulling on her coat, she picked up the letter for the letting agents. They were only down the street so she could pop it in, along with the keys, and then pick up a taxi from the rank a few doors down. She was going home. Just until she got her strength and looks back but she was going home … to her mum.

* * *

Kings Cross was busy. It was Friday and crowds of people, having left work early, were on the move for the weekend. Katrina pushed her way through the masses, dragging her suitcase behind her, her bag tucked tightly under her arm. She felt giddy and sick, a couple of times almost passing out but with grit and determination, managed to throw the feeling off, although she had to sit down on a bench once or twice on her way to the platform for the York train. She would have to change there for Harrogate, which was a bind and prayed the platform she arrived at and the one to depart from York wouldn't be too far away from each other. She had sent a text to her mother, saying she was on her way home and Vicky had promised to pick her up from Harrogate so all she had to do was get herself on the train and then she could collapse for a few hours.

It took an age to find the right platform and stepping onto one of the escalators, she was terrified she was going to faint as the giddiness returned but eventually she reached her train, hauling the suitcase behind her into the nearest carriage, finding a space for it on the luggage rack near to an empty seat.

By the time the train pulled out of the station fifteen minutes later, it was packed. Katrina's whole body was aching and she was desperately in need of sleep. She shut her eyes and allowed the swaying of the train to lull her into slumber.

She woke up two hours later just as the train was pulling into York. She stood up unsteadily. She was far too hot and probably had a temperature. She wanted to throw her coat off but it looked chilly outside as the train glided into the railway station. People were pushing and shoving to get off the train and Katrina felt too ill to compete. She allowed them to pass, waiting until the gangway was clear before she moved. Eventually she could see the luggage rack opposite her and peered at the space where her suitcase should be with horror. It wasn't there. But it had to be. She could feel the panic rising. She didn't give a fig about the clothes and personal possessions but it was all that money … and the jewellery she had taken from Summer's room. God, if she lost all that her dream of jetting off to Hollywood was going to be seriously set back.

She began to wonder if she had placed her case in another luggage rack. After all, she wasn't feeling well and could have become confused. She rushed along the carriage, searching madly, people looking at her in bewilderment as she screeched, "my case … my case. It's gone!"

She stumbled backwards and forwards, crying now, desperate to find it but to no avail. It wasn't there. Some bastard had walked off the train with it. She should never have fallen asleep. She should have kept her eye on it at all times. How stupid she had been.

Eventually the guard, summoned by a worried passenger, headed into the carriage and took her arm.

"Are you sure you left it there?" he asked kindly, pointing at the rack opposite her seat.

"Yes, yes!" she sobbed. "I know I did. It was next to that purple one there … see." She pointed at the suitcase, wondering why that one hadn't been taken instead. Why, oh why, had it been hers?

"In that case, you need to report it to the Transport Police, madam. Let me escort you off the train and show you where to go."

"What colour is it?" he asked as they stepped off the train and he propelled her down the platform towards an office with a Transport Police sign outside. He was looking at the luggage of people around them. Katrina did the same, her eyes wide with panic.

"Black," she said with mounting despair, realising there was very little chance of getting hers back as nearly all the suitcases were the same colour. She was stuffed, well and truly stuffed, as she only had a few coins and two twenty-pound notes in her purse.

She thought of all the hours she had put in at that blasted studio, having to endure degrading and undignified treatment at times. She had humiliated herself for absolutely nothing and now she had nowhere to turn but to her parents. God, she felt so ill. She put out a hand to clutch onto the guard and then it all went black.

* * *

"They wanted to send you to hospital," said Vicky as she sat beside Katrina in her bedroom at the Beeches later that evening. After collecting her daughter from Harrogate railway station, Vicky had driven her back to the Beeches as fast as she could, shocked to see how dreadfully ill she looked. She had helped her have a bath, dressed her in a favourite pair of pyjamas Katrina had left at home and tucked her up in a bed warmed by an electric blanket. Then she had fetched a hot milky drink and a bowl of soup, which Katrina was trying to force down.

"I know. I wouldn't let them. When I came around after I fainted, I told them I just wanted to get back here and that you were meeting me. They weren't happy about it but they let me come, although one of the guards kept an eye on me, just in case I passed out again."

"What are they going to do about your suitcase?"

"Nothing. They took details, naturally, but it has no distinguishing marks and there is very little they can do so I just have to accept it's gone. God, why did I fall asleep? I feel so cross with myself."

"You're not well, darling. Still, you're safe and sound and that's what matters. We can always buy you new things ... now go to sleep. I'll come up and check on you later ... perhaps you will feel able to eat a little more after a good rest."

Vicky planted a motherly kiss on Katrina's brow and left the room, shutting the door softly behind her.

Katrina ground her teeth, unable to believe what had occurred during the last twenty-four hours, unable to believe she was home and as her mother had just said, safe and sound. Summer wasn't safe and sound. She was dead, thanks to Bill and Roger, pimping her out to God knows who and if she had stayed in London, she doubted very much if she would have been in too good a condition either once they caught up with her. But what if they came looking for her here to seek revenge? It wouldn't be too hard to track her down. They knew she was the daughter of Lady Victoria, who in turn was the daughter of a former Duke of Canleigh. They had wanted to play on her aristocratic lineage for the filming but on that point she had been adamant. If they wanted her, they would have to keep her identity a secret. After seeing her in action, they had reluctantly agreed.

On the other hand, they might just leave her alone … although they had all those blasted films. There must be an awful lot now as she had lost count of how many times she had been expected to perform. Would Bill go through with his threat to send them to her parents? She fervently hoped not. She would be so humiliated and ashamed if they ever got to see her in the throes of passion with all in sundry. She hadn't been too bothered at the time but now she had left London and all the seediness behind, she began to desperately regret what she had done over the last few weeks. It had been a crazy, stupid mistake to have visited Starlight in the first place and once she had gone inside and they had their hooks into her, she had been trapped.

Burying her head in her hands, she groaned, turned over and allowed the paracetamol her mother had given her to take effect. Her whole body was trembling but slowly, gradually, with the warmth of the electric blanket, the hot milk, soup and the painkillers, she began to relax and drifted off to sleep, her last thought being she would think about it all properly tomorrow when she felt back to normal.

* * *

"I'm quite worried about Katrina," said Vicky to Alex a few moments later when she found him in his office, going over the monthly accounts.

"She seems to have lost a lot of weight and looks really ill. Oh, I know, she has the flu, but I think there's something else on her mind … and she's terribly upset about having her suitcase stolen. Although I suggested having a shopping spree to buy lots of new clothes, she wasn't pacified … she said she had a load of cash and jewellery in it but when I said she didn't have to worry about money while she was here with us and I would buy her some more jewellery, she wasn't mollified. I would love to know what's on her mind and what she's been up to for the last few weeks … but then again, perhaps I wouldn't," she sighed, running a hand through her thick dark hair.

Alex smiled ruefully. "Darling girl, once she's over the flu and you've fed her up a bit, she will be fine. You know what she's like. Tough as old boots and always bounces back readily from whatever life throws at her."

"Well, I don't want her going back to London. I think she should stay here now and we'll give her a job."

"Oh," he raised an eyebrow. "Doing what? You know she's not remotely interested in the hotel trade."

"I'll think of something … but I want to keep her close … I want to make sure she can't get herself into any trouble."

"You have to remember she's old enough to make her own decisions. You can't keep her here if she doesn't want to stay."

"We will just have to think of something so she does," replied Vicky glumly "and if we can't, perhaps Lucy can … or Ruth. I'll discuss it with them in the morning as we're having coffee at Dingle Dell. Now, husband dear, how much longer are you going to be? It's terribly late and it really is time we were in bed."

"Not long … you go and I'll be right behind you."

CHAPTER 11

David Jenkins, General Manager of Canleigh Hall Hotel and fiancée to its owner, Lucy Canleigh, was doing his rounds. He had been up since 5.00 a.m., had run a lap of Canleigh lake with the aid of a torch as it was pitch dark and then did fifty lengths of the pool, which he had all to himself this early in the morning. It was rare a guest would want to swim before 7.00 a.m. whilst they were on holiday and the staff, who were allowed use of the pool in their spare time, didn't normally take advantage of it until late afternoon or in the evening.

Following a shower and dressing with much attention to detail with his gold cufflinks and matching tie pin to complement his navy suit and then adding his Rolex watch, he headed down the main stairs to his office off the entrance hall. The first thing he did when coming on duty was to check on who was leaving and who was arriving that day and if they had any special requirements so the staff could be notified as soon as possible. He then moved through the dining room and the lounges, stopping to chat to guests who were beginning to appear for breakfast, quietly nodding to those who were reading newspapers or books and didn't want to be disturbed. He checked for dust, running fingers discreetly along the tops of the furniture, noted any light bulbs that needed replacing, that the windows were sparkling clean, that the heating was the right temperature; satisfying himself that everything was as it should be and if it wasn't, the staff concerned were in for a hard time. He was a stickler, was David, for wanting things to be just so. There was a place for everything and everything should be in its place was his favourite motto, which he brought into his daily working life too and if the workforce didn't play ball, they didn't last long but he was proud of the staff he had hired since his arrival at Canleigh when Lucy had opened it as a hotel. The majority appreciated what he was trying to achieve and complied readily, taking as much pride in their work as he did. As a result, they had built a thriving hotel and he couldn't have been more pleased and now he and Lucy were engaged and were to be married in the spring, he was happier than he had ever been in his life. He loved Canleigh Hall as much as he loved Lucy and to know that he was going to be able to work here with her by his side for the rest of his life gave him enormous satisfaction.

He had fallen in love with Lucy gradually. It hadn't been an 'eyes meeting across a crowded room', scenario. Initially, working with her was a real pleasure and then gradually and slowly their relationship grew warmer, mainly during the sessions in his office when they would work side by side, playing Mozart on the CD player. Lucy adored Mozart and so did he and on discovering there was going to be a performance of The Requiem in Leeds, he asked her to accompany him. It had been a wonderful evening. They were enthralled with the music and then went for a late supper at Rendezvous, the newest French restaurant in town which stayed open until the early hours.

They suddenly found they had so much to talk about, not only Canleigh but their interests in nature, history, travel and, of course, classical music. They were the last people to leave the restaurant and as they walked back to the car park for David's car, they automatically held hands and smiled at each other, completely comfortable and in tune and David knew he was falling heavily in love.

The relationship blossomed and David was ecstatic. Although he had a confident working manner, he was a shy man, especially with women. He could chat happily with guests and the staff on an impersonal level but serious relationships had been non-existent. A number of women had attempted to get close to him and he dated a few but had grown bored very quickly, preferring his own company to the amorous attentions they bestowed on him. His choice of career involved social chit chat whilst he was on duty but once his shift was ended, he liked nothing more than to settle down with a good book and just be quiet, listening to classical music on his stereo and enjoying a brandy or two.

He adored his flat, which had previously been allocated to serving butlers to the Canleigh family. It was on the top floor of the Hall with amazing views. It was cosy in the winter, with the drapes closed and the heating on, and in the summer it was idyllic with the windows open, especially first thing in the morning, when he could lay in bed and listen to the birds until it was time for his run. Most mornings, unless the weather was utterly atrocious or dangerous, he would circle the lake before his swim in the pool. The exercise set him up to deal with whatever occurred throughout his day. It also kept him slim. He had a robust appetite and was convinced that if he didn't run, he would soon turn to flab and he had enough pride in himself not to want that, especially now he was engaged to Lucy and had a wonderful life with her to look forward to. God, he was so very, very happy!

* * *

"Any suggestions on what to do with Katrina will be gratefully received," remarked Vicky to Ruth and Lucy as they settled in the lounge at Dingle Dell. Tina had taken Selena to school so the three women had the place to themselves.

"Is she interested in hairdressing ... or beauty ... if she doesn't want to learn the management side, she might be better working with Suzanne or that other girl you have who runs the beauty salon," said Ruth thoughtfully.

"Maureen ... it's a thought ... I don't think Katrina would be any good at hairdressing but she might ... just might consider the beauty side. You know how obsessed she is by her looks."

"Yes, but that isn't quite the same as having to administer to others. She might not like having to touch other women ... I'm not sure I would," Lucy grinned.

Vicky nearly choked on her coffee and placed her pretty pink bone china cup on its saucer while she coughed into her handkerchief.

Ruth sat up, ready to bang Vicky on the back but she put a hand up. "It's okay," she said, regaining her breath. "I'm fine … it's just … it's just that I don't think Katrina will worry too much about touching other women."

"What do you mean?" asked a wide-eyed Lucy. "Don't tell me she's a lesbian. I would never have guessed."

"No … of course not." She hesitated for a second before continuing. "I hate to say this but I think … I think she has been either working as a prostitute or making pornographic films … probably with men … and women … she had an awful lot of money when she was in London and wouldn't say where it came from."

"No …," whispered Lucy, twirling her long highlighted blonde hair in her fingers, always a sign she was agitated. "Not Katrina. She is too … too proud of herself … desperate to become a proper actress … in proper films."

"Well, I don't know for certain because she won't admit to it but I've a nasty suspicion that's what has been going on."

"I wonder why she's come home," remarked Ruth, taking a slice of cherry cake from the pretty china cake stand on the coffee table. "If she's been making good money, why didn't she stay in London?"

"That's what I want to know," replied Vicky. "I can't tell you how relieved I am to have her here, especially as she is so ill and I can look after her, but I do feel there is an underlying reason for her sudden decision to come home. I will certainly do my best to wheedle it out of her when she's feeling better."

"Well, until you do, unfortunately there is very little we can do to help," said Ruth.

Lucy looked at Vicky thoughtfully. "If Katrina doesn't want to work at The Beeches, we could always do with some help at

Canleigh, especially with Christmas coming up. She could help David keep an eye on things, do a bit of waitressing or help out in the office. I wouldn't dream of asking her to do chambermaiding duties," she laughed, knowing how Katrina would push her nose up at that suggestion.

"That's awfully good of you, Lucy, darling. She might well prefer that. She loves Canleigh ... she's always been envious of you, inheriting it. I'll certainly ask her," said Vicky gratefully. It would be a huge weight off her mind if Katrina was settled somewhere close to home.

"She could live in too. There are a few spare rooms on the top floor which we keep for staff if they need accommodation ... and it would save her driving backwards and forwards, especially if the weather isn't too good."

Vicky beamed at Lucy. "You, my darling, are a lifesaver."

* * *

Katrina was recovering slowly. The following day she actually got out of bed, dressed and ventured into the lounge of her parents' flat on the top floor of The Beeches. It was a chilly day and even though the heating was on, she turned the radiators up to their maximum. Her father had a habit of turning them down low as he hated being too warm and was always keen to save money where he could. He would have to lump it today, Katrina thought, hoping he would remain down in the hotel and wouldn't venture upstairs until the evening. She would have crept back to bed by then.

She settled on the sofa, pulling the soft red blanket her mother used to cover her feet and legs in the evenings, over her body. On the coffee table beside her was a box of tissues, a jug of freshly squeezed orange juice with a glass, along with a flask of coffee and a cheerful looking mug covered with red poppies. Two delicious looking croissants had also been left to tempt her appetite.

Katrina gave a wry grin. She had refused breakfast when her mother had popped into her room to see her before she went downstairs to start work but determined to get her daughter to eat something and build up her strength, she had left this out in case she had decided to get up for a while. It was nice to be home, and to be looked after. She had missed this.

"Ah, so you did get up then," her mother remarked two hours later when she popped her head around the door. "How do you feel, darling?"

Katrina grimaced. "Rotten."

"Well, flu does take it out of you. You need lots of rest and lots of fluids, darling and I am going to insist you have something to eat later," Vicky said, noting the croissants hadn't been touched. "Perhaps some nice scrambled eggs with mushrooms, you know how you always like that when you are ill."

"Um. Perhaps. I'll see how I feel." replied Katrina unenthusiastically, running a hand through her hair. It felt horrible, lank and greasy. She must look an absolute fright. She would have to make a supreme effort and have a shower so she could wash it. She knew she would feel a lot better.

Vicky moved further into the room, shutting the door behind her. She sat down in the chair opposite the sofa and stared at Katrina.

"What?" said Karina, glaring at her mother. "I know I look bloody awful but there's no need to stare."

Vicky cleared her throat. "Sorry. I didn't mean to and you don't look awful … you just look poorly. However, I do want to have a little talk."

Katrina groaned. "Oh God. Now what?" She hated her mother's little talks. They were usually about restrictions of some sort and she didn't feel up to arguing her corner right now. Perhaps that's why her mother was doing it while she was at her least resistant.

"Darling … I don't want you to go back to London."

"I'm not."

Vicky looked surprised. "Oh? I thought you had only come home because you were ill and were intending to go back once you were better."

"No. I really want to go to Hollywood ... you know that's all I've ever wanted," her voice rose at her mother's sigh of resignation.

"Oh, for heaven's sake, Katrina! You didn't have any success in London, at least with anything remotely decent, so how on earth do you think you will succeed in Hollywood? The competition is going to be fierce, bitterly fierce. You won't stand a chance and could get yourself into really hot water and being so far away, it won't be easy for us to help you out."

"By hook or by crook I'm going," pouted Katrina. "But I need money to keep me going until I get work. I had ... I had quite a bit saved ... it was all in my suitcase ... which I'll never see again ... so, I was wondering ... would you please lend me some? I promise faithfully I'll pay you back as soon as I start earning," she added in a rush before her mother could say a determined no.

Vicky stood up and walked to the window to look over the peaceful gardens below, then she turned to her daughter, who was wearing a pleading look with just a touch of defiance. "No. I'm sorry but no," she said with determination.

She put up a hand at Katrina's gasp of protest. "As you walked out of Radley without a thought in your head as to how you were going to survive, after all we had done to make sure you were comfortable during your time in London, I think we now have to insist you find a proper job. You're terribly young to go to America by yourself and I would never forgive myself if something happened to you. No, Katrina, we ..., your father and I have discussed it, and we want you to work here ... and if you don't want to do that, Lucy has kindly offered you a post at Canleigh. If you buckle down for a couple of years, we might think about helping you then, once you are older and wiser and anyway, in the meantime you might meet someone and want to settle down and have a family and knock this Hollywood idea out of your head for good ... and you can always join the local drama group and keep your hand in."

"God forbid" exclaimed Katrina. "I don't want to get married and have children. That's the last bloody thing I want ... and as for the drama group, no thanks. I have much bigger ambitions."

"Language!" retorted Vicky, despising profanities, especially from her own daughter. "And I don't want to hear any more about Hollywood. We're not funding you and that's that. Now, let's talk about other things. Suzanne wants to pop up and say hello but I told her not to, she doesn't need to catch your nasty bug, not with Daniel to look after ... and the salon ... she's doing so well in there. Anyhow, I told her to ring you so she is going to when she closes up around 5.00 p.m."

"That's all I bloody need?" replied Katrina, ignoring her mother's demands to clean up her language while sullenly mulling over the idea of working either at the Beeches or Canleigh. She didn't fancy either but it seemed she had little choice at the moment with no cash of her own and no other job on offer ... and now Suzanne wanted to talk to her. The damned woman who was going to take half her inheritance. She was the very last person she wanted to talk to ... apart from Bill or Roger ... or the Police of course. God, she was in a mess.

"Katrina! Please!"

Katrina glared at her mother. "You can tell your precious Suzanne that I don't want anything to do with her unless you re-write your will again and leave me what is rightfully mine and not hers."

"You, madam, are beyond the pale," seethed Vicky. "Your father and I have decided that to share what we have between you is the right and proper thing to do and if you don't like it, it's just too bad. Nothing is going to be changed. Do you understand?"

Katrina pulled herself upright and glared furiously at her mother, her eyes bright with anger. "No. I don't! She was going to have a few thousand pounds ... I could live with that ... but not half the bloody hotel and half of whatever you have stashed away."

"A few million ... which is quite adequate split between you," Vicky said, rubbing her brow anxiously. She wished Alex was by her side to back her up. He couldn't stand any nonsense from their daughter.

"Christ! How can you do this to me? It's just not fair! She isn't your real child and she has a blasted husband somewhere to keep her. And what about the hotel? How the hell can we split that? We'll have to sell it."

"Do calm down, Katrina," Vicky sighed, perching on the arm of the sofa. "Suzanne has simply nothing ... it appears Todd was thoroughly irresponsible and spent recklessly so she has no money and can't rely on him sending her anything ... and she has Daniel to bring up. She needs stability for herself and for him and she is doing really well here, setting up the salon. She is very popular and revenue has definitely increased since she joined us. She deserves to have her contribution recognised and she might not be of our blood but as far as your father and I are concerned, she is our daughter and we both love her very much."

"It doesn't mean you have to take away half of my inheritance," Katrina said sullenly. She had never rated Suzanne that highly and hadn't been a bit upset when she obtained a job on a cruise ship and then married Todd and settled in Australia. Good riddance as far as Katrina was concerned.

"For goodness sake, Katrina. It's a small fortune and even sharing it with Suzanne will make you a very wealthy woman ... and don't forget, although it's pretty unlikely as Lucy is such a young woman, you might very well end up with Canleigh one day. She can't leave it to Selena for obvious reasons, so she has a trust fund set up for her but the Hall ... and everything that goes with it ... if anything happens to Lucy it will come to me. You know that

… unless she has more children with David, of course and then that will change."

Katrina sat up abruptly, her head spinning, her mind in a whirl. "What? What do you mean, with David … do you mean that general manager of hers? Surely they haven't got it together?"

Alarm bells were ringing. She had known for a long time that her mother would inherit Canleigh if anything happened to Lucy and she was next in line as long as Lucy didn't remarry and have more children … normal ones at that but Lucy had never displayed any desire to get married again after that awful time she had with Jeremy, her first husband, so Katrina hadn't given it a second thought. Not that she would be able to get her hands on Canleigh anyway for a very long time. Her mother was still a healthy woman and as for Lucy, she could live for years, but if she was planning on remarrying and having more kids, then that would really put the kibosh on getting her hands on such a glittering prize. Christ, her morning was getting worse and worse.

"Yes, actually. David is a very nice man and he's given Lucy her confidence back. They work very well together and I'm sure will have a very happy marriage. He's also extremely kind to Selena and she loves him."

"How nice," Katrina grimaced. She had never rated David highly. He always seemed a little on the effeminate side and certainly wasn't her kind of man. She couldn't imagine him doing anything much to keep a woman happy in bed. "So, when is this wonderful marriage going to take place?"

"In the spring," said Vicky, relieved the conversation had taken a turn from Katrina's inheritance "but Lucy wants a quiet wedding, nothing like her last one," remembering how grand the occasion had been when Lucy married Jeremy.

Katrina grimaced again, sliding down the sofa beneath the blanket. She felt too ill to think about all this properly now but inside she was seething, especially about Suzanne.

Seeing her action and noting Katrina's pale face, Vicky decided it was time to withdraw. "Have a sleep, darling. Once you get over this ghastly flu bug you will feel a lot better, especially once we find something for you to do."

"Yes ... yes, I need to sleep," Katrina said, relieved when her mother slipped out of the room and shut the door.

Katrina let the tears of sheer frustration flow. Bloody, bloody Suzanne. Bloody, bloody Lucy. She was so angry. Why the hell should she have to share her inheritance with Suzanne ... and why the hell did flaming Lucy have to get married again? But what could she do to prevent it all? Nothing. Absolutely bloody nothing. For some reason an image of her aunt, Lady Delia, sprung into her mind. She wouldn't have put up with it. She would have done something about it ... although she had ended up in prison for years the last time she gave vent to her anger. However, that hadn't stopped her having Blairness and then marrying the most gorgeous man ever, becoming a Countess and living in a second fairy-tale castle in Scotland. Katrina was so very envious ... and jealous ... yes, jealous. All her family were doing all right apart from her.

She buried her head in the blanket and cried, tears of rage and torment. She had nothing and not much to look forward to either, only half of her parent's estate and she couldn't get her hands on that for years. Oh God. She had to get to Hollywood. She just had to. Once she was there and she could persuade anyone who was anyone that she was worth taking a chance on, she would be made. She would be a star. She would be rich and famous ... but would she? Would she really? Was she any good or was it all a pipedream? Was she only good enough for porn movies where she only had to perform with her body and not actually say anything? A chill went down her spine. She couldn't even do that now. She couldn't go back to London. No matter what Roger said, Bill would probably want to get even after giving him such a bashing and anyway, he was probably in a lot of hot water if the police investigated Summer's murder properly and enquiries led back to him, especially if he assumed she had given the police any information about him and what went on in the club. He was aware that she knew he and Roger were involved with drug dealers and she had seen a gun in his jacket pocket at one point when he whisked out his wallet to pay her. No. She couldn't go back there. So, what the hell was she going to do?

Just as she was about to burst into tears again, her mobile phone on the coffee table flickered into life. She hated that tune and really would have to change it. Summer had chosen it when fiddling with it one evening and it really got on her nerves. Her mouth dropped open when she saw who was calling. Leo. Whatever did he want?

CHAPTER 12

Leo had a dilemma as his job at Starlight was a thing of the past. Even though he had earned a good whack at the studio, he liked to spend as well and living the highlife in London certainly wasn't cheap. He needed a job and quick otherwise he would have to start to penny pinch and that simply wasn't his style ... and the only person he could think of who might be able to help him out of a hole was Katrina, who had disappeared rather surprisingly two days ago without a word to anyone, which was all rather mysterious.

He had wondered if it was because she had bashed Bill over the head and was too scared to come back. He hadn't been at the studio that day but found out when he went in the next morning. Bill and Roger were in the office with the door open and talking loudly as he was passing. Leo had been able to hear the whole conversation.

Bill was growling that he was going to get his revenge on her. "Presents ... you've given the cow presents!" he was yelling at Roger. "I'll give Katrina, bloody Gregory, presents. I'd like to smash her blasted face in! I tell you, Roger, as soon as she's no use to us any longer, I'm going to get even with her for attacking me. Six stitches I've got in my head thanks to her and the headache of all flaming headaches. I tell you, one day I'll sort the little bitch out and her life won't be worth living!"

However, Bill's tirade had come to an abrupt halt as, without warning, the door from the reception area along the corridor burst open and two men in suits waving warrant cards and a piece of paper, followed by six uniformed police officers made their way purposefully towards Leo.

"William Struthers?"

Leo shook his head and pointed to the office door. "In there," he had uttered, his gut telling him that this was the end of his lucrative job at Starlight.

The eight police officers flooded into the office, leaving the door wide open, allowing Leo to see and hear it all.

Bill's mouth had dropped open when the first one, a middle-aged man with dark hair and a determined look, stared straight at him. "William Struthers?"

Bill nodded, clutching the wound on his head. It hurt like crazy.

"I'm Detective Inspector Conway and this is Detective Sergeant Williams," he stated, as both men held up their warrant cards. "I understand a woman by the name of Summer Masters has been working here."

"Yes," Bill croaked, not wanting to move his head again. What the hell had the stupid girl done? He had sent her off to sleep with those Germans … four of them apparently, so she should be knackered and fit for nothing after keeping them happy all night so what the hell were the police doing here … and in such numbers. He began to tremble. It looked damned serious by the stern looks on the faces of the two detectives and the uniformed lot weren't looking too cheerful either.

"I have to inform you that Miss Masters' body was discovered early this morning. She has been murdered. Her flatmate, Miss … Gregory," D.I Conway stated, referring to his notes, "has been informed and advised us that Miss Masters had been working for you and was out visiting Germans last night. I believe they are your … clients ...., Mr. Struthers."

Leo, who had been joined by Maria, wanting to know why the police were here in such numbers, stood silently in the corridor, surprised to hear Bill had been pimping Summer out and horrified to hear she had been murdered.

"We need you to come down to the station with us, Mr. Struthers, and answer some questions. Are you able to do that … or do you need to go to hospital?" asked D.I. Conway, staring at the wound on Bill's head curiously. He would be very interested to know how that had happened.

"I've been to the blasted hospital ... look," Bill spat, bowing his head so the detective could see the stitches.

"Right, well, we'll get someone to have a look at it before we interview you ... and I must also inform you that I've a warrant to search these premises so while we're at the station my men are going to spend quite a bit of time finding out exactly what has been going on here as we have reason to believe there may be drugs or weapons on site."

"And who the hell told you that?" Bill snarled. He knew the drugs were safe, Roger had them stashed away well away from the studio but there was the bloody gun ... in his desk. The bastards would find that for sure and with his previous, he would go down for it. Bugger, bugger, bugger!

"Just say, a little bird," the police officer smirked.

Enlightenment dawned on Bill. "It was that flaming Katrina. It was her that whacked me over the head. I want her charged ... grievous bodily harm. Do you hear?"

"For your information, it wasn't Miss Gregory ... she only advised us that Miss Masters worked here. It was another source entirely."

"And why don't I believe that," growled Bill, his eyes glittering with anger. "It was her. I bloody know it was ... and I'll definitely get the little bitch one day ... and I don't care what you say, I want her charged for attacking me."

"Yes, well, we'll see about that, now wind it in," said Conway. "And get a move on. We're busy men and haven't time to waste."

Bill stood up shakily, clutching onto the desk for support. If he could make out he was in a real bad way, that little tramp would go down as well. He wasn't going to let her get away with it.

Both Bill and an ultra-quiet Roger were escorted off the premises by the two detectives while the remainder of the officers donned rubber gloves and began their search of the office. As there was no reason for him to remain, Leo left, having given his details to one of the policemen in case they wanted to get hold of him again. The rest of the staff had been told they could go home too; the two females he was supposed to be working with, Kevin, the cameraman, and Maria.

Leo had little hope that things would be back to normal the following day and he was right. Maria and Kevin were staring hopelessly at the sign on the door of Starlight when he arrived the next morning.

"We're out of work," remarked Maria dismally, her face a picture of misery. She hadn't particularly enjoyed her job but Bill and Roger had been generous and she would find it hard to receive such a good salary elsewhere.

Leo stared at the notice in the window. 'Due to unforeseen circumstances, this studio is closed until further notice.'

"Oh, shit!" he exclaimed. "I presume Bill and Roger are still being held then."

"Yes. I rang the police station to find out," Maria replied. "They've been charged with possession of a firearm and living off immoral earnings i.e. Summer. They're in court later today but as they've both got records and the studio is still being ransacked for anything else incriminating, I expect there will be more charges, especially when the drugs are found. They'll definitely go down."

"Well, if there's nothing doing here, I'm off," said Kevin. "I've a few contacts I can ring to see what jobs are about so I better get cracking. Good luck, you two. It's been nice working with you," he grinned, turning on his heel and heading back down the street

"Lucky him," said Maria sorrowfully as she and Leo watched Kevin walk away. "So ... what will you do now?" she added, looking up at Leo.

"I think I'll go and see Katrina. After all, she needs to know about Bill in case she's worried he's gunning for her."

"I've been ringing her but she's not answering so good luck with that one. To be honest I wouldn't be surprised if she hasn't done a bunk because if it was her who turned informant, Bill will definitely go after her at some stage. He's not good at forgetting or forgiving."

"I know ... but at least she'll be safe for a while if he goes down. Bye Maria ... and good luck," said Leo, as he turned to head towards Katrina's flat nearby. He liked Katrina. He had a lot of time for her and didn't like to think of her being frightened. He also liked shagging her. She was a damned good lay and he had really enjoyed their sessions together. Some of the others he had been expected to work with had been so wound up and terrified, it had been a nightmare but Katrina ... she was different ... really made a meal out of playing up to the camera. He wondered if she had any idea of how well the films sold, both in the UK and abroad ... and thinking about it, Leo began to have a few ambitions of his own. If he could persuade Katrina to jump on board with him, they could continue where they had left off. Kevin would probably be up for the filming, or would know someone else who would be. Maria would know who had purchased Bill and Roger's films and could help on that front. Then they could sell them themselves and make a packet. Cut out the middleman. Bloody hell! What a damned good idea!

Leo began to feel really excited. Losing his job at Starlight might not be such a hit after all. This might be the opportunity he had been waiting for. His train of thought steamed ahead as he neared Katrina's flat. All they needed was somewhere private to work. Somewhere classy though. Not a seedy little room in the basement of a street. No. Somewhere posh with big, beautiful beds, expensive furnishings and furniture. The bubble of excitement was growing by the second. If he and Katrina performed in and sold the videos themselves, they could end up pretty damned wealthy. He, too, had grown up with ambitions to be a famous name in Hollywood but he was realistic. He and Katrina were both good eye candy, oozed sex appeal and could make a scene really steamy but as for dialogue and real acting, he knew he was hopeless as he could never remember his lines and

Katrina was too wooden and stilted. No, the likelihood of him … of either of them making it in the big time was just a pipe dream … but they could become affluent and want for nothing making their own porn films, and when they grew too old or bored with it, they could hire others to take over their roles … but only those who were willing … he didn't want to be like Bill and Roger, drugging girls to make them compliant. He wanted girls who wanted to do it, to enjoy it as Katrina did.

Leo was suddenly feeling optimistic about the future and couldn't wait to run his idea past his sexy, auburn haired porn partner. Please God she would be up for it. He reached the flat and came to an abrupt halt. There was a 'For Let' sign on the door with details of the letting agent. Maria was right, Katrina had gone. He pulled his mobile from his pocket. He would have to ring her. He had to speak to her. She was damned important if he wanted to make his future business a success.

* * *

Katrina had been somewhat relieved not to have Bill or Roger contact her but was more than surprised to see Leo was ringing her. What did he want? She debated on whether to answer. Had they persuaded him to contact her to find out where she was? But she liked Leo. She wasn't sure if she could trust him but she was bored and lonely upstairs now that her mother had gone back downstairs to the hotel. She pressed the answer button.

"Katrina?"

"Hi Leo. You okay?"

"Yeah. You?"

"Yes … apart from this blasted flu bug."

"Where are you? I've been round to the flat but there's a notice on the door saying it's to let … you haven't done a bunk because you clobbered Bill have you?"

"Well, that and also the little matter of Summer being murdered. I don't particularly want to end up like her …"

"You won't," said Leo quickly. "Bill and Roger have been arrested and charged with possession of a firearm and living off immoral earnings. They're going to go down for that, and for the drugs when the cops find them, so they won't be around for quite a while … and the studio is all shut up."

"Golly," said Katrina, taking a moment to let the news sink in. How things had changed in just a matter of a day or so.

"I presume you've gone home," said Leo. "To Yorkshire."

"Yes," she sighed. It didn't matter about him knowing where she was now as he was obviously ringing her because he wanted to and not because Bill or Roger had coerced him into it.

"Listen, Katrina. I've an idea how we can make ourselves some money. Can I come up and talk to you about it … please?"

"Well, it had better be a lot of money," she groaned. "I had my suitcase stolen on the train and everything I had stashed away has gone. I'm completely broke and relying on my parents again … and they won't fund me for Hollywood for a couple of years … until I've grown up a bit," she pulled a face. "All they can offer is a lousy job either here at The Beeches or at Canleigh, my cousin's hotel. I'll go demented. I know I will."

"Well, I might have the perfect solution and set ourselves up for life with what I have in mind. In a few years we could retire … and you won't even have to go to Hollywood," Leo almost sang. He nearly had it in the bag.

"Sounds interesting," Katrina grinned. "So, what's your idea then … bet it's something to do with taking my clothes off," she giggled.

Leo laughed. "Got it in one, darling girl."

"Well, you better get your arse up to Yorkshire and tell me all about it," she urged. "Come and stay here … at The Beeches. I'll tell the parents you're a good friend who helped me out in London and they'll be ever so grateful and give you a complimentary room."

"Great. I'll come up one day next week, after I've sorted everything here. I'll let you know when. Bye, Katrina … and thanks."

"No, Leo. Thank you … I think you're going to save my sanity."

* * *

"Yes, of course he can stay … but as he's your guest, he can join us up here … he can have Jeremy's old room," said Vicky when she and Alex came upstairs at the end of the day. She was pleased to see Katrina appeared a little brighter and was sitting upright on the sofa, reading a book on acting technique. She had put it down immediately her parents entered the room and mentioned her friend Leo wanted to come up from London for a few days.

"Thanks," Katrina said gratefully, although she had no idea what they would make of him. Leo oozed sex appeal but could be utterly charming too so hopefully he would ingratiate himself pretty quickly but if they ever got wind of what she and Leo had been up to in the last few weeks it would make life pretty difficult so he couldn't stay here long in case he let something slip.

"What does he do, this Leo?" asked her mother, pouring a glass of Chablis for herself and Alex. She waved the bottle at Katrina but she declined, preferring to stick to orange juice for a day or so.

Well, that's the thing … he's out of work at the moment. He was working in a hotel in London … in the bar … but they're not doing too well and he's been laid off. Would there … would there be any work for him here?"

Alex rolled his eyes as he took the glass Vicky offered him and sat down in his favourite chair by the fire. Vicky drew the velvet curtains, shutting out the cold, miserable November night and sat in the chair opposite her husband.

"You mean you want us to not only give you a job, but your friend too," Alex grinned.

"Oh, Daddy. Don't tease. Is there anything for Leo … he's really nice and very good looking … he will keep all the ladies very happy."

"I'm afraid not," said Alex ruefully. "We're fully staffed at the moment but I have an idea Lucy has an opening at Canleigh. I'm sure I heard her say Trevor was leaving and he couldn't have picked a worse time of the year to do so. He's run their bar since Lucy turned the Hall into a hotel. He will be sorely missed. Perhaps your Leo, if he is experienced enough, could be a good replacement."

"Oh, that's marvellous, Daddy … I'll ring Lucy and ask her … and I've been thinking … when I'm better and if Lucy still wants me, I will go and work at Canleigh. It will be much better than being here … it won't seem like a proper job with you two watching every move I make. It will be much better at Canleigh and I do so love the place."

"That is a very good decision," said Vicky with a smile. "Ring Lucy now and see what she says."

Lucy was delighted. "Oh, Katrina. That will be fabulous. David badly needs some help, especially over the Christmas period … and longer, if you want to stay. Let's see how we go until then … and as for your friend, if he knows what he's doing behind the bar, which seems to be the case from what you've told me, he can have a week's trial and if David thinks he has done okay, the job is his."

Katrina put down the phone with a huge smile of delight. Lucy had no idea what was coming. Leo and her … porn stars … working at Canleigh Hall, the epitome of grace and propriety. What an absolute hoot!

* * *

Leo arrived a week later. He was dressed in tight black jeans and a leather jacket and a backpack was slung casually over his right shoulder. His dark hair was slicked back and the spray tan he had invested in a week ago was still working its magic. He looked amazing, thought Katrina as she eyed him up and down when he walked into the reception at The Beeches, his eyes lighting up when he saw her sitting on one of the sofas by the window drinking coffee. She was feeling much better today, had gone for a little walk this afternoon, the fresh air helping to blow the cobwebs away and then wanted to sit and wait for him in reception, hoping to waylay him before her parents set eyes on him.

The reaction to his arrival amused her. All female eyes swivelled in his direction, many quite blatantly ogling the handsome young man and highly envious when they spied Katrina standing up and waving at him from her seat at the window. He hurried to her side, let the backpack slip to the floor and enveloped her in a crushing hug, brushing her cheek with his lips and smiling widely, showing off the most beautiful white teeth.

"Gosh, it's good to see you," he murmured. "I really missed you, you know … where the hell is your bedroom?"

Katrina laughed gaily and pulled away, suddenly aware that her mother was watching from her office window. "That, my darling Leo, can wait until later … much later."

He laughed too, feeling utterly pleased with the way things were going. They had spoken again on the telephone yesterday and he had told Katrina exactly what he intended their immediate futures to be and she had accepted his idea readily, being keen to make as much money in a shorter time as possible … and she had managed to wangle him a place to live and a job which would be the perfect cover.

"Until then," she was saying, "you have to put on a nice chaste show for my parents ... and then we're going over to Canleigh.

We're going to see David ... he's the general manager ... to introduce you and see what your duties will be."

Leo grimaced. "That's something to look forward to ... a job behind a bloody bar ... and the pittance that will pay."

Katrina sat down, waving at a waitress to bring more coffee. "Yes, but you will have free board and meals and as I'm going to work there too and can bag a room near to yours, we will have ample opportunity to get your plan into action. The sooner we start making serious money again, the better. I certainly don't want to be skivvying in a hotel for longer than necessary, believe me, even though that hotel might be Canleigh Hall."

Leo sat down beside her, crossed his long legs, and run his hand through his hair in a gesture that could only be described as exceedingly provocative to the women who were still throwing glances his way.

"I wonder if any of them have seen our films," he grinned.

"Christ! I hope not!"

"Why? I am the perfect Adonis and you have the most fantastic body ... you're absolutely gorgeous and boy can you shag ... you should be very proud of yourself ... and your parents should be very proud of you too."

"Um. I don't think having it away with you in front of a camera is quite what they had in mind for their one and only precious daughter. In fact, it's not quite what I had in mind for myself either," she mused. "Oh, Christ, Leo, this will work won't it? I want so much to get to America and find a company who will see my real talents."

Leo stared at her. He still couldn't believe how she deluded herself that she had a real future as far as stage and screen was concerned. If she ever did get to Hollywood she was in for a very rude awakening.

"Hello," said Vicky at their side. She smiled at Leo, struck by what a stunning looking young man he was. If Katrina was hoping to keep hold of him, she would have her work cut out. "You must be Leo," she said, holding out her hand for him to shake.

Leo stood up and held out his. Their eyes met and Vicky's breathing quickened as their hands touched. His was big and warm and firm, very firm and she felt almost faint with desire. What the hell was the matter with her? She was a happily married woman. She shouldn't be feeling like this.

"It's very nice to meet you, Lady Victoria," he smiled, his eyes twinkling at her, guessing from her expression what she was thinking. "I've heard quite a bit about you ... and may I say, what a fabulous place you have here," he added. "It's very impressive."

"Thank you, Leo," replied Vicky, removing her hand from his, ashamed to realise that she was doing it quite reluctantly. "But if you think this is impressive, wait until you see Canleigh ... our family home ... where you will be working if the interview with the general manager is successful."

"I'm really looking forward to it," he smiled at her and flickered a wink to Katrina.

Gillian, the receptionist, was beckoning Vicky to the reception desk, which gave her the excuse to get away from this unsettling young man and recover from her confusion. "I'll see you later then. I look forward to hearing how you get on at Canleigh and what you think of it."

Leo sat down again and grinned at Katrina. "Now I see where you get your fabulous looks from. Your mother is a real stunner too. I wonder ... would she like a new career in the porn industry?"

"Leo ... behave!" Katrina giggled, trying to imagine her prudish mother in the throes of passion with a couple of men ... and women. It didn't bear thinking about.

* * *

The visit to Canleigh and the interview with David was a success. He was immediately impressed with Leo's confidence behind the bar and his knowledge of mixing cocktails as Leo answered all David's questions with aplomb and enthusiasm for the chance to work in such a grand and luxurious venue. David could see instantly that Leo would be a big draw for the females who frequented Canleigh, as long as he didn't get himself into hot water with any of them and cause any scandals. However, they were desperately in need of experienced bartenders and David took a deep breath and offered Leo the job, albeit on the trial period suggested by Lucy.

David had already interviewed Katrina the previous day and she was moving into her room at Canleigh over the coming weekend and commencing her duties the following Monday.

He shook hands with them both, welcomed them to the team at Canleigh and left Katrina to show Leo around the Hall and the grounds.

"Wow. This place is absolutely perfect," breathed Leo, as they moved from room to room. "I can just see you now, draped over that sofa … or that one …," he enthused, "naked as the day you were born and being well and truly ravished by yours truly. We can wear masks to hide our identities so no-one would ever know it was us."

"And when do you think we could do that down here? There is always someone around … Lucy does have night porters you know … so the possibility of us not being caught is exceedingly remote. Although the gold drawing room and the ballroom are usually locked up unless there is a function on, so we might well be able to sneak in there as I don't think the night porters bother to patrol there and I know where the keys are kept. Anyway, we'll find out but until then we'll have to make do with the privacy of our bedrooms."

"What about the grounds? It would be good to do something outdoors."

"It's all open to the guests so we could be disturbed at any moment and any lights we used at night would be seen from the Hall so that's out."

"Shame," sighed Leo as they wandered around the lake and then stopped to look back at the Hall. "Your cousin, Lucy, is a very lucky woman ... having all this ... and she's still very young, isn't she?" He could vaguely remember Katina mentioning that Lucy had inherited Canleigh in her early twenties and that was only a few years ago.

"Yes, but she looks and acts much older. I suppose it's the responsibility of taking on Canleigh and she had a terrible time with her last husband and his lovers."

"Oh yes, I remember you saying but David appears to be a nice guy ... quite normal ... so maybe she will make a good marriage this time around."

Katrina felt the jealousy rising in the pit of her stomach. Bloody Lucy. She had Canleigh and all the wealth she could possibly want, plus Dingle Dell, which was fabulous, and now she was getting married again ... to someone who might not be the sexiest guy in the world but he was certainly charming and kind ... and would probably make an ideal husband and help Lucy produce a load more offspring. Katrina could spit. In a year or two's time she could probably kiss goodbye to any hope of ever having Canleigh herself ... unless something happened to Mother ... and to Lucy before she produced another child ... and there was little chance of that!

Their steps had taken them all around the lake and they were back at the Hall, taking a long meander around the impressive parterre on the south side of the building, with the statue of Pegasus in the centre and the fabulous view of the lake and the woods.

"Well, I'm really glad I made the decision to follow you up to Yorkshire," remarked Leo with a grin. "I think, my dear girl, we might just have landed on our feet here. I think we had better get cracking on filming though, just in case we don't make it through our probationary periods. If we can get as much filming done as possible in the next few weeks, and sell the videos promptly, we should have enough to hire somewhere decent to work in if we get kicked out of here. So, I need to contact Kevin as a matter of urgency so he can get himself up here pronto."

"How are we going to explain his presence? It's going to look a little strange if he's always turning up, and we all disappear to the bedrooms."

"Yes. You're right," pondered Leo. "We'll have to get him a job here too, as a cover. Perhaps I can persuade David I need an assistant. I believe Kevin has done some bar work in the past."

"Good. I can't wait to get started and get some real cash flowing again," said Katrina, not looking forward to commencing her duties at Canleigh Hall. She really wasn't cut out for such menial work.

"How do you fancy a bit of practice … have a rehearsal for what is to come … after all, you know what they say, if you don't use it, you lose it," grinned Leo, running a finger down her cheek. "We can go and christen my new bedroom in the auspicious Canleigh Hall."

Katrina grinned back. She really liked Leo. She really fancied him. She really liked having sexual encounters with him. "I can't think of anything I would rather do."

Linking arms, they sauntered back into the Hall via the rear entrance which was for the use of staff and up the backstairs to the top floor and to Leo's room on the north side. Leo shut the door firmly behind them and turned the key.

"Now, Katrina Gregory, future star of film and stage, get your clothes off and lay on the bed," he said with a wicked smile.

CHAPTER 13

"I'm not cut out for this," moaned Katrina as she passed Leo in the busy commercial kitchen at Canleigh. "I hate waitressing. My feet are absolutely killing me and I keep forgetting things people want … and I loathe clearing tables of dirty crockery, yuk, and …."

"Stop complaining," whispered Leo, grabbing two ice buckets from a counter top and throwing a glance at the other staff to make sure no-one was listening. "Just a few weeks, and we will have enough to escape."

"It can't come soon enough," she grumbled, scraping off leftovers from a pile of lunch plates into the bin beside the industrial dishwasher. She slipped off her right shoe. Her footwear was leather and flat but her feet were hot and sore, especially her big toe, which she had stubbed on a chair leg when a customer had stood up quickly from his table right in front of her. He had been mortified and apologized profusely but it hadn't taken the pain away. She rubbed it ruefully. It looked swollen.

"As much as I love Canleigh, I never envisaged waiting on tables if I lived here. I had something much more wholesome in mind."

"Just be patient," hissed Leo. "I must go. It's someone's birthday and they're ordering a hell of a lot of champagne," he said, waving the ice buckets in front of him.

Katrina watched him disappear towards the bar. He was actually enjoying his job. All the ladies loved him and every evening there was a bevy of women who wanted to sit near to the bar and ogle him. It was pathetic, the way they giggled every time he looked their way, behaving just like silly schoolgirls and some of them were old enough to be his mother.

"Katrina," shouted Sidney, the head chef. "Wake up! The mains for table 9 are ready."

Katrina sighed, put her shoe back on her foot, wincing with the pain, and hobbled over to the counter to pick up the braised lamb livers. How could anyone eat them? What horrible people they were.

* * *

David watched Katrina with exasperation. He wished to goodness Lucy hadn't cajoled him into giving the girl a job. She was pretty useless in whatever task he gave her to do ... or in some cases wouldn't do. She flatly refused to do any cleaning or chambermaiding work and he couldn't really argue with her because of who she was. She was useless in the office and annoyed the secretaries by doing her nails and preening herself in the mirror on the wall rather than getting on with her work and when she did, she didn't concentrate on what she was doing and messed up a couple of bookings and annoyed four new guests who probably wouldn't want to return. He had resorted to putting her behind the bar with Leo but whereas he was brilliant and a real asset to the hotel, she spent more time than a little leaning on the bar flirting with male customers. Resorting to putting her on waitressing duties had been the last option but that was not her forte either as she wasn't quick enough and displayed little interest in making sure diners were happy. David really didn't know what else he could give her to do and prayed she would become bored and decide to leave. He had told Lucy of his misgivings but she brushed them aside.

"Darling, David. I know Katrina can be difficult ... she's always been more concerned with her appearance than anything else but she needs to settle down and get this nonsense out of her head that she can make it in Hollywood. According to Aunt Vicky, Katrina is a useless actress and won't stand a chance, especially as she gave up any hope of learning anything at Radley ... and I did promise that I would try and give her something else to think about. I was hoping that once she got used to being properly employed, she would want to learn more and become a really useful member of the team, especially with her gorgeous boyfriend working here too. Just be patient with her please, David. I'm sure that in a few weeks her attitude will change and if it doesn't … well, we will have to think again."

"That's all very well but I think she's going to have to work behind the scenes because we can't risk her upsetting the guests any longer by her sloppy attitude."

Lucy thought hard. "How about putting her down in the stable block, either in the plant or gift shop or even the hair salon? I'm so grateful to Suzanne having advised on the set up and managing to find us some good stylists … it's such a shame she can't be spared from The Beeches to run it … she's done marvels over there."

"Yes, but that's hardly being behind the scenes, is it?" argued David. "But then again, apart from chambermaiding or cleaning, there really is little else where she won't have to deal with the general public and she flatly refuses to do either of those jobs."

"How about the beauty treatment room … there must be something she can do to help out there … she's obsessed with makeup and skin care so that could be of particular interest … or how about supervising the pool? She's an exceedingly good swimmer and won a few school medals and did a lifesaving course."

David stared at her with relief. "Perfect … I'll have a word with her in the morning and see what she thinks … mind you, I think she will agree to anything after her unsuccessful stint as a waitress."

"Well, I hope she finds it all to her liking," Lucy replied. "I've a nasty suspicion Aunt Vicky isn't too well at the moment and I don't want her worrying about Katrina."

*　*　*

Lucy's suspicions were correct. Vicky had a secret and even Alex hadn't been told. A week ago, she had found a lump in her left breast. The shock of finding it when having a shower had been traumatic. She had stood for ages, touching it, prodding it, praying she was mistaken. She had gone cold all over, real fear penetrating her whole being. She didn't know what to do. Her instincts were to get dressed, carry on as normal and hope it would go away but she knew it wouldn't. She had to get to the doctors, which would then start the whole ghastly rigmarole of hospital visits and the possibility of losing her breast. She would be maimed and scarred for life … in her panic she totally forgot about reconstruction. She might even be one of those women who couldn't beat it and she was too young to die and wanted so much to grow old with Alex. Oh God, Alex. As much as she wanted his support, she couldn't tell him. She couldn't tell anyone. She couldn't mouth the words because if she did it would make it real and she would have to deal with it.

For a number of days, she alternated between pretending the lump wasn't there to being convinced she was going to die, even avoiding sex with Alex in case he found it, carefully turning over in bed so that his hands didn't rest anywhere near it but as she sat in her office that morning, staring unseeingly out of the window, she knew she had no choice. It wasn't going to go away and she had to get a grip. She had friends who had gone through the same hell. Two had survived, although one had split up from her husband which had sent the poor woman into a spiral of depression and taken a long time to overcome … but then there had been Marilyn. She had died, leaving a devastated husband and three small children.

Vicky thought about Alex, Katrina and Suzanne. The girls would naturally be terribly upset if the same thing happened to her but both were strong and would adapt to life without her but Alex … how would he cope on his own? They were so close. They lived for each other, totally and utterly. He would be shattered. Oh God, she didn't want to be the cause of any pain for him. She loved him so much. She laid her head on her desk and cried.

Raising her head minutes later and wiping the tears away with a tissue, she knew what she had to do. She had to see the doctor, see a specialist and find out exactly what was going on. After all, it might not be cancer. It might only be a cyst or something. A rush of hope raised her spirits slightly. Of course. She might be panicking for absolutely nothing. It could be something quite simple. She picked up her phone.

* * *

Katrina wasn't sure if she was enjoying her new job or not. David had called her into his office and given her instructions regarding her new duties.

"I'm afraid I really don't think you're suited to the traditional hotel positions," he stated blandly as he gestured for her to sit down on the opposite side of his desk. "However, Lucy and I have come up with a proposition for you, which might suit your talents a little more."

"Oh?" Katrina had queried, glad to hear she wouldn't be expected to waitress any longer. Her feet were so sore she had booked a pedicure in the beauty salon, hoping that would help ease the pain. "So, what delightful work am I expected to do now then?"

"We thought you could have a variety of jobs, to make it more interesting. A few hours down in the stable gift shop, the plant shop and the new hair salon … we won't ask you to do a stint in the stable cafe as you're obviously not suited to that kind of work. Then you could help out in the beauty salon and assist in the spa up here at the Hall … I understand you have lifesaving skills so you could certainly take a turn supervising the pool."

"Oh," Katrina perked up. This was a bit more like it.

"I've had a word with all the supervisors of those departments," David continued, "and we've come up with a rota."

He handed her a piece of paper detailing where and when she had to be for the next seven days. "You can start in the beauty salon today. You can help greet guests and fetch them drinks and snacks while they're waiting for treatments or relaxing afterwards and you can help out on reception and sell the beauty products. I do hope all this will be more to your liking, Katrina."

She grinned and held up her hands. "Anything rather than waitressing. God, I hate it so much and being behind the bar is just as bad. This all sounds a little better."

It all went reasonably well. Katrina didn't particularly enjoy pandering to the needs of other women but the calming atmosphere of the beauty salon with its soft music and perfumed air was far more relaxing than the busy kitchens, dining room and bar. This was more up her street, although she would much prefer being the one to be pandered to but one day ... oh yes, one day. They would all be kowtowing to her, falling over each other to do her bidding. She couldn't wait!

CHAPTER 14

It is a tumour, I'm afraid," announced Mr. Fellows, the Consultant Oncologist, with a great deal of sympathy. "And the sooner we get you in to deal with it, the better."

Vicky sat on the leather chair on the opposite side of his desk in stunned silence. She had been so convinced he was going to say it was only a cyst, could be removed without difficulty and this whole ghastly worry could be forgotten.

She left Mr. Fellows' office, hardly able to take in that she was booked into his private clinic in Harrogate for surgery the following morning. She had no choice now. She had to tell Alex … and Katrina and Suzanne … but she couldn't do it yet. She had to talk to someone else … a woman … Ruth. She turned her red Volvo V40 towards Leeds. It wouldn't take long to get to Tangles. It was Wednesday and as far as she knew Ruth had no engagements today and would be at home, probably painting. With tears pouring down her cheeks and her insides frozen with fear, she put her foot down once she hit the open road and the car took off like a rocket.

Philip was just leaving the lovely old Tudor house as Vicky pulled up beside him. He was looking so old and frail these days, thanks to the damage Delia had inflicted on his body. Every winter he seemed to get smaller and weaker and Vicky knew Ruth was terribly worried about him. There had recently been talking of them moving abroad for the warmer weather … possibly to Italy … but nothing concrete had been decided. However, they were going to Spain over Christmas and New Year so perhaps they would consider a permanent move to Europe when they were relaxing in the sun, although Vicky couldn't imagine how Philip would cope without Tangles, the stables and the sanctuary in his life.

She smiled at him, hoping he wouldn't notice she had been crying. "Hi," she said as gaily as she could. "I need some company and was hoping Ruth was in."

"She's in her studio ... the parents of one of my clients commissioned her to do a painting of their child on one of our ponies so she's busy finishing it off. Go on up. She'll be pleased to see you."

"Thanks," she said, heading for the front door of Tangles while he eased himself painfully into the driving seat of his Volvo V70, started it up and headed down the lane towards the stables.

Ruth was concentrating hard on the canvas in front of her. A happy looking young girl in a hard hat and jodhpurs was astride a grey pony in a paddock, fields and woods behind her. Satisfied with the finishing touches she had just applied, Ruth looked up as Vicky entered the room and smiled.

"Hello. Come to have a look? I'm really pleased with this one ... my first attempt at a portrait," she laughed. Then she saw the look on Vicky's face, stood up abruptly, ripped off her paint covered tunic and placed her brushes on her palette. She strode towards her step-daughter and threw her arms around her. "What is it? Whatever is the matter? It's not Alex is it?"

Vicky burst into tears and clung onto Ruth for support, trying to get the words out in between taking big gulps of air. "Oh, Ruth. I'm so scared."

"Why? Tell me," demanded Ruth, becoming frightened too. "Come and sit down," she added, propelling Vicky towards a sofa in the corner of the room, covered with a multi-coloured fleece throw. She sat beside Vicky and held her hand, waiting for the sobs to lessen.

"I ... I've got breast cancer," Vicky gasped. "I've got to go in tomorrow and have a mastectomy. I don't know how to tell Alex ... and how he will take it."

"Oh, Vicky darling. I'm so sorry ... but why are you worrying about Alex? He will be thoroughly supportive. You know he will. He adores you and will do anything to make you happy."

"But ... but I won't be the same ... I shall be deformed," Vicky gasped. "I shan't ...,"

Ruth held up her hands to ward off any more negative talk. "Vicky ... you will not be deformed ... surely you will have reconstructive surgery ... and I sincerely don't think Alex is shallow enough to let this blight his love for you. You must give him more credit. He's a lovely man and won't let this get in the way of what you have with each other. You have a very strong marriage ... you know you do."

"But ... but what if I die? I can't bear to think of him grieving for me for the rest of his life ... and Katrina ... and Suzanne. I don't want to leave them."

Vicky burst into tears again and Ruth wrapped her arms around her, wanting very much to cry herself.

"And you're not going to. You're going to get over this operation, recover and go on to live a long and happy life with your gorgeous husband and your children."

Ruth stood up and crossed the room to fetch the box of tissues she always kept by her easel. She handed them to Vicky, whose sobs were beginning to ease.

"I do hope you're right, Ruth. I don't want to die yet. There's still so much I want to do ... with the family ... with you and Philip."

"Exactly. We're all going to grow old together," Ruth smiled. "And don't forget, when you've had enough of work, you and Alex are going to retire, join us somewhere nice ... I still have a hankering for a villa near to Lake Como ... and have lots of fun in the sun and I'm not missing out on your company then, believe me."

Vicky wiped away her tears with a couple of tissues and attempted to smile. "That would be so nice ... I'd love to find a lovely villa like our last one. It was so kind of Daddy to leave it to me and I was so sorry to have to sell it but we needed the funds to buy The Beeches. It would be fabulous if we could buy another."

"Yes," mused Ruth, glad the conversation was taking a less morbid turn, giving Vicki time to regain her equilibrium. "Yes, I loved it too. Your father and I had quite a few holidays there. It was so lovely and I'd love to buy another too ... I shall have to look on the internet and see if there is anything for sale. Even if we didn't retire as such, it would do Philip good to get away from here more, there's no need for him to work so hard, especially in the winter when it's so cold. Jim, his assistant manager, will look after the business and the sanctuary. He's been here for years and can run everything with his hands tied behind his back."

"I shall miss you over Christmas and New Year," said Vicky sorrowfully.

"I know, I'm sorry but neither of us would enjoy it, knowing Delia and Brian are just up the road. We wouldn't sleep at night. Even though Delia's probably not a threat any longer, and Lucy is adamant she isn't, we won't rest easy knowing she's so near. It's best if we go away ... and then Lucy can enjoy being with her mother without worrying about us too."

"Actually," Ruth looked up with delight, "I have the perfect solution. You must come and recuperate with us. You won't be able to work for a few weeks after your operation and if you stay at The Beeches, you will fret that you should be working ... I know you ... but if you come with us, you can relax properly and come back fighting fit."

"But Alex ... I can't be apart from him at Christmas!"

"Bring him too."

"But The Beeches ... it's our busiest time, Ruth. We can't be away."

"Why not? You're always there. You work so damned hard ... both of you. Why not get a temporary manager in? You have the connections and you can afford to get in the best people so you know nothing will go wrong. Come on, Vicky. Think about it. It will give you and Alex precious time together and get used to what has happened without the pressure of The Beeches."

"But Suzanne and Daniel ... it's their first Christmas back in the UK. How can we desert them?"

"Suzanne has a sensible head on her shoulders and will understand ... and I can always ask Lucy if she would include them for Christmas lunch at Dingle Dell. They've always got along well and Delia is no threat to Suzanne so there'll be no worries on that score."

Vicky's face began to brighten now she had something nice to look forward to and even though she was still frozen inside and terrified of what was to come, if she could close her mind to it and focus on spending a lovely Christmas in the sun with Ruth, Philip and her beloved Alex, she might just be able to get through the next few days. All she had to do was go home, tell the family and get through the dratted operation in one piece. Not much of a challenge really!

* * *

Suzanne was desperately saddened by Vicky's news but Katrina was non-committal.

Alex had asked them both to visit him and Vicky at their flat at The Beeches that evening, having wanted to be alone with his wife after she had broken the news to him just after lunch. He had downed tools and stayed with her all afternoon, hugging her tightly, letting her cry, reassuring her that nothing would ever deter him from loving her and nothing the surgeons could do to her would change that. But the girls had to be told, prior to the following morning when Vicky's surgery would take place, so they were summoned to the flat, Suzanne having left Daniel in the cottage in the care of Josie, one of her stylists who had offered to babysit. Katrina had driven over from Canleigh, curious as to what was so important to drag her over to The Beeches so suddenly. Her father had refused to enlighten her on the phone.

"I need you and Suzanne both here and I will tell you both then and not before," he had said firmly. "Just make sure you are here at 7.00 pm. Sharp," he had added.

Katrina had arrived at The Beeches at exactly 6.55 pm and dashed up to the flat, waving hello at Gillian on reception as she hurried towards the stairs. She could have taken the lift but it was quicker, and better for her figure, to race up the stairs. She entered the flat bang on 7.00 pm to be rewarded by a glance from her father who looked, with raised eyebrows, at his watch. For his daughter to actually be on time was a miracle.

Suzanne was already there, sitting beside Vicky on the sofa, who was dressed in a beautiful turquoise negligee, looking fragile and tired. She was devoid of makeup and appeared to have been crying. Alarm bells began to ring in Katrina's head, especially as her father looked ... she wasn't really sure but she hadn't seen him like this before. He was actually nervous, which was an emotion alien to him. He was always so self-assured and steadfast. A rock in all storms.

He had been drinking too. She could smell the brandy on his breath as he bent to kiss her cheek. That was really unusual as he never had a drop before dinner at 8.00 p.m. and that was another point, why was her mother in her negligee? She was usually preparing some grand concoction in the kitchen with her apron on at this time of the evening.

"Aren't you feeling well, Mother?" she asked, looking at Vicky curiously. She hoped to goodness it wasn't a bout of flu or some other kind of bug. She didn't want to catch anything now Leo had finally persuaded Kevin to come up to Yorkshire to get cracking with the filming over the coming weekend.

"Your mother and I have something to tell you," interrupted Alex. "Would either of you girls like a drink? I think you are going to need one."

"Just a very small one for me," said Katrina, her curiosity really aroused. "Vodka and plenty of coke, please, Father ... I can't have much as I'm driving."

"True but you can always stay the night if you have to," added Alex, heading to the drink's cabinet. "Suzanne? What would you like?"

Suzanne, picking up on Alex's nerves and deeply concerned about Vicky, shook her head. "No, thank you. I'm fine."

Katrina sniffed. She had forgotten what a goody two shoes Suzanne could be, especially in front of her parents.

Alex handed Katrina her drink and gestured for her to sit down in a chair opposite her mother and Suzanne. Vicky was looking at him beseechingly as if she didn't want him to speak. He noticed, sat down on the arm of the sofa next to her, took her hand and glanced at the girls. He looked haggard and drawn, and for the first time Katrina noticed lines on his face and on her mother's too. Her parents were both energetic, fit and extremely good looking, which is probably why she had turned out with such good features, but tonight they suddenly looked old, tired and almost ... defeated.

"Your mother has breast cancer," he said gently. "She's going into hospital first thing in the morning ... to have a mastectomy ... we wanted you to know as she is going to be pretty poorly over the coming weeks and will need all your support."

"Oh, Mum," cried Suzanne, throwing her arms around Vicky. "I am so sorry ... but you will be absolutely fine. Hundreds of women have this every day and go on to lead perfectly healthy and normal lives ... and we will do anything ... absolutely anything to help you get better again."

Vicky hugged her back. Suzanne had always been such a support when she had been growing up with them and she obviously hadn't changed.

Katrina didn't say a word. She sat glued to her chair, her mind in a whirl of speculation. If her mother died, it was another obstacle out of her way. That would only leave Lucy but she was still young and might have children; normal, healthy children, not like that brain-dead Selena ... but what if she didn't? What if she died early, like her mother was probably going to? Canleigh would really be hers then ... and all those flats, houses and office blocks in London and other parts of the country. Suddenly the glittering prize she coveted was there before her. Canleigh Hall could really be hers at some point in the future. She could be the one to queen over it instead of Lucy. She wouldn't have to worry about making it in Hollywood. She would be tremendously wealthy in her own right and wouldn't have to work at all if she didn't want to. She could just enjoy herself, spending all that lovely lolly ... and turning the Hall back into a private home was the first thing she would do. Her home. Her very own stately home. The hotel would be no more. Oh, yes! She couldn't prevent a smile.

"Katrina ... aren't you going to say something?" queried her father, looking at her with a puzzled expression, unable to understand why she was smiling. The news he had just imparted was certainly nothing to look happy about.

She shook herself, coming back to reality with surprise. She was still a skivvy at Canleigh, her mother was still alive and Lucy was about to marry David. How damned frustrating!

CHAPTER 15

"I'm not coming back to Canleigh tonight. I've had too much to drink and daren't drive so I'll stay here ... oh, and I think my mother is going to die," remarked Katrina to Leo on the telephone when she was alone in the lounge an hour later. Suzanne had returned to the cottage to relieve the babysitter and her parents had gone through to their bedroom, which meant dinner was not forthcoming and as drinking alcohol always made her hungry, she was starving and would have to raid the fridge in a minute.

"Oh, no," Leo said, the shock very real in his voice. He actually liked Lady Victoria. She had recovered her equilibrium well after their first meeting when he knew he had made a real impact on her and she had made him very welcome, even though he knew he wasn't exactly what she would have liked as a boyfriend for Katrina. "Why? What's the matter with her?"

"Breast cancer ... it's one of the biggest killers," Katrina sighed, almost with glee, wandering over to the drinks cabinet and pouring another large vodka and very little coke, outwardly to dull the pain of her mother's illness but in reality, to celebrate the possibility of Canleigh becoming a step closer to being hers.

"Well don't sound so pleased about it," lectured Leo with surprise. "That's dreadful news."

Katrina didn't see or hear her father enter the room as she was staring out of the window across the gardens to the cottage where Suzanne and Daniel now lived. The curtains weren't drawn and the lights were on. She could just see Suzanne talking to the babysitter in the lounge.

Katrina giggled. "Yes, darling Leo, but if Mother pops her clogs, the only person standing in my way of inheriting Canleigh is Lucy ... and I'm wondering exactly what can be done to help her arrive at the pearly gates too. Then I shall be made for life."

Alex, desperately low, upset and depressed couldn't believe what he has hearing. He had tucked a tearful Vicky up in bed and made sure she was asleep before he left her, then returned to the lounge, in need of another drink. To open the door and see Katrina, with her back to him, waving a glass in one hand and her mobile on loudspeaker in the other, and hearing her mouth such obscene comments, was tantamount to walking into hell itself.

"Katrina!" he boomed. "How could you? What the hell is the matter with you, you evil, nasty girl?"

"Oh whoops. Got to go," Katrina said quickly and snapped her mobile shut. "Sorry, Daddy, darling. It's the drink ... of course I didn't mean it. I was just being silly."

Alex, usually so calm and level headed, was boiling mad and full of grief for his wonderful wife who had made him so very happy for all of their married life. They had so desperately wanted a child in the early years and certain it was not to be, had adopted Suzanne and Jeremy. It had been a disaster with Jeremy but Suzanne had turned out to be a fabulous and loyal daughter but this one, the one he and Vicky had yearned for and had come along a few years later, who was of their blood and should have been utterly steadfast and loving, was standing there, mocking her mother's illness and actually wishing her dead for her own ends. He was shocked to the core. The only other person who had made him feel like this in his whole life was Delia, Vicky's evil sister and Katrina's aunt. He knew his daughter had possessed an unhealthy interest in Delia from an early age but to hear her talking like this, was the woman personified. Please God Katrina wasn't going to turn out like her.

Katrina flung herself onto the sofa, drink in one hand and fishing in her bag for a cigarette in the other.

Alex saw the gesture. "You are not to smoke in here! You know the rules, Katrina."

"Oh, for goodness sake, don't be so damned stuffy," she grinned a little lopsidedly, beginning to feel quite drunk. Perhaps she should have added more coke to the last vodka.

"Christ! Why can't you be more like Suzanne? She's so supportive but you, you, who are actually our child, you are a self-centred, self-obsessed girl with no care for anyone. How you could talk about your precious mother like that, I have no idea. Actually wishing her dead, for your own ends. I despair of you, Katrina, I really do. Your mother is the sweetest, kindest person I've ever met and she dotes on you, would do anything for you. You know that. You've always known that!"

Alex was so angry, he could have hit his own daughter. He had never felt like this in his life but to hear her talk in the way she had about his darling Vicky was too hard to bear, especially as they were all about to go through one of the most traumatic times of their lives.

"Oh, keep your wig on, Daddy and anyway, that's not quite true is it? She won't give me the money to go to Hollywood. She's making me work at Canleigh … skivvying … when I should be doing far more exciting things in America."

"Oh, do grow up, Katrina. Your mother and I agreed after the debacle you made of your education at Radley, we will not help you out again until you have made some effort to buckle down and work. We made it quite plain why we wouldn't fund this nonsensical idea of yours so for God's sake stop whinging like a small child. We now have far more important things to think about than your ridiculous wish to become a film star."

Disgusted and dismayed by his daughter's self-obsession, whining about Hollywood yet again when her mother lay sick and terrified in the bedroom down the corridor, was hurting him badly. He had expected far more of her but why? She had never shown either of them much affection, whatever they did for her, so why should it be any different now?

He had moved to the drinks cabinet but suddenly the walls started to close in and he needed air. He didn't want to remain in this room with this horrible, selfish girl for a second longer. "I'm going outside," he muttered, heading for the door.

"That's right, Daddy," called Katrina sarcastically. "Leave me to it as usual. Don't concern yourself with my feelings and what I want."

He turned back to her, his face red and angry, clashing with his scarlet tie, "Your feelings! God, Katrina, you make me feel utterly sick. Why you can't be more like Suzanne I have no idea. She is a complete credit to this family and utterly loyal and grateful for what we have tried to do for her ... but you ...,"

"Oh yes, bloody Suzanne, little Miss goody two shoes, who can do no wrong ... and if you think I'm going to share my inheritance with her, you have another think coming. I shall contest it when the time comes, believe me, I will," snarled Katrina.

"Well, you won't get anywhere, Katrina and if you're not careful I shall sign the whole damned lot over to her, which will prevent you receiving anything at all ... ever."

Katrina's eyes flashed as she stood up and walked towards her father. "Just try it. If you do, you won't live long to regret it."

Alex recoiled as she snaked towards him, a look of sheer hatred on her face. She looked terrifying; her mouth taut, her eyes blazing, her auburn hair catching the light from the chandelier above her head, making it look as if it was on fire. It was as if a devil woman was walking towards him. Not his daughter. Not the child he and Vicky had so wanted and so loved. What the hell had they spawned?

* * *

On entering the cottage, Suzanne was feeling lower than she had for a long time. Even losing Todd hadn't been as bad as the fear of losing Vicky, one of the two people she had heavily relied on for most of her life. They had rescued her and her younger brother, Jeremy, from a life of misery, being constantly on the move from one foster home or children's home to another and the stability and the love they had provided had been awesome. Even after Katrina had been born and Vicky and Alex had been over the moon with their child, Suzanne had been able to share in their excitement and help care for the tiny baby. Jeremy hadn't been interested and as a result had felt left out and isolated, which had probably led to his dreadful behaviour when he grew up. But Suzanne had never felt that way. She had never been jealous of Katrina, in fact she had idolised the baby nearly as much as Vicky and Alex.

It was such a shame that Katrina had turned out to be a spoilt brat. Vicky had indulged her more than she should and as a result Katrina did play up so she could get what she wanted more easily, knowing Vicky would usually back down.

However, it had been highly disturbing tonight, to see Katrina appearing to be unconcerned about Vicky's illness; just sitting there, drinking vodka with a peculiar glint in her eye … and not for one moment did Suzanne think it was a tear about to fall. The girl hadn't uttered one word of sympathy to her mother, nor helped her to bed. Of course, it could be that she was desperately upset but Suzanne had a suspicion that wasn't so, especially when she noticed just a hint of a smile playing around Katrina's heavily lipsticked mouth. The girl had looked almost pleased at the news of her mother's terrible illness.

Suzanne had reluctantly left Vicky and Alex in the bedroom, having watched Alex tenderly tuck his wife up in bed, his face a picture of misery. She had kissed Vicky, promising to pop over early in the morning before she left for the hospital. Then she left the hotel and crossed the lawns to the pretty stone cottage, covered with Virginia creeper, which in the few short weeks she had been back at The Beeches, she and Daniel had come to love.

It was old, as old as the Beeches itself and in the days before Vicky and Alex had bought the hotel, had been left to rot and was virtually derelict. They had restored it beautifully. It wasn't particularly big; three bedrooms and a bathroom upstairs, with a decent sized lounge, a dining room and a well-equipped kitchen downstairs but it was perfectly adequate for her and Daniel and they were particularly looking forward to the summer when they could sit outside in the lovely little garden and just enjoy the utter peace it would provide.

Josie was curled up on the sofa in front of the wood burner, reading a novel.

"That didn't take long," she said with a smile, popping her book into her bag.

"No … no, it didn't. Thanks, Josie. I'm really grateful. I hope Daniel was good."

"Oh, yes. He went to bed with a book and I popped in a little while ago and he's fast asleep. You have a lovely little boy there, Suzanne. You're very lucky."

"Yes, I am," Suzanne smiled. "He's a real treasure and I have no idea what I would do without him now."

Josie smiled back, realising that Suzanne was shattered and in no mood to talk. She picked up her bag and coat. "I'll leave you to it then. See you in the morning."

"Yes," replied Suzanne with a tired smile. "Yes … and thanks again."

Locking the door behind Josie, Suzanne walked quietly towards Daniel's room and popped her head around the door. Her son was fast asleep. She went back to the lounge, closed the curtains, sat on the sofa and let the tears she had held back all evening flow freely.

CHAPTER 16

Lucy was shocked to hear about Aunt Vicky's illness from Ruth and desperate to do whatever she could to help and support her.

"She's devastated, obviously," said Ruth. "But I'm sure she'll be fine and we all have to remain positive for her."

"Of course we do," agreed Lucy, feeling an icy chill. She loved Aunt Vicky nearly as much as Granny Ruth. They had been so supportive of her during her childhood and teens when her own mother was incarcerated in prison. Vicky, Alex, Ruth and Steppie. What would she have done without them all?

"What can I do?" she asked.

"Nothing. She's going in for surgery first thing in the morning and probably won't be allowed visitors, apart from Alex of course and possibly Katrina and Suzanne. We can go the next day and see her together if you like, take her some flowers and cheer her up a bit."

"Oh, poor Uncle Alex. He must be so worried ... and Katrina and Suzanne ... I bet they're feeling scared."

"No doubt. I feel for Suzanne, just having split from Todd and coming home to start a new life and now this. She's always been so close to Vicky."

"I wonder how Katrina will react. She isn't particularly warm hearted so I don't suppose we'll see much emotion from her."

Ruth snorted. "No. You're right there. She's always been a bit of a cold fish, totally self-obsessed and selfish. I wouldn't be surprised if she isn't too concerned and I certainly can't see her wanting to look after Vicky in any way, can you?"

Lucy grinned. "No. God help poor Aunt Vicky if she did. Sympathy and empathy are not traits that Katrina has in abundance."

"No. Anyhow, Philip and I are taking Vicky and Alex off to Spain for Christmas and New Year to help with recovery. The last thing Vicky needs is to be at The Beeches over such a busy period.

She won't be able to resist working and it will just be too stressful for her."

"Who will they get to run it?"

"A temporary Manager. It will cost them a fortune to get a good one but they can afford it. However, this is going to leave poor Suzanne and Daniel without any family for Christmas … and Katrina for that matter, so, I was wondering darling, I know you have your mother and Brian staying with you and Selena, but would you be able to invite Katrina, Suzanne and Daniel for Christmas lunch? I know Vicky wouldn't feel so guilty about going away then. Would you mind?"

"Of course not. Suzanne and Daniel will be very welcome … and I am sure Katrina will be delighted to be invited. You know how she has this morbid fascination for Mother, who was quite irritated by it at her wedding … gosh, do you realize Mother and Brian have been married for five years now. It's gone so quickly!"

"Well, all I can say is that Brian must be an absolute saint and needs a medal to have lived with your mother for so long. He must have nerves of steel and a very kind and understanding heart."

"He has. He really has," enthused Lucy. She loved Brian very much and was more than grateful to him for keeping her mother on the straight and narrow and making her so happy.

"So, having extra guests won't upset your plans for Christmas Day?" asked Ruth.

"No, and Selena will love having a houseful of people, especially as she'll probably receive loads of presents … and her and Daniel get along so well … he is so patient with her … so it will be nice … and I am positive Mother and Brian won't mind one bit. I just hope the rest of you will have a nice time, Aunt Vicky especially … going away to recover is the best thing for her and if David and I can do anything to help at The Beeches, just say the word. I know Canleigh is going to be frightfully busy but David has it all in hand and I could always pop over and check all is as it should be."

"That would be lovely of you, darling … and Suzanne will be there, apart from Christmas lunch, so she can keep an eye on things too."

"Good. So it's all sorted then. All we need now is for Aunt Vicky's operation to be a success and for her to make a quick and full recovery."

* * *

Alex had spent a restless night although strangely enough, Vicky hadn't. She had slept like a baby in his arms to begin with but had eventually turned over, which had left him feeling somewhat bereft. He imagined what life would be like without her. It would be awful. He didn't know if he would be able to go on. He had loved her so much since the first day he had set eyes on her at University but she had been besotted by Barrie at the time, who had turned out to be rotten to the core even before they were engaged, sleeping with Delia on a weekend visit to Canleigh. Stupidly, as Vicky often said, she eventually forgave and married him. Alex had been heartbroken at the time but had managed to stay close when Vicky and Barrie had set up their first club in Kensington and asked him to be their partner. He had leapt at the chance to be beside Vicky every day and was glad he had been as when Delia was taken to court for shooting her brothers, Richard and that Rocky fellow, Barrie had stepped in, put up the bail money and then when her trial collapsed due to lack of evidence, commenced a torrid affair with her which resulted in them viciously assaulting Vicky, then fleeing to Canleigh. Just days later Barrie had driven his car down the drive and smashed it into a tree, leaving Vicky a young widow.

Alex had been appalled and shocked to the core at Vicky's treatment at the hands of her husband and sister but was glad he had been there to pick up the pieces. He had gradually put Vicky back together with his love and commitment and to his delight, following Barrie's untimely demise, she had finally fallen in love with him and agreed to be his wife. Their marriage had been the best as far as he was concerned. They had hardly ever had a disagreement, even over their businesses, which had expanded and grown over the years into quite an empire but once they sold all their clubs around the country and just concentrated on The Beeches, which meant he was at home all the time, they had been really settled and happy. Now that might all change. His darling wife might die ... a lot of women did but then a huge number survived, he kept telling himself ... and Vicky would be one of them ... and he didn't care a jot about how she looked, as long as she was alive and able to enjoy life with him until they were really old and grey and surrounded by grandchildren and great grandchildren.

That made him think about Katrina. He was so disappointed and angry with her. He knew she had probably had too much vodka after she had been told about Vicky but she hadn't been so inebriated that she didn't know what she was saying. To dismiss her mother's illness so lightly, for her own ends and to wish her dead, was not only appalling but deeply worrying. Whatever went on in her head? He had always known Katrina wasn't the most empathetic of people but to say what she had was distinctly concerning. Surely she didn't really wish her own mother harm so she could be in with a slim chance of inheriting Canleigh? If so, he would be terrified of leaving Vicky alone with her and that was crazy, not wanting to leave them together, mother and daughter. No. She couldn't have meant it ... likewise her words that he would regret it if he signed everything over to Suzanne. It had been terrifying, seeing the hate in her eyes but it must have been all the vodka she had drunk. It must have. He would get up early and have a word with her when she was sober and she would be contrite and apologetic but would she mean it? His stomach flipped over nervously.

* * *

Alex never had the chance for a word with Katrina. Even though he rose at six thirty, he discovered when he went along and knocked on her bedroom door, that she had risen even earlier and left The Beeches. That made him angrier than ever. That she could depart without a kind or encouraging word to her mother on one of the worst days of her life was unforgivable. He really would give her a thoroughly good talking to when he caught up with her.

* * *

Katrina had guessed her father was going to try and talk to her before he took her mother off to hospital and she couldn't face it. With a crashing hangover as she had taken the vodka bottle to bed with her and downed the lot, she was well aware she shouldn't be driving but leaving so early, there wouldn't be too many people about and it should be possible to skip back to Canleigh without any mishaps if she was careful.

It was still dark and she had to concentrate hard on the road as her head was thumping madly and her eyes were as heavy as lead but the further she travelled away from The Beeches, she felt a little better. She couldn't have handled a confrontation with her father, nor watched her mother being carted off to hospital looking feeble, weak and tearful, perhaps never to return, or if she did, possibly for not very long. She wound down the window and allowed the early morning air to wake her up and sharpen her mind. She was intrigued to think she could consider her own mother's death with such detachment. She didn't feel particularly sorry for her, she didn't particularly care if she never saw her again. Why? Why did she feel like this? Why wasn't she more caring? Surely she should be devastated her mother was having to go through such an awful time with her life hanging in the balance.

She thought about her childhood. No real problems there, apart from Suzanne and Jeremy, vying for her parents' attention. It had been better after Suzanne had disappeared over to Australia and Jeremy had married Lucy, moved to Canleigh and was then killed in that car crash. It had been good being the only one at home, the one that both of her parents focused on and did all they could to make happy. So, why wasn't she grateful? Why didn't she love them more? Was it because her mother had spoiled her ... perhaps given her too much ... until now? Yes, they had sent her to Radley and paid for that lovely flat but now they were digging their heels in about Hollywood and also making her share her inheritance with Miss Goody Two Shoes, which made her mad as hell. They had never said no to her or put obstacles in her way before and she didn't like it. How could they treat her like this?

As she drove through Canleigh village, the street lights still on, she tried to imagine what it must feel like to be Lucy and own the Hall. Could it ever come to her? Could it? Only time ... and a little effort and manipulation on her part ... would tell.

CHAPTER 17

Vicky was petrified when she got out of bed the next morning. Even though the heating was on she felt terribly cold and couldn't stop shaking. She could hear Alex having a shower, and tried to compose herself before he emerged, not wanting him to see how frightened she really was. She needed to put a brave front on for him, as she knew he would for her.

She sat on the bed and waited, looking at the clock on the bedside table, ticking away the seconds, the minutes, her life. Would she survive this? Would they find the cancer had spread and nothing could be done? Would they tell her she only had months to live?

"Oh, you're up, darling," said Alex, walking towards her, rubbing his hair dry with a towel. "How are you feeling?"

"Ok," she said quickly. "I'll just have my shower. We haven't much time if we have to be at the hospital by 8.30 a.m. ... and you know what the traffic is like at this time of the morning."

Alex stood back to let her pass, noticing her glassy eyes and wishing so hard she didn't have to go through this. He knew she was scared out of her wits and he was too. Today was going to be one of the longest of their lives.

* * *

Ruth laid in bed looking at the clock beside her. Philip had departed down to the stable over an hour ago but she had nothing of importance to get up for this morning and could enjoy a lie in. Not that she was enjoying it, worrying about Vicky, what the outcome of this morning's operation would be and how Alex was bearing up.

She had rung him last night to see how telling the girls had gone but his phone was switched off. Assuming he was with Vicky, she had just left a message on his answerphone to say she

152

was thinking of them and if Alex wanted some company at the hospital today, he only had to ring her and she would go straight over. Hopefully he would have found the message but if he hadn't, she would ring him later.

Too restless to remain in bed she got out and looked out of the bedroom window. It was a grim November day. It had rained through the night and was still drizzling, a mist lingering around the trees in the distance. It didn't look at all inviting. This was a day to spend in her studio, pottering about and indulging herself with hot coffee, soup and rolls but Vicky and Alex were far more important and whether he needed her or not, she decided Harrogate was where she was headed.

* * *

Lucy was wondering what to do. She loved Aunt Vicky so much and wanted to be there for her but they couldn't all go this afternoon. Granny Ruth had said she would ring her later with any news. In the meantime, she would pop over to Canleigh and sign a pile of papers David said were there for her attention. Selena had gone off to school with Tina so she had a few hours to herself. She might have a swim while she was at Canleigh too. Exercise always raised her spirits and at the moment she was feeling pretty down with Aunt Vicky being so poorly … and she didn't want that feeling to take hold. She had been fighting depression since the terrible end of her marriage to Jeremy and on tablets to help her cope for a long time. Since her engagement to David, that awful debilitating feeling had passed and she had been able to wean herself off the tablets but the slightest concern or worry about anything could easily send her down into that dreadful spiral again and she would do anything to prevent it.

She flicked through her array of swimming costumes and decided on a cheerful pink one which always looked good with her blonde hair … and that needed touching up as the darker roots were just beginning to show. She would ring Suzanne later and make an appointment. They could have a chat about what they could do to help cheer up Vicky when she came home from hospital.

She thrust her costume into the pretty little waterproof bag she kept for swimming sessions, flicked a comb through her hair, picked up her car keys and handbag and left Dingle Dell, smiling as Coco, Selena's little brown and white cat Steppie had given her, shot out of the door in front of her and sat down on the grass to lick her paws.

"Bye Coco. Don't get up to any trouble today," she warned, settling into her silver Mercedes. "We'll see you later."

* * *

Not having to be on duty until 10.00 a.m., Leo was only just getting dressed as Katrina banged on his bedroom door and entered immediately, looking like death warmed up. "How's your mum," he asked, pulling on black trousers and a crisp white shirt. "You look awful. Have you been up all night with her?"

"Thanks," Katrina said sulkily, throwing herself on the bed and emptying her handbag to find her cigarettes and lighter. "And no, I haven't. I just had too much bloody vodka last night."

"So, how is she?"

"No idea," she replied casually, miffed at him raising an eyebrow questioningly. "She didn't look too good last night but I left too early to disturb her this morning."

"Don't you care," he asked with astonishment. He adored his mother and would do anything for her and if she were so ill, he would have stayed by her side, not get smashed and then walk out.

"At this moment in time, not really … I'm damned angry with my parents … they intend giving half of my inheritance to bloody Suzanne … and I can't tell you how livid I am."

"But she's your sister … surely she's just as entitled to it as you are."

"She's only bloody adopted … and she has a blasted husband somewhere … he should keep her … anyhow, if and when the time comes, I'm going to contest it in the strongest possible terms. I'm damned if I'm sharing it all with her! Then there's not funding me for Hollywood. So, as my beloved parents treat me as if I am of no consequence, I can reciprocate. No doubt mother will be okay anyway. They can afford to pay for the best care and the hospital has a good reputation."

"That's as maybe but you really should be there to support her. David will give you time off for this, you know he will, especially as he's soon to become family."

"Umm. That's another fly in the ointment."

"Oh?"

"Well, think about it, Leo. If David marries Lucy and gets her pregnant, then there is no hope, no hope at all that I shall ever inherit Canleigh."

"I didn't know you were likely to anyway," he said with surprise.

"Yes. If anything happens to Lucy, providing she doesn't have any children who aren't brain-dead, it will go to Mother and then to me."

"Blimey!"

"Quite."

"But it's all possibilities and probably won't happen as your mother will hopefully come through her ordeal okay, Lucy is still going to marry David and probably have healthy children and will live to a ripe old age. Anyway, what about Hollywood? I thought you wanted to focus on that, not about the remote chance you could inherit this place."

"I've been thinking about that … I'm not so sure I want to go now. There's too much going on here and I want to be around. I want to get rid of any chance Lucy will marry David and even …

get rid of her." There she had said it. She took a long drag of her cigarette and watched Leo's expression change to one of sheer horror as he took in what she meant.

"Whoa ... you can't mean that. You wouldn't ..."

"Yes," she said firmly, "I would ... and I want you to help me."

"Look, Katrina." He was standing up now, facing her full on. "I might be many things but a murderer ... no. You can rule me out on that one ... and especially Lucy ... she's one of the loveliest, kindest people I have ever met."

"Okay," she said flippantly, grinding her cigarette into the ashtray beside his bed. "That's fine. I'll do it on my own. Just make sure you forget all about this conversation ... or you might just join her. Any hint that anyone knows what I'm planning and I'll say you had something to do with Summer's death and you were in cahoots with Bill and Roger. Do I make myself clear?"

"Crystal," Leo croaked, unable to believe how this conversation was going. Katrina had been someone he had considered a friend and fun to be but she had hidden, sinister depths and he didn't like it, not one little bit. He had really rated her, even considered a proper relationship with her, especially as the sex was so good, but this was a different ballgame, this was a different woman to whom he thought he was becoming attached and it was blatantly obvious she wasn't someone to be trusted and he would have to watch his back.

Suddenly she burst out laughing, the sound reverberating around the room. He looked at her, astonished by the sudden change of demeanour.

"Got you there, didn't I?" she grinned. "You really thought I was going to blackmail you and do away with the delightful Lucy Canleigh."

"You crazy bitch," he uttered, furious with himself for having felt threatened and with her for what she had said.

She laughed again. "I know. Isn't it fun? You have simply no idea what I am going to come up with next, have you, darling Leo?

Of course, I'm not going to bump my lovely cousin off but I do want to prevent her marrying David … and I do want you to help me do that … it won't mean anyone being physically hurt … just a little manipulation … a little raunchy fun, … and you're very good at that, aren't you, darling?" she grinned as she wrestled with the belt of his trousers. There was always one way to get Leo to do anything she wanted. "And with Kevin arriving soon to start filming, we had better get in a little practice, don't you think."

She licked her lips as she undid the buttons on his shirt, and he groaned with desire. He was hers for the taking and she could get him go do anything she wanted.

* * *

An hour later Lady Victoria was wheeled into the operating theatre and the operation to save her life began.

CHAPTER 18

Lucy loved Dingle Dell, the purpose-built bungalow she had commissioned to be built in an isolated field on the Canleigh estate four years ago. Suffering from depression following the trauma of what Jeremy and Felix had put her through at the Hall, she found it impossible to remain living there. She could never forget the pain, the fear and the anxiety they had caused and as much as she loved Canleigh and always would, she could no longer reside there or she would never be able to put what they had done to her behind her. Also, once the alterations had commenced to turn the building into a hotel, it just wasn't practical with a small child who had learning difficulties.

She had pondered on moving into the Dower House but although she had been happy there as a small child, it was impossible to forget what had happened in the drawing room with her mother bashing poor Steppie nearly to death. Therefore, the only sensible solution to her problem was to actually build a home which could be designed especially for her and Selena.

Granny Ruth and Steppie aided in her search for a suitable site on the estate and between them, they decided on a field just over a mile along the lane from Tangles. It had been used for sheep grazing by a tenant farmer since before Lucy was born but as he was about to retire, it was the perfect time to take complete possession and build a beautiful new home.

Lucy had enjoyed all the sessions with her architect, designing all the rooms exactly how she wanted them. To make it safer and easier for Selena, it was decided a bungalow would be more practical than a two-storey dwelling. On entering the solid oak front door, with rectangular windows at either side, a long, wide corridor ran the whole length of the property to a floor to ceiling window at the far end. On the left of the entrance was a spacious drawing room with French windows facing south with Lucy's study next door. To the rear was a utility room and an enormous kitchen with every mod con. Then there was the dining room and a smaller, more cosy drawing room, both with French windows leading onto the west gardens and providing magnificent views over the fields and woods at the rear. Five bedrooms ran the full length of the north side; three for guests, one for Selena and in the north east corner with double aspect windows was Lucy's. Outside there was a lawn to three sides, pretty flower beds and a couple of young copper beech trees which Lucy was looking forward to seeing grow to maturity. There were tall black wrought iron gates at the front entrance from the lane and a gravelled drive with enough parking space for ten cars in front of the bungalow. It was perfect.

Lucy had revelled in making Dingle Dell a safe and pleasant place for her daughter to grow up in and even though she had to visit the Hall most days because of the business, it was so good to be able to drive away from the memories of what had happened there. She had been so terrified and intimidated by Jeremy and Felix and in her heart of hearts wasn't sorry she would never see any of them again.

Selena had thrived at Dingle Dell and grown from a happy baby into a happy youngster, thanks to the care and attention of not only Lucy but Tina too. Tina had been the much-loved nanny to Lucy and young Stephen, the last and final Duke of Canleigh, who had so sadly died in that awful attack in London when he was on a night out with his military friends but when they had no need of a nanny any longer, Granny Ruth who was in charge of Canleigh at the time, had kept Tina on as housekeeper. However, once Selena was born, Tina reverted back to the role she adored, exceedingly protective of her new charge who so sadly suffered from learning difficulties.

Once Lucy and Selena moved to Dingle Dell, Tina cared for Selena every morning as Lucy spent a few hours at the Hall before returning home to spend precious time with her daughter in the afternoons. Sometimes, if the weather was nice, they would play in the garden or go for long walks or even drive over to Tangles so Selena could have a riding lesson on Noddy, one of the rescued Shetlands, Steppie had taken in. If the weather was unkind, they would either stay indoors, playing games or watching DVD's or sometimes they would venture into Leeds and visit the cinema if there was something on which would hold Selena's interest.

That was until Selena had started school last year. Lucy had managed to find her a place in a highly recommended private special school in Harrogate, which catered for the child's needs perfectly. Selena, under the care of the kind Mrs. Timmins, the Headmistress, loved it. She liked learning new things and was making friends easily and Lucy liked to invite them back to Dingle Dell, with their parents, on the odd occasion. It was good to mix with people who were dealing with the same issues as herself and Lucy was more than happy with her decision to send Selena to Dawney Wood.

And there was another reason to be happy, thanks to one special person in her life who had certainly helped ease the depression that had dogged her for so long. Lucy hadn't thought she would ever trust a man again after what Jeremy had put her through but surprisingly, David Jenkins, her General Manager at the Hall, had managed to find a way through the invisible armour she had placed around her heart.

David's role was to steer Canleigh Hall in the right direction once it was up and running as a hotel. He had all the right credentials, having been brought up in a public house near Brancaster in Norfolk where he helped out behind the bar during his holidays from the University of East Anglia. On completion of his business degree he had decided he wanted to have a career in hospitality, obtained employment in various hotels in London over the next few years, and ended up as general manager of the famous six-star Varzi hotel owned by an Arab sheik. However, by the time he was in his early thirties, he was becoming tired of frenetic London life and when he happened, quite by chance, to see the advertisement in The Lady for a general manager at Canleigh, he had applied without hesitation.

Lucy would never forget her first sight of him. He was utterly gorgeous with a tall, athletic figure, thick brown hair with gold highlights and fabulous dark, kind eyes. He wore a Savile Row navy suit, a crisp white shirt, gold cufflinks and a gold Rolex watch. From the moment he walked into the office at Canleigh Hall, Lucy was bowled over. He looked every inch the person she wanted to be in charge of her hotel and as the interview progressed, she discovered he was utterly charming, kind and solicitous and she was intrigued to discover he was deeply religious, and went to church without fail every Sunday. He showed great interest in St. Mary's, just a short walk across the lawn and Lucy, after showing him around the Hall and gardens, walked with him across to the church, knowing her search for a general manager was over as they were so at ease with each other.

He told her a bit about his personal preferences, that he kept fit by running every morning, followed by a swim and he had no desire to socialise in his spare time, having spent hours every day talking to guests and staff. Once his shift was over, he liked to lead a quiet life; reading and listening to classical music.

She wondered why he was still single, for a moment wondering if he was gay, recalling how Jeremy had fooled her for such a long time. With hesitation, she asked if he was married or there was a prospect of him being so. After all, as his employer and as he would be living in, she had a right to know.

"So, there is no Mrs. Jenkins," she said, as they neared the church, wondering why his answer was suddenly of great importance to her.

He had smiled. "No. I've never met anyone I wanted to settle down with …. and I quite like being single, being able to do as I please when I please … in my free time of course," he added quickly.

Lucy had appointed him without hesitation. She had other people to see but with David's experience, his quiet presence and his eagerness to help her build the business at Canleigh, there could be no other competition ... and she had been right.

He soon had the place ticking like clockwork. The staff idolised him and the guests adored him as he was so keen to make sure all were being looked after to the best of his ability. He could literally charm everyone, from the sternest businessman to the hoity toity elderly ladies who often stayed at Canleigh. They were all thrilled by his careful attention to their welfare and Lucy had to admit, he was the perfect man for the job and she couldn't have chosen better.

Canleigh, as a luxury spa hotel, soon gained an excellent reputation. With David's expertise and with the help and guidance of Aunty Vicky and Uncle Alex, who had years of experience with The Beeches, along with suggestions from her own mother, Lady Delia, Lucy had managed to give Canleigh Hall a really special feel to all those who were lucky and wealthy enough to spend some time there. It was certainly appreciated as they returned again and again and the lavishly styled hotel was nearly always running at one hundred percent occupancy with the diary containing firm bookings for rooms for the next two years, along with weddings and business functions.

Lucy had hired one of the most highly acclaimed interior designers in the country and the result was simply stunning. All the bedrooms on the first floor were decorated luxuriously and those which didn't possess them, were given bathrooms, all with extra-large walk-in showers and jacuzzi baths with gold fittings. Every room had four poster beds, along with plasma televisions, built-in wardrobes with full-length mirrors on the doors and deep gold drapes, bedding and carpets. The whole effect was elegantly grand and relaxing and Lucy loved seeing how guests reacted when occasionally, if the staff were too busy, she escorted them to their rooms when they arrived.

The ground floor had been relatively easy to sort out. The green drawing room immediately to the left of the front door, followed by the Italian room, gold drawing room and ballroom were only used for weddings and functions. The remaining rooms on that floor were utilised every day.

The mahogany dining table, along with the precious Chippendale chairs which had been in the dining room since the Hall was built, were removed and placed in storage in the basement. Smaller tables were acquired, covered with pristine white damask tablecloths and dotted around the room, providing more privacy if diners didn't wish to converse with others at mealtimes. The library, the state sitting room and state bedroom also had their furniture placed in storage and large, comfy sofas and occasional tables, covered with the latest newspapers and magazines, allowed guests to relax and unwind and gaze out over the pretty parterre to the lake and the woods.

The rooms on the west side of the building, overlooking Lucy's grandmother's precious rose garden, were used for various activities, such as yoga, dance and exercise classes. The crimson drawing room and sitting room were now offices and a massive semi-circular oak desk to the left in the entrance hall, was reception.

At great expense, the swimming pool had been extended and now boasted a steam room, sauna and jacuzzi, along with extra changing cubicles with showers, hairdryers, an array of expensive toiletries, thick white towels, bathrobes and slippers. A number of thickly padded reclining chairs by the pool were added for the comfort of the guests.

Lucy was thrilled to discover how quickly the business expanded and how many famous people liked to partake of her hospitality. There were well known actresses and actors, politicians, heads of corporations from abroad as well as from the U.K and best of all, two members of the royal family had also stayed for a weekend and promised to return. Her decision to turn

Canleigh into a hotel had been a good one and she was thoroughly pleased with the result.

However, the most exciting development in Lucy's life had been the burgeoning friendship with David, which ultimately led to romance. Their relationship remained strictly business-like for four years but gradually they became closer and took to walking around the lake on sunny days once Selena was at school and there was no need for Lucy to rush home. Ostensibly, their walks covered business topics but gradually their conversations meandered into more personal things. Lucy found David so easy to talk to. He didn't judge. He didn't criticise. He just listened and nodded and occasionally put a hand on her shoulder and eventually she found she was telling him about Jeremy, Felix and Matthew ... not all the ghastly details but enough for him to guess what had really gone on and what she had endured. Then she had burst into tears a few months ago at the sheer relief of being able to talk about what she had kept bottled up for so long, he had thrown his arms around her, let her cry and then kissed her. She would never forget that kiss. It had been so tender, so loving and she had known as she opened her eyes that he loved her ... and she loved him.

Their relationship cemented as the months flew by and Lucy became more and more light-hearted, so much so that she discussed the possibility of giving up her anti-depressant tablets with her doctor. He was cautious and put her on a reduction plan which would take many months but she was nearly there and had a feeling she would never need them again, not now she and David were engaged.

He hadn't asked her to marry him. As much as he wanted to, he hadn't dared. After all, she was his employer, she was the one who owned Canleigh Hall, she was the one who was rich. What could he offer her? He had been open and honest one evening after they had taken Selena to Filey. It had been a lovely family day, lots of shrieks and laughter from Selena as they played in the sea, David made sandcastles, pretending one of them was Canleigh

Hall and then they ate a big pile of fish and chips in a cafe in the town. They had driven home in Lucy's Mercedes, tired and happy, with Selena fast asleep in the back.

Back at Dingle Dell, having put Selena to bed, the two adults curled up together on the sofa in the lounge, drinking wine and devouring the big box of chocolates David had bought the day before.

"I wish ..."

"What do you wish?" David had murmured, kissing her brow.

"I wish we could do this all the time ... I wish you didn't have to go back to the Hall. I wish you could live here ... with us ... there, I've said it," she said, feeling the blush spreading all over her face.

David smiled lazily. "Yes, lovely Lucy. I wish that too but it wouldn't be right ... I couldn't just move in. Think about the gossip ... and no doubt the press would have something to say about it ... you know how they like to make a mountain out of a molehill and they are always wanting to know what's going on at Canleigh."

Lucy sat up and looked at him, taking all her courage into both her hands. "What if we were ... what if we were married? That wouldn't raise any eyebrows."

David looked at her, his expression one of sorrow. "Of course that would be fine but I can't ask you, Lucy ... as much as I want to. I've thought about nothing else for weeks but I can't. I have nothing to offer you ... I'm just your general manager for goodness sake. I know I have quite a bit put by but it's nothing compared to what you have. It would look as if I am just a gold-digger ... and believe me, I'm not. I really do love you, Lucy. More than you will ever know but I can't ask you to marry me. I'm so sorry."

Lucy threw her arms around him and kissed his cheek hard. "You silly, silly man. I don't care a fig about money, status or anything else for that matter. All I care about is you, you and

Selena ... and I want us to be a family, a proper family. So, David Jenkins, will you do the honour of marrying me?"

The incredulous expression on David's face had made Lucy hold her breath while his brain took in what she had just said.

"I don't know," he uttered eventually. "Lucy, it's such a big step ... I love you ... and Selena ... so much ... but ...,"

"There, if you love us, there is nothing else to be said, is there? Apart from yes. Just say yes ... I promise you'll never regret it," she added, terrified he was going to turn her down, not wanting to dissolve into pathetic tears in front of him.

He took her in his arms and looked her straight in the eyes. "If you are absolutely sure ... totally and utterly ... I never want you or anyone to think I was marrying you for your money ... it's you, Lucy. You are my world ... you and little Selena ... and I can't imagine either of you not in it anymore and if you really want me to be a permanent fixture in your lives, then yes. Yes, I'll marry you."

Lucy was happier than she had ever been in her life and was so certain that she had done the right thing for her and Selena. They would become a proper family in the spring, with a quiet, romantic wedding at Gretna Green. She didn't want to marry again at Canleigh and although her mother had offered to have the ceremony at Blairness or Glentagon, Lucy had visited Gretna Green on a trip up to Scotland and fell in love with the idea of marrying there. David had agreed readily as it would be relatively low key with only his family and Delia and Brian as guests and little Selena as bridesmaid. Then Delia and Brian were going to take Selena to stay with them for a couple of weeks while Lucy and David honeymooned in a remote cottage on the Isle of Skye, taking time to explore the Western Isles at their leisure. It would be absolutely perfect and Lucy was really looking forward to it. A whole new chapter of her life was about to begin and this time, this time, it was going to be right and she would never need another anti-depressant ever again!

CHAPTER 19

David was standing by the lift when the door slowly opened and Leo emerged to head towards the bar where he was to start work in a few minutes time. Leo had been startled to see David; his lips parted to smile but his eyes looked wary, almost embarrassed …. yes, that was the word, David decided. Leo had looked shifty and embarrassed. But why? David watched him cross the reception area with a puzzled expression. He had been impressed with Leo so far and hoped he wasn't up to no good and would blot his copybook. If he did, it was probably something to do with Katrina. She was so damned up herself and would no doubt land herself into a hell of a lot of hot water at some point. He hoped it wouldn't be here at Canleigh while he was in charge.

* * *

Leo felt decidedly uncomfortable under David's scrutiny. If the man knew that Katrina was planning his downfall, he would run a mile. For a split-second, Leo wondered whether he should tell him but he knew that if he did, Katrina would hit the roof and probably exact some ghastly revenge on him, just as she had promised. No matter what she said, he didn't trust her now. He had seen that ugly glint in her eye and she wasn't just playacting. She had meant it, however much she protested otherwise. If he said anything to anybody, she would crucify him. He hadn't had anything to do with Summer's death but he had worked for Bill and Roger for a long time and the police might well believe her. Blast the bitch. He would have to go along with her plans for now but as soon as he could he was going to extricate himself from her clutches. He didn't trust her any longer and he was a total believer in self-preservation.

David followed him into the bar and watched while Leo unlocked the shutters and cranked them up.

"I'm looking forward to meeting your former colleague, Kevin ... Latimer ... is that right? I must say I hope he is as good a bartender as you are, Leo. You've been a real asset to Canleigh Hall in the short time you've been here."

"Thank you," Leo replied warily, wondering what was coming. "I'm sure you'll be impressed with Kevin and give him the job."

"I certainly hope so, Leo. It's difficult to get really good staff these days. It might seem a great place to work ... which it is, but you know, as I do, that some of our ... more demanding guests ... can be pretty overbearing at times and it takes a lot of skill and patience to deal with them. Not everyone has those qualities," he finished, a vision of Katrina growing frustrated when waiting on tables springing to mind.

"Speaking of which, I see Mrs. Roberts-Fry is beckoning me," he said under his breath, with a hint of a smile. "I do hope she has found nothing to complain about this time."

He headed off to where a middle-aged woman with bleached blonde hair and too much make-up was teetering on massively high heels and wearing an exasperated expression on her face.

Leo breathed a sigh of relief. He had bigged Kevin up more than a little to David. If his own plan of getting the porn films off the ground was to succeed, Kevin had to have access to the staff quarters and how better than to get him a job here. Kevin had experience, having worked in pubs when he was young, so it wouldn't take much to teach him about cocktails and they wouldn't be here long anyway, just time to make enough with the videos to be able to hire a studio somewhere, possibly back in London. Although he had made up his mind he didn't want Katrina accompanying them. He really wouldn't ever feel at ease with her again.

* * *

Kevin was on the train heading for Leeds from London. He was grateful to Leo for thinking of him and wanting to work with him again. He had jumped at the chance. Having worked for Bill and Roger for over a year, only because the money was good and he liked to keep up the appearances of a decent lifestyle, he was dashed to find that the few jobs he had been offered since Starlight was shut down weren't exactly well paid and money was becoming a little tight. He had already had to shift from his decent sized flat in Greenwich to a tiny studio apartment in what could be described as the more run-down side of the area. Not only had his living accommodation been less inviting, but so had the neighbours and he was keen to move again as soon as possible but needed money to do so. Now, if all went well with this interview today with the general manager at Canleigh Hall, he would have a job and somewhere to live for a while and once Leo sold some of the films they were intending to make, earn much more on the side.

He also liked the idea of working with Katrina again. She was a natural in the bedroom, one of the best he had ever turned a camera on … as long as she didn't speak. She certainly couldn't act, in the true sense of the word, but she could show anyone a good time in the sack and he envied Leo, who had given her a good seeing to so many times in front of him. He wouldn't mind having a piece of the action himself and wondered about setting up the camera so that he could join in this time. He grinned. He was becoming aroused at the mere thought.

* * *

Katrina was deliberating on her future. She wasn't needed in the spa until 11.30 a.m. so was chain smoking in bed, thinking about all the people who stood in her way of owning Canleigh and The Beeches and what, in the grand scheme of things, could be done to improve her position.

For now, there didn't seem much she could do about her inheritance and Suzanne ... and she supposed, Daniel, as if anything happened to his mother, he would be next in line to inherit. She had time to think about it as even if her mother kicked the bucket, her father was still hale and hearty and probably wouldn't succumb to the grim reaper for a good few years yet. However, when the time came, she would fiercely contest the will and because she would quite likely be rich by then, would have the cash to hire the best law firms to deal with it.

There was also the possibility that Suzanne, in the meantime, would marry again and if so, would have someone else to support her and wouldn't be in dire need. So, she wasn't going to worry about her inheritance for a while, although having to relinquish half to Suzanne would make her bridle every time she thought about it.

However, Canleigh, was a very different matter and far more urgent. David was supposed to be marrying Lucy in the spring and within days could have her pregnant. That had to be prevented at all costs and the only way she could see of doing that was to discredit David totally and utterly in Lucy's eyes so that she would finish their relationship and even dismiss him from Canleigh.

Then she could decide what to do about Lucy. Could she bump her off? Was she brave enough and if she was, how could she do it to make it look like an accident? She thought about Aunt Delia. Everyone in the family were positive she had transpired to kill her brother, Richard, and her half-brother, Rocky, on purpose, although it couldn't be proved. If she had, how had she managed it? It would have had to have taken meticulous planning and an element of luck but then she had ruined it all by attacking Granny Ruth and Grandpa Philip in a heated rage and ended up spending nearly two decades in prison. That wasn't going to happen to her. Whatever she did had to be thought through carefully. Nothing must go wrong ... and it wouldn't if she kept her head. She knew she had a terrible temper, which was difficult to control at times so she mustn't let it get the better of her, just as Mother was always urging.

Mother. Would she survive very long after this operation? If she didn't, there really would only be Lucy standing in the way but if Mother made a full recovery and inherited Canleigh if something happened to Lucy, that would slow things up until she did pop her clogs. Perhaps it was time to buckle down and pretend she was taking a real interest in the business side of Canleigh instead of Hollywood and then her mother might be persuaded to relinquish it to her much earlier. If she did survive this cancer scare, her mother would be weakened by it and might want to start thinking of early retirement. Running The Beeches was exhausting. She certainly wouldn't want to take on the responsibility of Canleigh too.

Gosh, there was a lot to think about and decide what exactly to concentrate her efforts on. Canleigh or Hollywood? Canleigh or Hollywood?

She began to think about Hollywood seriously. Beneath her brashness and the desire to be a rich and famous film star, she was fully aware her acting skills really weren't up to much. It had been obvious at school as although she had been given the best parts, courtesy of that stupid drama teacher desperate to get her knickers off, some of the other kids had been far better than her and everyone knew it.

The students at Radley were also far more talented than her, were aware of it and disliking her arrogance and snobbery, had teased her relentlessly, ending in that final day when she had walked out.

Now, thinking calmly about it, she had to admit everyone, including her own mother, may probably be right and if she did get to America, she might well be in for more depressing rejections and end up bitter and broke, with no choice but to return to the U.K with her tail between her legs. So, perhaps it was time to give up that particular dream and concentrate her efforts on becoming the chatelaine of Canleigh so that in a few years' time she wouldn't be sitting up here with no money and no property. She would own a little empire and be filthy rich … if she played it right … if luck stayed with her.

So, David was her first target and with Kevin arriving today and filming in their bedrooms starting this weekend, an idea of exactly what she could do to discredit David was beginning to take shape and she felt a real thrill of excitement that she could actually achieve it ... and it would be fun doing it. She would have to run it past Leo and Kevin as they were pivotal to how it turned out but she could either use the threat of blackmail regarding Summer or promise them something to make it worth their while … but what? She didn't have anything. No. It would have to be blackmail. It had worked with her drama teacher at school. It would work now. She just had to keep a cool head.

Seeing the time, she rolled off the bed and dressed in her spa uniform; white trousers and a pale blue shirt with her gold name badge. She put her hair up, as all staff with long tresses were expected to do and glanced gleefully in the mirror. She looked good but when she was the owner of the Hall and could hold lots of balls and parties and sweep around in a gold ball gown, she would look even better. It would happen. She knew it would. She just had to get rid of David and Lucy and work on her mother. Not much really.

CHAPTER 20

The whole family were furious with Katrina. She hadn't visited Vicky once since the mastectomy and both Ruth and Lucy had tackled her about it.

"Your mother has been through hell in the past few days," Ruth seethed when she found Katrina folding towels in the spa at Canleigh. There were no guests in the immediate vicinity as it was lunchtime and they were all in the dining room so she was able to speak freely. "Why haven't you been to see her? She's very upset."

Lucy, having been slowed down by a chat with David when entering the Hall, came up behind Ruth and glared at Katrina too. "Don't make the excuse you've been too busy," she said crossly. "You know you can always have any time off you need to spend with Aunty Vicky."

Katrina gave a snort. "I don't want to see her. She has enough family pandering to her whims. She certainly doesn't need me … and I don't need her either. She's made it perfectly plain I'm of no consequence … pushing me aside for Suzanne and giving her half of what I am entitled to. I'll never forgive her … or my father for that. They've hurt me badly and if I'm hurting them, it's just too bad," she said, knowing how childish and belligerent she sounded but it was true. It was how she felt and she just knew she couldn't waltz over to the hospital or to the Beeches and pretend all was well and behave like the nice little girl they wanted her to be. She was hurt and angry and if they didn't like it, it was tough.

"I always knew you were a selfish child but I had hoped you would grow up at some point," remarked Ruth, wanting to grab hold of the girl and shake her hard. Vicky had cried in her arms last night because Katrina had been nowhere near her and she didn't know why. It was so remiss of Katrina, to hurt her own mother like this. It was unnecessarily unkind.

"Oh, I have, Granny Ruth. I finally accepted that whatever I want, my precious parents aren't always prepared to let me have."

"God! You are beyond the pale. They have spoilt you terribly and this is how you have turned out, expecting to always get your own way in all things."

"Naturally," smirked Katrina "and if I don't … well, whoever doesn't play ball will have to suffer the consequences."

Her eyes glittered maliciously and Ruth recoiled, banging into Lucy behind her. It was like confronting Delia again. The dark eyes, flashing dangerously, were the same, the lift of the lips to show teeth threatening to sink into flesh. She had seen it before … on her stepdaughter … Delia. Ruth felt physically sick and in shock. She turned away quickly, grabbing Lucy's arm.

"This is impossible," she hissed. "We're getting nowhere. Let's get out of here."

Katrina watched them leave the spa, two old women clutching onto each other for support. She grinned to herself. That told them and hopefully that would be the end of anyone begging her to visit her mother and it might, just might be the way to get her mother to change the will now, rather than have to hang on until both parents died and then go through the process of contesting it. This might just work. If her mother was so keen to see her, her parents would have to change the will. There. Problem sorted. She just had to stick to her guns.

The timing would have to be right though. Should she just ignore all pleadings for a couple of weeks to wear them down and then visit and demand a will change or would it be better to do it now, while her mother was at her weakest and her father at his most vulnerable? If they didn't play ball, she would flatly refuse to visit them again, which would really upset her mother and get her father to cave in. That might well work and would finally rule Suzanne out of the picture, apart from parting with a reasonable sum of cash, just as before.

Katrina folded another towel with a triumphant flourish. Yes, she could solve that knotty little problem just by being stubborn, and quicker than she had expected … and as for David and Lucy

… she had a funny feeling their romance was going to come to an abrupt end very soon.

She was smiling widely as two female guests wandered into the changing room. They smiled back, assuming her sunny expression was for their benefit. They were wrong.

* * *

"You can go home tomorrow, Lady Victoria," announced Mr. Fellowes as he sat down on the chair beside her bed with her notes in his hand. "All looks well to me and you just need to go home and rest. Obviously, you need to come back for your regular check-ups and I do want to see you again next week but there is no reason why you can't go on to lead a full and healthy life as we are as certain as we can be that we operated early enough to prevent the tumour spreading."

"Will … will I need radiotherapy or chemotherapy?" asked Vicky tremulously.

"No. I don't see any reason to go down that route at this time. I am more than happy with what we achieved in the operating theatre but obviously we will keep a strict eye on you … and if you are concerned about anything, anything at all, you must ring me immediately."

"Thank you so much," she whispered, eyes shining. It was so annoying, this need to burst into tears at the slightest little thing. She supposed it was because she was so weak but that would change once she got home. She smiled at Alex, sitting in the chair nearest the bed. He was holding her hand firmly. He, like her, had been so nervous about this meeting, praying that the surgeon wouldn't give them any more bad news. But he hadn't. All was as well as it could be and Vicky slumped back onto the pillows with relief. She could go home … and she wasn't going to die … not yet anyway.

***

"That's absolutely brilliant," breathed Alex, gripping her hand tighter after Mr Fellows had left the room and they were on their own. "We can get you back to The Beeches and then look forward to heading off to Spain with Ruth and Philip. I've managed to secure the services of a well recommended general manager for two months so everything should run like clockwork while we are away so you can relax now and concentrate on getting better. It will do us all good to have a decent holiday ... get some sunshine .... and sangria," he smiled.

"And what about the sex," Vicky sobbed. "I'll never be the same ... it won't be the same ... I'm so sorry."

Alex rose from his chair and took her in his arms. "You silly goose. We don't have sex ... we make love ... and that will never change ... I love you so much, Vicky, and always will. You are the most precious thing I possess and nothing will ever change that, do you hear," he asked, planting gentle kisses on her head as he cuddled her close, wary of hurting her damaged side.

She lifted her head and stared at him through her tears. "Oh, Alex, you will never know how much I love you," she sighed "and how much I want to go home. It will be lovely being back with Suzanne and Daniel ... and Katrina ...why hasn't she come to see me? Suzanne has been in every day, bless her."

Alex shifted uneasily. He didn't want to lie but Vicky didn't need to know exactly why their selfish daughter couldn't be bothered to visit.

"They've been particularly busy at Canleigh and couldn't spare her. She will come over when you're at home."

"I certainly hope so. I've really wanted her here ... to help support you at the very least."

"Don't you worry about me. Ruth, Philip, Lucy and Suzanne have been a tower of strength."

"Good. I'm glad. We have a lovely family ... and I'm so looking forward to getting away with some of them ... although it will be strange not being in Yorkshire for Christmas and New Year."

"It will be good to be in a warm climate in the winter for once, and somewhere quiet ... it's a peaceful little village Ruth and Philip have picked and we have a big detached house to rattle around in so we won't get on each other's nerves."

"Sounds perfect," Vicky whispered, suddenly feeling very tired.

Alex took her cue. He laid her gently back down on the bed, tucked her in and kissed her, promising to return in the evening. He left the room and stepped into the corridor. He took out his mobile and rang his daughter yet again. He had rung her repeatedly over the last few days but she blatantly refused to answer. He had left message after message but again, no reply. He was utterly disgusted with her and when he did catch up with her, she was going to receive a very large piece of his mind!

* * *

Katrina was having lunch in the staff dining room in the basement when she heard her phone and looked to see who was calling. Her father. Again. She grinned and ignored it, allowing it to go through to answerphone, for the umpteenth time. His previous messages had been a mixture of anger, despair and pleading and this one would no doubt be something similar but she didn't care a jot. She decided her parents could stew for now as she had other things to think about. David had appointed Kevin and tonight, the three of them; Kevin, Leo and herself, were going to meet up in her bedroom and start filming. The sooner she started earning decent money again, instead of the mere pittance she was paid at Canleigh, the better and if that was the only way she could earn it, so be it.

She was also going to run her idea of how to degrade David past them this evening as their assistance was vital to its success. Then, with a bit of luck, the general manager would be leaving Canleigh pretty soon with his tail between his legs ... and she knew the perfect time to set it in motion ... during the night of Sunday 9th December. The hotel would be full to capacity that weekend as there was a big charity event on the Saturday evening, the beauty salon was booked solid for treatments and there were very few tables left for lunch, dinner or afternoon tea. The weather forecast was also reasonably good which meant there would be a number of non-residents who would visit the grounds and spend well in the shops and cafe in the stable block following their ambles around the lake and gardens.

David would be exhausted by Sunday evening but would still insist on sitting up half the night, counting and checking the takings and bagging it all up ready for collection by Securicor first thing on Monday morning ... and with the hotel so busy, there would be far extra to deal with. Usually Pete, the assistant manager, would assist David but it was his birthday that day and he was going home to Manchester to celebrate with his family and wouldn't return until early Monday morning. So, David would be alone to check the takings. Tired and alone. Brilliant!

Katrina grinned. David, the demure, strictly correct man, had no idea what a treat he had in store for him and how, instead of spending a boring evening counting money, he was going to star in a porn film. She chortled happily to herself while she ate her lunch. Some of the other staff in the staff dining room stared at her. No-one wanted to sit with her, no-one wanted to be her friend. She was above them in station as she was related to Lucy Canleigh but even so, she wasn't very nice ... usually sarcastic and arrogant. No-one would miss her if she left.

CHAPTER 21

Saturday 1st December 2003

Filming in secret in Katrina's bedroom had gone well since the first session a few weeks ago and they were beginning to make some serious money, thanks to Maria sending Leo the names of Bill and Roger's contacts. They had considered it more prudent to use their own rooms rather than the more luxurious hotel bedrooms just in case they were caught ... and anyway, the type of people wanting to watch the videos wouldn't care too hoots ... all they were interested in was the action ... and there was certainly plenty of that. Even though Leo was now wary of Katrina, she still had the power to make him desire her body. She was so damned sexy. It oozed out of her and as she gyrated on the bed with him, he knew he would never find another woman who could turn him on like she did.

Kevin was in his element, filming two people who needed no direction and listening to Katrina panting and Leo groaning, he could easily have joined them if he didn't have to get the best shots he possibly could. He wanted, as much as they did, to make a success of their new venture and even though he had only been at Canleigh for a short time, he had already decided this was the life for him, not as a mere menial but someone with money, able to do whatever he wanted, whenever he wanted. He was fed up with having to scrape by and this idea of Leo's was a good one, could be pretty lucrative as they were going to split the profits three ways but he was already wondering what else he could gain from being in such a luxurious place, how he could turn being here into a real opportunity to get everything he desired.

"We could command a pretty penny for this one," remarked Kevin, taking the can of Carlsberg Katrina offered him from the fridge in the corner of the room at the end of the session. "You were both pretty sensational ... better than you've ever been."

Leo was pulling on his underpants and jeans. "Yeah ... I suppose it's not having to worry about Bill and Roger any longer ... this is our business ... and no-one can take it away from us."

Katrina grinned, wrapped herself in her dressing gown and lit a cigarette. She opened a window and blew the smoke outside. "And I want you to help me do something else in a fortnight's time ... have a little more fun."

"Oh?" queried Leo and Kevin simultaneously, looking at her curiously.

"I want David to join us."

"David!" Leo looked startled. God, was this her plan to scupper the man's engagement to Lucy? And how the hell did she think she was going to get him to romp around with them? David was a paragon of virtue, straight-laced, church on Sunday type. He would never, not in a million years, consider it and would more than likely give them the sack instead for having the audacity to use Canleigh for their new venture.

Katrina grinned and took a deep puff of her cigarette. "Yes ... David. Blimey, Leo, you do have an annoying habit of repeating everything I say. Now, I want you both to listen carefully. This has to go like clockwork. Nothing, I repeat nothing, must go wrong or else we will all be for the chop. Do you understand?"

* * *

David was tired. It had been a hectic few days preparing the hotel for Christmas. All the decorations were up, food, alcohol, especially champagne, ordered and some already delivered. Every room in the hotel was booked and presents for the guests from the management had arrived. Lucy always insisted that from the beginning of December until the big day, every room had a small, beautifully decorated, Christmas tree and underneath would be a gold wrapped present for each guest and if they brought a dog, a cuddly toy and a packet of doggie chocolates would be included.

Carol singers were booked to perform in the entrance hall every evening until Christmas Eve and with all the doors leading from room to room propped open, they could be heard throughout the ground floor.

As David walked through the entrance hall to his office, nodding to the two night porters sitting at the reception desk, he felt quite uplifted when he passed the massive Christmas tree in the corner. It always looked good but this year it seemed to sparkle much brighter than it usually did. He felt much the same, now he and Lucy were engaged. He loved her very much and even though he knew people would assume he was only marrying her for her wealth and status, he knew and she knew, he wasn't. He adored the very ground she walked on and would do anything for her.

He had known about Lucy's dreadful previous marriage and how she had suffered terribly at the hands of her husband and his gay partners. It had been common knowledge at the time, splattered all over the newspapers in the days following the crash that killed the men, but Lucy had also talked to him about it one evening when they had cuddled up on the sofa at Dingle Dell when Selena was tucked up in bed. He had felt so sorry for her and vowed never to let anyone hurt her again and assured her he would do everything in his power to make her happy. It had been a wonderful night, the first they had slept together and it had felt so right and now he was so looking forward to the day, just a few short months away, when they would venture up to Gretna Green for their wedding.

He stepped into his office, locked the door, checked his desk was clear, unlocked the safe and took out the hessian bags various members of departments had brought in earlier with their takings for the day. This was always his last duty, counting it and recording it all. It usually took him around an hour and then he could go to bed. He yawned. That time couldn't come soon enough.

* * *

"I can't believe you want to do this." Leo was aghast. He actually liked David. He had given him a job, had encouraged him and always took the time of day to stop and chat for a few moments to ask if Leo had any problems. To trick him, as Katrina wanted to do, seemed grossly unjust and for what?

"I'm not going to consent to this unless you give me a really good reason," he said firmly, sitting on the bed and glaring at Katrina, who had lit another cigarette. He wished she wouldn't. He had given up smoking since arriving at Canleigh and hadn't realised until now how he hated the smell. It always seemed to linger on his clothes and in his hair. He would be glad to get back to his room and have a shower.

Kevin was putting away his camera equipment but stopped and looked at her. He also liked the general manager. He seemed like a fair man and relatively easy to work for as long as his instructions were carried out properly. So, what was Katrina up to?

"I don't want him marrying Lucy," she announced belligerently. "If he marries her and she has any more children, that puts any hope of me inheriting this place right out of the window."

Leo exchanged a look of bewilderment with Kevin and then looked at her with surprise. "But … but …,"

"Look," said Katrina impatiently, stubbing out her cigarette in the ashtray by the bed and then sitting down next to Leo. "If anything happens to Lucy, Canleigh goes to my mother and then to me. However, my mother is ill and may not live long so that ostensibly rules her out so that means there is only Lucy between me and Canleigh but if she has more brats, my chances are blown. Whatever happens, she mustn't marry David …. so, if you help me do this, discredit him in her eyes, that will be one little problem solved as he will be so mortified, he will sling his hook or Lucy will help him on his way."

Kevin and Leo were staring at her with amazement. They had always known she had a bit of a wild streak but this was distinctly cunning and so cold blooded, especially the way she talked about her mother, as if she didn't care a fig about whether she lived or died.

"So, what's in it for us?" said Leo slowly, not taking his eyes from Katrina's.

She smiled wryly. "I was waiting for you to ask. Well ...,"

"Nothing, I suppose. Well, forget it then," spluttered Kevin, heading for the door.

"Wait," Katrina hissed. "How does £5,000 each sound?"

Leo whistled. "And where do you propose to get £10,000 just like that. I thought you were skint?"

"Let's just say I have the ways and the means ... and you don't need to worry your heads about it. Now, I'm planning on doing it two weeks tomorrow evening ... when David is shattered as we have such a busy weekend with the charity ball and the hotel is booked solid for the weekend."

"Why then?" asked Kevin, wishing she would get to the point. It had been a long day and he was looking forward to getting to his bed in the room along the corridor.

"Well, David counts and records all the cash every night but on that Sunday there should be an enormous sum and I happen to know that Pete, who usually helps him will be away as it's his birthday, so I am going to step in and offer to help and while I'm closeted in the office with him, I'm going to slip him some of our nice pills that Kevin has so kindly supplied," she grinned wickedly, "anyway, leave the rest of the details to me. I'll fill you in when I've sorted it all ... now are you in ... or not?"

Leo was looking at her with a horrified expression. "You're not going to steal the takings? I'm not being party to that! I've no intentions of going to prison because of your crazy scheme ... and how do you think you'll get away with it, anyway?"

"Oh, do keep calm, Leo. It's not the takings … I have another source to tap into to pay you so don't you worry about that. I have it all worked out, down to the last tiny detail and I'll divulge all the nitty gritty when the time is right but again, are you two in or not?"

* * *

David yawned, willing himself to stay awake until he had finished recording the takings. This was one task he liked to do himself so he could see exactly how things stood before he retired for the night. There was never much actual cash anyway, as most non-residents liked to pay by card at the end of the evening and residents paid their bill at the end of their stay. However, it would be an entirely different matter in a couple of weeks' time as they were hosting their annual charity night for Philip Kershaw's animal sanctuary, which was an event Lucy had devised the first year she had opened Canleigh as a hotel. It was always held in the ballroom, and included an auction, the most desired item being a four-week cruise of the Caribbean; and a raffle with prizes Lucy had purloined from all over the country, and then all the usual donations of course. The event was always successful as Lucy and her family knew a great many influential people. All in all, the evening generated thousands of pounds and there was always a great deal to be counted in the early hours of the morning. Pete always helped him on such busy weekends but would be on leave this time so he would have to ask another member of staff. Lucy had offered but it was silly for her to come out late at night on a chilly December evening and it would also mean she would have to get a babysitter. No, that was out of the question and he would manage. There were still a few days to decide on which member of staff would be willing and able to help him.

* * *

Katrina remained motionless under the scrutiny of Leo and Kevin. They were perplexed by her demand, horrified by her careless disregard of her poor mother and shocked by her wish to make David look bad in Lucy's eyes

"Well," she demanded again, "If you're not up for this, I shall have to find some other way to knock David out of Lucy's good books and believe me, I will. I've told you, I have it all planned out quite neatly and it will work, if you both do as I tell you. You don't have to worry about a thing, I promise … on the other hand, if either of you feel the need to tell anyone at any time, either before or after the deed, I promise I'll make your lives bloody difficult and you'll both join Bill and Roger in prison with regard to Summer's demise."

Kevin's mouth dropped open but Leo stood up and glared hard at Katrina. "Don't be so bloody ridiculous. Neither of us had anything to do with it and there isn't a shred of evidence we did."

Katrina gave a hollow laugh. "Oh, don't be too sure about that, Leo darling. I can certainly engineer some if I really have to."

"God! You're a devious bitch," Kevin said, horrified to discover the girl he had considered to be seriously okay, was such a treacherous, unprincipled, poisonous human being. He looked despairingly at Leo, who had slumped on the bed, with a look of complete defeat. It was no good, they would have to go along with Katrina or God knows what she would do. Kevin gulped, his feelings mixed. He had no intention of seeing the inside of a prison and certainly liked the sound of receiving a lot of cash for just making a film of David having it off with Katrina … after all, filming was what he came up here to do and did it really matter who was performing, as long as he got paid?

Leo looked sadly at Katrina, wondering how he had got her so wrong.

CHAPTER 22

Monday 3rd December 2003

Delia was fed up. She had wanted to go Christmas shopping in Edinburgh with Brian this weekend, intending to be laden with presents for Selena and Lucy on the trip down to Canleigh. She loved beautiful, old Edinburgh, steeped in history. There was always something new to learn and she adored wandering up and down the Royal Mile, visiting the castle, Holyrood Palace, St. Giles Cathedral and all the shops and alleyways in between. She had even dragged Brian onto a ghost walk one evening last year, which she had found amusing and he thought was plain ridiculous but they had enjoyed a good laugh with the other participants and went home with a few ideas for Crystal to incorporate into the ghost tours she did at Blairness, which had proved to be very popular and a good source of revenue.

They hadn't been to Edinburgh for a few months and she had really been looking forward to it, staying in their favourite five-star hotel, wandering down Prince's street, visiting the theatre, eating, drinking and having delicious sex, not that that would be any better than it was here at Glentagon. However, she had come down with a damned cold and didn't feel up to going and their trip would have to be delayed but a couple of good gallops around the estate should blow all her germs away in the next day or so.

However, she hadn't had the strength for riding today. All she had managed was to walk the dogs around a couple of fields, pay a visit to the stables to give poor Charlie a few carrots and ask Griselda, one of the gardeners who had experience of horses and cared for Charlie as part of her duties, if she could take him out for a while. Just doing that had exhausted her so here she was, tucked up on the sofa in the scarlet drawing room, books and dogs by her side and waiting impatiently for Brian to join her so they could go through the Christmas card list.

She knew where he was. In his office with that damned new highly attractive secretary, who had the audacity to flaunt herself and flutter her well-mascaraed eyelashes at him. It thoroughly annoyed Delia and she had suggested on more than one occasion since the woman's appointment a few weeks ago, that she should be dismissed but Brian had been reluctant.

"Let's give her a chance," he had urged. "You know there's not much work around these parts and she is the Vicar's daughter, so I feel we have an obligation to help ... and to be fair, she is damned good at the job."

"Um. She's probably desperate to get out from her father's scrutiny and have some fun in her life and I hope you aren't the fun," was Delia's caustic remark. "I wish Trudy hadn't decided to retire. She was much more suited to the post."

Trudy had been Brian's brother's secretary for many years, knew the estate inside out and was an enormous asset but had regretfully decided to retire in the summer. They both missed her. Brian, because she was a fantastic secretary and he had relied on her more than he had realised and Delia because she genuinely liked the older Scottish woman who was down to earth and said what she thought. This new young woman was a different kettle of fish entirely. Twenty-six years old, recently divorced from her Glaswegian husband, which was the excuse for returning to her roots, and obviously desperate for a man but if she thought she was going to try her luck with Brian, Delia would have no hesitation in sending her flying out of Glentagon no matter what he said.

She sniffed and blew her nose, feeling sorry for herself. She ached all over, even though she had taken paracetamol and wondered if it might be a good idea to return to bed but she felt wobbly and faint and didn't know if she could make it without Brian to help her. Where the bloody hell was he? He had promised to join her over an hour ago. She played with her mobile, her finger hovering over his number but she didn't want to sound like a bothersome wife. She put it down again, closed her eyes and lay listening to the crackling of the fire.

* * *

Brian was sitting on one side of the great oak desk in his office, with Melanie the other, shorthand pad on her knee and a pencil in her hand. They had dealt with all the day to day correspondence but he still sat there, mulling over a knotty problem he was having with the wife of one of the tenant farmers who was way behind on the rent. He knew why, of course. Nothing was much of a secret in these parts. Everybody on the estate knew everybody's business. Suffering from depression, McGregor had walked out on Nancy and her elderly mother who had moved in with them when she had suffered a stroke and although Nancy was working long hours on the farm, she didn't seem to be able to cope and was having real difficulty paying her bills.

He had been advised by his accountant that he couldn't allow the situation to continue and should really give her notice but he hadn't the heart. Being around the same age, he had known Nancy and her husband since they were all young and had even attended their wedding. The pair had worked the farm ever since their marriage and up until McGregor had walked out, had made a real good job of it.

He sat brooding about dictating the letter that would be the death knell for Nancy. Melanie waited patiently, gently tapping her pencil on the side of her notepad, her long red talons making it hard for her to hold it. How she managed to write with those, he had no idea, and they looked ridiculous. Long painted nails had never attracted him. He shuddered, imagining them raking down his back. Ugh. He much preferred Delia's undecorated hands, the only thing slapped on them being a big dollop of hand cream at bedtime. Delia, oh bloody hell. He looked at the clock. He had promised to join her about an hour ago and she wasn't feeling well. He stood up abruptly.

"That's it for now, Melanie, thank you."

"Didn't you want to write to Nancy?"

"Yes, but I want to think about it a bit longer. I'll leave it until tomorrow. If you type up what I've dictated now, I'll pop back later and sign everything."

He left the office, uncomfortably aware of Melanie watching his every move. She was beginning to make him feel a little uneasy and he wondered if Delia was right and he should dispense with her services. He knew how insecure his wife could be and he never wanted her to feel threatened in any way … there was also a nagging feeling that it wouldn't take very much to wake the sleeping giant in her … and that was the last thing he wanted to do.

* * *

"Where have you been?" asked Delia petulantly, sniffing into another tissue, knowing she looked a sorry picture.

"Sorry, darling. I was wondering what to do about Nancy. I really don't want to give her notice. She's been on that farm for years and has her disabled mother to look after. I really am at a loss to know what to do about it."

"It's easy."

"Oh?"

"Yes. Just let her live there for a peppercorn rent. Let's face it, Brian. You don't need the money … we're hardly poor … oh, I know it's not good business sense but this is your estate and you look after people on it. Bugger what accountants and solicitors urge you to do. Use your heart."

"I agree but if we do it for one family, we would have to do it for others and then where would we be?"

"Swear Nancy to secrecy then. No-one need ever know about it apart from her and us ... the accountants ... oh, and Melanie I suppose as she will have to type up the agreement ... although that might not be a good idea. She might just tell someone in the village."

"Well, I'll type it up myself then and she won't see it ... and I'll take it over to Nancy and discuss it with her on the farm rather than asking her to pop into the office."

Delia smiled. He obviously didn't trust his new secretary that much then. Maybe her days were numbered after all ... and she wouldn't be too unhappy about that decision.

Brian sat down beside her and took her hand. "How are you feeling now?"

"Pretty rotten," she grimaced. "I think I need to be in bed really ... I need to knock this on the head ... we still have to get to Edinburgh for the Christmas shopping and I don't want to go down to Canleigh feeling like death and spreading my germs."

"Canleigh," Brian murmured, staring at the flames leaping up the chimney. "It will be lovely spending more time with Lucy and Selena ... and getting to know her David a little better. We haven't had much to do with him yet."

"Well he's always been so busy at the Hall when we've been down. He seems a decent enough chap though, works damned hard and is a worthy partner for Lucy. I'm so pleased they are together. He's made her bubble again and the depression she has suffered should become a thing of the past now. I must say I'm really looking forward to the wedding too. It will be fabulous to actually play mother of the bride this time. I never told her but I was so disappointed not to be able to go when she married Jeremy at Canleigh and I was banned from going anywhere near."

Brian wrapped his arms around, uncaring whether he caught her cold. He loved her more than he could ever say and was so pleased that she had Christmas and the wedding to look forward to and her rotten past was well behind her.

CHAPTER 23

Monday 3rd December 2003

Alex parked the car as near to the rear door of The Beeches as he could so Vicky could avoid walking through the front and into reception. She wasn't up to facing anyone other than family yet, however well-meaning they were, and wanted the privacy of their own flat as quickly as possible.

He took her arm as soon as she stepped out of the car, terrified she might buckle over, and she clung on to him for support in the lift, both relieved when they reached the flat and she could sit down on the sofa in the lounge.

She looked out of the window and smiled at the sight of the gardens stretched out in front of them. The trees might be leafless and the shrubbery devoid of flowers but it was so good to see it, to be back here, alive and with a future to look forward to. She had been so convinced she was going to die, so terrified, so frightened but the surgeons had done a terrific job and as far as they were concerned, she had many more years to look forward to … to be with her wonderful husband … her children. Her children! Katrina!

Her tummy lurched sickeningly as Alex excused himself to pop down to the office to collect some files so he could work up here with her.

"Put your feet up, darling. I'll only be a minute and then I'm going to wait on you; hand, foot and finger. I'll put the kettle on and we'll have a nice cup of tea and I've had some scones sent up too." Alex smiled tenderly, so pleased she was home where she belonged. He had missed her dreadfully. The flat had seemed so quiet, so empty and he had felt so alone but thank God she was back now; alive, talking and breathing. He wasn't going to lose her yet.

Alone with her thoughts, Vicky laid back on the large, soft cushions and thought about Katrina. Katrina who hadn't set foot in the hospital the whole time she had been there, who hadn't rung, sent a card, sent flowers ... or visited. How could her daughter be so cruel? Whatever had she done to deserve such coldness from the only child she had ever born?

Suzanne had been at the hospital every day, bringing flowers and chocolates, bringing Daniel with his little gifts of fruit and posies. She had chatted happily, about the salon, about the guests, about Daniel's successes at school, doing her best to keep Vicky's mind off the fact that Katrina hadn't turned up. Bless her. What a lovely girl Suzanne was. Vicky was so glad she hadn't remained in Australia when her marriage broke down. It was so good to have her and Daniel here.

For some reason she burst into tears, annoyed with herself for being so pathetic. She really had nothing to cry about now ... apart from Katrina ... and she did feel hurt, really hurt, by her lack of consideration and when they did eventually meet up, she was going to tell her so.

* * *

Alex was thinking the same thing as he beetled down to his office, reluctant to leave Vicky for longer than necessary. She was so vulnerable at the moment and needed her family around her now. When he caught up with Katrina, he was going to give her a right telling off in no mistake and if she thought she was going to change their minds about the inheritance with her current behaviour, she really must have a screw loose. Blast the girl.

He saw Suzanne, just making her way out of the salon to take her morning coffee break. She waved and came straight over. "How is she?"

"Okay. I've put her on the sofa upstairs for now. I'm going to take some work up so I can stay with her."

"Should I pop up, do you think? Say hello … or will it be too much? I can always come up later."

"No, you go. Have your break with her. She will love it and it will give me a chance to have a word with a couple of the staff while I'm down here and clear one or two things up."

He watched her slim figure hurrying up the stairs. She never took the lift, using the stairs as an extra exercise to keep her body in trim. What a lovely girl she was, in nature and in looks. Whatever Katrina did or didn't do, at least they had Suzanne.

* * *

Vicky was looking at the holiday brochures Alex had left out on the coffee table when Suzanne knocked and pushed her head around the door.

"Hi. How are you doing?" she asked sunnily, pleased as punch to see her mother home, even though she did look exhausted and ready for her bed.

Vicky smiled and put down the brochure she was reading. "Darling … do come in. It's so nice to see you … and to be here. The hospital staff were lovely, of course, but there really is no place like home."

Suzanne settled on the white leather pouffe beside Vicky, not wanting to sit on the sofa in case she jarred Vicky's wound. She took Vicky's hand. "I can't tell you how good it is to see you here too. We've all missed you so much … not just the family but the staff. They all ask about you every day."

"I know, bless them. They sent me a huge bouquet while I was in hospital and just look at all those … I think there's one from just about every member of staff," Vicky smiled, waving her hand at the sideboard and mantelpiece, on which stood a vast array of get-well cards.

"So, what's this?" asked Suzanne, staring at the brochure on Vicky's lap. "Is this where you're going with Granny Ruth and Grandpa Philip? I must say ... it does look lovely."

Vicky nodded, hoping she would be up to it. She hadn't long to regain her strength for the journey. They were leaving on Thursday.

"We're taking it really easy because I shan't be able to fly. We're taking the train down to the south coast, where we're going to stay for a couple of nights and then we're taking the boat over to France and then catching another train down to Spain. It will be much easier than driving as we can move about, especially Philip, as he can't sit in one position for long. Hopefully, the journey won't exhaust me too much and once we get there there's nothing to do but sleep, eat and relax. It shouldn't be too hot either. Warm but not hot. Just perfect. I'm so sorry, Suzanne, that we won't be here for you and Daniel ... on your first Christmas back in the UK," she added. "And I do hope Delia behaves herself while she is down with Lucy ... although as you have nothing she wants, you should be perfectly safe and have nothing to fear. Thank God I shan't have to worry about bumping into her. I really don't want to set eyes on my sister ever again," she shuddered.

Suzanne looked at Vicky curiously. She had always known what a dreadful person Lady Delia was and naturally knew all about her being in prison for so many years and why but Lucy had let her back into her life and they seemed to get on extremely well, and as Vicky was such a kind and loving person, it was strange she hadn't done the same. Anyway, she would meet the woman for herself on Christmas Day as she and Daniel had accepted Lucy's invitation to lunch, although she wasn't sure whether or not she was looking forward to it. What with having to meet Lady Delia and her husband, the Earl of Glentagon, and then Katrina being there too ... and she and most of the family were feeling pretty angry with the girl right now, that didn't bode well. She sighed. Why the hell did life have to be so damned complicated?

* * *

While Suzanne was upstairs with Vicky, Alex took the opportunity to try and contact Katrina once more. Yet again she refused to answer her phone and in desperation he rang Canleigh, asking to speak to David. He was put through straight away.

"David, I've been trying to get hold of Katrina for days. Is she working, do you know, or has she disappeared off the face of the earth?"

David glanced at the rota on the wall in front of him, "She's in the spa all day. Do you want me to ask her to call you? Perhaps her phone is playing up."

"So it might be, but there are other phones she could use to find out how her mother is doing," Alex snapped, frustrated to know there had been nothing to prevent Katrina contacting them. "Sorry, David. I don't mean to take it out on you but I'm so cross with her. Vicky has just come home from hospital and she hasn't had a word from Katrina since she went in. It really isn't good enough."

"No. I agree. That's appalling," said David. "But she's been working very hard over the last few days, which has been good to see after her somewhat shaky start. She suddenly seems to have decided to buckle down."

He had to admit he had been impressed by Katrina's unexpected desire to do well. She was moving around far more quickly now, eager to please the guests, always wearing a sunny smile and nothing seeming too much trouble. He hadn't pondered on why there was this miraculous change but it was certainly very welcome and certainly made life a lot easier. She had even brought him a cup of coffee yesterday, announced she was doing nothing after her shift had ended and was there anything she could do to help him in the office? He never would have believed it of her a few days ago.

"Well, that's something, I suppose," remarked Alex begrudgingly, "but if you could mention that I had rung her, just in case her phone isn't working properly, I would be grateful. Tell her that her mother has returned home and would dearly like to see her."

"Yes, of course. I'll go right down to the spa and inform her now," David offered.

"Thanks," Alex finished, switching off his phone. His anger with his daughter hadn't abated but he was genuinely pleased to hear she was beginning to settle into her role at Canleigh. If that stupid idea of hers to get to Hollywood could be knocked on the head, at least until she was older and less likely to be swayed by unsuitable people, it wouldn't be a bad thing.

* * *

David made his way down to the spa, nodding and smiling at the guests he passed on the way, his eyes darting here and here, checking as he always did that all was as it should be; the staff were working to full capacity, there wasn't a cushion out of place, no dirty crockery or cutlery left on any of the side tables, newspapers folded neatly, a stain on the carpet had been removed. It was all in the fine detail. Everything had to look perfect at all times. The guests were paying well for the privilege of staying in such opulent surroundings. They expected the best and he was determined they would receive it.

Through the glass doors leading to the pool, he could see Katrina talking to a young female guest, pointing out the jacuzzi, steam room and sauna. He waited until she had finished and then opened the door and called to her. He couldn't go in unless he took his shoes off and donned pool slippers and as he considered it was undignified to wear them with a suit, he stayed where he was until Katrina joined him.

She smiled and he smiled back, gratified to see she was still on the right wave length. He still didn't entirely trust her not to revert to her old ways.

"Katrina ... I've just had a call from your father. He's been trying to get hold of you for days apparently ... about your mother ... she's home now and he would dearly like you to go and see her."

A cloud crossed Katrina's eyes for a split second but David didn't notice as he was removing a bit of fluff from his jacket.

"Oh, okay. Thank you, David. My phone has been playing up, I think I need a new one. I'll ring them as soon as my shift has finished," she said meekly. "I'm so pleased Mother is home. She must be very relieved."

"Yes, I'm sure she is," David replied, noticing a pile of used towels spilling out of a bin by the pool. "Please remove those towels, Katrina. They look dreadful."

"Yes, David. I'm so sorry. I didn't notice them," she said as he nodded, closed the poolside door and headed back to the main building.

"Whatever you say, David, whatever you say," she muttered as she turned to deal with the towels. "But the boot will be on the other foot very soon, believe me and I can't wait to see you squirm, panting and desperate to get laid. Oh yes, David, darling. You're about to have more fun than you've ever had in your life and then we'll see who is cracking the whip ... quite literally," she giggled.

CHAPTER 24

Thursday 6th December 2003

They were finally in a first-class carriage on the train heading south out of Leeds, all four of them; Philip, Ruth, Alex and Vicky.

Vicky sat holding hands with Alex, looking more her old self than she had for a while, watching the Yorkshire landscape through the window, looking forward to the next few weeks away with some of the people she loved most in the world. She still hadn't seen or spoken to Katrina but Alex, had insisted she forget about their errant daughter for a while and not let her spoil this precious time they were going to have together. Vicky smiled up at him now, her wonderful, wonderful rock.

None of them spoke for the first part of the journey, all immersed in their own thoughts. Ruth was just pleased to get away and wanted the trip to benefit Philip and Vicky. Philip was running over and over in his mind all the instructions he had left for Jim, his assistant manager and the remainder of his staff. They were all highly skilled and competent and he could trust them implicitly to look after the animals properly but even so, he knew he would ring them every day to make sure nothing was amiss.

Alex closed his eyes and tried to unwind. Recent weeks had been so stressful with Vicky's operation and Katrina's lack of consideration for her mother, then there had been the induction of the temporary general manager to care for The Beeches. The man was well experienced and more than capable of making sure the hotel ran smoothly over the most important holiday period of the year but like Philip, Alex would always have a niggling feeling that something might go wrong and he should have been there to supervise. He didn't think he would ever truly relax away from their business and perhaps it was time to start thinking of early retirement. Spend more time with Vicky. Her cancer had been such an awful scare and every day they were together was even more precious now. If they retired, sold the hotel, and bought a villa in Italy, as Vicky often said she would like to do, they could have a lovely life and all the stresses of building up such an empire as they had over the years, with not only The Beeches, but also all their clubs, could be put aside and they could really reap the rewards of all their hard work. He sighed and smiled at Vicky beside him, who was watching the scenery flash by. He would discuss it with her properly while they were in Spain. He was convinced she would agree.

* * *

Lucy told Katrina that her parents had departed earlier that morning for their trip to Spain. She had driven over to the Hall to speak to David and bumped into Katrina, who was just leaving the office.

"I do wish you had said goodbye, at least," Lucy said, not wanting to be too forceful and make Katrina mad, after all it was just over two weeks to Christmas and she didn't want a falling out before the big day.

"Oh, they will have such a fabulous time, they'll forget all about me," sang Katrina gaily, flashing Lucy a wide grin, thinking how upset Lucy was going to be next week when she discovered just what her precious David had been up to. "David is in his office, if it's him you're looking for."

Katrina headed towards the door for the spa and Lucy watched her go with sadness. She knew how upset Aunt Vicky and Uncle Alex were about Katrina's refusal to see them and if she could work on Katrina over Christmas and make her realise how selfish she was being, hopefully the situation could be rectified when they came home.

"Hello, Lucy," said David, emerging from the office, fiddling with one of his cufflinks. "Can you do this for me, please. It came loose and now I'm having trouble doing it up."

She did as she was asked, looking up into his eyes with love. He was such a lovely man, so steady, so loyal, so in love with her. He would never treat her as Jeremy had. She looked up at the stairs in the middle of the entrance hall, remembering that horrendous night when she had discovered Jeremy with Felix, their butler, in the throes of a sex act in his bedroom. How she had flown away from them, down the corridor, heading for the stairs, while she was heavily pregnant. She remembered the ghastly sensation of flying through the air when she tripped over her flowing negligee at the top. She shuddered and David noticed. He put a hand on her arm. "Are you okay?"

She gave a relieved smile. It was a long time ago. Jeremy and Felix were dead and could do her no more harm ... and now she had David. Wonderful, trustworthy, kindly, generous, loving David. She really had won the lottery this time.

* * *

Suzanne had been very sorry to say goodbye to Vicky and Alex before she started her shift in the salon. She hadn't let it show, of course, knowing how much they needed this break, especially Vicky.

Even so, she was a sad that the first Christmas she and Daniel were home, they couldn't spend it all together. However, she had done her best to make their little cottage as festive as possible. They had visited the local garden centre yesterday afternoon and bought a real tree, nearly six-foot-high, and lots of pretty baubles and beads to dress it with, along with ceiling decorations and lots of tinsel to drape around the mantelpiece and all the pictures on the walls. Daniel's face had been wreathed in smiles as he chose what to buy and he hadn't been able to get home fast enough to make the tree look wonderful and decorate the lounge and his bedroom.

Once he was in bed and positive he was asleep, she had taken out all the presents she had bought him during the previous couple of weeks, which had been under lock and key in her wardrobe in case he decided to investigate. She wrapped them up in glittering Christmas paper, remembering how miserable and angry she had been last year when Todd had promised to help her but had gone out with friends instead and hadn't returned all night. She had cried, knowing he was probably with another woman and because the atmosphere between them was so bad, it had ruined Christmas for her. Things would be different this year and in future years now he wasn't in their lives any longer. She hadn't heard from him, even though she had sent him text messages to give him their address but he hadn't bothered to reply. What a complete and utter rotter he was. She and Daniel really were better off without him.

She smiled. Thanks to Vicky and Alex she could bring Daniel up in a warm and loving environment, earn a decent living and have the lovely little cottage to live in. Her husband need never enter their lives again. She felt sad for Daniel, not having his father in his life but then Todd wasn't exactly the role model she wanted for her child. Daniel was much better off here, with Alex and Philip to look up to, and David, Lucy's fiancé. He was in the same mould; kind, solid and thoroughly dependable. Lucy was a lucky girl to have found him.

* * *

Delia was feeling a lot better. The cold had virtually disappeared overnight and she was now well enough to ride and blow the last remnants away.

She mounted Charlie and called the dogs. She intended to gallop up the hills this morning, circle the estate and then return home. It would take around three hours but she had nothing else to do and Brian was busy with the accountants who were preparing the yearly tax return for Glentagon.

However, the remainder of December was going to be pretty busy. They had the Christmas staff dinner at Glentagon on Saturday evening. It was usually a quiet affair as most of the staff, with the exception of darling Melanie, were nearing retirement and weren't interested in dancing the night away so Delia hired caterers and put on a lavish dinner in the dining room, followed by drinks in the sapphire drawing room, when she and Brian would hand out presents. It was always a lovely occasion which they both looked forward to and this year was no exception, although Delia sincerely hoped Melanie wouldn't spend the evening eyeing up Brian.

Then, after a rest on Sunday, they were travelling down to Blairness on Monday to stay for a few days before continuing on their journey to Canleigh. She was so excited. Returning to her very own castle, especially at Christmas, was such a joy and such fun. As there were far more staff as the castle was open to the public, and they were much younger than those at Glentagon, Crystal always insisted on a spectacular Christmas party in the entrance hall, which reminded Delia so much of her wedding day when the room had been decorated just the same. The evening always started off with a banquet, followed by Brian and Delia handing out presents and then the table would be cleared and moved to the side of the room and the ceilidh would commence, never finishing until the early hours of the morning.

Delia loved re-acquainting herself with everyone and hearing all the news; who was having a romance, who was engaged, who had started a family, etc., etc., as well as discussing the business. Crystal, Connie and Gerald Ponsonby, Brian's replacement as estate manager, were all running Blairness like clockwork. Every summer since Delia and Brian had moved to Glentagon, had been frantically busy with the house open to the public every day of the week now Delia wasn't in situ, the caravan park was always full, as were the cottages they rented out to locals and the golf course was well used.

The only thing on Delia's agenda which hadn't been achieved, was organising an annual equestrian three-day event but there was no reason why it couldn't be done and she was going to talk to Brian about it while they were away. It had been put on the backburner for too long and she wanted to do it. It would mean a lot of work and she would have to spend more time at Blairness but that wouldn't be a problem as Brian could come with her most of the time. They could have held it at Glentagon but it was their tranquil, family home and somehow it would have seemed wrong to have hordes of people, horses and dogs all over the place, even if it was only once a year. No, Glentagon was private to them and that was the way it was going to stay. Blairness was the working castle and thanks to all the effort that they and the staff had put in over the last few years, it had proved to be highly lucrative, provided much needed employment and given brilliant holidays to tourists.

As she cantered out of the stable yard and headed up the hill in front of her, Delia grinned to herself. She was so bloody happy, she could burst. Her heart was singing with joy. She was back on Charlie again, the dogs were running by her side, she had a great ride to look forward to and a loving husband to come home to, she was going to see her beloved Blairness in a few days ... and then her lovely daughter and granddaughter ... and Canleigh. Bloody hell, life was so bloody good!

CHAPTER 25

Friday 7th December 2003

At 1.00 a.m. in the morning, Katrina made a trip into Leeds. No-one knew she had gone out, no-one knew where she was going. She had crept down the back stairs from the top floor of Canleigh to the basement and let herself out of the kitchen door with the key everyone knew was kept in an old biscuit tin on a shelf beside it. It was old and rusty but luckily, still worked.

Earlier that day she had parked her car in the back lane, just down from the stable block, so that when she started it up no-one from the Hall would hear and wonder who was going out at this time of night.

Not used to wandering around the estate in the dark on her own, she didn't feel very happy. There was a stiff breeze which made things rustle and move, making her jump as she scanned her surroundings nervously, waiting for rampant men to jump out at her from behind trees.

"Get a grip, for God's sake," she murmured to herself, waving her torch around, almost crying with relief when she saw her car just a few feet away. If anyone asked why she had parked it down there, she was going to say it had suddenly cut out on her and she had to leave it there but so far no-one had said anything.

She shot into the driver's seat and locked the door, letting out a huge sigh of relief. Her hands were shaking and it wasn't from the cold as for December, it was a fairly mild night. Even so, she started the car, desperate to turn the heating up as high as it would go. She nearly jumped out of her skin when a raunchy song by the Rolling Stones blared out loudly.

"Shit," she hissed, banging the radio knob quickly, pushing the gear stick into first gear and letting off the handbrake.

It took her half an hour to get to the other side of Leeds, the seedier side, the side where girls walked the streets, night after night, most of them desperate to make enough to buy drugs to get them through the next day. Then it would all be repeated tomorrow night. Poor sods. Apart from the pills Roger and Bill had plied her with, she had never touched drugs in any shape or form. Thankfully, they didn't appear to be addictive but then she didn't need them anymore anyway. It didn't take much to get her going in the sex department and now she had Leo on tap, she was well satisfied.

She headed into Talbot Lane. She had never been here before but knew of its reputation as *the* place to find a prostitute easily. The street lights were not very bright but she could make out one girl standing in a doorway of a tatty looking newsagents, another on the corner of a side street, two lolling against a wall. They were all smoking, and dressed in short, tight skirts and high heels.

Katrina stopped the car and stared at them, wondering which one would be best to approach and what kind of reception she would receive. They would probably be extremely suspicious of her, a lone woman, wanting their services. They would probably think she was a lesbian and nothing could be further from the truth. She gripped the steering wheel tightly as she observed them. The girl standing outside the newsagents looked a vicious piece of work and the one on the corner looked way out of it and probably wouldn't understand what the hell she wanted anyway. She stared at the two who had stubbed out their cigarettes on the ground and were lighting two more while their eyes cast around for possible punters. Two cars cruised down the street, one stopping by the first girl and the other by blondie at the side street. Katrina watched, fascinated, as the girls spoke to the men through the car windows and then got in. The cars headed off down the road and disappeared around a corner, leaving the final two girls alone.

Katrina was deep in thought. They were young, these two, both probably not long out of school, which meant they might be reasonably pliable, although that wasn't to be relied upon as if they had been born and brought up around here, they could be as hard as nails. Still, she had to take a chance.

They had noticed her staring across at them and were watching her under their eyelashes, wondering what she was doing there. She obviously wasn't a tart and didn't look like the old bill neither.

Katrina decided to bite the bullet. She drove across the road and stopped right beside them, winding down her window.

"Whadda you want?" mouthed the dark haired one. "We're not into girls ... although if you have enough cash on you ... we could force ourselves," she said, throwing back her head and laughing loudly.

"No. That's not what I'm after," said Katrina, shuddering at the thought of having a sexual encounter with these two as neither looked very clean. No wonder the two punters had ignored them and headed for the other two girls. However, that wasn't a problem for her. The seedier the recruits she managed to get hold of, the better as far as she was concerned.

"So, whadda you want then ... you're not an effin social worker are you, or a do-gooder? If so, we don't need you and we're both old enough to do what we want ... so bugger off ... you're bad for trade," hissed the one with her fair hair in a ponytail. Katrina could see her reasonably well in the pool of light from the street lamp above their heads. Her makeup was thick and black around her eyes and her lipstick was a glaring shade of scarlet. She couldn't have been more than sixteen and looked a right tart, which she was, of course. Katrina could almost feel sorry for her. What kind of life was this and how long would it be before she caught some kind of nasty STD, became hooked on heroin, was beaten up or even murdered? What a depressing, dreadful life.

"I've a proposition for you," Katrina said quickly, not wanting to antagonise them further. "There's a good wad of cash in it for you if you're interested."

"Doin' what?" demanded the older, dark haired one, blowing smoke rings in the air.

"Giving a gentleman a good time on Sunday night … it's a birthday present for him."

"Could be," they said in unison.

"Good. I'll have someone pick you up … around midnight … to take you to a private house and entertain this gentleman for a couple of hours … you'll be filmed … but it will never be released to the general public … it's for private use only … and you'll be paid really well for doing it."

The girls looked at each other. "Is that all? No kinky stuff?" asked the fair haired one.

"No. I promise you. Just straight sex. My friend … he's wanted to have it off with a couple of women for a long time but he's shy and doesn't have the nerve to arrange it so I thought I would do it for him … and it's to be filmed so he can keep it and look at it as it's doubtful he would have the courage to do it again."

"Umm. So how much?" demanded the dark haired one.

"A thousand each … and that means keeping your traps shut about me in the future … just in case any questions are asked … not that they should be," she added. She didn't think for one moment that David would ever try to get to the bottom of how he had ended up in bed with these two and Lucy would be so appalled, she wouldn't want to mention it to anyone.

"A thousand," breathed the dark haired one, her eyes shining with anticipation. That would be more than enough to pay off Micky Brent, the loan shark, and still have some left over. She had borrowed two hundred quid from him last month to help pay her rent and he was breathing down her neck for it and would be giving her a good pasting if she didn't make enough this week to pay him back. This woman was offering her a lifeline.

"Done," she said, nodding at her friend, who was also thinking what she could do with a thousand and how she needn't come out on the streets for a while. "So, what do we have to do exactly?"

"As I said, just be here around midnight on Sunday evening and you'll be taken to meet this gentleman. He's very nice … just needs to be shown a good time and I'm sure you two will fit the bill very nicely. Here," Katrina said rummaging in her bag. "Here's a deposit to keep you going … you'll get the rest once the job is done. Now, do we have a deal?"

"Oh yes," breathed the dark haired one, grabbing the cash from Katrina's outstretched hand. She had given them two hundred quid. She could give her hundred to Micky immediately and that would get him off her back for the rest of the week. She grinned at Katrina. "Thanks … we'll be here."

"Good. Just write down your first names and phone numbers on here so I know how to contact you," Katrina ordered, passing out a pad and a pen.

They couldn't give her the information fast enough, handing the pad and pen back to her, having scrawled their details in barely legible writing. She nodded goodbye, wound up her window, started the car and moved off, glancing at them in her rear-view mirror. They shoved the money into their bras and then walked quickly the other way. No doubt they were going home to celebrate their luck. She was going to do the same.

CHAPTER 26

Friday 7th December 2003

Following her trip into Leeds, dumping her car back down the lane near the stables, running as fast as she could back to the Hall and creeping up to her room via the backstairs, pumped so much adrenaline around her body, Katrina was unable to sleep. Her mind was overly active, plotting and planning and hoping she had made the right decision with those girls. Using them was taking an enormous risk, anything could go wrong, especially if they realised exactly where they were being taken. It could go to their heads and they might decide to show off and blab to all in sundry. But she couldn't do the deed with David herself. The family would all find out and Lucy would never forgive her, ending all hope of ever getting her hands on Canleigh or her inheritance in the future.

So, no, she had to use them and they would all have to go somewhere the girls wouldn't associate with Canleigh. She thought and thought, wondering whether it would be an idea to hire a hotel room but that would be too public, getting them all in and out. No, it had to be somewhere quiet and out of sight of anyone. She considered the properties on the estate but all bar one was occupied at the moment. The Dower House. It would be perfect. The girls could be brought in via the back lanes so probably wouldn't have a clue where they were, especially in the dark and no-one would query what was going on as the house was so isolated. Also, Lucy had spent a lot of time and money furnishing it beautifully for the guests who used it as a holiday cottage, and as soon as she saw the video of her beloved cavorting with two prostitutes, would know instantly where it had been shot. Perfect.

Katrina hugged herself with glee. The first step of her grand plan was going to work like clockwork. The next, ridding herself of Leo and Kevin was the next and would be slightly more complicated. She knew what she really wanted now and it didn't include them and making porn films for the rest of her life. She could have a damned good lifestyle here if she played her cards right but she would have to get rid of them pretty soon as the longer they hung around Canleigh, the more likelihood there was that they might blab too. So, she had to pay them off and send them on their way and hopefully, never set eyes on either of them again.

However, money was the problem. Although they thought she was going to steal the takings to pay them, she wasn't. She had a better idea what to do with that and discredit David even further, really putting a nail in his coffin, so she would have to find the cash for them from elsewhere and what she had in her bank account certainly wouldn't do.

There was only one other possibility. She knew the on-line passwords to get into both the personal and business accounts of her parents. She had known them since the day she had been sitting beside her mother when she was paying the fees for Radley out of the personal account. The silly woman had actually said the username and password out loud and they had fallen about laughing when she revealed the password was rectum.

"Well, it had to be something I would never forget," Vicky had laughed, "you know what I'm like, head like a sieve for passwords, and I didn't want to write it down anywhere."

"Don't tell me you use the same for your business account," Katrina had joked.

Vicky had nodded. "Yes, but don't for goodness sake tell anyone. They would be horrified."

So it was easy. Katrina switched on her laptop, searched for Barclays bank and typed in the security details. Bingo. She was in and hell, her parents were rich. She had always known they were wealthy but this was a revelation indeed. There was a couple of million in the business account and over twenty-three in their personal account. Shit! Then she thought about all their personal effects; the cars, her mother's jewellery, the life insurance ... and The Beeches must be worth a small fortune ... God, it went on and on. She couldn't understand them. Why on earth did they still work with what they had amassed? They must be mad. They could go anywhere, do anything.

Without further ado she transferred twelve thousand pounds from their personal account to hers to pay the girls, Leo and Kevin. Her parents probably wouldn't discover it had gone for weeks. Of course, she could transfer much more, millions in fact, and do a complete bunk. Run away with it, disappear abroad, live the high life. They would never prosecute her; her father might want to but her mother wouldn't let him.

She considered the idea. She could do it now and go tomorrow. Catch a plane somehow hot and inviting, live a luxurious life. It was tremendously appealing but if she did, she could never come home. They would never forgive her, none of them and although she didn't care too much about that, she did care about her home, about Canleigh. She had always loved the place, always been fascinated with it even though it was now a hotel. If she had her way and it was hers, she would turn it back into a private home. Her private home. Not a bloody hotel for all these damned annoying guests. But she couldn't do that unless something happened to her mother and Lucy … and just how could that be engineered without it looking as if she had something to do with it?

She glanced at a photo on her dressing table. It was of Lady Delia, her wicked, evil aunt. What would she have done?

* * *

At 9.00 a.m., David was busy checking all was as it should be on his rounds of the hotel, finally popping into the spa, pleased to notice Katrina smiling nicely at two guests who had never stayed with them before as she told them exactly what was on offer. She saw him and gave a slight wave. He nodded back, pleased to see she hadn't reverted to her former sloppiness and disinterest.

He finished his rounds, had a word with Veronica on reception to see exactly who they were expecting today and who was leaving and at what time. He liked to be on hand for arrivals and departures so he could personally greet and say goodbye to all their guests. It was important that they received his attention.

He headed into his office, closed the door and sat down at his desk, overlooking the main drive. It was a reasonable day for December. No real bad weather yet but it was coming. The forecast had said so. Heavy snow and ice, which meant the gardeners would have to be informed to put plenty of salt on the main steps at the front entrance. They didn't want any accidents.

He called his secretary in for a half an hour of dictation and then made a few calls before Veronica alerted him that the guests who were leaving had made their way into the entrance hall and were at the reception desk paying their bills.

There were three couples and two ladies this morning and as all of them arrived downstairs about the same time, it didn't take him long to make sure they had enjoyed their stay, wish them all a good journey home and offer a hope that they would return one day.

As the last couple made their way out of the front door, he turned to see Katrina standing behind him.

"David," she said firmly. "Please could I have a word with you."

"Of course," he nodded, putting out a hand to indicate she could go through to his office. He followed her and closed the door.

"Take a seat," he said, moving round to his chair. "What can I do for you?"

"I've been thinking … yes, I know I don't do enough of it, my parents are always telling me so," she forced a sunny smile, "but I really have … about my future."

"Oh?"

"Yes. I really don't think I'm cut out for Hollywood after all. It's a stupid, childish dream and I think I'm finally beginning to grow up … it's since I've been working here."

"Well, might I suggest that if you are 'growing up', you say a good word to your poor mother. She really has been through the mill during the last few weeks and has been terribly upset by your lack of consideration." He said it before he could stop himself.

Katrina hung her head, pretending shame. "Yes, I know. I have been terribly selfish and self-centered … and I will. Today. I'll ring her when my shift is finished." She wouldn't, of course but he wasn't to know that.

"Good. I'm glad to hear it … but you didn't come in here to talk about your parents so what is it, Katrina? I really am very busy today and haven't much time."

She raised her head and looked him straight in the eye. She had to gain his trust as she needed to work more closely with him over the next few days so he would agree to her helping him count the cash on Sunday evening. Then she would have the opportunity to drug him and get him over to the Dower House … and this was the only way she could think of doing it, although she was going to lie through her back teeth.

"Okay. I've decided I want to learn the hotel trade … properly and here … not at The Beeches, before you suggest it. I really don't think I could work with my parents but I do want them to be proud of me and I love Canleigh, always have." At least that part of it was genuine. "So, I was wondering," she continued, "would you consider allowing me to work with you … as a trainee manager … please."

David looked at her, astonishment written all over his face. "Really? Are you sure about this, Katrina? It's a complete turnaround if you're serious. It was only a few weeks ago you were complaining bitterly about waitressing and refusing to do any housekeeping duties."

"Yes. I know but as I said, I have been doing a lot of thinking and I really want to get to grips with something, something worthwhile. I want to have a proper career and I would dearly like it to be here, learning from you."

"Well. I am quite, quite flabbergasted," David said. The last thing he had expected to deal with today was this request from Katrina. He sat and stared at her, thinking hard. She looked serious enough and he had been impressed with her over the past few days. If this was really what she wanted and she was prepared to work really hard, he was more than willing to help her and he knew Lucy … and Vicky and Alex would be enormously pleased.

"Okay," he said, with a smile. "But on a trial basis at first … say a month. See how it goes but I warn you, Katrina. You will have to work exceedingly hard. No messing about. No moaning and groaning if I ask you to do something you don't like and strictly no flirting with the male guests."

"You have my word," she replied, smiling widely. "Thank you so much, David. I am really very grateful … when can I start."

"Tomorrow. I want to see you in here at eight o'clock in the morning, dressed in a navy suit and a white blouse. I want you to be alert and willing to do anything I ask of you. Is that clear?"

"Yes … and thank you again," she said, standing up with a big grin on her face. "I really do appreciate this."

"Let's see if you're so happy at the end of the probation period," he smiled, picking up the telephone as she left his office. He was going to ring Lucy and tell her the good news. She would probably be as astonished as he was.

CHAPTER 27

Sunday 9th December 2003

Sunday night duly arrived. The hotel had been heaving all weekend as they had all expected, especially with the charity ball for the animal sanctuary at Tangles. Ruth and Philip were normally in attendance but, in his absence, Lucy had stepped in to host it and did a fine job. The staff were rushed off their feet from Friday morning through to Sunday evening and were all relieved when their shifts ended and they could all go home to recover.

Katrina, in her new role as trainee manager, had to admit she was feeling the effects of such long hours over the weekend too. She had been on her feet constantly, David asking her to help him keep a check on every aspect of service to their guests as she was the only other member of management apart from him, with Pete having left to celebrate his birthday. She constantly paraded from room to room, overseeing what was going on, half of her mind on her job and the other on what was going to happen later. Nothing must go wrong.

Then it was here, the evening she had been waiting for, when her plan to discredit David was going to become a reality. It was quiet as a number of guests had checked out earlier in the morning and those who remained were tired and just wanted to relax in the spa, dining room and lounges. They chattered amongst themselves but by 11.00 p.m. they were in their rooms, enabling Leo and Kevin to clock off, leaving only the night porters, David and Katrina still on duty.

Katrina saw Leo and Kevin leave the bar and head upstairs to their rooms, pretending they were off to bed. They now had two hours to get everything in place. Leo was going to use Katrina's car, drop Kevin at the Dower House to set up all the equipment and then head into Leeds, fetch the girls, drive them over to join Kevin and then come back to Canleigh to help her with David.

She felt distinctly nervous and jittery but tremendously excited now her plan was under way. It wouldn't be long now before the righteous David was past history.

"You might as well go on up, Katrina, thank you. It's been a tough few days and you must be exhausted. I know I am," said David as they stood in the entrance hall having said goodnight to three guests who had just left the bar for their rooms. "Once I've checked the cash, that's where I'm heading," he added.

"Well, if you let me help you, you'll be finished much quicker," Katrina said, trying to sound as concerned for him as she could. "I'm tired but I doubt if I will get to sleep very quickly so I might just as well help you … and we will be sitting down," she grimaced, slipping off her shoe and rubbing her foot. There was a blister coming on her big toe from being on her feet all day. It hadn't burst yet but it did hurt.

"No, really," said David. "I can manage."

"No. I insist. You look shattered … and I can't let cousin Lucy think I don't support you … after all, you will very soon be family," Katrina grinned, heading over to his office door and opening it. "Come on. Let's get it done and then we can both go to bed."

David shrugged. He would have preferred to do the cash with anyone bar Katrina but there was no-one else, he was terribly tired and if she was offering to help, it would be foolish to refuse, especially as there was Saturday's takings as well as todays to check. He had managed to count Friday's but last night he had been too exhausted after the ball and had slung the money bags into the safe, hoping to find time to do it today. That hadn't happened so now he had to face a long slog counting and checking it all as Securicor would be here first thing to take it away.

They entered David's office and as a precaution, he locked the door before he opened the safe. Katrina settled down at the big table on the opposite side of the room to his desk, where they sat for staff meetings and where he always counted the takings.

David dumped the money on the table. There were several bulging hessian bags containing the takings from Saturday and Sunday. Two from each of the departments; the bar, beauty salon, the cafe in the stable block, plant shop, gift shop, hair salon and the last, containing auction and raffle ticket cash from the charity event on Saturday evening.

David commenced with Saturday's bar takings, tipping out all the cash and notes Leo had carefully placed into the little plastic bags supplied by the bank for the different coinage. The notes were held together by a plastic band with the completed nightly cash-up sheet on top.

Katrina gulped as David spread the cash out on the table. "You start counting the coins and I'll do the notes," he instructed.

"Actually, I'm really thirsty, David," she said, with her hand in her pocket, fiddling with the pink pill in the cellophane wrapping Kevin had given her earlier. "Would you mind if I have a drink before we get stuck in?"

"Of course not," he said, waving at the drinks tray in the corner of the room, which was useful for when he didn't want to take visitors through to the bar. "Help yourself but no alcohol mind, not when we're counting money."

"Okay. I'll have an orange juice. How about you?"

"Nothing for me now, thank you. I sometimes have a quick brandy when I've finished."

She poured herself an orange, checking there was plenty of brandy. She would give him one as soon as the counting was all done and slip the pill into it. She looked at her watch. Leo should have dropped Kevin by now and be on his way into Leeds. He was going to text her as soon as he had the girls at the Dower House and was on his way over to the Hall.

As expected, an hour later, with most of the money bagged up ready for Securicor, her mobile pinged.

"Good heavens, whoever is sending you a text at this time of night?" David looked up in surprise.

"Oh, it's one of those annoying messages from the phone company. They drive me nuts," she remarked with a grin. She read it rapidly. According to Leo, the girls were safely at the Dower House, along with Kevin; Leo had parked the car down by the stable block and was on his way up to the Hall. It was time. The pills worked quickly so David had to have one now.

"Now we've just about finished, do you think we could have that stiff drink?" she asked. "I don't know about you, but it will help me sleep."

"Of course. Pour a brandy for both of us. I could really do with one now, "he agreed, writing up the takings in the accounts book.

It was easier than she had thought it would be. He was taking no notice of her whatsoever and she slipped the pill into his drink. It dissolved immediately and she stirred it quickly with her finger. She handed him his glass and he smiled, snapped the accounts book shut, slipped the top on his fountain pen and sat back in his chair.

"Thank you, Katrina, for assisting me tonight. It probably would have taken another hour if I had been on my own."

"Good. I'm glad I could help. Now, drink up and then we can go to bed," she urged.

He raised an eyebrow and she laughed. "I didn't mean together. Goodness, David. What are you thinking?"

He blushed. "Sorry … I."

"Oh, don't be so straight-laced," she grinned. "But you do need to loosen up a bit, David. You don't want Lucy to get bored."

He took a big gulp of his brandy, a bit uncomfortable as to where this conversation was going. The sooner they were out of the office the better. He finished it quickly, wondering why she was grinning from ear to ear as she watched him. She didn't touch hers.

He stood up but there was a sudden ringing in his ears. He gripped the side of the table. He felt most peculiar. Not ill but queer

… and much to his astonishment he began to imagine what Katrina would look like devoid of all her clothing.

There was a soft tap on the office door and Katrina moved quickly across the room and unlocked it. Leo slipped in, a grim expression on his face.

"Let's move," he said, staring hard at David who was looking a little wobbly on his feet. "I've just told the night porters that I've been out to get some air and have seen movement and torchlight over by the church. They've just gone over to have a look so we haven't much time."

"You go with Leo," Katrina said to David urgently, grabbing his glass and shoving it in her bag. She didn't want anyone checking it in the morning and finding there was something mixed in with the brandy.

He stumbled around the table, grinning stupidly at her, throwing an arm around her waist and trying to kiss her. He missed her mouth and planted a wet, sloppy mouth on her cheek. She grimaced.

"Gosh, Katrina, has anyone ever told you how drop dead gorgeous you are?" he purred, bending his head to nuzzle her neck.

"All the time," grinned Katrina, "now go … and we can promise you a right good time in a few minutes. You're going to party like you've never partied before."

"Oh, bring it on," he said gaily, trying to undo the buttons on her blouse.

"Not now, David and certainly not here. Go with Leo. He's going to take you somewhere quiet, where we can really have fun."

She turned to Leo. "Did you give the girls the masks I gave you earlier?"

Leo nodded and grabbed David's arm while Katrina opened her handbag, stuffed in the £19,000 in notes that David had just counted, and then threw the remainder of the hessian bags containing the coins into the safe and slammed it shut, being careful to use a tissue so that if there was an investigation, any fingerprints would belong to David.

Checking the entrance hall was still empty, Leo guided David towards the backstairs as Katrina turned off the office light and locked the door, still using a tissue.

"Go down to the basement and wait for me. I'll only be a moment," Delia whispered, shooting up the stairs as they headed down. She ran as quietly as she could up to David's rooms in the west wing, opened his door with the key from his bunch she still had with her and shot into his sitting room. She stood for a second, looking around swiftly, wondering where to put the money. She had thought about under the mattress but then she saw his sports bag. Even better. She opened it, took out the £19,000 from her bag, pushed it into his and zipped it back up, just leaving one £20 note sticking out.

She flew back out, locked the door and ran swiftly down to the basement to re-join the two men, wiping the keys with a tissue and dropping them into David's jacket pocket. The three of them made their way out through the kitchen door and into the night, a bewildered David clutching onto Katrina, leering down at her in a way that she could only consider utterly ludicrous. If only precious Lucy could see her beloved David in this state … but then she would soon and in a worse predicament than he was now.

They reached the car. Katrina drove while Leo sat in the back with David, to prevent him trying to grab her. They reached the Dower House minutes later, Katrina pleased to see all the heavy drapes had been drawn and it looked like any occupants had gone to bed. She parked the car around the back, away from prying eyes.

"The Dower House … is the party here?" David said gleefully, hanging onto Katrina's arm and running a hand over her breasts. She brushed it away and with Leo's help, pushed him through the front door and into the drawing room on their left where Kevin was chatting to the two girls, both wearing the black lace masks she had bought for them while in Leeds on Friday. They both looked up with interest as the three made their entrance. Katrina noticed, with amusement, how their eyes lingered on Leo.

"This is David," said Katrina, putting a hand on his shoulder. "He's really looking forward to his party."

The dark haired one rose from her seat and sashayed over to David. She was wearing a short, tight black skirt and a low-cut sequined top with no bra. She grabbed his hand and placed it on her waist. "Hello, David. Should we go upstairs? Tricia and I are going to give you a really good time."

"Yeah," said Tricia, coming up behind her friend, grinning like a Cheshire cat. "Bev and I are just dying to get to grips with you."

They each took one of his hands and Katrina giggled as David shot up the stairs behind the girls, Kevin hard on their heels so he didn't miss filming any of the action.

"Should we go and watch the entertainment?" Katrina grinned at Leo.

"You can ... I'm staying here ... I'm not really sure I want to be part of this anyway. You're damned rotten, Katrina. Neither David or Lucy deserve this. It's going to devastate both of them ...and for what?"

"You know why. If they marry and produce children, I shall never get my hands on Canleigh," she pouted.

"Christ! You are an avaricious bitch! You'll probably never get it anyway as Lucy isn't much older than you. You're just going to cause a lot of misery for no gain at all. It's horrible. You're horrible."

"Oh, get a grip. You're not doing so badly out of this little caper tonight. I'm paying you all very well ... and just remember, if you ever open your mouths about any of this, I'll go through with my threat and tell the police you were implicit in Summer's death. Anyway, David is having the time of his life ... at least I hope he is."

Leo glared at her and sat down heavily on the sofa. He had been in the porn game a long time and he liked it but he didn't like what was going on upstairs. David had been a decent boss and Leo liked his job, even though it was a cover for the porn films. However, he was going off Katrina rapidly and it was time to move on. Yeah. Get tonight over with and then pack a bag and get out of here. He didn't think he could ever face David or Lucy again anyway.

Katrina delved into her bag and handed him a wad of notes. She'd had to rush to her bank in Leeds on Friday afternoon and take out all the cash she had purloined from her parents so she could pay everyone tonight. "Here. There's the ten thousand I promised you … don't forget to split it with Kevin. I think you'll find that makes it all worthwhile," she said.

"Christ, Katrina. It's the hotel takings. We could really get done for this."

"It's not. Don't panic. This is from a different source and you don't need to know where. As for the takings … I'm going to make it look as if David intended to steal them … I've dumped them in his room. I don't think for one minute that Lucy will contact the police. She won't want her darling David arrested and charged. Just think of the scandal and the effect it will have on the hotel. No, she will want to keep it quiet but just in case and I'm wrong and the police are involved, they might conduct a search, so I suggest you hide your cut off the premises … Kevin too … and for God's sake, don't put it in the damned bank!"

"Bloody hell! We're not that damned stupid!" he hissed.

"No … anyway, do what you want, just don't get caught with it. I'm going upstairs. I want to make sure those girls are earning their money."

He watched her go with distaste. Once he and Kevin left Canleigh for good, he definitely never wanted to set eyes on her again. If she could do this to members of her own family, what the hell could she do to anyone else? Katerina certainly wasn't a safe person to know and the sooner they left the better. He really didn't want to be around her any longer and certainly couldn't bring himself to touch her again. No, their acting career together was well and truly over. She was poison.

CHAPTER 28

The night of Sunday 9th December 2003

Katrina was pleased. The girls really had earned their money in the half hour they rollicked with David on the king-sized bed in the master bedroom. She had stood in the doorway, watching with amusement as David was pampered and petted, licked and caressed by the two naked women. He was enjoying himself hugely as he thrust into Bev while Tricia sat in front of them, playing with her breasts in full sight of David, who was leering at her, desperate to get his hands on her too.

"That's good, David, so good," Bev was purring. "God, you are wonderful. A real stud …,"

"Oh yes, David," Tricia joined in, leaning forward, her enormous breasts almost in his face. "I can't wait for my turn."

Katrina couldn't keep the grin off her face. Kevin was moving around the bed, capturing it all, making sure that there could be no doubt it was David in the throes of the action. He was doing a good job, as were the girls. David was well into it now with the pill well and truly in his system. The effects would last a good couple of hours but they had achieved what she wanted in a much shorter time but they couldn't leave until David began to come down and was too exhausted to care what happened to him. Then all of them, apart from him, could squeeze back into her car, deposit the girls back in Leeds and sneak back into Canleigh. David could be left here to sleep it off, which would mean he would probably be late in the morning as he would have to walk back to the Hall and would miss Securicor and the hullabaloo when it was discovered so much money was missing, probably by Pete, as he would be the first one on duty and would have to deal with it. It was going to be a hell of a morning after the night before and she was looking forward to it tremendously, especially when everyone realised David was missing and his room was searched and the takings were discovered. Yes, darling David would have a hell of a lot of explaining to do.

* * *

An hour later, David, physically and mentally shattered, was coming down. Katrina knew that feeling well, how after such an exhausting session sleep was desperately needed ... and he was already tired from an extremely busy weekend.

She yawned. She would be glad to see her bed after this little lot too. Kevin looked done in and the girls looked seedier than ever now their makeup was smeared and their hair in complete disarray. They dressed back into their cheap polyester garments as David fell into a deep sleep on his stomach, his head buried in a pillow and one arm hanging out of bed. Katrina covered him with a sheet.

"Sweet dreams," she whispered. "Enjoy your peace while it lasts."

She followed the girls and Kevin downstairs to where Leo was asleep on the sofa. She nudged him awake. "Come on. It's time to go, so let's get out of here. I don't know about you but I want my bed."

He rubbed his eyes and stumbled to his feet while the girls pulled on their coats and Kevin tucked his equipment into a canvas bag.

Katrina handed each of the girls a wad of notes. "There. That's what we agreed. Just remember. You have never been here. You have never seen us before and you never will again. If I ever hear a whisper that you have mentioned what went on tonight to anyone, you will be extremely sorry. Is that clear?"

They both nodded, took the notes and stuffed them into their handbags.

"What about David?" asked Leo, fiddling in the pocket of his jacket for Katrina's car keys.

"He's sleeping it off. He can walk home in the morning."

Leo glared at her, feeling a wave of pity for his boss. He had been duped and drugged into having sex with a couple of whores, and would wake up in the morning, remember what had happened, and then have to get himself back to the Hall where he might well be arrested for stealing the takings. Even if he wasn't, it was a damn sure thing he was going to lose his job and his fiancée. Leo was utterly staggered at the lengths Katrina had gone to. She really was an evil bitch.

He found the car keys and walked outside, followed by two weary girls holding each other up, Kevin with his canvas bag and then Katrina, still with a wide smile on her face as she locked the door and then pushed the key through the letterbox for David to find in the morning, thinking how she would love to be a fly on the wall to see his face when he woke up and realised what had happened. She was laughing gaily as she slipped into the passenger seat of her car, quite happy for Leo to drive. God, she was tired but what a brilliant night it had been. She had pulled it off and David would be gone very soon. Poor Lucy would be so upset but she would console her, be pull of pity and understanding, full of sympathy. Poor Lucy. Poor, poor Lucy. Katrina grinned at Leo, sitting beside her, grim-faced. He obviously wasn't happy about the way things had gone. But it was just too bad. He had his money and with that he would have to be content and anyway, she had a funny feeling he and Kevin wouldn't be around much longer. She had burnt her boats with them.

One of the girls coughed behind her. They would be fine. They understood and she didn't think for one minute they would say anything to anyone. It was just work to them, and they had been paid well. As the film wouldn't be seen by anyone apart from Lucy and David, and they wouldn't want it to become public, especially as David had so obviously been a willing participant, there would be no reason for anyone to contact the girls about it.

Yes, it was all wrapped up, quite nicely and she was very, very pleased with herself.

* * *

Lucy couldn't sleep, having to keep popping into Selena's room to check on her as she had been tossing and turning for most of the night, probably because she was so excited about Christmas as they had decorated the tree this afternoon and there were already a few presents on the carpet beneath it.

She tried to read but the book couldn't hold her attention so she got up and wandered through to the lounge. The tree did look a picture. Blue was Selena's favourite colour so they had used shiny royal blue baubles, silver tinsel, along with white lights and a pretty fairy perched on the top. Selena hadn't been able to take her eyes off it until it was time for bed.

Now was a good time to wrap some of Selena's presents, Lucy decided, returning to her bedroom where she had hidden them on the top of her wardrobe.

There was a new doll, with long blonde hair; a telephone, a china tea service and best of all, the doll's house with all the furniture; pots and pans and three little figures plus two dogs and a cat. Selena would love it. She had seen it in the toy shop in Harrogate in the summer when they had been walking past and had stared at it with ecstasy and Lucy had decided there and then it would be her daughter's Christmas present. She had gone back the next day and bought it and kept it hidden ever since. She debated on whether or not to wrap it up. It would be more exciting for Selena if she did.

She hauled it through to the lounge, took out her scissors and sellotape from a drawer in the dresser and began to wrap it, feeling a growing sense of excitement.

She was so looking forward to Christmas this year. It was going to be one of the best. Selena would be thrilled with her presents, David would be able to get away from Canleigh for a few hours to share it with them, they could start planning their wedding in more detail ... and her mother and Brian would be here too. It was a shame that Ruth and Philip, along with Vicky and Alex wouldn't be around but they were enjoying themselves in Spain; she had heard from Ruth yesterday, and they were all having a lovely time.

She finished the doll's house and sat back to have a look at her handiwork. Selena would have no idea what it was but was going to be so thrilled and excited when she found out. Lucy couldn't wait to see her face.

She yawned, feeling sleepy now. She looked at the clock on the mantelpiece. It was three o'clock. Time to go back to bed ... alone. It would be so nice when she and David were finally married and could go to bed together every night. That was one part of her marriage she was really looking forward to.

* * *

David woke up briefly. His arm was hanging out of bed and going numb. He rubbed it back to life. God he was tired and this bed was so damned comfy. He could sleep for a week. Once his arm recovered, he turned over, buried his head in the softness of the pillow and fell straight back to sleep.

CHAPTER 29

Monday 10th December 2003

Katrina only slept for an hour, woken by her phone which she had kept close to her ear so that she wouldn't miss the call she was waiting for. She looked at the clock. It was two minutes past 4.00 a.m. God, she was tired.

"They're ready," whispered Kevin. I'll drop three copies with you and then I'll scoot over to the Dower House and Lucy's before it gets light."

"Fine. Thanks," grinned Katrina, hauling herself out of bed and pulling her dressing gown over her naked body.

A couple of minutes later there was a light tap on her door and she opened it. Kevin thrust a brown envelope at her. He had two more in the pocket of his leather jacket.

Katrina took the package. "How did it come out?" she whispered.

"Perfect," he whispered back.

"Brilliant," she grinned. "You should be okay at Lucy's. She told me she's turned the security lights off as the badgers and foxes keep switching them on and it frightens her to death."

"Okay but I've got this, just in case." He produced a thick woollen scarf and put it over his face. No-one would recognise him with that in place.

"Good … get on your way then," she instructed, "oh, and here's another £200 for doing this for me," she handed him another package, containing some of her savings. "The bicycle is in the storeroom next to the kitchen."

He shoved the envelope into the inside pocket of his jacket and headed back down the corridor towards the back stairs. He would have much preferred to drive to the Dower House and Dingle Dell while playing postman but as Katrina had said earlier, someone might see or hear a car, especially tenant farmers who might be up and about this early in the morning. A bicycle would be silent and could easily be hidden behind trees if need be.

Katrina shut the door and turned on her light. She pulled the dvd case out of the envelope Kevin had given her, opened it and slipped the disc into the dvd player beside her television. Kevin had surpassed himself, catching the threesome at the best angles, which would leave no doubt in anyone's mind that the male participant was David. The masks the girls wore had worked well and even with their exertions, had stayed in place and anyway, Kevin had concentrated more on close-ups of their breasts, genital areas and naturally, the sex act itself with an intense look of concentration and pleasure from David as he eagerly thrust into each of them in turn.

She turned the machines off with a deep sense of satisfaction. She had done it! All hell was going to break lose today and she couldn't wait to see events unfold. Giggling to herself, she got back into bed and curled up. She didn't have to be on duty until 8.30 a.m. but it was doubtful she was going to get any sleep between now and then. Her mind was simply buzzing!

* * *

Lucy saw the package on the mat at the front door when she came out of her bedroom in her dressing gown, on her way to wake up Selena before Tina arrived to take her to school. She picked it up and looked at it curiously. It must have been delivered during the night. How very strange. She opened it to see a dvd in a plain cover. Stranger still. However, as intrigued as she was, she hadn't time to watch it now as she had to get Selena ready and she had a lot to do today as well. There were the preparations for Christmas and she also had to pop over to the Hall for her weekly business meeting with David at around eleven. They would discuss important hotel matters for an hour and then have lunch in the dining room. They always met on a Monday as it was the quietest day of the week and they could be fairly sure of not being interrupted too often.

An hour later, Tina and Selena had departed for Harrogate and Lucy was on her own. She looked at the dvd on the kitchen worktop where she had left it earlier, her curiosity now getting the better of her. She really should get on with other things such as preparing one of the guest bedrooms for her mother and Brian. Then there was the food and drink to order, their presents to wrap and a hundred and one other things that needed doing before she drove over to Canleigh.

Oh, bugger it. She would have a quick look. It was probably some stupid advertisement for double glazing or something similar. She placed the breakfast things in the dishwasher, wiped the top of the kitchen island, picked up the dvd and crossed over to the little television and dvd player in the corner and set it all up to play.

She really, really wished she hadn't when, with a sickening jolt, she realised what she was looking at. She sat down heavily on one of the breakfast chairs, nearly tipping it over in her haste. It rocked for a split second and then righted itself. She sat, staring wide-eyed at the television, watching her naked fiancé allowing two masked women, also devoid of clothing, to fondle him. He was moaning and panting, with an ecstatic look on his face. He was thoroughly enjoying it, stroking their breasts, sucking their nipples. As much as she wanted to, Lucy was unable to tear her eyes away, as all her hopes and dreams for a bright and loving future with this man, crashed around her ears.

She could hear it, the drumming in her head, similar to that which had come over her when she had seen Jeremy and Felix having sex, that dreadful night when her world had fallen apart and she had tumbled down the stairs at Canleigh trying to get away from them.

She felt sick and knew she was going to throw up. She just made it to the sink, heaving, gulping for air, grabbing a nearby tea towel to wipe her mouth. She stood staring out of the window at the field at the rear of the property, the field where during the summer she, David and Selena had enjoyed a picnic, David showing Selena how to make a buttercup chain. He was so patient with her, so keen to help her. How could he do this? How could he do this to her? How could he do it to Selena, who loved him too?

The dvd was still playing. She could still hear him, groaning with desire, the women whispering and encouraging him. Who the hell were they? Where did it take place … and when?

Girding her loins, she turned back to the television, determined to watch it, determined to find some clue as to who her fiancé was with and where but it was impossible to tell who the women might be, although they did possess broad Yorkshire accents so must be local tarts he had picked up.

She stared at the surroundings but as most of the filming was concentrated on the writhing threesome, there wasn't much of a clue. The bed was obviously a king size and it had a nice headboard, which looked vaguely familiar but she couldn't think where she had seen it before and then with a crashing sense of realisation she knew. It was the bed in the master bedroom at the Dower House. The bed she had bought when the old one had needed renewing. It had cost a pretty penny and she hadn't intended to have it used in this way, by her fiancé and his whores.

Anger began to take over the deep sense of yet another huge betrayal. She felt like murdering David for hurting her so badly. God, she was so stupid! To be duped by a man again but even with all the evidence in front of her, she couldn't quite believe it of him. He was such a strong and determined man where business was concerned, but in his private life he was a true gentleman, deeply religious and kind to everyone. She had known him for a number of years and she would never, not for a minute, think he would do something like this. It wasn't in his nature. But then did one every truly know another? She hadn't thought Jeremy was bisexual. God, she was so naive.

The disgusting film finished, just after one of the women and David reached orgasm. It clicked off, the kitchen suddenly deathly silent.

Lucy knew she was in shock. What was she going to do? She didn't know. She wished Granny Ruth wasn't abroad. She would have gone straight to her. She deliberated on phoning her in Spain but why ruin her holiday? It wouldn't be fair. There was her mother, of course, but Lucy was never keen to tell Delia anything that might make her mad, always frightened about how she might react, never wanting to be the cause for her mother to lose her temper and do something to send her back to prison. No, she couldn't tell her either. She was going to have to be a big, brave girl and deal with this herself ... alone ... but how? How was she going to face David, after what she had just seen?

She sat down again, defeated and utterly shattered. She had been betrayed in the cruellest way ... again. She hated men with a vengeance and would have nothing, absolutely nothing whatsoever to do with any of them on a personal level in the future. She put her head in her hands and cried piteously, for herself and for Selena, who would never have the joy of knowing a decent father. They would be alone for the rest of their lives. The deep, dark depression she had thought was in the past began to descend again like a black cloud.

***

David stirred. It was daylight. He could see pinpricks of light at the side of the heavy window drapes. He stared at them, trying to think where he was. The room looked familiar but it wasn't his. He lifted his head and groaned. It was throbbing painfully, he felt nauseous and his body was like lead. He could barely move and his private parts were damned sore.

Puzzled, he reached out for his phone, which lay beside him and switched it on. It blinded him for a second with its bright light and then he could see the time. Christ, it was just gone nine o'clock and he was supposed to be on duty as from eight and he didn't even know where he was. He hauled himself off the bed, wondering why he was completely naked, heading to the window to draw back the curtains. As soon as he did, he realised where he was instantly. God it was the master bedroom in the Dower House, the bed was in an unholy mess and his clothes were all on the floor and that was extremely odd. He was meticulous about folding his clothes properly when he undressed and he never, never, threw them on the floor. What the hell had been going on?

A ping from his mobile indicated he had a text message. No doubt it was the hotel, wanting to know where he was. Well, they would have to wait. He had to get himself decent first. He dashed into the bathroom and had a shower. He would have to send someone from housekeeping over to clean the place up but he was still puzzling what he was doing here. Last night was so fuzzy. He could vaguely remember Katrina being part of it. He could remember them counting money in his office but after that, it was all a bit of a blur. Did he get in a car with her? Was Leo there … and Kevin? Had they been to some sort of a party?

Tiny bits began to resurface in his mind. He began to recollect a couple of women, their faces obscured with black lace masks, and with ample breasts. Naked breasts. They were on the bed with him. No. No! He hadn't! He couldn't! He would never do such a thing. He wouldn't dream of it. He was an engaged man. He loved Lucy. He would never stoop so low.

With mounting horror, he dressed quickly, desperate to get back to the hotel. He dashed downstairs to see if there was anyone else in the building but he was alone. He stood in the hall wondering what to do. It would take ages to walk or run back to the Hall … and it was beginning to rain. He hadn't a coat or a brolly. He was going to get soaked. He'd have to ring for a taxi.

As he pulled his phone out of his trouser pocket, he glanced at the front door. There was a brown envelope on the mat. He bent down to pick it up. 'Watch me, David' were the instructions in thick black lettering on the front. His heart beat loudly and his mouth went dry. He just knew this was going to be something bad but even so, he did as he was told.

* * *

Katrina hurried downstairs to reception at 8.30 a.m., eager to see if there were any developments. Pete was on duty from 8.00 a.m. so would have discovered the takings were missing. He would be in a right panic, especially with the disappearance of David who was probably still snoozing happily away at the Dower House. There was no sign of Kevin or Leo as she left her room but then they didn't have to start work until ten so could have a lie in.

Her first duty this morning was to head to the dining room to make sure all the guests were enjoying their breakfast and nothing was out of place. She smiled and nodded at the girls on reception, the night porters having clocked off at seven. There was a light on in the office and a seriously worried looking Pete emerged as Katrina was about to pass. He saw her and grabbed her arm.

"Katrina." His tone was anxious and she had a job not to laugh. "Have you seen anything of David this morning?"

"David? No. Why? Is something wrong, Pete," she asked. Oh, it was so very hard not to giggle.

CHAPTER 30

Monday 10th December 2003

Pete was dumbfounded. He had entered the office at the commencement of his shift to find the table where they held their meetings and counted the takings was in disarray, which was most unusual as David was a stickler for tidiness and always cleared everything away before he retired. Something must have gone wrong last night as the table was littered with till rolls, empty plastic money bags, rubber bands and paperclips, along with the accounts book, which the general manager would never leave out for anyone to see.

Pete knew Securicor would be arriving around 11.00 a.m. to collect the weekend's takings, which must have been considerable as the hotel had been so busy. With trepidation he opened the safe. The hessian bags were there and he breathed a sigh of relief but relying on his instincts, he pulled one out and looked inside. The coins had obviously been counted and placed in separate plastic money bags ready for banking but there were no notes. He checked the remaining bags. They were all the same. No notes in any of them.

Christ! He sat down abruptly in David's chair. Where the hell was David. He was never, never late and the safe was virtually empty. What the hell was going on? He looked at his watch. It was ten minutes past eight. David was usually sat at his desk well before then preparing for the day but it was obvious he hadn't been down this morning as the first thing he did was turn on his desktop and check the bookings. Pete touched the machine. It was cold and obviously hadn't been switched on. Likewise, the coffee machine and that was very strange as David said he couldn't function properly if he didn't have at least two cups of decaf after his run around the lake and goodness knows how many lengths of the pool every morning.

Pete sat and chewed his lip and wondered what to do. Should he ring the police or should he ring Lucy or should he rush up to David's room and demand to know what had been going on. Perhaps the man had been taken ill. There had to be a good explanation.

Locking David's office behind him, he moved quickly up the backstairs to what had been the servant's quarters. Katrina, Leo and Kevin had rooms in the east wing but David had the whole of the west wing to himself. Pete, who lived in the village, and wasn't au fait with the top floor of Canleigh, stood for a second, looking at all the doors in front of him, wondering which one led into David's flat. He banged on the first one. No answer. He banged on the second. No answer again. He did the same all along the west corridor but David didn't appear. He shouted as he banged but it didn't make any difference. Then he noticed the last door was slightly ajar. He pushed it open cautiously. It was obviously David's quarters as he recognised the sports bag on the floor beside the sofa. David always used it when he went down to the pool.

"David," he called loudly, heading through the lounge into the kitchen and then back through into the bedroom, wondering if he was going to find a dead body because this scenario was so damned unusual for such a punctual, meticulous man.

The bed hadn't been slept in. Pete looked around in despair, wondering what to do. Perhaps David had stayed at Lucy's last night. That was a distinct possibility and common sense told him he should ring her and find out. If David wasn't there, then it would be time to become really alarmed. He went back through to the lounge, nearly tripping over the sports bag. Something was poking out by the zipper. He moved closer to have a look ... it was a twenty-pound note. He couldn't resist it. He pulled the zipper back quickly and couldn't believe his eyes. The bag was stuffed full of notes; fifties, twenties, tens and fives ... and they could have only come from one source. What the hell was David playing at?

* * *

"Lucy. It's Pete. I don't suppose David is with you, is he?" Pete asked in despair, just knowing what she was going to say but then if David had stolen the money, why the hell had he left all the cash here for anyone to find? It didn't make sense.

Lucy was still sitting in the kitchen at Dingle Dell, numb with shock and grief. She couldn't understand what Pete was saying for a second or two. She couldn't bring herself to think of anything but the awful images of her fiancé on the television screen.

"No. No, Pete. He's not here. Isn't he at the Hall?"

"No. He's not … and there's more. It looks like we've had a load of money stolen from the safe … or at least, not stolen, as it's in David's room."

"What? What are you babbling about, Pete?" she asked with exasperation. "Why do you think it's stolen and what do you mean, it's in David's room and where is he, anyway?"

"I've no idea," said Pete, hating what he was having to do. "But something isn't right and Securicor will be arriving mid-morning to take the cash away and I've no idea if what is in David's room is the correct amount of the weekend's takings … the coins are bagged up in the safe but there are no notes … they all seem to be here … but why … and why, in David's bag. It's all very puzzling and I'm really wondering if we should call the police."

"I'm totally confused … I'm coming over. Don't do anything until I get there," Lucy demanded, grabbing her car keys and her bag and turning off her mobile as she left Dingle Dell. It seemed her fiancé had a hell of a lot of explaining to do.

* * *

Katrina was checking a booking with the reception staff when she saw Lucy arrive and march straight into David's office where Pete was waiting for her. Lucy looked pale and miserable and just for a fleeting instant, Katrina felt a little sorry for her. She'd always been good to her, like a big sister really, but needs must. Lucy mustn't marry and David had to go ... and so far, it seemed everything was working ... there was definitely a panic on and more to the point, he still hadn't turned up. It was chucking it down outside and if he had finally woken up and was on his way, walking up from the Dower House, he was going to get pretty wet and would look like a drowned rat when he arrived.

As Katrina grinned at the thought, out of the corner of her eye she saw a taxi draw up outside the front door. David was alighting and handing a ten-pound note to the driver. Grim-faced, he dashed up the steps and into the entrance hall.

"Good morning," she said lightly, flashing him a grin. "Where have you been all night then? Been partying, have you?"

"You little bitch," he hissed through gritted teeth. He had never condoned violence in his life but to see Katrina with a wide smirk on her face, fully aware of what had occurred during the last few hours, made him want to raise his hand and give her an almighty whack. "It was all your idea, you little tramp. If Lucy has seen that blasted film you will have ruined my whole life ... and why? What have I ever done to you? I only ever tried to help you."

"I'm sure I don't know what you mean, David darling. But if I was you, I would pop into your office where Pete and Lucy are waiting for you as I think they want to know what has happened to rather a lot of money."

David stopped in his tracks. "What?"

"David?" said Lucy, her voice icily cold, emerged from the office, having heard his voice. "Please, can you come into the office? I want a word."

David rounded on his heel and did as Lucy asked, throwing Katrina another furious stare. The office door closed behind them and she virtually skipped into the library to make sure the morning papers had arrived.

* * *

Lucy couldn't look at David. All she could see in her mind's eye was him cavorting with those two women … in the master bedroom at the Dower House. The place she had lived so happily with her mother all those years ago. She felt the searing pain, ripping through her, just as it had the night she had seen Jeremy with Felix. What was wrong with her? Why did men do this to her? Why? She had never done anything wrong. She had loved them both and thought they loved her. How wrong she had been. How deep was her despair?

David was standing with the door behind him. He was looking at the disarray on the table, at the open safe door, at Lucy, at Pete. He couldn't take in what was happening. His brain was foggy, he felt desperately tired and just wanted nothing more than to go upstairs and sleep. But he couldn't. He had to deal with what was going on here first.

"The takings … from the weekend," Pete was saying. "There's nothing in the safe bar coins. The notes … they are in your room … in your sports bag."

"What?" exclaimed David. "What on earth do you mean? Katrina and I counted it all last night and put everything in the safe … there should be just under £19,000 there … look, I recorded it in the accounts book," he said, crossing the room to pick up the book. "I'm sure I did."

"Well, if you did," said Pete, "the page has been ripped out and some of the till rolls are missing so we can't check."

David looked at Lucy, who still had her back to him. "Lucy … surely you don't think I had anything to do with this? Surely you don't think I would steal from the hotel … from you?"

"Quite frankly, I don't know," replied Lucy, turning to Pete. "Pete. Would you mind leaving us and put the 'do not disturb' sign on the door please."

Pete nodded and left the room, turning the sign outside as instructed.

Lucy crossed to David's chair and sat down at his desk. Her legs felt weak and she hoped she wasn't about to faint. She had to be strong now; really, really strong. Leaving all feelings for David aside, she had to remember she owned this hotel and not only had he cheated despicably but he had also intended stealing from her. Obviously, something must have gone wrong or he would have been gone by now but even so, he wouldn't have got far once the police were on his tail.

"Why, David?" she asked wearily, running a hand over her brow but still not looking at him. She couldn't bring herself to meet his eyes, to see the deceit in them. She didn't particularly want to hear his voice either, to hear his lies, but she was going to have to. She couldn't leave things as they were. She needed to get the truth out of him and then he would have to leave. It was going to break her heart to dismiss him, to see him walk out of her life but there was no other way. She could never forgive any of this and could never, ever trust him again in any capacity whatsoever.

"Lucy, I am so sorry … I really don't know what happened … Katrina and I counted it all last night …,"

"Well, it's lucky for you I have already spoken to Katrina and she confirms what you say and that there was £19,000 in total. However, she says she left you here, drinking brandy, and went to bed."

"Well, that's a lie … well, not all of it … we both had a drink and then I suddenly felt very strange … quite … well, not ill, but odd … and she and Leo helped me out of here."

"Leo?"

"Yes. Both of them."

"And you all went to the Dower House," Lucy stated.

He looked aghast. She knew where he had been. God! Surely she hadn't seen that ghastly film. If she had, he was well and truly done for.

She looked at him then, garnering the courage to raise her head and meet his eyes. "Yes, David. I've seen it. Someone, goodness knows who, had the kindness to post it through my letterbox during the night."

He sank into the chair opposite her and groaned. "Oh, God, Lucy. I am so sorry. I don't know what came over me. It wasn't me … I wouldn't do that to you."

"But you did, David. You did … and now you have to bear the consequences."

"I think … I think I was drugged in some way … Katrina …,"

"Katrina, Katrina … for goodness sake, David, stop going on about her. You are a person in your own right. You and you alone are responsible for your own actions … and it wasn't her with you on that bed, was it? So, stop blaming her!"

Her voice was rising uncontrollably. Her distress was showing. She took a few deep breaths, trying to stop her heart pounding so quickly.

"Well, it's true, Lucy," he said quietly. "Katrina must have done something to my drink because it wasn't long after that I started to feel most peculiar."

He was trying really hard to remember exactly what had happened. He couldn't clearly recall leaving the office or how he had arrived at the Dower House but although fuzzy, he could now remember the lurid sex session, how he had suddenly been unable to stop himself wanting those two women, how he had actually enjoyed it. How he could have given in to such sheer carnal pleasure was a mystery and he was deeply ashamed. He had never done such a thing before and would never do it again but how to convince Lucy of it? He knew she would never believe him. The trust between them was gone. He knew what she had gone through with her first husband. It had taken him a long time to boost her self-confidence and self-esteem and make her aware that she was worthy of great love. All that now lay in tatters at his feet. He had destroyed their relationship in one foul swoop and he still couldn't understand how he could have done it. He had to have been drugged. There was no way he would have behaved as he had if he had been in his right mind ... and it had to be Katrina. He just knew it. She was the one behind all of this and he would dearly like to get his hands around her neck ... and squeeze.

CHAPTER 31

Monday 10th December 2003

Lucy left the Hall minutes later. She didn't want to hear any more of David's grovelling excuses and apologies. Her heart was cold and she could never forgive him. He was utterly dead to her now.

"As a result of all the good work you've done here since I opened Canleigh as a hotel, and how you've raised its credibility and profile, I shan't prosecute you for attempting to steal the takings," had been some of her last words to him.

"But I …"

She had put her hand up to stop him, physically disgusted by his appearance. He had obviously showered before coming in as his hair was wet, unless that was the rain, but his normally impeccable suit and shirt were crumpled and she could distinctly smell cheap perfume.

"I don't want to hear it, David. Whatever comes out of your mouth now, I can't believe so you might as well stay quiet and just listen. As I said, I shan't prosecute. However, I want you to go upstairs, pack and leave here immediately. I want you off the premises by lunchtime and if you're not, then I might reconsider my decision not to contact the police."

"Is there anything I can say?" he asked pitifully, knowing in his heart what the answer would be.

"No," replied Lucy. "I never want to see or hear from you again. I shall ask Pete to accompany you to your room to make sure you only take your personal belongings."

"What about the hotel … it's Christmas, Lucy. We're fully booked … it's going to be all hands to the deck."

"Yes, and it won't be your hands. Just leave, David. The Hall and what goes on in it is of no concern to you any longer. Just get out."

"Can't you see I've been set up," he said, trying for the last time to make her change her mind.

"Even if you have, David, I've seen that damned film ... and you were hardly an unwilling participant ... God knows what you might have caught from those tarts and if you think I would ever want to touch you again after seeing that, you must be mad. There is absolutely nothing you can say that will make me change my mind."

She had stood up, picked up her bag and keys from the desk and strode past him. He put out a hand to stop her but she shrugged him off and continued out into reception, leaving him, a dejected, utterly defeated figure.

Pete was hovering around the reception area, waiting to say goodbye to the departing guests and wondering what to do about the Securicor collection. Lucy saw him as soon as she left the office and walked straight across to him, giving a weak smile to the reception staff, who were agog to know what was going on. Pete hadn't told them a thing but it was obvious something serious was afoot.

Lucy drew Pete aside. "Take David up to his rooms, stand over him while he packs and then see him off the premises, please, Pete. Then I want you to take over his duties until we decide what can be done to get some help for you. Katrina can assist you. She's proved able enough in the past few days ... and the responsibility should be good for her. I'll make some calls and get back to you later today ... oh, and can you and Katrina check the cash in David's sports bag and get it off to Securicor sometime today please."

Pete nodded and Lucy, unable to keep her sorrow in check for much longer, hurried down the front steps, got into her car and drove down the back lanes towards the Dower House.

She had no idea why she was being drawn there and when she finally drew up outside the front door, she remained in her car, staring at the lovely old building where she and her mother had been so very happy when she was tiny. She fished in her bag for the set of keys she always kept with her for various cottages on the estate that were rented out as she never knew when she might want to check one over. She found the one for the Dower House, got out of the car and walked up to the front door, unlocked it and stepped inside.

She went into the drawing room first. There were signs people had been there very recently. The cushions on the sofas were askew, there were cigarette butts in the ashtrays and dirty wine glasses along with two empty bottles of Chardonnay on the coffee table. Two of the glasses, with bright red lipstick imprints, made her shudder with disgust.

She looked around numbly, thinking that while asleep last night, she had been blissfully unaware of what was going on here and what her fiancée was doing. She still couldn't believe it. In fact, if she hadn't seen the film with her own eyes, she wouldn't have done. David simply wasn't the type, or at least she hadn't thought he was. That was one of the reasons she had loved him so much. He had seemed so stable, so solid, so dependable. How wrong she had been to think that of him. She really was a terrible judge of character, especially of men ... but it wouldn't happen again. There would be no more. It was her and Selena after this and no-one would be allowed to get close to her again.

She moved back out into the hall and looked up at the stairs which would take her to the master bedroom where her fiancé had dealt the fatal blow to their relationship. Knowing it was a stupid thing to do, but unable to help herself, she walked up the stairs, turning right at the top and stood outside the bedroom door which was closed. Tentatively, she put her hand on the doorknob and turned it.

It had stopped raining outside and the room was bathed in winter sunshine, making her blink for a moment as it streamed through the two sash windows overlooking the front gardens and her car below. Her eyes went straight to the huge king-sized bed.

The sheets and duvet were a rumpled mess and she felt sick just looking at them. More dirty glasses sat on the bedside tables, more cigarette butts in a saucer as there was no ashtray. It was a rule that there was no smoking in the bedrooms and to discover that David had allowed it, made her seethe. The room stunk of perspiration, smoke and sex. Suddenly the bile rose up in her throat and she just made it to the sink in the ensuite. She heaved and heaved, tears pouring down her cheeks as she strained. The pain pierced her heart, tearing it apart, like a red-hot poker rushing through her. It was unbearable. Utterly, utterly unbearable.

* * *

Leo saw Pete escorting David up to his room. Pete looked embarrassed and uncomfortable, David looked the object of complete misery. Leo's heart turned over. He felt incredibly guilty at the part he had played in David's downfall but even if he wanted to say anything to Lucy to help his former boss, he doubted very much if she would forgive the man and anyway, it was impossible as he would then drop himself, Kevin and Katrina in it too and that simply wouldn't be a wise move. No, poor David was finished. Not only here, but probably his whole career because it was doubtful if Lucy would give him a reference ... and it was all down to flaming Katrina. God, she was rotten to the core and the sooner he got away from her the better.

He had thought last night that he might stay at Canleigh until after Christmas but he wasn't so sure now. It was obvious Lucy wasn't going to call the police about the attempt to steal the takings as the place would have been crawling with them so if he and Kevin did decide to leave, it wouldn't arouse any suspicions that they were involved. He had his share of the money Katrina had handed out last night and he had quite a bit in the bank from the films they had already made. He could afford to get out of here and he was pretty sure wherever he went, Kevin would follow. There would be no point in him staying here anyway as there would be no more filming with Katrina. That was a complete and utter certainty. Once he left Canleigh he didn't want to set eyes on her ever again. He would think about it today and talk to Kevin this evening. Perhaps they could do a bunk tonight. Bugger Canleigh! Bugger Katrina!

* * *

Katrina was in the office, yet again counting the money, as Pete had asked her to do. She bagged it all up, placed it all in the safe ready to be collected by Securicor later that afternoon as Pete had arranged, wrote the total in the accounts book and with great satisfaction looked around the office.

This room had been a drawing room before the place had been turned into a hotel. When she became the owner, it would be again. When she became the owner. She licked her lips. She was one step closer with David out of the way and it was Lucy's turn next but it might not be necessary to do anything to her. Lucy had suffered from depression for years and had looked quite ill when she left here this morning. Perhaps this would tip her over the edge. Perhaps she would commit suicide. How convenient that would be … and if she did, there would only be Mother to deal with.

Katrina felt a huge excitement taking hold of her. Canleigh really could be hers one day if luck stayed with her. Then she would be rich beyond her wildest dreams, turn the Hall back into a grand home and she, and she alone, would live here with a load of servants and she could wear a fabulous gold ballgown and hold grand parties, balls and soirees, just like they had in the old days before she was born, at least she supposed they had. She really didn't know much about her ancestors. Anyhow, that didn't matter. She sat mesmerised, planning her future life at Canleigh, wondering which bedroom she would have … the big one at the rear, overlooking the lake. That would be ideal.

"Have you finished counting the money?" said Pete, hurrying through the door and striding straight up to the window.

Startled, Katrina nodded and stood up to join him, wondering what was so interesting outside. It was David, stepping into his car, having thrown a couple of suitcases in the boot. He looked sheepish and miserable as he shut the door and started the engine. Katrina badly wanted to give him a cheeky wave but it wouldn't look good in front of Pete so she kept herself in check.

"Bloody idiot," murmured Pete. "He had it all. What the bloody hell was he thinking of to throw it all away?"

"There's nowt queerer than folk," replied Katrina with a Yorkshire accent.

Pete grimaced. "Um. That's true. Now, can you please do the rounds and make sure everyone is being looked after properly for lunch. David had a meeting with the tourist board regarding bookings for next year. I will have to take his place. Can you cope for a couple of hours? Lucy said she's going to get some help so hopefully she will get back to us this afternoon with some kind of solution otherwise we're going to have a pretty mad couple of weeks with all the Christmas bookings."

"Yes, I'll be absolutely fine," said Lucy. "You go to your meeting and don't worry about a thing." She grinned. "Believe me, I have it all in hand."

CHAPTER 32

Monday 10th December 2003

Delia always felt a thrill of excitement when turning up the drive for Blairness. It wasn't long and it was straight, so the castle was immediately in sight when driving through the wrought iron gates. The centuries old stone building was so beautiful it always made her catch her breath and it was all hers. Whatever happened, no-one could ever take it from her.

She beamed at Brian, who was driving, and he beamed back. He loved Blairness too, having spent a lot of years caring for it while she was in prison and then helping her to put it on the map once she was released. They had fallen in love here and married here. It had special memories for both of them.

They pulled up outside the front door and got out of the Range Rover which was packed to the hilt in the rear with presents for the family at Dingle Dell and for the staff here at Blairness.

"Halloo," yelled Crystal from the floor above, waving at them through an open window. "Oh, it's lovely to see you. Mildred has prepared tea … with her famous fruit cake. Go on through to the red drawing room. I'll be down in a second," her head of red hair disappearing back inside.

Delia laughed. "Oh, that's great. I can just sink my teeth into that cake and I'm dying for a good cup of tea."

They left the presents in the car as there were too many to carry in one go. Brian just carried their suitcases, followed Delia into the entrance hall, and left their luggage near the stairs to take up after they had enjoyed Mildred's offerings.

"I can never walk in here now without thinking of our wedding day," remarked Delia, looking around, remembering how the big room had looked on the most special day of her life. In three days, it would be their fourth wedding anniversary but she could still remember every minute of that day as if it was yesterday. How she had felt coming down the stairs, seeing all their guests assembled but focusing on Brian as he stood waiting for her. The room had been decorated for Christmas and adorned with greenery from the estate, much as it was now, and looked simply wonderful.

Delia sighed and Brian took her in his arms. "That was the best day of my life," he said. "And I can't thank you enough for making me so very happy over the last few years."

"And I you," she said softly, her eyes gentle and loving as she stared up at him. It was amazing how this man made her feel. He had such a calming effect on her and it had made her a much kinder, thoughtful person. If she had only met him when she was young. If only he had been the one she had first fallen in love with. How different life would have been. Still, there was no point in thinking like that. They were together now and always would be and Delia's heart sang with joy. He had made her the happiest woman on earth the day they had married and she still felt the same. He was her everything and she knew she was his.

"Gosh, are you two still totally besotted with each other?" joked Crystal, appearing at the top of the stairs and grinning down at them.

Delia and Brian grinned back. "Naturally," Delia laughed. "And we always will be … don't be jealous."

"Me? Good heavens, no. I have no need to be jealous of anyone," she grinned, waving her left hand over the banister as she moved downstairs. The light from the chandelier above their heads caught the ring on her finger and it sparkled brightly. "Meet the soon to be Mrs. Gerald Ponsonby," she giggled. "Mrs. Ponsonby … whatever would all the Holloway lot think of that?"

"Oh, Crystal. I'm so pleased for you … I really am. Gerald is such a great chap and I'm sure you will be really happy," exclaimed Delia, clapping her hands together and then hugging her former Holloway cellmate as she stepped onto the highly polished oak floor of the entrance hall. "I knew you two were close but didn't realise it was this serious. I'm so pleased for you but this doesn't mean you're going to give up your job, does it? Finding a replacement for you will be a daunting task."

Crystal had proved to be an amazing custodian of Blairness and had driven up visitor numbers and revenue since she had been put in charge four years ago. It would be extremely difficult to find anyone who could replace her with the same passion and energy that had really helped the castle become one of the most visited stately homes in Scotland.

"Don't panic," replied Crystal. "I love my job too much and will be here as long as you'll have me … although I'm going to have to reconsider living arrangements."

"Yes. I suppose you will want to go and live with Gerald down at the cottage but that's okay. I can't see any problem with that. The castle is well secure at night now we have put in all the new alarms and anyway, the McFrains are still in situ so it won't be completely empty at night … on the other hand, Gerald could always move in here with you."

"Thank you … but as much as I love living here, it's not exactly homely … and Gerald and I have been thinking about buying a rather nice house in Elvington which has just come on the market … it will be perfect for us, especially if we decide to have children, and only takes a few minutes to drive here so we won't be far away. Anyway, you're here for a few days so we've plenty of time to discuss everything properly … come on through. I'm gasping for a cup of tea and as for that cake … we only get it when you come so it's a real treat."

Delia and Brian exchanged smiles as they followed Crystal into the red drawing room. Even though Delia owned Blairness, they were often made to feel like visitors by Crystal but didn't mind a bit. She was one of their stalwarts and if she wanted to queen it over the place, she could do so with their blessing.

* * *

Lucy had left the Dower House in floods of tears that morning and how she had managed to drive back to Dingle Dell without crashing the car, she had no idea. It was just as well she met no other vehicle on the back lanes of the Canleigh estate.

The first thing she did on entering Dingle Dell was to ring the agency to see if they could find her a temporary general manager for the next few weeks until there was time to interview for a permanent replacement for David. That would have to wait for a while as she wasn't brilliant at obtaining new staff … look how it had turned out with him! She didn't trust herself to appoint another general manager on her own. She wanted Aunt Vicky and Uncle Alex to assist her so the process would have to be delayed until they returned from abroad … and anyway, she wasn't in the right frame of mind to interview anyone at the moment. She was far too distraught and couldn't think clearly.

The agency was helpful. They had a number of men on their books who didn't want to settle anywhere as they enjoyed the freedom of working for short periods in one hotel or another, gaining experience and expertise as they did so. Two were free for the Christmas period and both could start immediately.

"Just send me the best you have," said Lucy, her head throbbing and her heart broken. "Tell him to report to Pete, the assistant manager. He will show him around. I … I have a family crisis and I can't meet him until tomorrow."

After sending a text message to Pete to advise that help would arrive later that day and could he make sure the temporary manager had every assistance, she headed for the kitchen and took a bottle of white wine from the fridge. Tears prevented her from reading the label but she didn't care what she drunk, as long as it was alcoholic and could help ease the dreadful piercing pain that was encompassing her whole being. She had never in her life felt like this. What Jeremy had done to her had been really bad but this was killing her. It had taken her such a long time to put her faith and trust in anyone again but David had got under her skin and she had succumbed. Stupid! She was so stupid! She slapped her head hard with her hand, again and again, moaning with despair, aching with misery and dejection.

She drank one glass of wine within seconds and poured another. She picked up the glass and went through to the lounge, bathed in glorious winter sunshine. It was hard to believe it had rained so relentlessly only a few hours ago.

She looked at the Christmas tree in the corner of the room, at the presents beneath. It all looked so gay, so exceedingly warm and cheerful; so snug, so enticingly homely. Oh, God. How was she going to cope with the festivities? Entertaining her mother, Brian, Suzanne, little Daniel and Katrina. How was she going to be jolly when all she wanted was to shut herself away in her room to nurse her bleeding heart?

Her mother and Brian were at Blairness and would be staying there until Sunday and then travelling down to Dingle Dell ... so she only had six days to pull herself together and there was still quite a bit to do but how was she going to be able to concentrate, feeling the way she did? It was going to be a complete disaster. She knew it was. Her heart wasn't in it anymore ... but there was Selena to think about. She was so looking forward to Christmas, was so excited and had already put up her stocking by her bed. If there was one person in the world Lucy couldn't let down, it was Selena. She had to put on a front for her. She could cry in private but when Selena was around, everything had to be perfect for her. Lucy took the bottle of wine back to the kitchen and returned it to the fridge. She took a deep breath. David or no David, life had to go on however much she was hurting.

She sat, calmer now, at the breakfast bar in the kitchen, thinking a little more clearly about what had gone on, remembering pieces of what David had said. Why had he kept harping on about Katrina? What could she have to do with his misdemeanours? There had been no evidence of her in the film. It wasn't her that was having sex with David, so why did he seem to think it was her fault? It was a complete mystery. Perhaps she should have listened to him instead of just shutting him up … but even so, whatever Katrina may or may not have done, she had not been on that bed in the Dower House with him.

She pondered on whether it might be a good idea to have another word with Katrina to see if she could shed more light on it, especially as she was probably the last one to have seen him last night before he ended up at the Dower House … and how had he got there anyway? His car was at the Hall and he had arrived this morning in a taxi. Unless he had taken a taxi last night. Yes, that was it but why would he have cleared off, leaving all that money in his room and the office in such a mess? It was so out of character but then did one ever really know another? Perhaps he had been cavorting with prostitutes for a long time. Perhaps he had used the Dower House on more than one occasion … perhaps it had been a regular occurrence, whenever the place wasn't booked up … and perhaps he had never been filmed before. But why this time? And who would have sent it to her? What malicious person could want to tarnish David's reputation and put his livelihood at risk? Whoever it was would have known she would finish with him immediately, more than likely dismiss him and his career would be over. Why would anyone be so cruel?

She sat thinking, chewing her lip, the clock on the wall ticking away the seconds and minutes. She had missed her lunch but she wasn't hungry. She didn't think she could ever eat again.

She took a pad and pen from the drawer in the kitchen island and doodled for a while, thinking hard about who would benefit from David's dismissal from the Hall. There was Pete, of course, but then he wasn't experienced enough to become general manager yet. Maybe in a few years but then he was such a nice lad. She couldn't see him being so devious and there wasn't anyone else, apart from Katrina … and she certainly wasn't ready for promotion … and what other reason could she have for getting rid of David?

She sighed with exasperation. From what she could see, there wasn't one. In conclusion, David was just a pathetic man, unable to deny his lust. In a way, it was just as well she had found out now what he was really like. If it had happened after they were married, it would have been much, much worse. Even so, her heart was bleeding, and she had never felt so depressed and miserable in her life. She couldn't help it, she put her head in her hands and sobbed piteously for yet another man she had lost.

CHAPTER 33

Monday 10th December 2003

"I don't think Lucy is going to call the police in," announced Leo as he and Kevin walked up the backstairs to their rooms at the end of their lunchtime shift.

"No, She's not. I had a quick word with Katrina when I bumped into her in the kitchens just now. All the money has been recovered from David's room so there's no need to involve the police on that count and as far as our little escapade last night is concerned, it appears Lucy just wants to keep that as quiet as she can as she hasn't mentioned it to anyone. Poor woman. I feel dreadfully sorry for her."

"So do I," agreed Leo, "and for David. Neither of them deserved what we did to them. I don't know about you but I feel pretty rotten about it ... and the sooner I get away from Katrina Gregory, the better. If the police aren't being summoned, I think I might just pack a bag and go tonight."

"Tonight?" Kevin looked at Leo, startled. He hadn't expected his friend to say that.

They had reached Leo's room. He opened the door and pulled Kevin inside.

"Yes. Tonight ... and I think you would be wise to come with me."

"But why? We're on to a good thing here."

"Not any more, we're not. I don't trust Katrina any longer. If she can do what she has to David, one of the most decent men I have ever met, she won't hesitate to do something similar to us if her back is against the wall. She could really drop us in it if she wanted to. She's bloody twisted. Don't forget Summer died and we were questioned. Katrina has already threatened to implicate us in some way if we open our mouths about last night but I wouldn't put it past her not to do it anyway, just to get shot of us."

"But … the hotel … it's busy … we can't just walk out."

"Why the hell not? I'm all for self-preservation, even if you're not. Come on, we can get back to London tonight, doss down with Mark and Will for a few days while we get set up somewhere … then we can find some more girls and get cracking on the videos again."

"Oh, shit. I like it here. I like the routine, the food, the room. I know the pay isn't much but it's warm and comfy … and clean. You know what Mark and Will's place is like … a flamin' doss house."

"Look, that's preferable to waiting around to see what Katrina has up her sleeve to get rid of us. I really don't want to get sent down for conspiracy to murder … do you?"

"Who … who have we murdered?"

"Oh, for Christ's sake. No-one but Katrina will make it look as if we had something to do with Summer's death. I just know she will."

"But why?"

"Christ, Kevin, you can be bloody thick at times. Get your brain into gear. We know what she did to David, not only with the delightful scenario at the Dower House, but trying to implicate him in stealing from the Hall. We could spill the beans at any time and she knows it, however much she tries to bribe us … and now she will turn her attention to Lucy and if something untoward happens to her …, or Lady Vicky come to that … she knows it wouldn't take us much to put two and two together … no, we're safer getting as far away from here as fast as we can and disappearing from Katrina's orbit for the rest of our lives."

"Bugger, Leo. Do we really have to go?"

"Yes … and the sooner the better. We'll do our shift tonight and then grab our stuff, get a taxi into Leeds and get back to London. I'll give Mark and Will a ring in a minute. God, I'll be damned glad to get away from that cunning little bitch!"

* * *

Adrian Valentine arrived at the Hall just after 3.00 p.m. He drew up outside in his new Mercedes, which was costing him a fortune every month in repayments but as he had wanted a Merc since he was a small boy, he didn't care. It was his pride and joy and if he had to work hard to keep it, so he would. He got out, opened the rear door and carefully lifted Cherub out and placed her on the ground. She looked so cute in her little pink coat and her diamante necklace and everyone would love her, as they always did, wherever he went with her in tow.

He had just completed six months at a prestigious five-star hotel in London, taken a break for two weeks and was now eager to get cracking again and hadn't been able to believe his luck when the agency rang this morning and asked if he would consider doing a stint here, at Canleigh Hall. He had been delighted. He was from Yorkshire originally, from a little village near to Whitby, and being a reasonable driving distance from his family home was a real bonus, especially at this time of the year. He might just be able to pop over and see them at some point, if only for a couple of hours. He also had Cherub to think about and this place would be ideal for her with all the lovely walks in the grounds. He sighed with satisfaction as he eyed up the vast lawns in front of the Hall.

"Perfect, my little darling, absolutely perfect." he smiled at the pure white little Bichon Frise. She wagged her tail back and smiled with her eyes. She didn't mind where she was as long as she was with her master.

They walked up the steps together and into the entrance hall. Pete was standing just inside the door and opened it for them.

"Hello," said Adrian. "I presume you must be Pete Williams? I'm your new temporary general manager, Adrian Valentine … and this is Cherub," he added, nodding down at the little dog.

A very attractive girl with auburn hair, dressed in a tight-fitting blue suit and white blouse shot from behind the reception desk, making a beeline for Cherub.

"Oh, what a lovely little dog," she said, stroking Cherub's head. "She is so cute."

"Yes, she is," said Adrian, used to such adoration for his best friend. "And you are?"

"Katrina … Katrina Gregory … I'm the owner's cousin … and trainee manager … and if there is anything, anything at all, I can help you with, please don't hesitate to ask."

* * *

Katrina was amused to see that the fair-haired temporary general manager, dressed in a grey suit and wearing gold rimmed glasses, was obviously gay. That would no doubt upset Lucy even more, reminding her of her Jeremy and Felix and her ghastly time at their hands.

He was tall and thin with exceedingly long arms and fingers, which made the effeminate waves and the frequent touching of his hair more obvious as he talked quietly to Pete, who introduced him to the reception staff and then escorted him into the office, Cherub following closely behind. Adrian had removed her lead but she still remained as near to her master as she possibly could in this strange new environment.

It was time for afternoon tea and Katrina was needed to supervise the dining room so she made her way there through the drawing rooms, nodding to the guests and straightening newspapers and books left on coffee tables.

She was still feeling tired from lack of sleep last night but she was also elated. Her plan to get rid of David had worked swimmingly and now she could move on to thinking about what she was going to do next but she would leave it for a while, otherwise it would begin to look suspicious. She would enjoy

Christmas; working here and having lunch with Lucy and the family at Dingle Dell, although that might not be the cheery occasion they had all expected now that Lucy's hopes and dreams for an idyllic future with David had been shattered. Oh well, she would have her lunch and then leave. She had the brilliant excuse that she was needed back here so no-one would question it.

Glancing through the library window, she saw Adrian mincing along the path outside with Cherub, obviously giving the tiny dog time to have a wee and possibly a poo. The new GM was going to be a pushover, there was no doubt about that. He had looked quite taken aback when she said she was Lucy's cousin. She would make sure he never forgot it!

* * *

Delia and Brian had enjoyed a nice lunch with Crystal and Gerald, discussing what had been done at Blairness this year and what was planned for next. Then Brian and Gerald decided to take a drive around the estate and Cheryl had an appointment with her hairdresser.

Delia didn't want to go out. It was bitterly cold and an afternoon curled up in the red drawing room where there was a lovely roaring log fire and ringing Lucy was far more appealing. She hadn't spoken to her for a couple of days and wanted to let her know roughly what time they would be arriving at Dingle Dell next Sunday. They had to remain at Blairness until then as it was the staff Christmas party on Saturday and Delia didn't want to miss that for anything.

She kicked off her shoes, put her legs up on the sofa, and dialled Lucy's number on her mobile. It rang a long time before Lucy answered, which was unusual, and Delia nearly gave up, thinking her daughter must be busy. Then, suddenly, she answered.

"Hello," she said quietly, her voice hardly definable.

"Lucy? Are you alright? You sound a bit weak and feeble."

"Yes ... no, I'm not really. Something has happened ... and I'm really not feeling very happy at the moment."

"Why, what's the matter?" Delia demanded. "Is Selena okay or are you ill ... do you want us to postpone coming? We can always stay here, at Blairness, if you're feeling rough and can't cope with us."

"No ... no, please come. I'm not ill. I'm ... I'm just ...,"

"Just what, darling. For goodness sake, spit it out. You're getting me really worried now."

Lucy burst into tears at the other end. "'It's David. I've sacked him ... he's behaved appallingly. He no longer works for me and the engagement ... the engagement is off."

CHAPTER 34

Monday 10th December 2003

Arm in arm, Ruth and Vicky ambled along the sandy beach in the cove just down from their hotel. It wasn't hot enough to sit about as there was a chilly wind but it was pleasant enough to stroll and breath in the fresh sea air. Alex and Philip had driven inland for the day to visit an old castle but the women had just wanted to relax by the sea.

Vicky was looking better and better as their holiday progressed. Her skin was glowing, her hair was thickening up again and she had more energy. She was getting back to normal fairly quickly and they were all so pleased and relieved for her.

"I don't think I ever want to go home," she said, looking wistfully at the gentle waves lapping around their bare feet.

"We always say that but when we get there, we soon slip back into our normal routine," replied Ruth, thinking about her painting and how she wished she had brought her oils with her. She wondered if it was possible to buy some in the local vicinity. The scenery was breath-taking and she wanted so much to capture it.

"True but we, that is, Alex and I, we work so damned hard … always have … and this cancer … well, it's made us think more about what's important and it's us. Even though Alex is now based at The Beeches, we still work long hours … and we're not getting any younger. We've been talking about it since we've been here and decided we are definitely going to sell up and move to Italy. No more waiting until we retire. We want to do it now so we can spend as much precious time together as we can before it's too late."

"Oh gosh," exclaimed Ruth. "We will miss you so much. I can't imagine you both not being so near … but what about Katrina … and Suzanne …especially with her only just returning to the UK?"

"I know. I feel a bit rotten about that but I'm sure she'll understand and it won't be for a while anyway. I don't expect it will be very easy to sell The Beeches so it won't be imminent … and we'll make sure she and Daniel are okay … we can buy them a house, because the new owners might not let her live in the cottage, although, hopefully, they will let her stay working there … but if they don't for some strange reason, we'll buy her a salon in Harrogate as I expect she will want to stay in the area because of Daniel's schooling. Anyhow, whatever she would like to do, we will make sure she is okay."

"And Katrina?"

"Oh, Katrina," Vicky sighed and looked out to sea. "I heard from Lucy that she's buckling down at last at Canleigh and doing okay … actually taking a real interest. I do hope so. She could have a really good career in hospitality if she wanted. She's bright, smart, very attractive … she could do well."

"I wonder what she will say when she hears you want to sell The Beeches."

"Oh, she'll probably scream some more about her inheritance … and be thoroughly jealous of whatever we do for Suzanne. Alex is becoming very fed up with it all and apparently threatened to disinherit Katrina entirely. That must have been a sharp shock for her."

"Gosh, yes. Especially if he intends it all going to Suzanne. Katrina would be incandescent with rage if that was the case."

"Yes, you're right. She would go mad. I think when we get home, we're going to have to talk to both the girls properly again and see what we can come up with to secure both their futures and make Katrina understand that she just can't have it all and she is going to have to share. We have a responsibility to Suzanne … and Daniel … and we're not going to shirk it".

"I see a few storms ahead," murmured Ruth. "And I don't mean here and now."

Vicky grimaced and shivered as the breeze suddenly turned colder. It was like someone had walked over her grave. Stupid expression that but even though she was tremendously excited and happy about the plans to move to Italy, she had a deep sense of foreboding that it wouldn't be an easy transition, especially where her immediate family was concerned.

* * *

Lucy felt a fraction better once she had told her mother about her broken engagement. Luckily Delia hadn't asked why or how it had happened so Lucy had been able to brush it aside for now … but she had no doubt that over the Christmas period, Delia would worm it all out of her.

It would be common knowledge by now that David had intended taking the money and that was why he was dismissed but she had no idea how many people knew about the disgusting film. Obviously she did and whoever had sent it but who was it and would they keep it a secret? Why had they done it anyway? What was the purpose? What did they hope to gain?

The questions went constantly around and around in her head. Who could it be? Who were those girls?

It was grinding her down, constantly nagging at her, wondering, wondering, wondering. She couldn't imagine any of the staff at the hotel being involved … apart from Katrina … it always came back to her. David had been so sure it was her but Lucy couldn't credit it. Her brain felt as if it was about to explode. Would she ever know who had set out to destroy her happiness and her future? Would she?

* * *

Delia told Brian as soon as he returned from his trip around the estate with Gerald.

"I feel so damned sorry for Lucy," she said. "I really thought David was going to be so good for her after all that terrible trauma she went through with Jeremy.""

"So why did he break it off?" asked Brian, settling down beside her on the sofa in the red drawing room and pulling her close. He had missed her this afternoon.

"I've no idea. She just said he had left Canleigh in a hurry and that was that. She's had to get a temporary manager in for the Christmas period until she can find time to interview for a permanent one."

"Bloody hell. What a time to lose the general manager ... at the busiest time of the year. Will we have to go in and help out, do you think? I'm up for it if you are."

Delia grinned and punched him playfully. "You would, wouldn't you ... I can just see you, pandering to the whims and fancies of all the guests and wouldn't they be totally chuffed and flabbergasted to find out they were being fawned over by the Earl of Glentagon?"

He grinned. "It might be rather fun."

"Yes, it could be ... but not if anyone recognised me ...,"

He hugged her. "It's not going to come to that. I expect this temporary manager will be fine ... we'll just have to jolly Lucy along at Dingle Dell. I expect she's pretty devastated, poor girl. What a rotter, doing this to her ... especially now."

"Yes ... but I've a feeling there's more to this than meets the eye. She was very reluctant to tell me exactly why David had departed so abruptly but I'll get it out of her when we get there. Blast the man. That poor girl has been through enough. She didn't need this. Goodness knows what it is going to do to her. After Christmas is over, I think we should suggest she and Selena come to stay with us for a while ... perhaps for the rest of the winter ... help her get over it ... I hate the thought of her being so far away and just sitting there brooding about what might have been. She loves it at Glentagon and it would be good to have her and Selena close for a while ... and Selena might well be able to go to the village school for a few weeks."

Brian nodded. "I think that's a superb idea and I'll be very surprised if Lucy doesn't take you up on it."

* * *

Ruth was incredulous. "David can't have ... he wouldn't. I don't believe it of him. There must be some mistake," she blustered over the telephone, unable to take in what Lucy was telling her. Ruth had really liked and respected David and considered he was a perfect match for Lucy and he had done so well looking after the interests of the Hall. It was crazy to think he would have risked it all to steal the takings out of the safe. He was paid well, had no real expenses as he lived in so all his utility bills were included, as were his meals so he certainly wouldn't need the money. It didn't make sense.

"There must be more to this," she said. "What is it you're not telling me, Lucy?"

Lucy went completely silent at the other end. She couldn't speak about that vile film. It was haunting her badly. In her mind's eye that was all she could see; David, gyrating on that big bed with those two tarts, thoroughly enjoying himself, with no thought for her. It was lucky, in a peculiar way, that the excuse for sacking him was that he had tried to steal money, which meant she didn't have to mention the film but there were people like Granny Ruth, who had known David well, who were going to question it more deeply and she was right, it didn't make sense. Lucy still had no idea why he had tried to take the money and did such a bad job of hiding what he was doing.

"I'll tell you when you get home. There's no need to spoil your holiday."

"Lucy! If you don't tell me, I shall be spending the rest of the holiday worrying anyway so please tell me now."

"Oh God. It's so awful," Lucy cried. "I don't know if I can."

Ruth's heart plummeted as she recalled the horrendous time Lucy had endured at the hands of Jeremy and Felix. It had taken the girl a long time to recover and trust again and God forbid she wasn't going through another hellish experience at the hands of a man.

"Darling, do you want me to come home? I will, you know. You only have to say the word."

"No ... no, you mustn't. It wouldn't be fair and anyway, Mother and Brian will be here in a few days and you won't want to bump into them."

"Have you told her ... your mother ... what has happened?"

"Only as much as you."

"Okay ... well be careful, Lucy. I know you love Delia but she's damned unpredictable. I don't know what she would do if she thought you were hurting again. She couldn't do anything about Jeremy and Felix as they were killed before she found out what they were doing to you but David will still be around somewhere and if she's angry enough, I wouldn't be surprised if she didn't track him down and make him pay for whatever he's done to you."

"I know but Brian is so good at calming her down and she still worships the ground he walks on so he will make her see sense."

"I just hope you're right. Now, my darling, remember, if you do need me, I will be on the first plane home. Philip can always stay here with Vicky and Alex. He will understand."

"Thank you, Granny Ruth. I feel a little better just talking to you. I'm sorry I don't feel able to tell you exactly what went on but I will ... eventually. It's just too raw at the moment."

"Okay, darling ... and I am so very sorry. Give my love to Selena and give her the best Christmas you can."

"I'll try."

"Good. Keep your chin up, darling and we'll be home straight after New Year."

Ruth switched off her mobile and looked at Philip, Vicky and Alex, who were sitting around the veranda table beside her. Relaxing over coffee and liquors after dinner, they had been listening intently and were desperate to know what was so wrong.

"What's happened ... what's David done?" asked Vicky anxiously. "Is Lucy okay?"

Ruth told them exactly what Lucy had told her, about David attempting to steal the takings from the weekend. They all agreed it didn't seem possible. They all knew him well and not one of them thought he was stupid enough to ruin his career for this, let alone upset Lucy and put their relationship at risk.

"Whatever else he's done must have been pretty bad if Lucy can't even talk about it," said Alex. "What on earth could it be?"

"I really don't know ... Lucy was really clamming up but she did say one thing that had me puzzled," remarked Ruth.

They all looked at her, waiting for her to expand.

"She said that David intimated Katrina was behind it ... all of it ... but again, that just seems ludicrous."

Alex looked sombrely at his relatives. "I'm not so sure. That damned daughter of ours is up to something. I didn't want to mention this, darling," he looked despairingly at Vicky, "but I think you should know. I was checking our bank balance this morning ... Katrina has managed to gain access to it and has transferred £12,000 to her account."

"What?" Vicky gasped, her mouth dropping open.

Ruth and Philip were staring at Alex aghast. Why on earth would Katrina do such a thing ... steal from her own parents?

"She can't remove anymore," Alex said quickly. "I've changed the passwords but when we get home, that girl has one hell of a lot of explaining to do."

CHAPTER 35

Tuesday 11th December 2003

Even though Katrina had decided not to continue with her plan to grind Lucy down until after Christmas, she couldn't resist the temptation. Kevin had given her three spare dvd's of David's escapade and she decided to send Lucy another, by first class post this time. She popped into the outskirts of Leeds in her coffee break and found a little shop which also contained a post office and sent the dvd by first class post.

The postman covering the Canleigh area always delivered very early so the dvd would most likely be sitting on Lucy's hall floor when she emerged from her bedroom in the morning. Would she watch it? She might not if she thought it was exactly the same as the last one but then she might, as there was a chance it was something different. Lucy would have a dilemma. Katrina could imagine her, standing in her dressing gown, staring at the dvd, frightened of what it contained.

Lucy wasn't a strong person, kind but a bit weak and watery for Katrina's tastes, and having suffered so badly from depression for so long, it should be relatively easy to send her into a downward spiral again and what did serious depression lead too … invariably one trying to end one's life ... and that would be very handy, very handy indeed.

Katrina grinned. Knowing Lucy was reluctant to involve the police in any part of the affair with David, Katrina felt safe to have a little more fun and just see if she could tip Lucy over the edge. It would certainly save her having to do anything physical to her but would it work? Well, it was certainly worth a shot she decided. If her ruse worked and Lucy did sink low enough to attempt suicide … and succeeded, no-one would ever link it to her. Then she would be virtually home and dry with only her mother and father to deal with and at that moment in time, she had no idea what she could do there ... not yet, at any rate.

"Have you seen either Leo or Kevin this morning?" asked Pete as he passed her in the dining room. Breakfast was over and Katrina was supervising setting up the tables for lunch.

"No ... aren't they in the bar?" said Katrina, looking at her watch. It was 10.30 a.m. They were usually down by now to re-stock, organise the servery and have time for a coffee before it opened at noon.

"No ... and they better get a move on ... we've three big parties coming in for Christmas luncheon and we don't want to be running out of anything. Would you mind popping up and giving them a prod in the right direction, please, Katrina?"

Katrina sped up the back stairs and banged on Leo's door first and then Kevin's.

"Rise and shine, you two. The bar needs opening and you don't have very long."

Neither of them answered, which was strange. She usually got a grunt or two, especially from Leo, who was never good at getting up. She hammered on his door again and rattled the door handle, surprised to discover it wasn't locked. She opened the door and stepped inside, all ready to shake a sleeping Leo awake but his bed was made, which was damned unusual. She looked around, puzzled. Something didn't feel right and for a second or two she couldn't think what and then it hit her ... all his personal possessions were missing. She shot through to the bathroom but all his toiletries had been removed. There was nothing of his in the little kitchenette or the bedroom. All the drawers were empty, as was the wardrobe. The bugger had done a bunk and has not given her a hint of what he intended.

She knew Kevin would be gone too. There was no way he would stay without Leo. Even so, she knocked on his door and walked in, only to find his room was exactly the same.

She sat on his bed, chewed her lip and pondered. Did it matter to her that they had done a bunk? Not really, in the grand scheme of things. Yes, they had known what she had planned and executed for David but they had been paid handsomely for their silence and now they were out of the picture, she couldn't see any reason why they would ever tell on her. They had their money and wherever they had gone, and she suspected it was probably back to London, they wouldn't want any dealings with her again and she was safer with them out of the way. She smiled, shut Kevin's door and went down to tell Adrian and Pete that they needed more bar staff as a matter of some urgency.

* * *

Tina duly arrived to take Selena to school. Lucy and Selena, just finishing her porridge, were in the kitchen, both dressed for the day, when Tina opened the front door with her key and walked along the hall to the kitchen at the far end. She smiled and handed Lucy a package she was holding.

"I met the postman coming down the lane. Poor man is in a bit of a flap as he's having trouble with his van this morning."

Lucy stared at the envelope and ran a hand over it, the shape and feel making it obvious there was a dvd inside. The scrawl on the front was the same, in black felt tip pen. Her tummy was doing somersaults.

Tina and Selena departed, Selena waving goodbye to her mother as the car swept up the drive and disappeared down the lane towards Harrogate. They wouldn't be back for hours as Tina was going to pick Selena up after school, take her into Leeds to see Santa, do a little Christmas shopping and have a special tea.

The house was deathly quiet without Selena's happy chatter. The peace usually settled on Lucy like a cloak of calm but today it didn't and she suddenly felt terribly lonely and isolated. She stared out at the big garden. There was no-one around and unless someone was specifically coming to visit her, no cars would venture down the lane. She was alone and lonely. Depression waved over her like a huge black velvet blanket and she sank slowly onto the kitchen floor and wept. She wept for the loss of David who had let her down so badly and for Selena who wouldn't have the security of a decent man in her life. She wept for the Hall which had just lost a brilliant general manager who could never be replaced. Then she wept at the bleak outlook for the remainder of her life, without a husband or more children and then she wept for the millionth time about Jeremy and what he had done to her. She would never ever recover from that ordeal and now, David's betrayal, had piled more misery on top of it. She obviously wasn't worthy of a man's real love. She was useless, unwanted, unloved. She was a waste of space. She wept uncontrollably. Great shudders enveloped her body and that was how Delia and Brian found her thirty minutes later.

* * *

Delia hadn't wanted to remain at Blairness any longer than necessary after Lucy's distressed call the day before, even though it would mean missing the staff party on Saturday. Instead, Delia asked Gerald to summon all the staff to the grand hall that afternoon, apologised profusely that she and Brian had to leave, thanked them all for their hard work and handed out their presents. They then had an early dinner with Crystal and Gerald, retired at a sensible time and left the castle at 5.00 a.m. this morning. Not wanting to bother the elderly McFrains, Crystal had hauled herself out of bed even earlier to prepare breakfast, not wanting to see Delia and Brian leave without something decent inside them on such a cold and miserable day. She saw them off, sad they were leaving but understanding Delia's need to be with Lucy. She was far more important and Crystal, who had a lot of time for Delia's daughter, hoped she would be okay. With Brian driving, they drove away, waving to Crystal, standing outside the front door in the floodlights, becoming smaller and smaller in their mirrors and then disappearing from view once they turned out of the gates.

Due to heavy rain there had been a little localised flooding which meant a couple of detours but once they were out of Scotland there were no more hold ups and the remainder of the journey down to Yorkshire went reasonably smoothly. They only stopped once at a service station for a quick coffee and for Delia to take over the driving from Brian. She drove faster than he and they arrived in Canleigh village just before 10.00 a.m. and then headed straight down the back lanes to Dingle Dell.

Delia had jumped out of the car first, eager to see Lucy and ascertain for herself exactly what state of mind her daughter was in. She knocked on the front door of the bungalow and then turned the knob and entered.

"Lucy?" she called, knowing she was probably around somewhere as her car was outside. "Lucy … it's us … where are you?"

She checked the lounge, smiling at the sight of the beautifully decked Christmas tree and the presents already beneath it. Little Selena was going to have a great time opening most of them. Then she went through to the kitchen.

"Oh God, darling," she moaned, seeing Lucy on the floor, sobbing her heart out, her face red and blotchy and her eyes sore from so much crying.

"Oh, I'm so glad to see you," Lucy cried, stretching out her arms for Delia to pull her upright.

Delia threw her arms around her daughter and hugged her close. "Come on, darling. Let's get you somewhere more comfy … and a drink. Coffee, I think, laced with a brandy. Where is Selena?"

"Tina has taken her to school," Lucy replied, her voice shaky. "Then later they are going into Leeds for tea and to see Santa."

"Good. That will give us plenty of time to get you looking a little more cheerful," said Delia firmly, propelling Lucy through to the lounge, sitting her down on the sofa and covering her with a multi-coloured velvet blanket which Selena often cuddled up in. "Now, you stay there while I make the drinks. Brian and I are in need of something too ... we haven't had anything for around three hours."

Brian had brought all their luggage into the hall and looked at Delia questioningly as she passed him on the way to the kitchen. She shook her head and pursed her mouth. "She's distraught ... go and have a word with her please, darling ... while I make the coffee."

Brian did as he was told. He loved Lucy as if she were his own and hated thinking of her being distressed in any way. He strode through to the lounge and straight up to her, knelt down and cuddled her close. He stroked her hair away from her face and kissed her cheek.

"Oh, Lucy. I am so very sorry. I never thought for one minute that David would let you down. I really thought you had found happiness this time and I was so pleased for you."

"I know. I can't believe it either," she gulped, trying to stop the flow of tears. She must really look a pathetic sight.

Brian took some tissues for the box on the coffee table and wiped her eyes gently. "Well, we're here now and we're going to help you in any way we can to get over this."

"Thank you," she whispered, wondering what they were going to say when they knew the whole truth.

Delia returned to the lounge carrying a tray with three steaming mugs of coffee and a plate of banana sandwiches. She knew they were Lucy's favourites, quick to prepare and would assuage hunger until lunchtime. She handed Lucy her mug, the aroma of brandy filling the air.

"Here. Drink this. It will help steady you and make you feel a little better," she commanded. "And when was the last time you had something to eat?" handing her the plate of sandwiches.

"I don't know," Lucy whispered, sipping the coffee, the brandy making her cough it was so strong. "Probably yesterday ... at breakfast," knowing full well she hadn't been able to touch a thing since she had seen David in his office yesterday morning.

"Well, that's not going to help, is it? So, eat those sandwiches for now and I'll make us a lovely lunch once I've poked around the kitchen to see what you have."

"The fridge is full ... so there's plenty of choice," Lucy said faintly, letting the brandy do its job. It was warming her, a lovely welcome glow going all the way through her body.

"Oh, you had left this in the kitchen," said Delia, picking up the envelope Tina had brought in earlier, from the tray. "It feels like a dvd. I hope it's something nice ... something to cheer you up."

Lucy took it shakily. She didn't want to open it but both Delia and Brian were watching her and would think it strange if she didn't ... and anyway, it might not be what she thought it was. But the plain dvd was exactly the same as the last one. She let out a cry of anguish and let it slip through her fingers on to the floor.

"Whatever is it, darling?" queried Delia, startled by Lucy's expression of sheer horror.

Without waiting for an answer, she picked it up and looked at it, turning it over to see if there was any indication of what it could contain or who had sent it. Nothing. No clue whatsoever.

"I think we need to see this," she said firmly, marching towards the television and dvd player in the corner of the room.

"No," whispered Lucy. "Please, no. I simply can't bear it," and dissolved into the most heart wrenching bout of weeping Delia and Brian had ever witnessed.

CHAPTER 36

"It's the same one," sobbed Lucy. "I just know it is. Why send it to me again?" Her hands were clenched and she was shaking uncontrollably.

"What do you mean ... again?"

"I .... I had the first ... yesterday morning ... before ... before I discovered David had tried to steal the takings."

Delia stared hard at her distraught daughter. She didn't want to do this but she had to know what had upset Lucy so badly.

"I'm sorry, Lucy ... but I need to know what the hell is causing you to be in such a terrible state," said Delia firmly, placing the dvd into the machine and switching it on, ignoring Lucy's groan of agony.

Lucy put her head in her hands, embarrassed and ashamed that her mother was now going to see David's degradation and there was nothing she could do to stop her.

Delia watched the film with mounting horror and disbelief. Brian shifted uneasily on the sofa beside Lucy, holding her hand tightly and in between glances at the television screen, watched the expression on Delia's face. It disturbed him more than he would have liked. She didn't just look angry, she looked at boiling point. She was breathing deeply and gritting her teeth.

"I think we've seen enough, Delia. Please turn it off," he said.

"No wonder you sent him packing, darling," said Delia quietly, hitting the stop button on the remote and turning to look at her daughter. "What a despicable thing to do to you ... and send you the evidence. I can't believe how cruel he has been ... and to send it to you twice, that is nothing short of sick ... and who are these dreadful women? Prostitutes I suppose, the way they are behaving. You are well shot of him, Lucy, that's for sure and if I ever get my hands on him ...,"

Brian looked grim. He had seen some pretty dreadful things in his time but to see someone he had liked and was looking forward to welcoming into the family behaving in such an appalling manner was sobering ... and now he was going to worry himself sick about Delia. He didn't like the way she was striding around the room, shaking her head and throwing her hands through her hair with exasperation.

"You can't let him get away with this, Lucy," Delia said forcefully. "Taunting you. If this is the second one you've received, it's harassment and needs reporting to the police. Did you mention it to them when you reported him for theft?"

Lucy looked at her mother with despair, terrified to see her so angry, knowing her next words were hardly going to calm her temper. In between desperate sobs, she took a deep breath. "I didn't call them."

"What?" Delia's voice was rising. "Why the hell not?"

"Because ... because I felt so ... so humiliated ... I just wanted David out of the Hall as soon as possible. I couldn't bear to look at him or be in the same room with him and I certainly couldn't take questioning from the police and then there were all the staff and the guests ... all wondering what was going on. The stealing was bad enough but if any of them got wind of this ...,"

"Oh, darling," Delia sighed, sinking to her knees beside Lucy and taking her in her arms. "I am so very sorry. What an absolute rotter he is ... he knew how vulnerable you were ... but he's done so much to boost you up ... so why is he shattering it now? It all seems extremely peculiar and what has he gained from it? He's had to skulk away with his tail between his legs and will have totally ruined his career. He'll never get another job in a decent hotel again. He's finished and it's crazy ... and why would he keep sending you the dvd? What does he hope to gain by it?"

"He wouldn't be so damned stupid ... it's someone else ... someone who really wants to upset you and break you and David up, Lucy. Have you any idea who it could be?" pondered Brian.

"No ... I'm going crazing thinking about it but in the end, it isn't really that important. The fact of the matter is that he's betrayed me in the most despicable way and could have been doing so for a very long time and thank God I found out before the wedding. God, I just hate him," Lucy cried, "and I could kill him for wrecking Christmas. I'm going to find it so hard to be cheerful, especially for the children."

"Oh yes, the children ... I had forgotten whatshername is coming ... and her boy," remarked Delia absentmindedly, her mind working overtime to think who could be behind this latest turn of events in her daughter's life.

Brian handed Lucy the box of tissues from the coffee table. She took a couple and wiped her eyes.

"Suzanne ... and Daniel. She's lovely and so is he. They've had a rotten year too with Todd walking out on them and then having to come home from Australia and re-start their lives."

Relieved to be able to change the subject and hopefully allow her mother's attention to be diverted from David and his misdemeanours, Lucy continued. "She's done a brilliant job at The Beeches, opening the hair salon ... she's a fabulous stylist and has built up the business very quickly. Aunt Vicky is thrilled with her. Suzanne's helped me with the salon down at the stable block too. It's all up and running beautifully down there now and doing very well."

"Thank goodness for that," Delia said. "I've been telling you that it's a wasted space for years and you should do something with it before it falls down around your ears."

Lucy managed a weak smile. "Yes, and while you're here you must have a look. I think you will be suitably impressed, especially with the coffee shop which has the best pies and pastries in Yorkshire. The whole scheme has proved highly lucrative as not only do our residents like to take a wander down there and spend but we have a large number of non-residents coming to the Hall for lunch or afternoon tea and then they very often have a walk around the lake and the grounds and pop into the stable block to buy a few things from the gift shop or plants, jewellery or beauty products before they leave."

"Well, that all sounds really good, darling. We'll definitely have to have a look, won't we, Brian?" Delia said quietly, pleased to see Lucy looking a little more in control of her emotions. She, however, was still seething inside and wasn't going to let it rest until she found out who was sending these dvd's. Who was it out there who wanted to hurt her daughter so badly? When she found out, their life wouldn't be worth living.

* * *

Katrina walked around all day with a smile on her face. She was rid of Leo and Kevin, she was rid of David and wondered how soon she could be rid of Lucy.

She was busy all day, having to do a turn in the bar until the agency sent two girls to take the place of Leo and Kevin. She pandered to the guests, was pleasant to the staff and crept around Adrian by making a huge fuss of Cherub and offering to take her for a walk around the lake during her break while Adrian settled himself in. He had a lot to acquaint himself with in a short space of time with so many guests arriving for the Christmas festivities. Pete and the rest of the staff were run off their feet, doing their best not to look harassed or stressed. Katrina just smiled. She couldn't help it. She was in her element and felt more in control of her destiny than she ever had. What a fool she had been, thinking she could make a career in the film industry, for which she would have to work bloody hard, when all she could ever want was right here, beneath her nose.

"Katrina ... would you mind waitressing this evening, please," said Pete, pouring over the rotas when Katrina appeared back in the office with a grubby looking Cherub, who had decided to try and greet the ducks in the muddiest patch of the lakeside path. "We're a waitress down as Sheila has sprained her blasted ankle this morning." He hated asking Katrina, expecting her to moan loudly as she loathed waitressing. To his surprise, she smiled.

"That's absolutely fine, Pete. I don't mind. I don't mind at all."

*　*　*

"I think we should go home," said Ruth to Philip that evening as they were dressing for dinner. "I'm really worried about Lucy."

"She'll be fine, darling. She has Katrina, Suzanne and Tina and it won't be long before Delia and Brian come down from Scotland either ... is it next Sunday they are due? They might even decide to travel down earlier in the circumstances and they will look after her."

"Um. That's true but I feel we should be near, just in case."

"Look, if Lucy wants us, we can be back in a matter of hours ... and she might be damned miserable, but she has got support. There is absolutely no need for us to go home. Now, promise you will stop fretting. You can always ring her again later ... just to make sure ... and if she actually says she wants us, then of course we will go but I really don't think there is any need."

"Okay. You're probably right ... as always," Ruth sighed, checking her makeup in the dressing table mirror. "I just feel so sorry for her ... after all she has gone through in the past ... and now this. It's so damned unfair. I just want her to be happy ... as happy as we are. She's such a lovely girl and deserves it."

Philip pulled her close. "I know ... and maybe it will happen one day. I do hope so."

"I just hope Delia doesn't lose her temper over this and makes things ten times worse."

Philip grimaced. "Oh God, so do I but thank goodness none of us will be in the firing line if she does go berserk again."

CHAPTER 37

Saturday 22nd December/Monday 23rd December 2003

Delia didn't mention anything about trying to find out who was behind what had gone on with David to Lucy again, although she had discussed it with Brian when they were tucked up in bed together. He was of the opinion that they should leave it alone. Whoever it was had had their fun and now David was out of Lucy's life, things should calm down.

"Yes, but she did receive that second dvd after David had left," insisted Delia. "What if she receives another? Do we stand by and do nothing then?"

"Let's just wait and see what happens, hopefully nothing … hopefully whoever it is will become bored if there is no reaction but if another dvd does turn up, we will have to try and persuade Lucy to contact the police. We can't sit back and let it go on. It will destroy her. Anyhow, whatever happens, we can get Christmas over with and on Boxing Day, or the day after, we will take her and Selena back to Glentagon. I've had a word with her and she's keen on the idea. I don't think she's been away from Canleigh and Dingle Dell since they last came up to us in the summer and it will do her the world of good to have a break and give us all something to look forward to."

Delia had to be happy with that and as the days wore on towards Christmas, she began to relax as no more strange packages arrived to upset them all again. However, she was deeply concerned about Lucy who was listless and showed little interest in anything that was going on around her, not even the Hall; letting Adrian, Pete and Katrina run the show without even querying if things were going well.

But then, on the morning of 22nd December, there was something else to think about. Brian woke her with a gentle kiss and murmured in her ear. "Happy anniversary, Delia ... and may there be many more."

Delia smiled and curled up in his arms. "Amen to that."

"I want us to drive up to Malham Cove today," he said. "I've checked the weather and it's supposed to be an okay day for December so I think we can enjoy a bracing walk there and then drive back via Bolton Abbey and have a bite to eat at the Duke of Devonshire's place ... the Devonshire Arms. I've heard it's rather good, to say the least ... and we might even book a room for the night," he grinned.

Delia grinned back. "That's a rather nice idea ... as much as I love staying with Lucy, it's a bit restricting on the sexual front. I know she's not listening ... probably doesn't care a fig anyway what we get up to but I would hate to think she could hear us enjoying ourselves when she is so damned miserable."

"I know. Poor kid. Poor us ... being so constrained for the last fortnight. We'll make up for it later today, I promise," he smiled, running his hand down her face. "You do know how much I love you, don't you, Delia?"

Her eyes locked with his. "Yes, darling. I know ... and I love you just as much too. You are the very, very best thing since sliced bread ... but why Malham Cove?" she added as an afterthought.

"Because that's one of our favourite spots ... and I want us to go back as there's something I want to give you and I think that's the right place to do it."

"Oh," she pulled herself up and looked at him questioningly. "What is it?"

He laughed. "You can beg and flutter your eyelashes as much as you like, but I am *not* going to tell you. As much as I know it pains you, you will just have to be patient."

"God, Brian Hathaway, you can be damned exasperating at times!"

"I know ... but you don't mind really as you love me so much," he grinned, running his fingers down her face. The scar, that awful mark which had ruined her right cheek for so long was virtually invisible now. Once they had married, she had been determined to look her best for him and endured three more painful operations to rectify the damage and it had worked. He hadn't wanted her to go through it. The scar hadn't concerned him one iota but she had insisted. She had been beautiful before but now, in her early fifties, she was more stunning than ever and he was tremendously proud of her.

She kissed him and slid back down the bed to be enfolded in the safe haven of his arms, closing her eyes with a wistful smile playing around her lips, letting her mind drift back to the last time she and Brian had visited Malham Cove. Even though the awesome beauty spot wasn't a million miles away from Canleigh, she had never been there until last year when they had been visiting Lucy in August, while Ruth and Philip were away and the coast was clear with no chance they would bump into each other. They hadn't intended visiting Malham but on returning from a fabulous day out at Aysgarth Falls, they had passed the sign for the Cove and decided to do a detour. It was a glorious evening by the time they reached it, parked the car and meandered in soft sunshine towards the majestic rock formation with such an amazing view. It had been one of the most romantic evenings of Delia's life and she would never forget it; Brian with his arm firmly around her waist, telling her how much he loved her, his head brushing hers, the gentle touch of his lips on her cheek, the birds beginning their evening twittering ritual. They had stood for ages, watching the most spectacular sunset, at one with the glories of nature and the environment. It was etched on her memory as being one of the most special moments of her life and she was pleased he had thought of going back there today ... although she was deeply intrigued, wondering what it was he was going to give her. She really had everything she ever wanted ... as long as he was by her side, she lacked nothing.

* * *

They left Dingle Dell just after 10.00 a.m., Lucy and Selena waving them off. Delia had felt a trifle guilty for deserting them for twenty-four hours but Lucy had been totally understanding.

"It's your wedding anniversary and you must spend it together. You certainly don't want to have us around you on one of your most special days of the year. I'm just so pleased for you that you found Brian and you are both still so happy. So, go, have a lovely time and don't worry about us. We will be absolutely fine. Tina is coming over to help with Selena and I am going to make a huge effort and go up to the Hall to see how the team are getting on. I really have been terribly remiss in that area of my life. Thank goodness Adrian, Pete and Katrina have it all in hand. Even so, I should show my face."

So, they had driven away from Dingle Dell and headed towards Malham, Brian teasing Delia all the way as to what he was going to give her. He had no packages with him that she could see so the nearer they drew to the famous Yorkshire attraction, the more curious she became.

"You'll have to wait until we're standing at the top, where we were before," he said firmly, turning the car off the main road and along the B roads towards their destination. "I'm so relieved it's a reasonably decent day. It wouldn't have been such a good idea if the wind was high or we had torrential rain."

It wasn't even particularly cold, just chilly but that didn't matter. Both wore thick wool coats and Delia had on her thermals, which she was rarely without during the winter months. They might not be sexy but were certainly very practical.

Just as they had on their last visit, they drove through the pretty little village and up to the tiny car park near to the gate for the

Cove. The sun came out to welcome them as they held hands and walked towards the massive rock formation. It bathed the ancient limestone rock formation in a glow of light, making it look even more spectacular.

Brian didn't say a word, just smiled secretively at Delia now and again. He knew he was driving her nuts but didn't care. He wanted her to remember this day until she took her dying breath.

Eventually they reached the spot they had stood on before, with the amazing view of the beautiful Yorkshire Dales laid out in front of them. Apart from a couple of hikers in the distance, they had the place to themselves.

He turned to her, holding her face in his hands. "I wanted to bring you here as our last visit was so very special and I wanted to make today even more so. You know how much I love you, Delia … and how I want us to remain as close as we are for the rest of our lives. I never want to be apart from you … ever … you are the most precious thing I have ever had in my life and that's why I want you to have this."

He reached into his coat pocket, brought out a small box and opened it. The eternity ring, encrusted with six diamonds, sparkled brilliantly in the sunshine.

"I want you to have this, as a symbol of how much I love you and how we really will be together for eternity," he said, gazing straight into her eyes. "I don't ever, ever want us to be apart … not in this life or the next."

It wasn't often Delia wanted to cry but she did now, the tears sliding gently down her face. "Oh, Brian. Thank you so much," she gulped as he took off her glove and slid it along her finger to sit with her wedding and engagement rings. "That's a lovely thing to say and do. I so want that too … to be with you … for always."

He gently wiped away her tears with his finger and kissed her brow, the tip of her nose and her mouth. His voice was gruff. "I think it's time we headed off to the Devonshire Arms. I want to spend the rest of the day and night making up for the last celibate fortnight. I want to make love to you again and again. God, Delia, I love you so very much."

* * *

They booked out of the Devonshire Arms the following morning, more in love than ever if that was at all possible, and although Delia adored her wedding and engagement rings, her new eternity ring was even more special and she couldn't stop looking at it on the way back to Dingle Dell. She would always think of the moment Brian had given it to her every time she glanced at it.

Lucy and Selena were pleased to see them, Selena even more excited now that it would soon be Christmas Day and it wouldn't be long before she could unwrap all the presents that sat beneath the tree in the drawing room.

"Lead me to the kitchen," joked Brian when they had said their hello's. "I'll make a start on preparing the food for the next couple of days ... and I don't want any help from any of you three ladies." He grinned at Selena. "You can all go off and play."

Lucy was tremendously grateful how Brian had taken charge of the kitchen for the last few weeks. He loved to cook and didn't often get the chance since moving to Glentagon so he was in his element at Dingle Dell, especially at such a special time of year and could really go to town over the next couple of days.

"That's a great idea," agreed Delia, looking at Lucy. "Let's wrap Selena up nice and warm and get up to Canleigh and walk around the lake. Would you like to go and feed the swans and ducks, darling?" she said to her granddaughter, who was sitting on her lap.

Selena nodded her head vigorously.

"Go and get your coat then ... and you, Lucy. It will do you the world of good too, getting some fresh air into your lungs," she said, looking at her daughter's pale and pasty face.

"Yes, you're right. It will," replied Lucy but with little enthusiasm.

They drove over to Canleigh in Delia's Range Rover, parking near to the stable block from where they could easily reach the path leading to the lake.

"Ice cweem?" asked Selena, peering hopefully through the entrance at the coffee shop.

"Not now, darling," said Lucy. "We're going to have a nice walk and then go home for tea … and I think there just might be some ice-cream for you then."

Delia stood beneath the arched entrance to the stable block and looked around wistfully. How different it was now with the little shops and such a lot of people milling about. Not at all like it had been when she was a child when this part of Canleigh had been so important to her; being here with the horses and ponies, learning to ride, helping to groom them, muck out, clean the tack … right up until that day she had tried to hang herself in Demon's stall. She shuddered and touched the three rings on her wedding finger. She had been in such a bad place that day and for years after. Brian had changed all that and if she had succeeded in killing herself, she would never have known the pure joy of being his wife. She really was a very lucky woman.

Even so, she couldn't help staring straight at the plant shop where Demon's stall had been, pushing down the urge not to cry. She still mourned the blasted horse. She had loved him so much.

Brushing away a tear, she turned to Lucy and made a huge effort to smile. "You've done an amazing job, darling. It's obviously proving popular and I'm so pleased you decided to take my advice with the old place."

They turned and headed down the path towards the lake. It was nearly midday and the walk would take around an hour, so they would be back at Dingle Dell just in time for the sumptuous lunch Brian had promised them.

They didn't talk much, Lucy because she was still finding it hard to make idle conversation and Delia because she wanted to soak up the atmosphere of the Canleigh estate. It was like drinking a beautiful thick syrupy nectar. It was tantalising sweet and wonderful, her old home. She adored Glentagon, she loved Blairness but Canleigh would always be deep in her blood and although she was more than happy for Lucy to be its custodian, her passion for the estate would never truly die.

The two women watched as Selena fed the ducks and swans that surrounded her as soon as they realised the little girl had a bag full of wild bird food for them. Lucy always kept some in for these occasions as she was well aware that they shouldn't be fed bread. Selena laughed as she threw it into the water and they gobbled it up greedily. Delia and Lucy smiled. The child's pleasure was infectious.

"Actually, I did want to talk to you about something," said Lucy thoughtfully.

"Oh?" said Delia, tearing her eyes away from her granddaughter to Lucy.

"Yes. I'm going to change my will."

Delia looked at her with surprise. "Okay, so what's brought that on?"

"Well, after the complete debacle I've made of my last two serious relationships, I don't intend to become entangled with a man again and, therefore, there will be no more children," she said sadly. "And Selena obviously can't be responsible for Canleigh. As you know, Aunty Vicky agreed to be my heir when I inherited it … you were out of prison but were still on licence and it just wouldn't have been wise, in the circumstances, to have left it to you. However, I've been giving it a lot of consideration lately, especially since Aunt Vicky hasn't been well. She mentioned to me months ago that she would like to retire early and move abroad and if something happened to me, she certainly wouldn't want the responsibility of Canleigh now.

"So, what do you intend doing with it ... not that anything is going to happen to you, you silly girl," Delia said fondly, her eyes firmly on Selena in case she stepped too far into the lake in her little red wellies.

"I'm going to leave it to you ... you've always wanted it ... so it's only right you should have it and if I do die, you'll be the best person for it."

"But ... but we live at Glentagon ... and I've got Blairness ... how the hell could I ever look after Canleigh too?" said Delia, bewildered and shocked at her daughter's statement. "And with Ruth and Philip living next door ... but anyway, this is ludicrous. You're not going to die before me. God, I'm years older than you and will be gone long before you are."

"You wouldn't have to live here ... run it as you do Blairness. Get the best staff to look after it ... look how well Crystal and Gerald have cared for Blairness. The same could happen here. I'm serious ... and if I know you're happy about it, then it will set my mind at rest. Honestly. This is what I want to do ...,"

Delia threw an arm around her daughter and hugged her close, unable to believe that she was actually being offered Canleigh, the one place she had hankered after owning since a small child but had given up hope of ever getting her hands on long ago ... and she certainly didn't want it if it meant Lucy wouldn't be around, although she could hardly say that now. The girl's mind had to be put at rest.

"Oh, darling. That is so very, very kind of you and yes, of course I would look after the place properly if anything awful happened, you know I would ... but nothing will, darling, nothing will. You're going to live to a ripe old age and quite possibly marry at some point and have more children."

"I don't think so but thank you ... I feel loads better now and I'm sure Aunty Vicky will be, when I tell her she's off the hook."

"What about Ruth and Philip though? They won't be at all happy to hear about this."

"I have a sneaky suspicion that they are going to move abroad too in the not too distant future … Granny Ruth has a hankering for Italy and whatever she decides, I am pretty sure Steppie will go along with it. They are as inseparable as you and Brian."

Delia wrinkled her nose. "That's nice."

Lucy managed a laugh. "Yes, it is, Mother dear," linking arms with her and giving her gloved hand a squeeze.

Selena suddenly gave an almighty sneeze and started to cough. Lucy handed her a tissue. "Oh dear, darling. I do hope you're not going down with a cold for Christmas."

Selena sneezed again. "Ice cweem," she said hopefully.

Delia grinned. "You don't give up, do you? Come on then. Let's get back to the car as we're getting chilly standing here and if you are a really good girl, I'll ask Grandpa Brian to give you some when we get home … I think there's some really nice chocolate ice cream in the freezer and I have a sneaky suspicion that it's your favourite."

Selena nodded enthusiastically as they all turned to head back to the car, walking just a little quicker than they had on the way down.

* * *

Suzanne was exhausted. It felt like nearly everyone in Harrogate wanted their hair done at The Beeches before Christmas and she would be jolly glad to get back to the tiny cottage and relax this evening. Knowing that she was working flat out until the salon closed for Christmas tomorrow afternoon, the parents of one of Daniel's friends had invited him to their home this morning for a sleep over tonight, so she didn't have him to worry about, which was extremely helpful. The salon was closed on Christmas Eve so she was planning to spend the whole day with Daniel, just him and her, as they would be with the family at Dingle Dell on Christmas Day.

However, it would be strange being without her son this evening although it would provide the chance to finish wrapping his presents and then put her feet up and watch television and if there wasn't anything decent on, there was always one of her favourite dvd's ... anything which starred Hugh Grant would be a real treat. Then, just a few hours at the salon to get through tomorrow, a cosy evening with Daniel to look forward to and then it would be the big day itself. Daniel could open his presents, they could have a light breakfast and attend church in Harrogate before driving over to Dingle Dell for lunch.

Suzanne had mixed feelings about spending Christmas day at Dingle Dell. It was so kind of Lucy to invite them but it would be a bit daunting. However, it would be nice for Daniel to have little Selena to play with. She wondered how poor Lucy was going to cope with having a houseful of people. It wouldn't be easy for her, trying to be jolly when her heart was probably breaking.

Suzanne wasn't sure how she felt about meeting Lady Delia and her husband, the Earl of Glentagon, who were an unknown quantity. Suzanne knew all about Delia being the black sheep in the family with the horrendous past, although supposedly, she had changed dramatically since her marriage ... and Lucy obviously loved her ... so hopefully spending a few hours in her company wouldn't be too taxing.

And then there would be Katrina ... so intensely jealous, so self-centered, so damned selfish. The girl needed a good shaking for the anguish she had put her mother through recently and it was going to be pretty difficult being civil to her.

It was going to be a strange Christmas lunch in no mistake, with a somewhat difficult set of people to share it with. Thank goodness it would only last a few hours and then she and Daniel could escape back to the cottage and she didn't intend sharing him with anyone on Boxing Day. They were going to have a marvellous time all on their own.

* * *

"Selena is asleep," announced Lucy, entering the drawing room to join her mother and Brian, having given her daughter a bath and put her to bed. "She's curled up with Coco as usual, still coughing a bit so I've given her some Calpol which will give her a good night's sleep. She's probably just exhausted, having had a pretty hectic time of it over the last few days with all the pre-Christmas excitement."

Delia smiled. "She certainly loves that cat, bless her."

"Yes, she does. I had considered getting a dog but I'm a bit like Aunt Vicky, I don't think I want to cope with all that mud and dog hair," Lucy sighed. "Coco fits in well. She's out and about most of the day and then curls up with Selena at night. She's really no trouble at all."

"It might be an idea to get a dog though, darling, now you don't put the security lights on at night because of the wildlife disturbing you. You're terribly isolated down this lane and living here, just on your own with Selena … it makes you pretty vulnerable, especially as you're so wealthy and well known," warned Delia. She hadn't been so concerned when she knew David was about to move in on a permanent basis but the prospect of Lucy and Selena being alone in the future was worrying, especially after this dvd nonsense. There might still be someone out there who wished Lucy harm.

"Um. You might be right. I'll give it some thought after Christmas and all our guests have gone home."

Lucy suddenly felt a deep desire to crawl into bed and cry. Depression, as much as she didn't want to let it take hold, kept descending on her. Her heart was heavy and she felt utterly exhausted. She didn't think she had ever felt so miserable in her life, even more than when she had been so badly treated by Jeremy and she had felt really bad then. This was ten times worse and she had no idea how she was going to get through Christmas day, having to put on a front for her guests. Boxing Day couldn't come soon enough.

CHAPTER 38

Christmas Day 2003

Katrina was looking forward to spending the day at Dingle Dell and to see how Lucy was faring. Hopefully she would be in the throes of despair and misery, hopefully she would be depressed and suicidal ... and if she wasn't, her unexpected present this morning might help her on the way.

She yawned. She hadn't had much sleep again last night, getting up at 1.00 a.m. to cycle over to Dingle Dell and post another dvd through the letterbox. It had been an exhilarating experience, cycling along the lanes, finding her way around the potholes with the aid of the bicycle lights, then creeping up to the bungalow and delivering her present.

"Happy Christmas, Lucy," she had whispered on her way back to Canleigh.

However, even though she was tired, she was awake early, packed all the presents she had brought for the family in her holdall, slipped the last remaining dvd of David's little party into her handbag and then left the Hall, waved a cheery goodbye to the reception staff who had just taken over from the night porters, and wished them all a happy Christmas. She was lucky to have the day off but Adrian and Pete had insisted as they knew Lucy would want her family around her at the moment. She blew a kiss to Pete who was just heading off to the dining room to supervise breakfast and popped her head around the office door to say farewell to Adrian and Cherub, whom she was growing exceedingly fond of. The dog might look like a lapdog and very twee in her outfits, but she had the heart of a lion and thoroughly enjoyed her romps through the woods with Katrina, who guessed the little dog had never had so much fun in all her life.

"Happy Christmas, Adrian ... and you, my little darling," she said, patting an expectant Cherub on the head, who always assumed that Katrina making an appearance would either mean being handed a biscuit or going for a walk.

"Happy Christmas, Katrina. Have a good day and give my regards to Lucy. Tell her everything is hunky dory here so she can relax and try to enjoy herself." Adrian had been filled in by the agency as to why David had been dismissed and the broken engagement and he felt desperately sorry for Lucy. He had had his heart shattered once and it was a horrible thing to happen, especially at this time of the year.

Katrina walked around to the side of the Hall where all the staff cars were parked, placed her holdall on the back seat of hers and drove off the estate. Just in case anyone happened to be watching her progress, she headed towards Dingle Dell but as soon as she was out of sight of the Hall and reached the fork in the lane where she could either continue to Lucy's bungalow or go through the back lanes to the main road for Harrogate, she chose the latter, putting her foot down as she wanted to get this little job over with as fast as possible. The roads were virtually empty this early on Christmas Day and it wasn't long before she pulled up at The Beeches.

She dashed through reception, raising a hand in greeting to Gillian. "I'm so stupid, I left a few things here that I need for today. I'm just popping up to the flat," she said in explanation for her sudden appearance.

She could have taken the lift but couldn't be bothered to wait and ran up the stairs. A pile of unopened Christmas cards lay on the hall carpet by the door and the flat felt sad and forlorn with her parents away. The heating was on and the place had a stuffy atmosphere, unusual as when Vicky was at home, she was always opening windows to let in fresh air.

Katrina moved to the window overlooking the gardens and at the far end, the cottage where Suzanne and Daniel lived. She stood and stared at it, feeling intense hatred for the woman who was going to receive half her inheritance. Blast her. Blast, blast, blast.

Why hadn't she remained in Australia when her marriage disintegrated? Why the hell did she have to come back here and ingratiate herself with their parents again? However, she was going to regret that decision. Katrina was going to make sure of that. She was going to set her up. The idea had dawned on her yesterday and now she was going to carry it out. Because Suzanne had been away from the family since she was around eighteen, none of them knew her as an adult very well so might not find it too difficult to believe she had something to do with discrediting David … when presented with the evidence … although why she would have done it was anyone's guess but that didn't really matter. She could have been jealous of Lucy … having it all, when she had just lost her home and her husband and had to start again. It really wasn't important. The fact that she might have been involved would be enough to make everyone think twice about her and not trust her so implicitly, that was if they ever found out.

Katrina nibbled her lip, deep in thought. Would Suzanne actually tell anyone about the items she was going to find in the next day or so? If she did, she was risking her innocence in the whole affair not being believed, which might lead to the police being involved. It would also result in their parents distrusting her and then being more easily persuaded to disinherit her. However, if Suzanne realised how vulnerable she was and kept her mouth shut, it would be tantalisingly easy to blackmail her into giving up her half of the inheritance, especially if little Daniel was threatened too. Bloody hell. What a fantastic way to get the damned woman off her back. Suzanne would lose whether she told or kept quiet. What a fantastic twisted end to the plot to get rid of David and Lucy and prove to her parents that Suzanne really wasn't worth bothering with, let alone leaving her half their fortune.

Turning from the window, she took a small bag from her room to give credence to her story that she was just picking up some things she needed and left the flat, running down the stairs to the ground floor. Gillian was still in reception, busy talking to a group of guests who were discussing arrangements for lunch. None of them noticed Katrina sidle into the hair salon. She quickly pulled the little package which would destroy Suzanne's hopes of a comfortable future, from her handbag. It contained the fourth dvd, the black felt tipped pen used to write on the envelopes and finally, the receipt from the shop where she had bought and paid for all the items in cash. She placed it into the drawer beneath the bookings desk. Thank goodness it was a cold day and she was wearing gloves so she wouldn't look odd. She had wiped her fingerprints off all the items earlier and when Suzanne opened the package to see what it contained, hers would be all over everything. Perfect!

On leaving the salon, she grabbed a comb from a display stand. Gillian was on the phone in reception, looking straight at her. Katrina waved the comb in the air. "Just borrowed this," she mouthed. Gillian put up a hand in acknowledgement and Katrina hurried outside to her car. She turned onto the main road but pulled into the first layby available. Delving into her coat pocket, she took out the new pay as you go phone which she had bought yesterday when she had managed to get into Leeds for an hour. She typed in Lucy's number to send her a text.

'HAPPY CHRISTMAS, LUCY. HOPE YOU HAVE TIME TO WATCH THE DVD TODAY. AM SURE YOUR RELATIVES WILL ENJOY IT TOO. XXX.

She sent it, slipped the phone back into her pocket and started the car, intending to turn up at Dingle Dell early and offer to help with the lunch preparations while watching events unfold. She drove back towards the Canleigh estate with a wide grin on her face. Quite a bit had been achieved this morning, especially dealing with Suzanne, who probably wouldn't discover the package in the hair salon for a day or two as it wasn't open again until the day after Boxing Day. The result of that would be something to look forward to in the next few days but for now she was off to see how poor, poor Lucy was faring at Dingle Dell with the arrival of the latest dvd and the anonymous text. What a Christmas this was turning out to be.

* * *

Suzanne had been woken by Daniel at six o'clock, eager to see if Father Christmas had visited their little cottage and yelling with delight when he discovered he had. At the foot of his bed was a great big red sack filled with presents and he dragged it through to Suzanne's room, bubbling with excitement.

"Mum ... Mum ... he's been. Look what he's left me," he yelled, jumping onto her bed and shaking her hard.

Suzanne grinned, rubbing her eyes, trying to force herself awake to share in his excitement.

"Oh wow. You must have been really good to receive all of these," she smiled, hugging her son. "Happy Christmas, darling."

"Happy Christmas, Mummy ... can I open them now please?"

Suzanne nodded and pulled herself up to a sitting position, propped up by pillows and settled down to share in Daniel's enthusiasm for each and every one of the presents he opened.

Half an hour later they were surrounded by discarded pretty coloured wrapping paper and although he loved all his other presents, Daniel was transfixed by his new laptop.

Suzanne left her delighted and happy son to play games suited to his age group while she showered and dressed and then went through to the kitchen to prepare a little something to eat. Lucy had rung her yesterday to check she and Daniel were still coming today and had mentioned that her stepfather, the Earl of Glentagon no less, was preparing a sumptuous lunch for them all. However, it was best to have a light breakfast to avoid tummy rumbles in church.

She filled the kettle at the sink and glanced across the lawns at the hotel. She could have sworn she saw someone in the window of Vicky and Alex's apartment at the top of the building ... but they were still away. She stared, trying to make out who it could be and then, as the person moved away, she caught a glimpse of the long auburn hair. It was Katrina. Why was she here? Not that it mattered, after all it was her family home.

Not particularly concerned, Suzanne forgot all about it, although she wasn't looking forward to being in such close proximity to Katrina over lunch. She wanted nothing more than to give the girl a good tongue lashing for being so horrid to Vicky. Yes, it was going to be really hard to be nice to Katrina today but the effort would have to be made.

* * *

Delia and Brian were seething. Lucy was distraught. "Why is someone doing this to me? What have I done that's so bad that someone wants to hurt me so much?" Lucy was crying.

She had woken and automatically turned on her mobile to check if there were any messages. There was one, from an unknown number. She couldn't believe it. She was going to receive another dvd. Whoever it was, wasn't giving up. How many more of the damned things was she going to be sent? She got out of bed and opened her bedroom door. It was there … on the carpet … yet another of those envelopes, with the now familiar scrawl of her name in black felt tip pen on the front. Her heart, already bruised and battered, sank like a stone for the umpteenth time since she had set eyes on the first dvd. The last thing she wanted to be reminded of today, when she had to make an enormous effort to be jolly, for Selena, if no-one else, was David's faithlessness. She had given herself a good talking to on going to bed last night and was determined to push him to the back of her mind but now the whole ghastly episode was firmly at the forefront, the painful hurt rushing back to hit her forcefully again.

White-faced and shaking, with the delicious smell of cooked bacon wafting down the hallway, she headed towards the kitchen where she could hear Delia and Brian chatting happily.

Brian looked up as she entered. "Good morning, Lucy. Would you like me to cook you breakfast?" he asked with a smile.

"No ... thank you," she gasped, holding out the envelope. "They've sent it to me again ... and there's a text on my phone ... look," she said, handing her mobile to Delia.

"No!" they said in unison.

Delia took the phone, read the message and passed it to Brian. "As soon as the shops are open, darling, I think you should get a new phone with a different number ... this has got to stop."

"I agree," remarked Brian firmly, taking the envelope from Lucy's shaking hand. "And this can go where it belongs." For good measure, he stamped on the dvd several times to render it useless and then threw the pieces in the kitchen bin.

"Now, turn your phone off and don't put it on again today. If anyone needs you urgently, they will ring here. We can nip into Harrogate or Leeds in the morning and purchase another mobile for you. Most of the shops will be open as it's Boxing Day ... and while we are there, I think you should report it to the police too."

"Oh God, I can't. I don't want them to see David like that ... it's so embarrassing ... so humiliating. No, whoever it is will get bored soon and stop it."

"I mean it, Lucy. You must report it ... you simply can't allow it to go on and on. We simply have no idea how many more of these blasted dvd's there are and who else might get their hands on them ... and we don't want it getting totally out of hand and something worse happening."

Lucy nodded reluctantly. "Yes, I suppose you're right but I'll only do it if you promise to be there with me."

"That's fine," Brian replied. "As I said, we'll do it all tomorrow morning ... before we leave for Glentagon. Now, would you like something to eat? You hardly had anything yesterday. You must be hungry."

Trying to prevent the tears taking hold at his kindness, she shook her head. "No, thank you. I really can't at the moment and I don't want to spoil my lunch," she added, knowing it was pretty doubtful if she would be able to eat much of that either. "I'll go and shower and get dressed ... and pop in and see if Selena is awake."

She left the kitchen, her shoulders sagging and her head bowed, looking the picture of misery. Delia's heart sunk to see her daughter enduring so much pain and anguish again. If she ever caught up with whoever was doing this to Lucy, the anger she had managed to hold in abeyance for so many years would definitely rear its ugly head because she would do anything, absolutely anything, to protect those she loved.

CHAPTER 39

Christmas Day 2003

Selena was still asleep, although Coco stirred when she saw Lucy, stretched and leapt off the bed to go in search of breakfast in the kitchen. Lucy checked Selena's forehead which was cool. At least she wasn't going to be ill, which was a blessing. She left her to sleep, placing Timpy, the new red and white teddy, a present from Tina, in the space Coco had abandoned.

Trying hard not to cry, she went back to her own room, considering a shower but deciding a bath would be more comforting. She felt deathly tired and her heart was heavy. Just a few weeks ago she had been so looking forward to today, to have a truly happy Christmas with her family ... and David, as her fiancé. It was hard to credit how things had changed in such a short space of time and how different today was going to be. Everyone was going to pussyfoot around her instead of being relaxed and jolly and she was going to have to make a supreme effort not to break down in tears. She badly wanted to crawl back into bed, pull the covers over her head and slip into oblivion with a few of the tablets her doctor had prescribed for her but she couldn't. She had to try and pull herself together, put on a brave act but it was going to be damned hard, feeling so lost and humiliated by David's treachery. God, she would be glad when today was over.

* * *

Katrina reached Canleigh village and turned the car towards Dingle Dell, feeling utterly pleased with herself, wondering what would happen when Suzanne discovered the package and what she would do. Would she actually watch the dvd? Would she torment herself wondering who had placed it in the salon and why? Would she show it to Lucy? Would she realise that she was being set up

... by her own ... *sister*? Katrina wrinkled her nose. *Sister*! She didn't want a bloody *sister*!

Katrina grinned as she passed the Dower House on the way to Dingle Dell. It was all shut up and looked forlorn and empty while it waited for new tenants who were moving in after the New Year. They would have no idea what had gone on there a couple of weeks ago and how it was shaking up the Canleigh family.

She turned up the lane towards Dingle Dell with a sense of excitement bubbling in her tummy. She couldn't wait to see Lucy ... to see the damage she had caused her ... and to silently gloat. An image of herself gliding around Canleigh Hall in a fabulous gold gown, sprang to mind. It was going to come true. She was going to hold a huge ball as soon as she was made the legal owner and she was going to wear that dress and everyone would know she was Katrina Gregory, the immensely wealthy owner of the Canleigh estate. She could see it now. It was coming closer and closer and she was so excited she could burst!

* * *

They were finally ready for church, the cottage was all locked up and all the presents for the family were in the car, along with Daniel who was buckled up in his car seat. However, Suzanne couldn't forget that figure in the top flat. Had it been Katrina? It didn't matter if it was, the girl had every right to be there and it was no business of hers but for some reason she felt a sense of unease. Katrina was a little bitch. Always had been and probably always would be and she didn't trust her ... and if it hadn't been her, it should be reported.

"I'm just going to have a quick word with Gillian," she said to Daniel, switching on the car radio. "Listen to some Christmas music, darling. Won't be long, promise."

Gillian looked up as Suzanne approached the reception desk. "Happy Christmas ... are you off to Dingle Dell now?" she asked.

"Happy Christmas, Gillian. Yes, in a minute … I just wanted to ask … was Katrina here a little while ago … I thought I saw her but wasn't sure."

Gillian nodded. "Yes, said she wanted something from the flat and then came down and went into the salon. She came out waving a comb, so I presume she must have forgotten hers."

"I see," said Suzanne thoughtfully, "so I wasn't dreaming then. Thanks, Gillian."

She walked back out to the car, a puzzled expression on her face. It seemed very odd that Katrina would want to take a comb from the salon. The girl was so vain, she never went anywhere without brush and comb and make-up. Oh well, never mind. In the grand scheme of things, it wasn't that important and if they didn't get a move on, they would be late for church.

* * *

"Well, hello," smiled Delia as she answered the door to Katrina. She hadn't set eyes on her niece since the wedding at Blairness but wasn't surprised to see what a beautiful woman Katrina had turned out to be. An exceedingly attractive teenager, she was now incredibly beautiful with her head of thick auburn hair, her high cheekbones and fabulous, unusual, violet eyes … and her figure was pretty good too with a slim waist and hips and a decent sized bust. She was dressed in a white top and an ochre coloured trouser suit teamed up with brown leather Gucci stilettos and handbag. In her arms were a pile of parcels in gold and silver wrapping.

Katrina smiled back. Aunt Delia didn't look any older than she had five years ago. She was still an amazingly attractive woman, especially now the scar on her cheek was virtually undetectable. Her long dark hair flowed around her shoulders, not a hint of grey as yet, her eyes were bright and clear, her figure as youthful as ever. Delia, the Countess of Glentagon, in a vermilion dress, diamond earrings and three rings on her wedding finger, looked fit and well and extremely good for a woman in her fifties.

"Hello," Katrina replied. "How are you? It seems such a long time since we came up to Scotland for your wedding. I've never forgotten it … that beautiful castle, the ceremony, your fantastic dress. It was such a special day."

"Yes. It was," agreed Delia, shutting the front door behind Katrina and pointing at the drawing room. "Go through," she said.

The enticing aroma of roast turkey and all the trimmings drifting through the bungalow made Katrina realise how hungry she was, having missed breakfast in her haste to get over to The Beeches. The drawing room was a haven of peace and calm with the Bang and Olufsen music system playing Silent Night, along with cinnamon candles on the mantelpiece and a real log fire roaring up the chimney. Coco was curled up in front of it, replete from a good breakfast containing extra bits of bacon Brian had mixed in for a treat.

"Where is everyone?" asked Katrina, placing her parcels with the pile beneath the tree.

"Selena is still asleep, bless her … she has exhausted herself getting so excited about Christmas so Lucy has left her in bed while she's having a bath. Brian is busy in the kitchen. He's in sole charge of lunch … won't let anyone help him," she smiled, terrifically proud of her husband, who she knew was having the time of his life playing chef since they had been at Dingle Dell. "Would you like a drink, Katrina … or coffee?"

"Oh, a sherry please, Aunt Delia. I shan't be driving until much later so I think I can have a small one."

Brian suddenly appeared at the door, Lucy's Christmas apron over his navy slacks and light blue shirt. He smiled widely at Katrina, thinking, as his wife had just done, what an arresting woman she had become.

"Hello," he said warmly, crossing over to shake her hand and kiss her on the cheek. "It's a long time since we saw you. You look wonderful."

Katrina grinned at Delia slyly, wondering how she would take her husband being nice to another woman but Delia looked totally unperturbed as she played with the diamond eternity ring on her finger.

Lucy entered the drawing room, smiled bravely and greeted Katrina warmly. Her dress in sage green did nothing for her pale complexion. Wearing no makeup, she looked quite washed out and defeated. Katrina was elated. Her plan was working.

They talked about non-consequential things while waiting for Suzanne and Daniel to arrive. It was difficult to know what to talk about without upsetting Lucy further, Delia realised. If they mentioned Katrina's work at the Hall, it would remind Lucy of David so it was wise to steer clear of any mention of it. Likewise, Vicky's state of health as Lucy was still furious with Katrina for ignoring her mother's pleas to speak to her. It was a minefield and Delia would be extremely glad when the day was over.

Suzanne and Daniel turned up two hours after Katrina, providing relief from a stilted conversation. They would have arrived earlier but the church had been packed and Daniel was difficult to drag away as he had wanted to exchange details of presents received with his friends.

Suzanne came in all smiles, kissed Lucy and hugged her hard, then turned to Delia and Brian, holding out a hand in greeting. "Hello, Delia … Brian. It's nice to meet you after all this time," she said, thinking what a handsome couple they made and Delia looked nothing like the ogre she had been made out to be.

Daniel looked at Lucy. "Where's Selena? I want to give her my present," he said, holding up a big box wrapped up in shiny red paper with a huge gold bow.

"Well, she was asleep when I looked in a few moments ago but you can go and look ... you know where her bedroom is," Lucy added, managing to smile at his enthusiasm.

The day passed without incident, although none could dismiss the distinct icy atmosphere that existed every now and again when the conversation died. Brian did his best to keep the conversation flowing naturally and Delia tried to back him up but with Lucy on the verge of tears, Suzanne uneasy and watchful of Katrina and Katrina obviously gloating about something which she wasn't going to mention, it was not an easy task.

By mid-afternoon when Lucy was beginning to think she couldn't go on pretending everything was normal any longer, Suzanne and Daniel decided it was time to leave. Selena was tiring quickly again after a busy day playing with Daniel and all their presents and fell asleep on Lucy's lap an hour after their lunch so he was growing bored and petulant and wanted very much to go home and play with his laptop.

As Suzanne began their preparations to leave, thanking Lucy for the hospitality and Brian for cooking such a delicious lunch, Katrina stood up. She had seen enough of Lucy's wretched face for one day and wanted to escape too, especially as she was on duty early in the morning. She wanted to get back to Canleigh and relax for a while, read a book in her room, plan her next move, not that she could do much for a while, apart from send a few more choice texts to her cousin. By the look of her, a few more messages mentioning that lovely little film should be enough to push her over the edge, help her on her way to oblivion.

Lucy carefully moved a sleeping Selena onto the sofa and followed the remainder of the family outside to say goodbye.

While Suzanne was busy buckling Daniel into his car seat, Katrina started her car, waved at Delia, Brian and Lucy standing at the front door and tooted to Suzanne and Daniel. She chortled gaily, heartily pleased with the results of her endeavours to provide a seriously good future for herself as she turned out of Dingle Dell

and headed back to Canleigh, the place she was going to call home
… her very own home … at some time in the future.

CHAPTER 40

Christmas Day/Boxing Day 2003

Suzanne took a tired Daniel home, something still nagging at her about Katrina. The girl had been quite odd all day, with a somewhat triumphant air, as if she was secretly pleased about something but had no intentions of sharing it … and as solicitous as she was towards Lucy, who was obviously deeply distressed and near to tears all day, her sympathy didn't ring true. Katrina wasn't given to showing compassion towards anything or anyone and for her to be so nice to Lucy was just plain odd. No, the girl was up to something and Suzanne wanted to know what it was … and she was still puzzled about her visit to The Beeches and the salon earlier. Katrina was too vain to leave anything behind when she went out, always checking her appearance in the mirror of her powder compact, and fiddling with her hair. No, she wouldn't have had any need to borrow a comb. So, what had she been doing in the salon? The question needled Suzanne all the way back to Harrogate and after she had parked the car, instead of going back to the cottage, she walked straight into the hotel, carrying the presents just received from the family in a huge canvas bag Lucy had lent her. Daniel trotted behind, cuddling a big floppy teddy bear which Delia and Brian had given him.

Suzanne smiled at Alan, the duty receptionist, Gillian having left for the day, wished him a happy Christmas and then marched into the salon, a disgruntled Daniel following.

"Why are we coming in here, Mummy? I want to go play games on my laptop," he whined. He had wanted to get to grips with it all day and any further delay was frustrating.

"We won't be a moment. Just sit there, while I have a look around," she said, standing in the middle of the salon and staring hard at everything. Nothing seemed amiss. Everything was just as it was when she had closed up last night. She moved to the appointments desk. Nothing. Without thinking, she opened the top drawer ... and froze. There was a strange package, nestled between the stapler and hole punch. It wasn't hers ... and it wasn't lost property ... and it hadn't been there yesterday. She knew instinctively, it had been placed there by Katrina. But why ... and more to the point, what was in it?

"Mummy," complained Daniel, bored and tired. "Hurry up."

"Okay, okay," she murmured, her train of thought still on Katrina. She picked up the package and pushed it into her coat pocket. "Come on then, young man. Let's go home."

* * *

With Daniel settled in their cosy little lounge, happily playing games on the laptop perched on his knees, the curtains drawn, the Christmas tree lights twinkling and the gas fire looking cheerful, Suzanne sat opposite him on her favourite chair and opened the package. Already concerned as to what she might find, she was perplexed to discover a black felt tip pen and a dvd in a plain cover, along with a receipt for envelopes, the pen and a set of dvd's, all paid for in cash ... with the faint aroma of Katrina's perfume. She turned the dvd over and over in her hand. What did it contain? She couldn't leave it until Daniel went to bed. She had to find out now.

With Daniel deeply into a battle between two futuristic gangs, she left the lounge and went upstairs to her bedroom where she had a small television and a dvd player. She made sure the bedroom door was firmly shut and sat down on the bed. She played the dvd, shocked to the core by what she was seeing ... David, having rampant sex with a couple of naked women with enormous breasts. It was unbelievable. She was rigid with horror. Poor, poor Lucy. How could David have done this? How could he be so stupid? Hadn't he realised he was being filmed? And who had been behind the camera? Surely not Katrina. The girl was a rotten little devil but surely she wouldn't go this far ... but it all stacked up ... her unusual visit to the salon, the perfume on the package ... and it would account for her somewhat triumphal attitude today at Dingle Dell. But why? Why would she do this to someone as lovely and kind and considerate as Lucy? A member of her own family ... her cousin ... someone who had supported her, given her a job. It beggared belief ... and more to the point, why had Katrina left all this in the hair salon?

With her mind in a whirl, Suzanne sat in the darkness of her room and switched off the dvd. She didn't want to see or hear David in the throes of passion. It was disgusting, obscene, and deeply disturbing but more to the point, so was Katrina for possessing such terrible evidence of David's treachery but why put it in the salon ... and had Lucy ever seen this? Was this the real reason she had broken off the engagement? David stealing all that money from the Hall hadn't felt right, especially as it had all been recovered in his rooms and could quite possibly have been some ghastly mistake ... but this ... if Lucy had seen this film, it would account for David's rapid departure and Lucy's terrible distress.

Without a shadow of a doubt, Suzanne knew Katrina was definitely behind it and she had to talk to someone to make sense of it before she went crazy. She was scared too. If Katrina had done this to get shot of David, she might do something bad to her too, being so mad about having to share her inheritance. Christ, she was going to have to be careful. What a little bitch Katrina was. What a completely evil little cow. Suzanne sat immobilised, the dvd in her hand, seriously alarmed for her own safety and that of her son.

* * *

She slept on it, not wanting to make any rash decisions until she had thought it all through properly. On waking early in the morning, she lay in bed and considered her options. She could get rid of all the evidence, chuck it in the lake or something and no-one apart from her and Katrina would ever know it had been at The

Beeches ... or she could show it to Lucy. She didn't want to do that. She didn't want to hurt the poor girl even more.

She wished Vicky and Alex or Ruth and Philip were at home. She would have taken it to them immediately, discussed the implications with them, receive proper, sage advice but that was impossible and she didn't want to ring them and ruin their holiday. They all needed their break, especially Vicky. No, she had to deal with this herself.

Then she thought of Delia and Brian. After all they were Lucy's parents ... albeit Brian was her stepfather but they were closest to Lucy and would want to protect her. She was loathe to talk straight to Delia, knowing her fearsome reputation but Brian ... he was calm and level headed and would help her think it through and decide what to do for the best ... but how could she get him on his own and talk to him?

Daniel made it easy.

"Brian said he would like to see my games ... and play with me," he said at the breakfast table, wriggling to finish his cornflakes quickly so he could get down and get back to his laptop.

"Did he? That was kind of him," replied Suzanne absentmindedly.

His words suddenly sank in.

"Oh, did he?" she repeated. "Then I wonder if he would mind if we popped over today for an hour or two ... I know they are going to Glentagon later today but Brian might be able to spare a little time. If not, you will have to be content with showing them to me."

Daniels face lit up enthusiastically. "Oh, Mummy, please ring him and see. He'll love the starship one ... it's really cool."

She looked at the clock on the wall. It was still only 8.30 a.m. but someone might be up and she desperately wanted to speak to Brian before the family left for Scotland. She picked up her mobile and rang Dingle Dell immediately, hoping Brian would answer rather than Delia or Lucy. She was lucky. Lucy was still asleep, cuddled up with Selena, and Delia had gone for a walk. Brian had just emerged from the shower but heard the phone and hoping it wouldn't have disturbed Lucy, hurried to pick it up.

"Dingle Dell," he said quietly.

"Oh, Brian. I'm so glad you answered," breathed Suzanne with relief. "Daniel was wondering … you apparently promised to have a game with him and he's dying to show you his laptop. Would it … would it be convenient to pop over this morning for an hour? And, actually, there's also something I need to talk to you about urgently," she added quickly.

Daniel had finished his breakfast, shot through to the lounge and was booting up his laptop. Suzanne shut the door between the lounge and the kitchen and sat down at the breakfast bar.

"I've found something, Brian … something I don't know what to do with … and I think it's something you should see."

"Oh?"

"It's a dvd … someone put it in my salon at The Beeches yesterday …,"

Selena heard Brian groan. "Oh, no," he said. "Have you watched it?

"Yes … it's David … it's disgusting."

"Oh, hell. Another one … Lucy has received three now … but why someone should have sent one to you is a mystery."

"Oh, no, poor Lucy. No wonder she's in such a state … I thought her breakup with David was just over him stealing from Canleigh … not this as well. It's truly shocking."

"She didn't want anyone knowing …," said Brian as quietly as he could, opening the front door and stepping outside so he could talk to Suzanne without Lucy overhearing if she had woken up. "She's desperately upset about it."

"I'm not surprised! It's horrendous … and I can't quite believe it of him. He seemed to love her so much. Why would he do such a thing … and why would anyone video it and then send it to us? It's totally malicious. Has Lucy told the police?"

"No ... she's been too embarrassed. However, Delia and I have persuaded her to and we're going later today ... we're not going to Glentagon until tomorrow now ... but I can't for one moment understand why you have been sent one of the blasted things," he added.

"Well, it's all a bit strange ... it wasn't just the dvd but there was also a black felt tip pen and a receipt, which included a set of dvd's, the pen and some envelopes ... like the one they all turned up in. I just don't understand it."

Brian was silent for a moment, his brain working overtime. "I hate to say this, Suzanne, but I'm wondering if someone has planted it on you, trying to make it look as if you're behind it all, which I am damned sure you aren't."

"Well, of course, I'm not," Suzanne's voice rose shrilly.

"No ... no. I don't think for one minute that you are. Come for lunch. Bring everything over here so we can examine it properly. This should finally convince Lucy that she needs to talk to the police if it's not just her receiving the dvd's. Even though she's promised to, she's still a bit wobbly on that front. Suzanne ... have you any idea who could have left it in your salon?"

"I hate to say it but I think ... I think it was Katrina ... but I'm at a loss to understand why she is being so malicious," she said sadly, feeling an overwhelming sense of helplessness as to how they were all going to deal with the girl and prevent her actions causing more misery and damage to the family, especially poor Lucy ... who didn't deserve any of this ... and then there was Vicky. When she found out what Katrina had done, she would be so desperately upset and Suzanne prayed it wouldn't have impact on her recovery.

"Christ!"

"I know. It's shocking, Brian ... I've always known she can be spiteful and nasty but I never thought she would do something like this ... and for what? I just don't understand it."

CHAPTER 41

Boxing Day 2003

Daniel took no persuading to jump into the car and return to Dingle Dell. With his precious laptop beside him, he chatted excitedly about all the games he was going to show Brian while Suzanne nodded, absentmindedly saying yes and no in the right places. Her mind was in turmoil, taking in what Brian had told her, the contents of the dvd, the chance that Katrina was creating chaos and unhappiness in the family and what for? She was a spoilt and spiteful girl and someone would have to do something about her before ... before what? Before she did something like Aunt Delia?

Suzanne shuddered, recalling all the tales she had been told about Lady Delia's past life ... how mad and bad she had been, although it was hard to credit it now. She appeared to be a thoroughly decent person and seriously in love with her gorgeous husband. Even so, it was hard to forget she had spent 17 years in prison for trying to kill Granny Ruth and Grandpa Philip in a fit of blind rage, with the whole family, apart from Lucy, convinced she had killed her brother and half-brother years earlier. What if Katrina was going to turn out like her? God, it didn't bear thinking about. She couldn't get to Dingle Dell quickly enough to talk it over with Brian and see if they could persuade Lucy to go to the police. Suzanne put her foot down on the accelerator.

They were nearly there now. They had passed the Dower House and were at the turn in the lane for Dingle Dell but neither Suzanne nor Daniel noticed Delia emerging from the woods on her way back to the bungalow. Delia waved and smiled but gained no response.

Brian had been listening for the car and came out to meet them, smiling at Daniel, brandishing his laptop. "Take it through to the lounge and set it up. I just want to have a quick word with your mother," he instructed, smiling as Daniel tumbled out of the car and rushed indoors.

As soon as the boy was out of earshot, Brian held out his hand for the package which Suzanne pulled from her handbag. "It smells of Katrina's perfume," she said.

Brian nodded. He could smell it too. Katrina hadn't covered her tracks very well.

"Have you ... have you told Lucy and Delia?"

Brian nodded. "I told Lucy immediately but Delia hasn't returned from her walk yet so doesn't know. Lucy is naturally flabbergasted and horrified but is keeping a lid on it for now as she has to see to Selena. It's been bad enough telling her of our suspicions but Delia is going to be another matter. It's going to be terribly difficult to keep her calm and the last thing I want is for her to blow her top."

"She's going to have to know sometime ... especially if you decide to go to the police."

Brian's expression was grim. "Christ, Katrina is going to have a lot to answer for. How the hell she could have the effrontery to sit here yesterday and pretend to be so nice ... what a nasty piece of work she really is. I want to go up to the Hall and ring her neck for putting Lucy through all of this ... and what for? What does she hope to gain?"

"I simply have no idea," said Suzanne, resting her body on the side of her car and grimacing. "Katrina has always been a law to herself and all in all, not a very nice person. I can't understand it .... with such lovely parents. She should be like them but she's not. She's horrible, spiteful, jealous ... oh, I can go on and on. She's certainly never been my favourite person and although I tried to be friends when we were growing up, she didn't want to know. I've tried again since returning to the UK but she blanks me at every turn. She's openly hostile and terribly angry that our parents have decided to split their fortune equally between us instead of her having the larger portion. You must have noticed how she avoided me yesterday."

"Yes ... I did wonder about it."

"Well that's why she has it in for me but Lucy ... what has Lucy got that Katrina could possibly want?"

"Canleigh?" suggested Brian, rubbing his chin, his eyes narrowing. "That place has caused such dreadful trauma for this family one way or another but I bet that's what it is ... Lucy had intended leaving it to Vicky ... and Vicky hasn't been well. Everyone also knows that Lucy has struggled with depression for years and she's terribly fragile ... it wouldn't take much ...,"

"No. You can't think Katrina is that evil," Suzanne whispered, terrified that his train of thought was mirroring hers. It made it far more possible if he was thinking along the same lines. "And anyway, Mother is getting better. Father rang us yesterday to wish us a happy Christmas and she came on the phone and sounded great. She's regaining her strength and recovering well ... and as for Lucy ... she's years younger than Mother ... so Katrina wouldn't get Canleigh for a long time anyway ... if ever."

"True but ... and I don't want to upset you ... but what if Vicky had a relapse ... and what if Lucy is sent crazy and demented ... which could be why Katrina is trying to send her over the top. Lucy is terribly vulnerable now ... I know she's mentioned suicide before."

"No! You don't seriously consider it's a possibility?"

"Well, the more I think about it, I do. If Lucy and Vicky were out of the way, Katrina would get the whole shebang, wouldn't she ... at least as far as Canleigh is concerned ... and as for your problem with her, that could be why she is trying to implicate you. If she can discredit you in her parents' eyes, that would put paid to you inheriting anything from them, wouldn't it?"

"Brian ... it's all set up ... are you coming?" cried Daniel, at the front door.

Brian pushed the package into his pocket and smiled at the boy. "Yes … coming." He turned to Suzanne. "Don't say anything to anyone for now, not until we have all had a chance to discuss it properly. I'll talk to Delia later … although I must say, I'm not looking forward to that conversation."

* * *

Delia shifted uncomfortably behind the rhododendron bush at the side of the bungalow nearest to the front door of Dingle Dell.

Having seen Suzanne and Daniel arriving, she had quickened her steps so she could be there as soon as possible after them. She liked Suzanne immensely and little Daniel was a delight and it would be nice to spend some more time with them.

She came in through the back gate at the far end of the lawns and walked around the side of the house. Brian and Suzanne were talking quietly beside her car. Intrigued, Delia stopped behind the dark green rhododendron bush and listened, wanting to know what they were talking about so earnestly.

She heard the whole conversation, first with disbelief and then a growing surge of anger. She could feel it, spreading like wildfire around her body. She itched to have Katrina in front of her right now, right this minute, so she could give her the trouncing she deserved. How dare she do this to Lucy? How dare she deliberately try to hurt her so badly that she might be tempted to end it all? As Brian and Suzanne entered the house and left Delia all alone outside, her fury was intense. She certainly couldn't go back indoors and pretend nothing had happened, that she knew nothing about what had been going on.

She stood and thought hard about Katrina … how she had behaved yesterday. She had had a glow about her, a self-satisfied one, and thinking about it, she had been watching Lucy a lot, albeit with a concerned expression but had that all been a front? Did she seriously wish her real harm? She had to find out. She had to tackle

Katrina ... and now ... she couldn't leave it a moment longer. She had to get up to Canleigh. Katrina was working this morning and should be easy to track down.

Stealthily she crept into the entrance hall, grabbed the keys for the Range Rover from the hall table and shot outside again. Within seconds she had started the car and was heading out of the drive and onto the lane towards Canleigh, the shingle spitting out from beneath the car tyres as she changed gear furiously and sped away.

Brian, who was just sitting down with Daniel by the largest window in the drawing room, saw it all and looked horror stricken at Suzanne. "Christ! I think Delia must have heard us ... she's taken the car and she's heading towards Canleigh ... Katrina's on duty today, isn't she?"

Suzanne's hand flew to her mouth. "Oh my God! Get after her Brian. Take my car ... stop her before she does something dreadful."

She handed him her keys and he didn't waste any time. He careered out of the front door, jumped into Suzanne's car and sped away after Delia, his heart thumping loudly. He had to catch up with her. He had to. If she let her temper get away with her, this could be the end for her. He put his foot down hard on the accelerator, praying he would reach the woman he loved more than anything on earth before she did something really stupid.

* * *

Katrina was in the office but was due on reception at any minute to cover for the lunch break. She would be glad when that little stint was over. She wasn't too keen on having to be nice to the guests who arrived and those who were leaving. The phone never stopped and there was always somebody wanting something. It was a real pain. She dreamt of the day she could dismantle that bloody desk and throw it away and have the entrance hall exactly as it was supposed to be, what it had been built for all those centuries ago. To receive her guests, in her gold ballgown, sweeping down the stairs, impressing everyone with her beauty and her wealth. She smiled to herself as she left the office, making it look as if she was pleased as punch to be taking over reception for an hour or two.

CHAPTER 42

Boxing Day 2003

Delia had never driven so fast and dangerously as she did now, speeding down the country lanes, taking the corners wide, praying she wouldn't meet any dog walkers or horse riders as it was doubtful she could stop the car in time.

She could remember many times when she had been explosively angry in the past, notably when her father had dismissed her offer to care for the estate, when Philip had let her down ... twice ... but this, this was different. This time she wanted to protect and stand up for someone she loved. There was only Brian, Lucy and Selena in her life who were vitally important to her and Delia would do anything in her power to make sure they were all safe from harm and at this moment in time, Lucy wasn't. If Katrina could do what Brian and Suzanne suspected, if she wasn't checked, she could go on and on, driving poor Lucy into a far more serious depression than she was already ... or worse. Bloody, bloody Katrina. She was going to rue the day she crossed Lady Delia Canleigh, that was for sure.

* * *

Katrina was really busy at Canleigh. There were lots of people checking out today following their Christmas break and more checking in for the New Year celebrations. The entrance hall was full of chattering, excited people, some with large families, others who had been before and recognised old friends from past years ... and the phone was constantly ringing.

Katrina was becoming flustered, exasperated and annoyed and would be jolly glad when her stint on reception was over. She wasn't very warm either with so many people coming in and out of the front door, some leaving it wide open, allowing blasts of cold air inside and even with the central heating full on, it hardly made an impact.

With all the chatter around her, she didn't hear Delia's Range Rover skid to a halt just outside the front door or see her run up the front steps but she did hear the door bang loudly as Delia virtually crashed into the entrance hall, making everyone stop talking and look to see who it was.

Katrina glanced at Delia and felt real fear descending on her. Delia's face was contorted with rage, her glinting eyes boring straight into hers.

"You little witch," Delia hissed, "you're going to regret what you've done," as she strode towards the reception desk, pushing people out of her way, others moving back quickly, intrigued or concerned as to why this demented looking woman was heading straight towards the poor, shaking girl on the reception desk. One or two of the men wondered whether they should intervene but decided not. Delia didn't look like someone to cross and then one of the women recognised her.

"'God, it's Lady Delia Canleigh," she whispered to the people near her. "She went to prison for years for attacking two people ... she nearly killed them ... Christ, I feel sorry for that girl. Do you think we should call the police ... and where is the manager? He should be doing something?"

Delia heard the woman but it didn't deter her from approaching her quarry, who was now standing rigid at the reception desk, her eyes wide with terror and her hands clutching the keyboard of the computer in front of her. Katrina couldn't move. She was transfixed, staring at Delia's angry face.

"What do you mean ... what have I done?" her voice was almost a squeak as Delia bore down on her, getting closer and closer until she was there, right in front of her, putting out a hand to grab her uniform and pull Katrina towards her. With their faces only inches apart, Delia lashed out with her tongue again.

"You know damn well what you've done ... ruining Lucy's hopes of a happy marriage ... sending her those God-awful films. You're nothing but a miserable little creature, trying so hard to hurt her, drive her crazy, just so you could get your hands on this place ... oh yes, madam, we've guessed what you've planned but it's not going to work. You're finished now.'"

Katrina was no match for Delia, who might be a good few years older but was far fitter and stronger. Ignoring the gasps from the onlookers, Delia hauled Katrina from the reception desk and dragged her across the entrance hall to the lift lobby, away from prying eyes. She hit the upward button.

"Now get up there and pack your things. You're not wanted here ... not now ... not ever ... and you're to keep away from my family and if we ever hear from you again, you'll be extremely sorry you meddled with me and my family."

"But you can't do this. I work for Lucy ... not you, you evil cow ... and don't pretend you're holier than thou. You spent years in Holloway for your crimes ... you're nothing more than a common old lag ... and how that gorgeous husband of yours can bear to let you into his bed, let alone touch you, is a mystery to me ... but he'll see through you one day and you'll be dumped for a much younger model ... perhaps it might even be me," jeered Katrina, seeing all that she had wished for crumbling around her.

Delia saw the red mist. She had seen it before, when she had trounced Philip all those years ago and then when she had urged Demon to attack Ruth. She lost all control and grabbed Katrina, hitting her again and again around the head, only vaguely aware that Katrina was not retaliating, just cowering, trying to shield her head with her arms.

"You bloody stupid little girl," Delia panted, bringing her hand back to smash it into Katrina again, "I'll bloody kill you first!"

Katrina, realising her life was in real danger and no-one was coming to help her, raised her arm fast and punched Delia straight in the eye. "Leave me alone, you bitch!" she yelled as Delia fell back, holding a hand to her face.

Maddened even further, Delia lashed out again, grabbing Katrina's hair with one hand and smashing a fist into her cheek with the other. Katrina let out a blood curdling yell, the pain excruciating as Delia was nearly pulling her hair out by the roots. She kicked out, landing a blow to Delia's shins, causing her to let go but as Delia's hand went out again, the door to the lift lobby crashed open and Brian flung himself at Delia, grabbing her by the waist and dragging her away from a cowering Katrina, who was rubbing her head with tears of fear and pain running down her cheeks. She really had met her match with Delia and was seriously terrified.

"Let go of me, Brian," yelled Delia. "I'm going to kill her."

"No. No, you're not. For God's sake, Delia, see sense. I don't want you going back to prison. We'll sort it properly … report it to the police … and she can be the one to go down."

"What for? I haven't done anything wrong," whined Katrina.

"God!" hissed Delia. "You really are deluding yourself."

"For harassment … sending indecent images … don't worry, Katrina. We'll find every scrap of evidence and we'll make it stick," said Brian, struggling to hold onto his wife.

"My parents will make sure that doesn't happen," Katrina's heart was thumping wildly with panic. Shit. It was all going wrong. She really was in trouble now and the only people who could and would help her, were her parents.

Delia's face was hard as she ceased writhing in Brian's arms. "I really don't think so, you crazy girl. Not once we've told them exactly what you've done. I know my sister thinks very highly of Lucy and Suzanne and once she knows, I can guarantee you won't receive any sympathy there. No, my dear. You're finished here. If I were you, I would get as far away from Canleigh as you can because no-one … absolutely no-one wants you here any longer

... and if you don't, I promise faithfully, I won't rest until I kill you."

"Delia," Brian warned. He looked at Katrina. "Get out of here as fast as you can and if you know what's good for you, don't come back. What you tell your parents is your concern but they will be told the truth ... we'll make sure of that."

Still rubbing her head, Katrina knew when she was beaten ... for now at any rate. She sidled past them and slumped into the lift, avoiding their eyes as she hit the button and the door closed behind her.

* * *

"Is there a back way out of here?" Brian asked Delia, not wanting to take her through the entrance hall. He could see through the glass door into reception that they were still being watched by a crowd of people and the new general manager was advancing on them.

Delia nodded, rubbing her painful eye. Katrina had delivered a damned good blow and it really hurt. "There," she pointed at the backstairs beside the lift.

"Which way?" he said, when they reached the basement, looking at the long corridor and several doors leading off it and what appeared to be a huge kitchen at the far end.

"We can get out of the kitchen door."

He propelled her along, hoping the general manager wasn't going to follow them. He had enough to cope with with Delia, let alone trying to come up with a decent explanation as to why she had attacked a member of staff. Christ, he hoped no-one had rung the police because if they had ... and if Katrina wanted to press charges, Delia would really be in the mire again.

They left the house and made their way down to the lake, Brian deciding it was best to leave their vehicles at the front of the Hall for now and walk back to Dingle Dell. It would help calm Delia and the cars could be picked up later.

The wind was getting up and it was threatening rain. Delia had a coat but Brian, having left Dingle Dell in such a hurry, was still in his shirt sleeves and was growing colder by the minute. He shivered, not sure whether it was from the chilly wind or the trauma of rescuing his wife from inflicting serious injury on Katrina. The whole episode had shaken him up badly. He loved this woman so intensely and if anything happened to her or she was put back into prison, he wasn't sure how he would cope.

Delia stopped in her tracks and looked at him. She put her arms around him, trying to warm him, feeling the deep sense of calm and security she always felt when she was so close to him.

"I'm so sorry, darling. Yet again, I let my temper get the better of me … and that was hardly the way the Countess of Glentagon should be acting in public. I've really let you down."

He pulled her even closer, kissing her eye which was taking on an interesting hue and looked pretty painful. "Darling, Delia. What the hell am I going to do with you?" he sighed.

CHAPTER 43

Boxing day 2003

Katrina sat on her bed, feeling a mixture of emotions; humiliation, anger, fear and sheer frustration. She wanted to cry but couldn't. She lit a cigarette instead, her hands shaking and hardly able to hold the lighter. She inhaled deeply, letting the smoke down into her lungs, allowing the feeling to calm her a little. She smoked it down to the butt and stubbed it out on the wooden floor, grinding it to a pulp with her shoe. She lit another and another while she thought and thought about her predicament.

She really didn't know what to do. She had completely blown it. She couldn't stay here. She couldn't go back to The Beeches. What the hell was she going to do?

She still had some money from what Leo had paid her for the porno films and her wages were due in a few days, which would be paid into her bank account … not that that amounted to very much. It would hardly enable her to live the life she had envisaged. Christ! She would have to go back to making porn films again, throwing herself on the mercy of strangers, as Leo and Kevin had disappeared from the face of the earth without a by your leave so obviously wanted nothing more to do with her.

Her thoughts turned to Hollywood. She had enough to get to America and try her luck but the travel costs wouldn't leave much left to live on and if she couldn't get a job quickly, she would really be in a pickle. Added to which, she hadn't the enthusiasm for it any longer. All she wanted now was Canleigh and thanks to her stupidity in overplaying her hand, she could kiss goodbye to that … and as for her blasted Aunt Delia … humiliating her in front of the staff and guests … she'd like to get to grips with her on a dark night when her precious husband wasn't there to protect her. She'd get the better of her then.

She rubbed her head where Delia had pulled her hair. Something sticky was on her hand. It was blood and Jesus, her scalp hurt. Rage against her aunt took precedence. She imagined how she would give Delia a good trouncing, smash her face in properly and not just give her a black eye. The woman was utterly crazy ... threatening her, humiliating her, physically hurting her ... ordering her out of Canleigh ... threatening to tell her parents ... how dare she? Who the hell did she think she was?

Katrina had never felt so angry in her life. Her blasted aunt had made life at Canleigh untenable ... and she was going to have to pay and would be grovelling at her feet by the time she had finished with her. But then it wasn't just her, was it? It was all of them ... the whole bloody family were against her. Delia, Brian, Lucy, Suzanne ... and soon, even her own parents ... once they knew what she had done, it was doubtful they would ever forgive her. They would be shocked and horrified and would finally wash their hands of her and flaming Suzanne would more than likely get her hands on everything they owned. Father had already threatened to give it all to her and that was without knowledge of recent events. He would throw a fit when he found out ... and there was the little matter of taking the £12000 out of their account. He was going to go crazy ... and that was a point ... should she take some more now? Should she clear the blasted account and just disappear and never return?

She went to switch on her laptop and then saw the blood on her hand. She rubbed her sore head again but the bleeding had stopped. She went through to the bathroom and bathed the wound on her head, washed her hands and took two aspirins to dull the pain. Then she turned back to her laptop. She was going to do it. She was going to clear her parents account and get well away from here and start a new life somewhere exciting.

She switched it on, impatiently waiting for it to boot up while she imagined a hot steamy climate with beautiful beaches. It didn't take long to find the website for her parents' bank ... but it wouldn't let her in. She tried three times but to no avail. Blast, blast, blast. One of her damned parents had discovered what she had done and blocked her. She couldn't transfer any more money. Her dreams of living permanently somewhere like the Caribbean faded fast and her anger returned.

Christ! She hated them all, every one of them, with a passion that was intensifying by the minute, although Delia topped the list. The woman she had been fascinated with ever since she could remember ... and she certainly believed all the stories she had heard about her now. All the rumours that she had killed her brother and half-brother but had got away with. The evil, mad look in Delia's eyes lent the whole story credence. The woman was bordering on the insane ... even Brian had found it hard to keep her in check ... he had really struggled to hold onto her just now ... even though he was bigger and stronger than her. Delia had been completely wild with rage and if he had not intervened, would probably have tried to kill her there and then.

She touched her head again. God, it was sore and she was damned lucky none of her hair had come out. Her face felt battered and bruised too from the hard slaps Delia had inflicted. She looked at the bed. The desire to crawl into it and nurse her wounds was overwhelming but she couldn't. She had to get out of here, with as much dignity as she could muster. The very thought of going back downstairs was torture. It would be utterly humiliating with all the staff and many of the guests aware of what she had done and how Delia had given her a good hammering. Everyone would know by now as those who hadn't been witnesses would have been told by those who had. She would never be able to hold her head up here again. All the staff and many of their regular guests had adored David and would really have it in for her when they discovered she had been the reason for his humiliation, dismissal and the break-up of his engagement.

Damn, damn, damn. She was going to have to get out of here but to where? She couldn't go back to The Beeches because word would have spread there too. Many of the staff at Canleigh knew the staff at The Beeches and phone calls would have been made and texts sent ... and then there was Suzanne. God, what a daft idea that had been to try and implicate her and not think it through properly. Of course Miss Goody Two Shoes would have gone straight to the family once she discovered the package in the salon and what was on the dvd ... but how did they know it was her? That was the puzzle. She had been so careful to wipe off her fingerprints and everything had been paid for in cash. Nothing had been left to chance, so how had they guessed? Anyway, it didn't matter now as she was finished ... with all of them. None of them would ever trust her again. Canleigh would never be hers now. They would make sure of that.

She could have kicked herself for making such a huge mistake. If she hadn't tried to implicate Suzanne and worked on Lucy more subtly, it could have been so different. She had been in too much of a rush, wanting to push Lucy over the edge quickly. She should have bided her time. Stupid, stupid, stupid!

A bang on her door made her jump. She wiped her face quickly, trying unsuccessfully to banish the tear stains. She blew her nose and moved towards the door. Then she stopped in her tracks. What if it was Delia again? What if she had escaped from Brian and had come back to finish her off?

"Katrina - it's me ... Pete. I've been sent up by Adrian to see if you're okay."

She gulped, reluctant to open the door and face her colleague. "Yes ... yes, I'm fine," she lied.

"Well, Adrian said to take the rest of the day off and he'll have a word with you later."

"Oh, okay. Thank you," Katrina replied.

"Is there ... is there anything you need?"

"No. I'm fine. I'll go to bed for a while. Thank you, Pete."

Katrina still didn't open the door. She couldn't face anyone, let alone Pete, who had never made any pretence that he liked her and had been a real admirer of David before his fall from grace. She heard his footsteps head back down the landing towards the stairs and sat back down on her bed. So, presumably she still had a job here ... but it wouldn't be for long once Delia and Brian discussed the situation with Lucy. She would want her out immediately. So, she was on her own, completely and utterly with no-one to turn to and nowhere to go.

* * *

During the walk back to Dingle Dell, Brian had managed to placate Delia and was confident she wouldn't try and return to the Hall to give Katrina another going over. He was just praying no-one had reported what had already happened to the police and they would come looking for her. He couldn't imagine Katrina would. She would be too scared they would ask the obvious question as to why Delia had attacked her in the first place and what it might lead to. No, she would keep quiet but there had been so many witnesses to Delia's outburst and some busybody might just think it was their business to intervene. Half expecting the police to be waiting at Dingle Dell for them, he was immensely relieved to see that the only car on the drive was Lucy's.

"God, you've been lucky," he said, with his arm tightly around Delia's waist. "It looks like your fracas with Katrina hasn't been reported."

"Thank God," whispered Delia. "I just didn't stop to think. I just wanted to get the little bitch for what she has done. I could still kill her."

"Delia! Stop it. You mustn't think like that ... please. I don't know what I would do if you were sent down again."

"Oh, thank goodness ... there you are," cried Suzanne standing at the front door. "I've been so worried. I didn't know whether to follow you in Lucy's car but she and Selena are still asleep and I didn't want to bring Daniel. What happened ... did you find Katrina? Has she admitted it?"

"I think we all need a stiff drink first ... and I don't mean tea or coffee ... and to get warmed up ... I'll just fetch a thick sweater ... I'm freezing," said Brian looking exhausted and shaking with cold. It had been a long walk and the temperature outside was plummeting quickly.

Suzanne rushed to the cocktail cabinet in the drawing room to pour generous shots of brandy into two glasses and handed one to Delia, who had taken off her coat and slumped onto the sofa, dishevelled and emotionally drained. Her eye was going a peculiar colour but although Suzanne was dying to know how it had occurred, she didn't like to ask. Brian joined them seconds later, having pulled on a pure wool bottle green sweater. He took the brandy from Suzanne and downed it in one.

"God, I needed that," he said, joining Delia on the sofa. He looked around. "Where's Daniel? Poor kid. I had promised to play games with him and then ran out on him."

"He's gone to a friend's house. Mark's mother rang my mobile a little while ago complaining he was bored so she was kind enough to come and get Daniel and have him for lunch so at least I don't have to worry about him for a while."

"I'm so sorry, Suzanne. I feel terrible, letting him down like that. I'll make it up to him. I promise."

"I'm sure you will ... but what happened ... at Canleigh?"

Brian gave her a brief account, keeping out how Delia had physically attacked Katrina but by the look of them both, Suzanne guessed more had gone on than he was letting on.

"Oh Lord. What will she do now? She won't want to stay at Canleigh ... that's if Lucy would even let her, which is pretty doubtful. Where will she go? She won't go back to The Beeches, will she? Come looking for me. Oh hell. I don't think I'm going to feel very safe going back to the cottage tonight."

"Stay in the hotel," suggested Brian, "although I shouldn't think she would do anything to any of us now. She knows we all know about what she has done so far. She's not going to risk making things worse."

"You don't know Katrina very well," said Suzanne, deciding a brandy might be the best thing for her too. She poured one for herself and sat down in the chair opposite Delia and Brian. "Katrina is a spiteful, nasty piece of work when she wants to be and I don't trust her one iota. She already hates me so what is she going to do now she knows I went straight to you with my suspicions and the blasted package she left in the salon. She will really have it in for me."

"If you're really scared, stay here," said Delia. "I'm sure Lucy won't mind and there's plenty of room. Stay until the situation has calmed down … until Vicky and Alex return if necessary. We were planning on taking Lucy and Selena up to Glentagon but in the circumstances that can wait … we'll go when we know you and Daniel are safe."

Suzanne felt a surge of relief. The very idea of returning to the cottage tonight was terrifying. She wouldn't be able to sleep, knowing Katrina might be lurking about outside, intending her and Daniel real harm.

"That's really kind of you. I'll go back to the cottage shortly and collect some things. I can fetch Daniel at the same time."

"We had to leave your car at Canleigh … I'll run you back in Lucy's to fetch it … we can leave the Range Rover until later … and you have to promise me you'll stay here," Brian said warningly to Delia. "I don't want you and Katrina setting eyes on each other again today."

She gave a weak smile. "I promise. The damned girl is probably miles away by now anyway and I feel filthy. I'm going to have a shower and then put something on my eye after I've made sure Lucy and Selena are okay."

Satisfied with her answer, Brian stood up. "Let's go, Suzanne. The sooner you're sorted the better and then perhaps we can start to put this whole matter behind us and concentrate on getting on with our lives.

CHAPTER 44

Boxing Day 2003

Katrina hauled her suitcases down the backstairs, and out of the back door nearest to the car park, hoping she wouldn't bump into any of the staff. She was lucky. It was lunchtime and they were either eating in the staff room or waiting on the guests in the dining room.

She threw her suitcases into the boot of her car and got in, not sure where to go but knowing she had to get out of sight of the Hall for now. She drove smartly past the house, her head held high in case anyone was looking, and up the drive towards the main road, not having a clue whether to turn left or right ... Harrogate or Leeds ... which way, she dithered ... which way? Automatically she turned towards Harrogate, although she knew she didn't want to go back to The Beeches and face that bitch of a so-called sister of hers. She might just do her a serious injury but she didn't just want to hurt her, she wanted to hurt all of them. She wanted revenge and at the moment, Lady Delia Canleigh was on the top of her list.

Suddenly she felt exhausted and drained, emotionally and physically, especially from the pounding Delia had given her earlier. She desperately wanted to sleep, her eyelids were drooping and she felt woozy. She had to find somewhere to rest. She thought about pulling over somewhere but it was cold outside and the temperature in the car would soon plummet and she had nothing to put over her to help keep her warm. As reluctant as she was to spend any money, she knew she had to find somewhere to relax and to think.

She was driving aimlessly towards Knaresborough when she noticed a house set back from the road with a sign indicating it was a guest house and had vacancies. It would have to do. She didn't want to go any further and if they recognised her and wondered what she was doing here, it was just too bad. She was too tired to care.

They didn't. The young couple who owned the guesthouse had only recently bought it, having moved down from Scotland. They had no idea who was who in the local gentry and greeted the tired looking young woman with warmth and concern and escorted her to a lovely room on the second floor which overlooked the garden.

"We only moved in last month," the wife said, "and as we've been concentrating on decorating and then celebrating Christmas, we haven't got around to advertising properly yet so we're nice and quiet … and you shouldn't be disturbed in here as there's no road noise. I can cook dinner for you this evening if you're hungry."

"That would be very kind … I'm … I'm a bit tired for now and want to sleep but no doubt I shall want something later."

"Right. Come down to the dining room at 7.00 pm and I'll have something delicious waiting for you … I love cooking so it will be a pleasure. There's plenty of tea and coffee in here for you, along with some biscuits and I'll pop up in a minute with some fresh milk and I've just made a madeira cake so I'll bring some of that too."

Half an hour later, Katrina was propped up in a very comfortable double bed, drinking a cup of tea, polishing off a large slice of madeira cake and gazing out of the window over the long garden which was lawned with shrubs near to the house and vegetables and a greenhouse at the far end.

Physically, she was feeling a tiny bit better. She had taken two more aspirins and the throbbing pain on her scalp was beginning to recede but the anger was still there. A seething, bitter fury that was consuming her and at the moment she had no idea what she was going to do about it. She couldn't think clearly. She put down her cup on the bedside table, slid down into the bed and fell promptly asleep.

* * *

Katrina woke at 6.00 p.m., feeling energised and hungry. She showered, applied fresh makeup and took two more painkillers. She had washed her hair in the shower and God, it had hurt as she gingerly applied shampoo and then rinsed it off. She could have cried with the pain. "Blast you, Delia Canleigh," she seethed, wincing as she tried to dry her hair with the lowest setting of the hairdryer, any hotter making the pain worse.

Dinner was delicious. Catherine, having told Katrina that's what she liked to be called rather than Mrs. Murgatroyd, was true to her word and was an excellent cook and Katrina soon polished off the steak and mushroom pie, mashed potato, broccoli and cauliflower, followed by golden syrup pudding and custard and lashings of coffee. She felt distinctly fat and full afterwards but stronger and more determined than ever to exact revenge on Delia Canleigh, having woken with a clear idea of exactly what she was going to do.

It was eight thirty by the time she had finished her meal, paid her bill and got back into her car. The Murgatroyd's had been surprised she didn't want to stay the night but she explained she was journeying up to Scotland and wanted to reach there before the heavy snow, which was forecasted for the next day or so, began. They waved her off, little knowing that they had just harboured someone who was about to commit murder.

* * *

She drove to the far side of Knaresborough and stopped off at a service station, hoping she wouldn't be recognised but the young man behind the till didn't bat an eyelid at her, even when she asked to buy two petrol cans. She filled them up and paid him, at the same time purchasing a thick woollen blanket from a nearby display unit. She drove away, realising she was on cctv but it was just too bad. She was past caring. She was just focusing on getting even with members of her family.

She drove back towards Canleigh. It was nearly ten o'clock by the time she hit the back lanes leading to Dingle Dell. She pulled into the nearest copse to the bungalow, stopped the car and turned off the lights. It was damned cold now, freezing hard and the snow that was forecast probably wouldn't be long in making an appearance. She would wait until midnight, wanting to make sure all were in bed in Dingle Dell. She pulled the blanket over her and settled down, hoping she wouldn't be nothing but a block of ice by then and unable to achieve what she had come here to do.

The minutes ticked by slowly. She was bored witless but daren't turn on the radio in case anyone heard so she sat in the dark, listening to the rustling of the trees and creatures of the night, keeping her seething resentment and hate alive, reflecting on the terror she was now about to inflict ... on Lucy and Delia in particular. Selena and Brian ... well, it was just too bad about them ... they would be collateral damage. It was a damned pity Suzanne and her brat weren't there too ... and her mother and father ... then she would have got the lot ... but she would deal with her flaming so called sister in an hour or so, when she had finished what she had to do here ... and as for the parents ... they would probably keel over with the shock of losing most of their precious family. Anyhow, this was top priority at the moment.

She didn't think about the possibility of not getting away with what she was about to do, totally focused on exacting her revenge. Her blood was up and she was going to get Lady Delia bloody Canleigh. She giggled. She would be doing the world a favour as her precious aunt wouldn't be trying to kill anyone ever again. She was going to be finished off for good.

It was midnight. Katrina moved gingerly, seeing if her body would work now she had been sitting in the same position in the cold for the last two hours. She was stiff but managed to get out of the car. It was bitingly cold in a chilly easterly wind and the grass beneath her feet was frozen solid. She was already togged up well for such a cold night with woollen outer garments but even so, as she took one of the petrol cans out of the boot, she couldn't believe how bitterly cold she was.

There was a faint moon but Katrina knew the way and didn't need much light. She hurried down the lane, her body gradually warming up, keen to get this task over with and then get over to the cottage in the grounds of the Beeches and finish off the job.

As she marched along, she had never felt so powerful, so in control, so in charge. She wasn't going to allow anyone to determine her destiny any longer. No-one was ever going to stand in her way again. She was going to do away with them all ... and unlike her evil old aunt, she was going to get away with it. No prison cells for her. She would do what she had to do and get out of Yorkshire fast, disappear in some big city. Not London. Perhaps Paris or Rome. If she could slip out of the UK by the back door, bribe someone to take her over the Channel by boat, she could get into Europe, change her name and appearance and ... and what ... she didn't know. She couldn't plan that far ahead and would deal with it later. All she was focused on at this moment in time was destroying Delia Canleigh and anyone else who happened to get in the way. She was damned if the woman was going to get away with humiliating and threatening her and ruining all her hopes of becoming the owner of Canleigh. To hell with her. She had to die.

She came to a halt by the front gate to Dingle Dell. Strangely there were three cars parked by the bungalow. Delia and Brian's Range Rover, Lucy's Mercedes and then, to her delight, Suzanne's little Fiat. So, she was here, was she? Too frightened to go home no doubt, scared what Katrina might do to her for dobbing her in. Well, she was going to find out very soon ... and it was going to save a job at The Beeches too. How damned convenient. What a hoot.

Karina giggled softly as she crept along the drive towards the house. All the lights were off so everyone must be in bed and fast asleep. She wondered if anyone would wake up. She hoped Lady Delia would and wished she could have been a fly on the wall and could see her face when she realised her end was nigh.

Softly she flicked open the letterbox, pushed the nozzle from the petrol can through it and poured the liquid inside. She could hear the faint sound of the petrol as it hit the carpet and prayed it wouldn't wake anyone up. She didn't want any of them to get away.

* * *

Suzanne and Daniel were in one of the guest bedrooms with twin beds, fast asleep, feeling safe surrounded by the rest of the family at Dingle Dell. Lucy had taken some of the Valium prescribed by her doctor to calm her nerves and she and Selena were cuddled up in bed together with little Coco, all three deep in slumber.

Delia and Brian were still awake, entwined in a passionate embrace. Brian knew the best way to distract Delia from anything was by making love and it had worked to a degree. She was still mad as hell at Katrina but lay languid and spent in his arms, having pushed her niece to the back of her mind for a while.

"I love you so very much," he murmured, kissing the top of her head which was nestled in his shoulder. "But I'll be damned glad when we get back to Glentagon and our bedroom is well away from the guest bedrooms and we don't have to worry about being overheard," he smiled.

Delia laughed softly. "I know. Me too, although it will be lovely to have Lucy and Selena up there with us for a while … and be able to relax away from all the stresses and strains of being here. It's been a minefield this Christmas. I'll be jolly glad to get away and I never thought I would say that about the Canleigh estate."

"Well, it won't be long before we can go … it's only a few days before Vicky and Alex return and Suzanne and Daniel can return to The Beeches without worrying ... and we can all sleep soundly in our beds, especially if we can persuade Lucy to talk to the police and leave it all in their hands". Brian sighed. "I do wish we could have done it today as we had planned but once she knew it was definitely Katrina behind it all, she wouldn't budge. Saying she wants to talk to Katrina first, if we can find her again after your little upset today, is understandable but ludicrous and possibly quite dangerous in my opinion".

Delia, feeling drowsy, turned into his arms and kissed his mouth. "I agree but there's nothing more we can do for now. Katrina is probably miles away by now. Let's try and forget it and get some sleep. I'm so very tired."

He cuddled her close and they closed their eyes but within seconds hers flashed open again. "What's that smell?" she asked, sniffing the air.

Brian breathed in deeply. "Bloody hell, it's petrol," he roared, throwing her aside and hurtling towards the bedroom door. An almighty whooshing sound and a massive ball of flame rushed down the hallway towards him and he slammed the door shut.

"Oh, my God, ... the damned place is on fire ... get out of the window ... NOW!" he yelled, his SAS training came to the fore as he grabbed his trousers and pulled them on, then dashed towards their en-suite to soak towels in water.

"But the girls ... the children ...," Delia shrieked, throwing her clothes on, "we've got to get to them ... they're probably asleep."

"Get outside," he ordered swiftly, "go around to their bedroom windows and bang on them, try and wake them up so they can get out that way. There's no point in trying to smash the windows, they're triple glazed and will need special equipment from the fire brigade. Take your phone ... ring for help."

"What the hell are you going to do?" she asked, throwing open the bedroom window and tumbling outside. The icy cold night air hit her, taking her breath away. She looked back at Brian, desperately needing him to follow her but he was wrapping the dripping towels around his body and his head.

"I'll try and get to them this way … now go, Delia … just bloody go. We haven't a second to spare."

He turned from her and opened the bedroom door, the flames flying down the corridor. He disappeared into them, leaving Delia gasping and gulping with panic at the danger he was placing himself in to save the girls and the children. She had to help him.

As she ran along the side of the house to Lucy's room, she pulled her phone from her pocket, pressed 999, sobbing and screaming that she needed the fire brigade and ambulance fast.

She reached Lucy's room and threw down her phone, satisfied that the emergency services were on their way but it would take them ages to get here, either from Leeds or Harrogate. They would be too late if she and Brian couldn't wake everyone and get them out.

Crying with panic, she banged as hard as she could on the window.

"LUCY!! LUCY!! Wake up! … You've got to get out … quick … the house is on fire!" she screamed, again and again, beating the glass with her fists. The room was in darkness and she couldn't see in, even though the curtains weren't drawn as Lucy liked to look at the stars when she went to bed. Delia couldn't see her daughter and Selena in bed, couldn't see Brian entering the room. Where the hell was he? Had he gone to Suzanne's room first? Selena … Daniel. Throwing one desperate look at her daughter's room, she charged to the next window, and did the same, screaming at Suzanne and Daniel to wake up but with no response. Were they all dead … from smoke inhalation? Oh God! Where the hell was Brian?

Delia had never been so scared in her life … not for herself … but for her whole family … her whole life was in this building … the whole reason for her living … if anything happened to them, she would die. But it wasn't going to. She would get them out.

Clouds scurried overhead, giving her a little light as they cleared the moon. She caught a movement in the corner of her eye ... a woman skulking in the trees ... Delia knew who it was immediately. Katrina. Her heart skipped a beat. It was her ... she had set fire to the place. Wanting nothing more than to charge over to her heinous, wicked niece and do her in, Delia resisted the temptation and turned back to the house, careering towards the back door, hoping to gain entry that way but it was well and truly locked and bolted. Lucy had spent lavishly on security when she had Dingle Dell built and it would take real force and the proper equipment to gain entry from the outside.

Delia, sobbing with desperation, ran back to the bedroom windows, hoping that someone would have woken up and were scrambling out of the windows. Suzanne's room was still in darkness and she banged on the window again with both hands, "SUZANNE! WAKE UP!" she yelled at the top of her voice.

She ran back to Lucy's room and burst into tears as she saw Brian crash through the bedroom door, flames billowing around him and lighting up the room as he dashed towards Lucy and Selena. Then there was a bang, an almighty bang like a bomb exploding and Delia went flying as the full force of it flew through Lucy's bedroom, taking the windows with it.

She came to, minutes later, stunned and shaking, her brain unable to take in what had happened. She could hear sirens in the distance, coming closer and closer, the air was freezing, the grass beneath her was frozen. She was shaking with cold and fear. Something awful had just happened but what? She pulled herself upright, checking herself for injury but she seemed okay.

She stared at the house, at the huge, flickering flames in Lucy's room, in Suzanne's room, the lounge, the kitchen ... everything was burning ... and she knew ... she just knew ... her whole family were dead. Lucy, her darling daughter and lovely little Selena ... who had never done any harm to anyone. Poor Suzanne and little Daniel ... the loveliest, warmest, kindest people she had ever met

... apart from Brian ... her wonderful husband ... her brave, wonderful husband.

"BRIAN!" she shrieked, tearing back across the grass towards Lucy's room but she could do nothing ... the flames were too strong. She couldn't see anyone beyond them. "Brian ... oh Brian," she cried, falling to the ground sobbing with grief. "No, no, this can't be happening. Please, please don't leave me ... please."

Men were running towards her, men in uniform and helmets with lights on. One of them grabbed her, hauling her to her feet. "Please ... come with me ... it's too dangerous being so close to the house," he said, his eyes kind and full of sympathy. He had seen people in her state before and it always got to him. His job wasn't exactly the easiest and he hated this part, dealing with grief-stricken relatives.

"My husband ... my daughter ... my granddaughter ... they are in there ... in that bedroom," she cried piteously. "Please, please get them out ... please save them."

"The men will do everything they can," he said reassuringly, guiding her towards the front of the bungalow where an ambulance was pulling up behind two fire engines. Firemen were running about, reeling out hoses, brandishing axes and other equipment in order to gain entry to the house.

The fireman who was with Delia, handed her over to the paramedics. "You stay here ... we will do everything we can," he repeated, as he turned to stride back towards the house, leaving her to watch and wait, knowing in her heart that there was absolutely nothing anyone could do to bring her family back to her. Nothing, absolutely nothing ... and there was only one thing for her to do now ... and that was to find Katrina ... and make her pay.

CHAPTER 45

Thursday 27th December 2003

Katrina heard the emergency services tearing down the lane and decided it was time to make her exit and leave the scene of such devastation and carnage she, and she alone, had set in motion. The bungalow was ablaze from the front to the back, huge flames leaping out of the windows which had exploded. Acrid smoke filled the air and even between the trees, yards from the building, it was affecting her, making her eyes water and it was impossible to breathe unless she held her scarf over her nose and mouth. What she was enduring was bad enough but to actually be inside the building must be hell indeed but so far no-one apart from her damned aunt had emerged … and she was now being fawned over by a paramedic as four firemen stood and assessed the situation and many more dashed about with equipment and hoses.

While the place was a hive of activity and all attention was on Dingle Dell, Katrina backed further into the trees and hurried down a track running parallel to the lane which would get her back to her car. She wasn't sure what to do now. She still had the second full petrol can in the car which she had intended to use on Suzanne's cottage at The Beeches but that wasn't necessary now as it certainly looked as if she and Daniel had been finished off tonight. So, what to do? First things first, she had to get rid of the can and then get cleaned up. She reeked of petrol, some having splashed onto her coat when she was pouring it through the front door of the bungalow. She also stank of smoke; in her hair and all her clothes. She couldn't go anywhere like this or she would certainly arouse suspicions and it couldn't be Canleigh, so it would have to be The Beeches. She could sneak in the back way, get up to the flat, clean up and spend the night, pretend she had been there ever since leaving Canleigh yesterday lunchtime. She wouldn't have any witnesses to prove she had but then again, there wouldn't be any to say she had been here tonight either. The only person who could incriminate her was the boy at the service station in Knaresborough but he had seemed a bit dim and why would he connect her with what had happened a good number of miles away? That was if he even read the newspapers or watched the news. Hopefully he wouldn't. So, apart from him, there was nothing to link her with what had occurred at Dingle Dell. Delia, of course, would no doubt accuse her but would anyone take any notice of her, a convicted criminal? And there was no other proof, at least there wouldn't be once she got cleaned up.

She reached the car, stripping off her clothes and removing the box of matches in her coat pocket. The air was freezing, making her shudder with cold. It wasn't a good idea to be naked in the middle of the winter in the middle of the woods. She washed her hands as best she could in some frozen grass, before opening the boot of the car, grabbing the second petrol can and the box of matches and ran deeper into the woods. She dumped her clothes in a pile under some trees, poured the petrol over them, lit a match and set fire to the lot, making the flames more intense when she hurled the petrol can and the box of matches onto the bonfire.

Realising the fire brigade might well see it from Dingle Dell, she flew back to the car, quickly washed her hands on the grass again, unzipped her suitcase and donned a clean, warm sweater, pulled on some jeans and found her leather jacket. It was only her smoke-filled hair that would give her away now.

She started the car and shot off down the lane. More emergency vehicles were coming up from the Harrogate direction. She took the left turning towards Tangles to avoid them, annoyed that it would take longer to get back to The Beeches. The sooner she was tucked up innocently in bed, the better.

* * *

Delia sat motionless in the ambulance with the doors wide open, watching and waiting to hear the news about her nearest and dearest, although she knew what the outcome was going to be. She was shaking with cold, terror and desperation. One of the paramedics had wrapped her up in a foil blanket but it wouldn't melt the ice in her heart.

The bungalow which had been burning brightly, lighting up the night sky and probably seen for miles, was a blackened ruin now the firemen had extinguished the flames. The air was putrid with smoke, making everyone without breathing apparatus, cough and choke. One of the paramedics placed an oxygen mask over her nose, which helped a bit and she sat beside Delia, her eyes full of sympathy, placing an arm around her shoulders and holding her hand. It was kind but meant nothing to Delia. Her whole being was being eaten up with sorrow and anger, a red-hot anger that was threatening to boil over at any minute. She kept looking at the spot where she had seen Katrina earlier but she must have gone as there was no movement now.

The police had arrived and were in earnest conversation with one of the firemen. They looked over to her, their eyes full of sorrow. Then she saw it ... another fireman was approaching the group, carrying a petrol can but the way he was waving it around, indicated it was empty. Delia recalled Brian's yell of warning that it was petrol she could smell in the bungalow. The bitch! Katrina had used it to start the fire. No wonder it had spread so damned quickly and killed all bar herself within minutes. If Brian hadn't insisted she clamber out of the window, or if they had been asleep, she would have been dead too and how she wished she was. The thought of living without him, Lucy and Selena was sheer torture ... and if poor Suzanne hadn't been so frightened of Katrina, she would have been alive too, tucked up safely with little Daniel in the cottage at The Beeches ... and it was all down to her completely mad niece. Delia knew it was. She didn't need anyone to confirm it.

She stood up abruptly, shaking off the paramedic, the oxygen mask and the foil blanket. She knew what she was going to do. She had the keys for the Range Rover in the pocket of her jeans. She was going to go after that little witch and finish her.

She headed towards the sombre policemen still in conversation with the two firemen. "I take it there's no-one alive," she stated, waiting for final confirmation of her fears, her face a mask. All four looked at her with sadness in their eyes. One of the firemen nodded. "I am so very sorry, Mam but no-one stood a chance. You were lucky to get out ... whoever set light to the bungalow meant you all serious harm, that's for sure."

Delia nearly choked. Nausea overcame her and she just managed to make it to the bushes before she was violently sick, the pain excruciating in her gut. A paramedic, who had been watching her, rushed over to hold her but Delia brushed her away. "Leave me," she demanded. "Just leave me ... I've something I must do."

"Please ... come with us ... you need to get checked out at hospital and the police will want to take a statement as well at some point."

Delia shook her head. "Not now. I have something to do and that's it. Just leave me be. I'm fine."

She wasn't fine. Nothing could have been further from the truth but she reeled away from the house, from the paramedics, the firemen, the police. They all watched her go, anxious and worried for her but knowing they could do nothing to stop her.

She stumbled up to the Range Rover and opened it, slumped into the driving seat, put her head down on the steering wheel, and gave way to her grief. It went on and on. She thought she would never stop, heart wrenching sobs racking her body. Then, suddenly, it ceased and she sat up, stared at the wild-eyed, demented looking woman in the rear-view mirror and knew what she had to do.

She started the car, racking her brains to think where Katrina would have gone. She certainly wouldn't have returned to Canleigh but there was every likelihood it was The Beeches. After all, it was her family home, and she could probably pretend she had been asleep there all night and had nothing to do with what had gone on at Dingle Dell. Also, Vicky and Alex were away so she could easily sneak in and out.

It seemed the obvious place and if Katrina wasn't there, Delia would find her ... even if it took the rest of her life. It was her mission now and she would be entirely focused on it and wouldn't rest until she made the girl pay ... and with nothing less than her life.

She headed for Harrogate, tearing around corners, putting her foot down on the straight bits, desperate to catch up with Katrina as soon as possible. Luckily there were no police about and the roads were quiet at this time of the morning. She looked at the clock on the dashboard. It was nearly 1.00a.m. An hour ago, she had been curled up in bed with Brian. Brian ... her soulmate ... she felt as if part of her, the best part was missing. She wondered if this was some ghastly dream but the stench of smoke in her clothes dismissed that one small hope and gave her the strength to continue on the path she had set herself. She should have been deathly tired with no sleep and so much trauma but she wasn't. The adrenalin was keeping her going. She was wide awake and deathly calm, with one purpose and one purpose only.

She found The Beeches easily, although she had never been there. Lucy had mentioned it was on the main road near to Fewston reservoir and there it was, her headlights had picked up the sign. The hotel was in darkness, apart from a light in the main foyer. Accelerating fast, she sent the Range Rover flying up the drive and couldn't believe her luck when she saw Katrina's car disappearing around the side of the building to where there was a rear car park. Delia paused at the front for a few seconds before following her, just giving Katrina enough time to get out of her car. Then she put her foot down again and shot around to the back to see her quarry locking her vehicle. Delia braked sharply, revving the engine hard, staring threateningly at the shaking woman in her headlights.

Katrina looked horrified as she recognised the Range Rover and its driver. She stood as still as a statue by her car, her keys in her hand and her eyes wide with terror.

Delia took her opportunity without hesitating, she took her left foot off the clutch and threw her right foot down, hard to the floor. The large vehicle smashed into Katrina's rigid body. Delia reversed fast, gratified to see Katrina slump on the ground, clutching her stomach and screaming with pain. Delia threw the car into first gear again and repeated her action. She did it three more times, until the woman, her very own niece, was nothing more than a bloody pulp on the ground, well and truly dead.

Alerted by the dreadful noises coming from outside, guests were lighting up their rooms and hanging out of windows to see what was going on. Night porters rushed out of the front door and round to the back, horrified to see the lifeless, bloodied body of Katrina on the ground beside her battered car and a Range Rover tearing up the drive to the main road.

Delia didn't feel a thing. She didn't feel pleased, she didn't feel sorry. She felt nothing. Numb. That was the only way she could describe it.

She kept heading for Skipton. The road was wide and with no traffic about she sped along, knowing where she was going and what she was going to do ... and she hadn't long to do it because everyone would know it was her who had just killed Katrina. They would be after her and this time she was not going to prison. Absolutely not.

The miles passed, she sped through the pretty little market town of Skipton and onto the road for Malham, where she and Brian had been so very happy only a few days ago. Where he had professed his undying love and given her such a fabulous eternity ring. Eternity. They would be together for eternity and much quicker than they thought.

She flew along the last remaining miles, round bend after bend along the B road leading to Malham. She drove through the village, all in darkness and up towards the tiny car park which at this time of the morning was empty. She stopped the Range Rover and slid out. She stood by the gate for a moment which led to the Cove. It was all so peaceful … so silent. She didn't feel cold even without a coat, although it had started to snow and was absolutely freezing.

She stumbled over the hard ground and stones in the darkness. It was quite a way and took a while to reach the Cove and as she staggered along, all she could think of was how she had felt just a few days before, when Brian was with her, holding her hand, smiling that wonderful smile at her when his eyes bore into hers and they knew they were soul mates. She could feel him here with her now, helping her along, urging her to do it, to be with him.

"I'm coming, my darling. I'm coming," she whispered.

Finally, shivering hard, she reached the top of the Cove. The moon was virtually obliterated by clouds but it was just possible to make out the shapes of the hills and valleys in the distance. Delia looked down … although she couldn't see it now, she knew it was a hellishly long drop to the ground below but she didn't mind. She was going to meet Brian. They would be together forever. She held out her arms and let her body drop over the side. It felt like flying as she plunged downwards but Brian was there … he was holding her, protecting her as he always had. He scooped her up in his arms and she sighed with sheer pleasure.

EPILOGUE

Dingle Dell was completely destroyed and the bodies the firemen found; two women, two children, a man and a cat, were all badly burnt. The body of Lady Delia Canleigh, the Countess of Glentagon, was found at the foot of Malham Cove the very next morning. Every bone in her body was broken but she had a smile on her face.

Vicky, Alex, Ruth and Philip were alerted by the Spanish police and headed home by plane immediately, Vicky uncaring whether she was advised to travel that way or not. This was a family emergency and she had to get home by the fastest way possible.

It took three weeks to conduct all the funerals. Suzanne and Daniel, after a church service at St. Mary's in Canleigh, were cremated and their ashes scattered in the grounds of The Beeches alongside Jeremy, Suzanne's brother. Lucy and Selena were buried in Canleigh churchyard. With respect for all those Katrina had killed and not wanting to place their daughter anywhere near them, Vicky and Alex drove Katrina's ashes to the Yorkshire coast and scattered them over Filey Brigg, praying she would now be at peace.

Brian's cousin, the new Earl of Glentagon, took Brian and Delia back to the estate and buried them together in the tiny churchyard just outside the castle walls.

A distraught Vicky, who was now the owner of Canleigh and Blairness, decided to sell them both. "I want nothing more to do with them," she told Alex. "My family are all gone and I never want to set foot in the Hall again … it's brought nothing but misery for years and I'm too tired to deal with running another hotel. No, Alex. Let's sell them both and retire, just as we said we would. Let's go to Italy and buy a lovely villa."

Heartbroken to have lost Lucy and Selena, Ruth and Philip followed them, finding they didn't want to stay in the vicinity of

Canleigh with so much sadness around them. With all the contacts Philip had acquired over the years, he found a suitable couple who wanted to buy Tangles, run the business and continue with the sanctuary. Within months of Vicky and Alex's departure, Ruth and Philip joined them in the enormous villa they had purchased on the shores of Lake Como. It was big enough for both couples and they finally found the peace they craved and tried to put the past behind them.

Canleigh Hall was sold to the Enchante group of hotels and went from strength to strength; always busy, always full of residents. However, guests often mentioned over lunch or dinner that very often at night, there were three ladies seen wandering around the rooms. There was a dark-haired lady in a black dress, a blonde-haired lady in a white dress and a red-haired lady in a gold gown. Who were they and what were they doing here?

THE END

LAST WORD

Thank you for reading the whole of the Canleigh series, which I do hope you have enjoyed and if you have, no doubt you are as loathe to let go of the characters as I am.

However, as you might or might not be aware, reviews of books are paramount to their success and, therefore, I would be enormously grateful if you could find a few moments to leave a short review on either Goodreads or Amazon as this will be so helpful, not only to me, but also to future readers. If you aren't sure how to do this on Amazon, just return to the page where you bought the book, scroll down to the reviews and just add yours. Easy peasy! Links are as follows:

Rejection Runs Deep:
US: http://www.amazon.com/dp/B076YZQW57/
UK: http://www.amazon.co.uk/dp/B076YZQW57/

Delia's Daughter:
US: http://www.amazon.com/dp/B07G47ZD3
UK: http://www.amazon.co.uk/dp/B07G47ZD3

Katrina:
US: http://www.amazon.com/dp/B07QBXWR7F/
UK: http://www.amazon.co.uk/dp/B07QBXWR7F/

Now, a real treat for you! **THE SECRET**, the shocking, dramatic prequel to **THE CANLEIGH SERIES** is now FREE for you to download. To obtain your copy, head over to:-
www.carolewilliamsbooks.com/sign-up

It's 1962 and Margaret, the Duchess of Canleigh, has a dark and dreadful secret. No-one must find out … absolutely no-one. If they do, she could lose her status, access to her husband's vast wealth, her children … not that she cares about them too much … but most of all her fabulous lifestyle … but someone does find out. Someone she hoped she would never see again and even worse, someone else close to home and she will have to risk everything, even her liberty, to keep them quiet!

On joining my mailing list, not only will you receive **THE SECRET**, but you can also download my FREE thriller short story. entitled **YES DEAR,** and will be informed of when further book releases, competitions and further freebies are available. I only send out emails when I have real news so you won't be bombarded with them, just an occasional one every couple of months or so.

Life was hard. She was always playing catch-up, always stressed, always at his beck and call … but he was in for a shock. She hadn't planned it that way. It just happened!!

THE PEESDOWN SERIES

PEESDOWN PARK

A PSYCHOLOGICAL THRILLER

(A BOOK YOU WON'T WANT TO PUT DOWN – A BOOK WHICH WILL MAKE YOU WARY WHEN WALKING ALONE!!

US: www.amazon.co.uk/dp/B08193FHW5

UK: www.amazon.co.uk/dp/B08193FHW5

If you want to make a lot of money, enjoy the outdoors for most of the day and be your own boss, become a professional petsitter someone had said. So, Miranda did ... but it wasn't all it was cracked up to be. No-one told her she would have to take her life into her hands, walking into people's empty houses to feed their cats when they were away with the possibility of bumping into a burglar ... or walking dogs in the woods in Peesdown Park where creepy men lurked about ... and she had no idea she had to be specifically aware of William ... the one man she thought she could trust ...but William was a killer. He had fled the UK after murdering his parents to gain their wealth but now he was back ... and residing near Peesdown Park ... and the locals were blissfully unaware that the nice, friendly old gentleman who integrated himself into the community so well would soon bring terror to their beautiful, normally peaceful recreation area ... and no-one, particularly Miranda, their bubbly petsitter, would be safe for long.

A GREAT READ: Loved this book. Left me wanting more!

GRIPPING: Just loved this book. Kept me engrossed.

A GREAT READ: Great characters and totally engrossing.

****

Books in the pipeline for 2020 are Panic in Peesdown, book 2 in the Peesdown series with possibly book 3 too. I shall also commence Darnforth, my next big family drama which begins in Normandy in World War II and then returns to Darnforth, a large Jacobean stately home in Yorkshire.

So, please sign up to hear news of when these will be available and to get your **FREE** copy of **THE SECRET** and **YES DEAR**.

www.carolewilliamsbooks.com/sign up

You can also follow me on:

Facebook - Carole Williams Author

Instagram - (carolewilliams.author)

Please email me at:

carole@carolewilliamsbooks.com

Many thanks.

Carole Williams.

Printed in Great Britain
by Amazon